.

A CURSED LOVE

Myths of Airren
Book Three

Jenny Hickman

Midnight Tide
PUBLISHING

Published by Midnight Tide Publishing.

www.midnighttidepublishing.com

Book Title / Jenny Hickman- 1st ed.

Paperback ISBN: 9781958673140

Hardcover ISBN: 9781958673157

Cover design by Cover Dungeon

AUTHOR'S NOTE

This book has scenes depicting grief and loss, violence, discussions surrounding suicide and suicidal thoughts, and contains some sexual content. I have done my best to handle these elements sensitively, but if these issues could be considered triggering for you, please take note.

Because all fairy tales
should end with
happily-ever-after

And all
happily—ever—afters
should be earned

PROLOGUE
RÍAN

EVERY TIME I CLOSED MY EYES, I SAW AVEEN PLUMMETING TO HER death.

Falling impossibly fast. Plunging into the waves. Never resurfacing. Swallowed by the seething sea.

Dawn spilled its golden light across the whitewashed cottage tucked between two fields. With the briny breeze tugging at my shirt, I racked my brain for some way to keep the precious woman sleeping inside safe from the inevitable. We may have won this battle, but I wasn't foolish enough to believe the Phantom Queen would let our victory stand.

I needed to return to the castle and inform Tadhg of what had transpired in the Black Forest. I'd be gone an hour, two at most. A lot could happen in two hours, and trouble had a way of finding these Bannon women. The thought of leaving Aveen all by herself made my chest ache. Or it could've been the recently restored organ doing that. Did having a heart always feel this heavy?

If only I could have gone back to yesterday and told myself not to go through with it.

With Tadhg's life force flowing through her veins, Aveen couldn't die unless the Queen got her hands on the enchanted dagger. And I'd hidden that cursed weapon somewhere no one would find it. But there were fates far worse than death for our kind.

No sense dwelling on it now. There would be plenty of time for that later.

A yawn escaped as I scrubbed at my burning eyes with a heavy hand. Phil the devil-goat peered up at me through one beady black eye before turning back to the thicket on the other side of the well.

My stomach churned as I forced my leaden legs to walk down the lane until I reached a wide enough gap in the high hedge to slip into the neighboring field. Morning dew clung to my boots as I crossed through the rock-riddled grass to the sleeping forest.

The dampened brown leaves carpeting the ground kept my footfalls silent all the way to the dry well housing Hollowshade's magical portal. The energy in this place would conceal any lingering signature my magic may leave behind, making it almost impossible to trace me back here for even the most experienced scryers. Handy, considering the Queen could never know my soul-mate lived nearby.

Instead of going straight to the castle, I evanesced to Ruairi's home in Tearmann, a stone dormer situated on a picturesque plot of land cut in half by a babbling brook. In the distance, you could hear waves greeting the shore. Some might have called this place peaceful or serene. I'd always hated it. The happy, chubby birds flitting from the laurel hedges. The pops of color in the flower boxes below the windows. I could still remember how his mother's laughter used to echo through these now-silent walls. What had he done to deserve the joy-filled life he'd been given while I'd been born to rot away in that cursed forest?

Ruairi answered on the third knock, his black hair matted to the side of his head. Nice to know someone had slept last night. "Get dressed," I said. "You need to guard Aveen."

He folded his thick arms over his chest, golden eyes flashing. "It's the crack of feckin' dawn, lad. I don't need to do anything besides sleep."

Of all the things I'd considered going wrong today, dealing with an obstinate pooka hadn't been one of them. He had to help me. If he didn't, Aveen would be all alone and there would be no one to protect her and—

My heart rate quickened. I pressed the heel of my hand against my chest, willing my thundering pulse to slow. "If the Queen finds her, there's no telling what will happen. I can't lose her. She'll take her from me. Please." The pooka in front of me went blurry. What the hell was happening with my eyes?

"Good god, man. Are you crying?"

Shit. "No." I swiped my traitorous eyes with a shaking hand, panic climbing my throat, choking what remained of my protest.

Ruairi sighed deeply before pulling the door closed behind him. "Where is she?"

Normally, the pity on his face would've incensed me, but not today. Not when I was exactly as pathetic as he thought. I summoned a tost before explaining where he could find Aveen.

He looked as if he wanted to say more, probably something uselessly optimistic or hopeful, but thankfully kept his gob shut. A moment later, I was on my own, just me, the quiet house, and the cheerful, glittering stream. I needed to get ahold of myself. Tadhg would never let me live it down if I fell apart in front of him.

Would Aveen have been better off in the castle? No. I'd made the right choice in bringing her to the cottage. She couldn't hide in Tearmann, not when my enemies were so close at hand. Look what had happened with Muireann. As much as I hated having my love so far away, she would be safer among the humans while I prepared for the Queen's inevitable retaliation.

To the best of my knowledge, the witch had never attacked without reason. Then again, I wasn't sure if she had ever been thwarted the way she had last night.

Only time would tell.

And as true immortals, we had nothing but time.

Until I found a way to end the Queen once and for all, we wouldn't be safe.

To think, a few short weeks ago I thought scuffing my favorite boot had been a disaster. How times had changed.

With a burst of magic, I evanesced to the castle gates. Tadhg's power and immortality had passed to Aveen when Keelynn had resurrected her with that cursed dagger. When my brother found out, he'd be on the hunt for a true immortal to kill so that he could keep his human as well.

I couldn't imagine wanting to be with that shrew for eternity, but Tadhg had never been right in the head.

A breeze whipped across the long grass, wrenching and twisting the lush green blades like waves on the ocean. A figure in a dark cloak waited at the crest of the next hill. My blood ran colder than the waters of the Airren sea.

The Queen had come for me.

At least Aveen was safe.

At least she knew I loved her.

At least—

The wind ruffled the ends of the woman's cloak, revealing blue skirts beneath.

A shaky breath escaped my dry lips. The Queen never wore anything but black. Still, when I inhaled, the air tasted of carrion and death, reminding me of the Black Forest. Except we were a bit far for the stench to be so pungent.

The figure slowly lifted her hands and removed her hood. Red hair danced like living flames around a pale face.

The woman's name lived on the tip of my tongue.

It couldn't be.

She was dead.

I'd watched the Queen tear her heart from her chest.

"Leesha?"

The woman's lips lifted in a familiar smile...

And then she vanished.

1

AVEEN

Do not murder the man you love.

That had become my mantra over the last five months.

Today, it seemed, would be no different.

I sat upright on the threadbare couch and scowled at the boards nailed to the window. They hadn't been there when I'd fallen asleep. With a weary sigh, I rolled to my feet, only to find the window above the kitchen sink blocked off as well. Somehow, he'd tacked boards to the window frames while I slept a few feet away.

Birds chirped from the other side of the barrier. The boards made it impossible for me to see them. I stretched my hands toward the ceiling and arched my back, feeling worse than I had when I'd passed out.

"Rían?" When no answer came, I stood and straightened my rumpled blue skirts. The scorch marks on the rug in front of the fireplace scraped the bottoms of my bare feet as I drifted toward the short hallway.

I found my wayward prince pacing the bedroom in a wrinkled shirt with the sleeves shoved over his corded forearms. His black breeches hung off his hips, and his single sock had a hole in the toe. My, how things had changed since we first met.

The floorboards creaked beneath me, and his head whipped toward the door. Dark circles lived beneath his reddened eyes, and a frown lived on his lips. I'd give anything to see him smile. Hell, even a smirk would've given me hope at this stage.

"Oh, good," he rasped, his fingers tapping against his thighs. "You're awake. I closed the windows. All that glass is far too easy to see through. It won't matter tomorrow, though."

I was almost too afraid to ask. "Why? What's tomorrow?"

He took a step toward me. That was when I noticed the small steamer trunk stuffed with dresses in front of the open armoire and the empty hangers discarded within.

Not this again. "I already told you, I'm not leaving Airren." Perhaps I should have gotten the words tattooed on his forearm, so he remembered them.

Rían grabbed one of my corsets from the bed and clutched the fabric to his heaving chest. "And I told you that every day we delay is one day closer to our doom. The only way to be together is to leave this cursed island. I've secured us passage on a merchant ship in the port. We sail with tomorrow's tide."

So many words and none of them good. I swallowed my groan.

Even if I wanted to sail off into the sunset with Rían, I couldn't leave my sister here all alone with Tadhg. I still wasn't sure the bloody Gancanagh was the best option for a husband or a protector. Some days, the man didn't seem able to care for himself.

I needed to speak with her and observe the two of them together to ensure this was what she wanted.

Besides, who was to say the Queen wouldn't send the merrow to sink our ship into the bay? Or that she wouldn't follow us to the ends of the earth once she learned her son had fled? "Rían, look at me." Bloodshot eyes met mine. "I understand," I said, hovering somewhere between wanting to hug him and wanting to hit him over the head with a candlestick. "I do. But knowing the Queen may be coming for us doesn't change my mind. However, if you want to go, you can. I won't try to stop you."

His hand jerked to the scar on his chest like it did every time he was on the verge of a panic attack—which seemed to be twice a day now.

"You don't want me here?" He started blinking rapidly. "I knew it. I feckin' knew this would happen."

This man. Always so quick to jump to the direst conclusions.

"Rían…" I wanted to reassure him, but one glance at the boarded-up windows and cache of weapons in the far corner, and the words turned to ash on my tongue. He didn't allow me to go to the garden or leave the house without an escort. I hadn't been alone in weeks.

I eased onto the mattress with a heavy sigh, and something hard rammed my hip. My stomach sank as I slid a long dagger with a serrated blade from beneath my pillow.

We couldn't keep going like this.

I closed my eyes and pinched the bridge of my nose to ward off the thumping in my skull. "Perhaps it would be better for us both if we took a break."

"I knew it," Rían muttered to himself, rubbing his hand over his chest. "I feckin' knew it. You've changed your mind."

"I haven't."

"You have." The corset fell onto the floor. "I'm sorry my love for you is such an inconvenience."

His love was a gift. His paranoia was the inconvenience. I never thought I'd say this, but I missed the man who didn't care about anyone or anything.

He jerked his curved dagger from its sheath and waved the handle at me. "Take it. Go on. Put me out of my misery and cut out my worthless heart."

"Stop being so bloody dramatic and put that thing away." I'd done my best over the past five months to handle him with care, but I was finished. Rían O'Clereigh needed some tough love, and since I loved him more than anyone, I had to be the one to give it to him.

He shoved his dagger back into the sheath with a vicious curse.

"As far as the Queen is concerned, I threw myself off the cliff and died." Sure, she might've learned that I'd been resurrected with Tadgh's life force, but the odds of her realizing that had made me a true immortal were slim.

His fingers resumed their tapping against his thighs. "When she finds out—"

"If she finds out."

"*When* she finds out," he ground out, "she will not rest until we both suffer."

Fine. If he wanted to doom and gloom, I'd go down that rabbit hole with him. "Can we stop the Queen?"

His lips pressed together in a slight grimace.

"If she came to the door right now, would these stop her?" I got up and kicked over the quiver leaning against the bedpost, spilling arrows across the floor. I didn't even know how to shoot a bloody bow. "What about this?" I stalked to the corner and tried to lift a broadsword. Bloody hell. Only a giant could have wielded such a weapon. From the way Rían avoided looking at me, I assumed I'd made my point. "Well? Does any of this give us a chance of winning against her?"

His jaw worked as he stared down at the rest of the weapons. There were daggers under the mattress. Daggers beneath the sofa's cushions. Daggers in the bloody privy.

"Answer the question, Rían."

He nudged an arrow with the toe of his boot. "I don't want to."

"Fine. Allow me." I let go of the sword, and the weapon fell against the wall with a shrill *clang*. "The answer is no. If the Queen comes for us, there isn't a damn thing we can do to defeat her. So why don't we stop worrying and start living? Why don't we do something productive with our time instead of hiding away like criminals?"

He'd barricaded the bloody windows, for goodness' sake. What was next? The door?

"How about instead of adding more daggers to your collection, you teach me how to defend myself using my magic?" The angrier I became, the more heat hummed through my veins. If only I knew how to wield it. "Or teach me how to evanesce." At least then I'd have a chance of escaping if the Queen came for us.

He shook his head, his cerulean eyes shuttering. "It's too—"

"Dangerous," I finished.

Apparently, practicing magic near the cottage could draw the Queen's attention since no recorded Danú lived in Hollowshade. You know how I solved that problem? By suggesting we take the portal elsewhere. Rían nearly had a heart attack. Heaven forbid I left this cage for more than a gulp of fresh air or a short stroll on the beach with a glamoured Rían trailing behind. He wouldn't even let me go down to the village for a loaf of fresh bread.

"Exactly," he agreed with a bob of his head.

"So I'm to live like this for the rest of eternity?" To be a prisoner in my home. To never see my sister again. To let him make all my choices in the name of "safety."

"Only until I kill the Queen."

"Something you haven't managed to do in over two hundred years."

"I didn't have the dagger."

"Ah, yes. A dagger you cannot wield."

"I'm working on it," he ground out.

He was working on it. Not me. Not us. Him.

My fingers closed over the cold hilt of the dagger on the bedside table. There was only one way to end this. Rían wasn't just breaking me. He was breaking himself.

I gestured toward the door with the gleaming blade. "Leave."

His chin jerked, and he stumbled. The heel of his boot caught on the quiver, and he slipped. His back slammed against the wall. "You don't mean that."

The horror in his wide, worried eyes nearly made me falter. But in order to save us, I had to destroy us first.

"I do. I want you to leave me alone. If you're so worried about the Queen finding me, then it's the best choice for us both. She'll have no reason to assume I'm still alive if we aren't together."

His trembling hands reached for mine. "You're not thinking straight."

On the contrary. For the first time in months, my head felt clear. "I can't be with you when you're like this. I've spent my whole life as a pawn, bending to the whims of men. You don't get to control me too."

Those hands that had held me so tenderly, that had brought such pleasure, fell to the wall, as if the plaster was the only thing keeping the man I loved upright. "I don't want to control you."

"Then let me be free."

He blinked. "You want to be free from me."

I nodded, knowing he'd taste the lie if I spoke the words aloud. This wasn't what I wanted, not by a long shot. Sending him away felt like prying open my ribcage and cleaving my heart from my chest, but I couldn't live like this anymore. Maybe a temporary separation would help him realize how ridiculous his demands had become.

"I hope..." His weak voice broke. "I hope you find someone who makes you happy. Someone who can give you the carefree life you want. The life you deserve."

Couldn't Rían see? *He* made me happy. *He* could give me a better life than I could've hoped for in my wildest dreams. But not if he continued to hold his fears closer than he held me.

Rían shuffled out of the room. The slamming door rattled the painting I'd picked up in the market. Guess what fell out from behind the frame? Another bloody dagger.

As if these weapons would do anything but incense the Queen.

My heart battered my breastbone in the stark silence. Suddenly, I was no longer in my room but on that cliffside. Terror clawed at my throat when I thought of the untold violence in the soulless black pits of her eyes.

That vile witch had stolen enough from me.

She couldn't have my sanity as well.

I smoothed my hands down my skirts until their shaking subsided and then I blew out a harsh breath.

I'd rather live a short, fulfilled life than an eternal, empty one.

Tightening my grip on the dagger, I braced one hand against the wall and wedged the blade between the boards covering my window. With a few twists and a bit of leverage, the nail holding the corner came free.

One by one, the barriers fell until nothing except muted gray light filtered through the grimy pane. I missed Tearmann's sunshine and warmth. Most of all, I missed the person I'd been while being held "captive" in Rían's castle. Unburdened, living in the moment, falling in love with a wicked prince.

A wicked prince I'd kicked out of my house.

He'd be back, though. Give him a week, maybe two, and he'd see the error of his ways. Then he'd return, and we could heal ourselves together and find happiness once more.

I left the bedroom to work on the boards blocking the kitchen and living room windows. Then I let the dagger fall to the ground and stepped outside.

Part of me expected to hit some sort of barrier, like the one around the castle in Tearmann. Instead, I sauntered straight into the dull day and filled my lungs with frigid, salt-laced air.

After growing up on the coast in Graystones, the rhythmic song and familiar scents of the sea lived deep in my marrow. But ever since my foray into the Black Forest, nothing about the ocean brought me comfort.

The waves no longer soothed, they smothered.

The olive-green fingers of seaweed looked as if they wanted to wrap around my ankles and drag me to the depths.

Instead of cooling, the relentless breeze made me sweat.

My insides quivered as I blew a breath through cracked lips.

Men had controlled me for my entire life, and I refused to let fear do the same.

I forced one foot in front of the other, walking away from the sea, over the bank, and toward the forest.

In a few months, my sister would return from the Underworld, and I vowed to be in Tearmann when she woke.

It was time to figure out my magic.

2

AVEEN

PERHAPS I HAD BEEN A BIT OPTIMISTIC THINKING I COULD TEACH myself to do something I had never done before. I'd spent all of two hours yesterday standing next to the portal like a fool, trying to call on the latent power smoldering in my chest and nothing had happened.

Unless you counted being shat on by a bird.

That was the moment I gave up and returned to my cold, empty cottage to try and get some sleep. And I had slept...until a creepy scraping noise startled me awake. I sat in that room with the quilt to my chin, cursing myself for sending Rían away. But after ten minutes of scratching and scraping, I figured if the Queen had come for me, she probably would have done so in a more dramatic fashion, and if the noise was a burglar, he probably wasn't that good at his job because it should not have taken that long to break into my cottage.

So I'd grabbed one of Rían's daggers, padded through the dark living room, rammed my shin off the coffee table, and then threw the door aside only to find my goat passed out on the stoop like a guard dog, his back hoof scraping against the doorframe as he twitched.

After a few more fitful hours of sleep, I returned to the well to practice. And by practice, I meant standing around with my eyes closed, trying to get this bloody magic to *do something*.

Just as I had that night in the alley when Robert had attacked me, I imagined the cool weight of Rían's dagger. The smooth hilt. The sharp, glinting blade. I swore I could feel the weapon in my outstretched palm, but when I looked, there was nothing there.

How had I managed to shift the thing without even knowing I possessed Tadhg's power?

I closed my eyes and tried again. And again. And *again*.

Each time ended in the same bloody result: an empty hand and disappointment in my gut. Where the hell was this magic when I needed it?

The budding trees creaked and groaned. I kicked a loose stone at the closest mossy trunk. At least no one was here to witness my complete and utter failure.

As if fate had heard my internal musings and laughed, a dark shadow moved in my peripherals.

When I realized what—or rather, *who*—it was, I couldn't help but groan. Did Ruairi honestly believe he could hide behind a sapling? Even sideways, his shoulders stuck out from the trunk.

"You know I can see you, right?"

With a muttered curse, Ruairi stepped from his terrible hiding place. His sharp fangs seemed to gleam despite the gloom in the woods. "This forest is nothing but feckin' twigs. Not a decent tree in the lot."

No sense asking what he was doing here. Rían must have ordered the poor man to stand guard. I considered sending him away, but since I hadn't made one bit of progress, a distraction from my dismal failure sounded brilliant. "Are you here to tell me to go back to the cottage?" If so, he'd have to drag me kicking and screaming.

His thick black brows raised toward his windswept hair. "Do ye want to go back to the cottage?"

I couldn't help the smile tugging at my lips. *Excellent answer.* "I will go back to that cottage when I am good and ready and not a moment before." Dampness seeped through my skirts when I sank onto one of the fallen trees. "How are things at the castle?"

Ruairi hooked a fallen twig between his fingers and used the end as a back scratcher. And to think, pooka were some of the most feared creatures on this island. "Eava misses ye. Keeps sayin' the place reeks of men. Gave out to R—" Ruairi cut himself off before saying my prince's name. "Gave out to *him,*" he amended with a quick glance around the trees, "for not bringing ye back."

Good. If anyone could help Rían see the error of his ways, it was their fiery kitchen witch. I missed Eava fiercely...and her cooking. What I wouldn't have given for a thick slice of chocolate cake right about now.

"And how is *he* handling this?"

With a heavy sigh, Ruairi leaned a shoulder against one of the skinny trunks, making the poor tree shudder and creak. "He's not impressed, I'm afraid. Already killed two merrow."

"You're joking."

He shrugged. "They were to be executed anyway, but Tadhg usually doesn't let it get that messy."

Lovely. Murderous Rían had returned with a vengeance. At least he'd stopped wallowing.

"I can see why ye'd be sick of him," Ruairi went on. "To be honest, I'm surprised ye lasted this long."

I wasn't sick of Rían. I was sick of him treating me as if I were some expensive glass bauble. As a true immortal, I'd never been less breakable. "Yes, well, he was being insane."

"In fairness, he's always been a little insane."

Up until this point, I'd enjoyed his particular brand of insanity. Now, though. I couldn't see us finding our way back to one another until he let go of this need to control me under the guise of protection. "So you're back to being my guard, then?"

Ruairi's smiling golden eyes dropped to his worn leather boots. "Maybe I'm just here for a friendly chat with a pretty lady."

The sentiment tipped my lips into a reluctant smile. We *were* friends. And friends helped one another, didn't they?

When I patted the log next to me, Ruairi's smile faltered. Who would've thought such a big scary pooka would look so unsettled by the prospect of sitting next to me. We'd spent countless hours together back in the castle, and this was no different. "Come on. I don't bite."

He hesitated for a moment before giving in. His wool-clad thigh grazed my skirts when he sank down. The scent of leather and sun-dried laundry drifted toward me.

"How are you?" I asked, feeling a bit guilty for not inquiring sooner.

"I'm grand."

Did he honestly expect me to believe that? Perhaps he didn't realize I could see his hands flexed into white-knuckled fists around the twig he still held.

Something must've been bothering him. If he didn't want to discuss it, I would respect his privacy. When he was ready to talk, I would be ready to listen.

He glanced sidelong at me. "How are ye?"

"I'm grand," I said with a smirk.

Snorting, he waved the stick toward the trees surrounding us. "Do I want to know why yer hanging around in a forest all by yerself?"

"That depends. Are you going to tell *him*?"

"Not if ye don't want me to."

Another brilliant answer. If Rían found out, he'd make it his mission to put a stop to my plans. One way or another, I had to get back to Keelynn. "I'm trying to figure out my magic."

"And how's that going?"

"I'm still sitting in a forest instead of a castle, so how do you think?"

One fang dragged across his lower lip. Then his face brightened. "Maybe I can help ye."

That sounded bloody brilliant. Still... "If he found out, he would murder you." Their relationship was tenuous at best. I didn't want to make it worse.

With a roll of his eyes, Ruairi launched his stick into the forest. "The lad's all bluster."

Said the man who'd literally just told me Rían had murdered two people. "You really want to help?"

"Sure, what else would I be doin'?"

He could have been doing just about anything, unlike me. "All right. Perhaps if you tell me how your magic works, I can figure out how to access mine."

His wide-set shoulders lifted and fell with a shrug. "Don't know, really. It's just there. Always has been. Comes out when I need it and stays inside when I don't."

In that alley, I'd needed the dagger, and my magic had come through for me. But Rían could shift anything, whether he "needed" it or not. Which meant I should have been able to do the same.

"What about shapeshifting?" Ruairi seemed able to change his form at will, much like the glamours Rían used.

He stared down at his hands, rubbing at the thick callouses on his palm. "It's not as impressive as the lads, but all pooka can take the form of a horse. Some can become a wolfhound as well. Others a hare or a hawk. The strongest of us can shift into all four."

"That's quite impressive."

His mirthless chuckle ruffled his shoulder-length black hair. "Yer with the glamour prince, I doubt a horse or a mutt impresses someone like ye."

"There's only one way to find out. Stand up and show me."

He glanced sidelong at me. "That's awfully forward of ye, human."

I slapped his arm, and he let out another gruff chuckle as he rose to his feet. Goodness, I'd forgotten how large he really was.

"Which one?" he asked with another sigh, looking over my head instead of directly at me.

I'd already seen him as a beautiful black stallion, so I chose something different. "Hound, please."

A flash of blinding light burst from his form. In a blink, he was no longer a man but a black wolfhound with intelligent golden eyes. From my seated position, he stood almost as tall as me.

Absolutely fascinating...

When I held my hand toward his snout, his wet nose bumped my palm, and he let out a little whimper that made me smile. If I didn't know better, I'd believe he really was a canine.

Ruairi's eyes closed when I scratched his wiry head. "Color me impressed."

With a snort, he ducked his head and slipped from under my hand. Another burst of light, and he was back to his human form.

I'd have loved to turn into a hound right about now. Then I could run straight across the Black Forest and get back to the people I loved. Since that couldn't happen, I needed to find another way to reach my sister before she woke from Tadhg's curse.

"Can you evanesce?" I asked.

His brow furrowed. "I can."

There it was, my ticket back to Tearmann. "Do you think you could teach me?"

His fangs gleamed when he grinned. "Suppose I can try."

3

RÍAN

Crows skulked atop lampposts, anxious to sink their talons into the bodies swinging from the gallows once the crowd dispersed.

Another miserable day brought seven more names to the register.

At the far side of the wooden platform, a wailing woman crumpled to the ground. No one asked if she was all right or stopped to offer condolences or words of comfort. They strolled right past, ignoring her and the corpses growing cold in the breeze.

Fat raindrops splattered on my forehead, the looming clouds no longer able to hold back their tears. No sense drawing the hood of my cloak. I longed to feel *something*, even if it was discomfort.

I brought my palm to the first man's knobby ankle and inhaled deeply. My well of magic swelled with what remained of his life force. If I could use this power to defeat the Queen, then their deaths wouldn't be for naught.

At least that's what I told myself as I withdrew the ledger from my coat and added his name.

Willie Breen. Half-fae. Seventy-three years of age.

Another round of sobs from the woman with mud seeping into her skirts brought a fresh wave of heaviness to my chest as I stepped over to the next victim in line.

Amie O'Dea. Witch. Eighty-five years old.

Dell Shelly. Grogoch. Two hundred and four.

Taren O'Dowd. Witch. Sixty-four.

Mary Brennan. Half-fae. Fifty-two.

Michael McMahon. Pooka. Forty-three.

I reached the end of the line, where the grieving woman had fallen silent, her chin tipped up toward the clouds, tears and rain-drops mixing on her ruddy cheeks.

The body in front of her belonged to a woman with a distended stomach beneath her stained shift.

Shit.

The sudden lump in my throat made it impossible to swallow. She'd been pregnant, and they'd hanged her anyway.

She didn't look familiar, and the letter that had arrived said there were to be six Danú executed. This woman made seven. Rounded ears peeked from behind mousy brown hair. She could still have been a witch or half-fae. Impossible to tell in death.

I knelt onto the stones next to the woman and offered her the handkerchief from my pocket. "Did you know her?" I asked, inclining my head toward the final victim.

Pushing to her feet, the woman dabbed the handkerchief beneath her red nose. "Her name was Polly McGill. She was my sister."

I rose as well and swiped a hand down my breeches to loosen the grit coating my knees. Another pair for the laundry. "What was her crime?" Not sure why I bothered asking since the woman was probably human. This damn heart made me too soft.

The woman's eyes narrowed. "My sister was tainted."

What the hell did she mean by that? Besides the tortured look on her face and glazed eyes, the dead woman appeared healthy to me.

"Polly's always been a good girl. Smart as whip." She lifted a pale hand toward the pooka dangling next to Polly. "Until that monster's magic seeped into her mind. Made her do unspeakable things."

Unless the pooka had somehow managed to steal the woman's heart, his magic wouldn't have been strong enough to influence Polly one way or another. Not that I could say that aloud. "What sort of things?"

"Abandon her good family to carry that *thing's* demon spawn," she spat.

Any sympathy growing in my heart for this vile woman evaporated.

"So she fell in love with a pooka." *That* had been her crime. Polly McGill had found the one thing everyone in the world spent their lives searching for, and she'd been killed over it.

Snorting, the woman shoved my handkerchief at my chest. The white square drifted into the muck at our feet. Her brown teeth flashed when she sneered and said, "No one can love a monster." Her skirts flung mud across my boots when she whirled and stalked toward the market.

No one can love a monster.

We monsters needed to stick together.

I opened my notebook and added Polly's name to the register next to the pooka's.

And then I named their child Regan and added the little one's name as well.

Aveen stumbled toward the cliff, her golden curls tangling in the wind. I stretched out a hand, catching her shoulder right before she reached the edge. She twisted toward me.

When I saw her swollen stomach, I startled and lost my grip.

She missed a step and dropped like a stone toward the gnashing waves a thousand feet below, screaming *Help me* until the sound was cut off by a sharp *crack*.

I flew upright, peering around the darkened room for a face I wouldn't find. Aveen was gone. Forever? I feckin' hoped not. Then again, it had been four months since she'd banished me from her life, so who really knew?

The candle on the desk had burned down to the candlestick. I hadn't meant to fall asleep, but that's what happened when you read books as boring as *This History of Magic*. I rested my elbows on either side of the thick tome still open on my lap and let my head fall into my hands. It didn't matter that I couldn't see the words written on the yellowed pages. The text hadn't been the slightest bit useful. No matter how many books I read, none of them held information on the fate of a mortal made immortal using a cursed blade.

I presumed Aveen would age as we did. She'd shifted my dagger, so she must have access to at least some of Tadhg's power. And she'd come back after the Queen had…

A shudder ran down my spine; the terror of watching her die still plagued my head and my heart. I didn't know how to let it go. The Queen could kill me a hundred times over and I'd find a way to move on. But knowing my love for Aveen put her in constant danger left me crazed.

I pushed the book off my lap and threw my legs over the side of the bed. On my way to the window, I hooked the wine bottle on the bedside table between my fingers. Stars winked far above, hiding secrets no one would ever know.

A figure waited on the knoll beyond the castle gates, holding a candle aloft, the shuddering flame bright enough to highlight strands of red hair tangling in the wind. I screwed my eyes shut and drank straight from the long neck until all that remained was another empty bottle.

When I opened my eyes again, the ghost had disappeared.

I saw Leesha almost every day now. Some sort of dark magic wielded by the Queen, no doubt. If my mother's aim had been to drive me mad, she'd succeeded. Even when I didn't see Leesha, her spirit still haunted me all the same. A constant reminder of how I had failed the woman I once loved. Of how I couldn't let the same fate befall my soulmate.

I wasn't sure how long I'd been standing there when Eava's soft humming found its way through the door. The old bat was the only person in this place who checked on me.

A knock rattled the bottles lying against the door. "Rían? I've made ye dinner."

I didn't want dinner. I didn't want anything but to be left alone. Still, she continued going through the trouble day in, day out. The least I could do was take a few bites to make her happy. "Leave it at the door."

"Come now, my boy. Wouldn't ye like some company?"

Aveen was the only company I craved, and she wanted nothing to do with me.

"Yer hair must be getting outta sorts," Eava went on. "I can give ye a trim while I'm at it."

I dragged a hand through my thick hair that grew like a weed.

Aveen loved weeds.

Sighing, I flopped onto the bed. The strands at the front fell into my eyes, but I shoved them right back. Probably should've cut it, but not tonight.

"Maybe tomorrow." That's what I told her every night she did this. Maybe this time, it would be true. I scratched my stubbled cheek. How did Tadhg stand it? My face itched so feckin' bad. Eventually I'd have to do something about that too.

Once Eava's shuffling steps faded into silence, I got up and kicked past the sea of empty bottles to collect a shirt from the floor. A tray of lamb stew waited in the hallway, along with a plate of cherry tarts still warm from the oven. I choked down what I could of the stew and shifted the tarts to the fireplace. I didn't need more reminders of what I'd lost.

I needed to make sure Aveen was all right.

I grabbed my pack from the floor and slung the strap over my shoulder. The thought of running into anyone downstairs made me want to hit something, so I evanesced out to the gates, crossed the wards, and went straight to the portal in Hollowshade.

The trees in the forest creaked and swayed, their moonlit shadows shuddering across the ground. My boots slipped silently down the frosty path toward Aveen's cottage. Smoke twisted from the stone chimney before vanishing with the sea breeze. Like an invisible hand had fisted the front of my shirt and yanked, I felt myself being drawn toward that blue door.

Would it really be so bad to give in?

All I needed was one night. One smile. One laugh.

I gave myself a mental shake. This was how life had to be. Aveen had been right to send me away. I never would've been strong enough to keep this distance on my own. As difficult as this was, I was determined to respect her wishes.

A feminine silhouette drifted across the kitchen window. My heart leapt into my throat, but I forced my gaze away, toward the darkness that loomed on all sides of that whitewashed cottage, searching for signs of trouble.

We'd retrieved my heart. By all accounts, we'd won.

And yet here I stood, on a frigid hilltop, unable to hold the woman I loved, as empty and alone as ever.

My pack hit the hard ground with a *thump*. I withdrew the blanket to cover the frosty grass. If only I could've built a fire to warm my bones. There'd be none of that tonight. I didn't deserve the comfort anyway.

Phil stomped toward me, his beady black eyes trained on the pack. I grabbed one of the apples and handed it to the smelly animal as a peace offering, so he didn't try to butt me with his crooked horn the way he had a few weeks back. *Rotten beast.*

Before I could withdraw a second apple for myself, movement along the forest's edge caught my eye. A tall, dark shape, moving quicker than anyone should. I told myself not to panic, that whomever it was could be heading toward the village.

Only this person wasn't turning toward the village but sprinting toward my human's cottage. Unable to evanesce without leaving a magical signature, I chased after the shadow, my heart roaring in my ears until I realized who had arrived.

A different sort of fire replaced the ache in my chest. One borne of rage and regret.

Not only had my brother's best mate come to call on my human, he had a basket swinging from his arm that smelled suspiciously like chocolate cake. Which happened to be Aveen's favorite.

When his glowing golden eyes met mine, he startled and then rushed to hide the basket behind his back. As if I wouldn't see the thing.

I shifted my dagger, really, really hoping he would give me an excuse to stab him as I gestured toward the basket with my blade. "Did Eava give you that?"

Ruairi hesitated. "Maybe."

Her betrayal felt like an iron pipe to the ribs. Eava, the woman I considered my real mother, had given this bastard something to help him woo my feckin' soulmate.

Ruairi tried to walk around me, but I met his step with my own, blocking the gate. "You're not going inside." Not a feckin' hope. He could go right back to his house and wallow like me.

The dog smirked his last feckin' smirk. "Last I checked, bringing cake to a friend wasn't illegal."

"Tadhg is your only friend."

His fangs flashed in my face, and I had to control the urge to tear them out one by one. "Not anymore, lad."

When I'd told Aveen to find someone who could give her the life she wanted, I hadn't feckin' meant it. And I certainly hadn't wanted her to pick some hairy feckin' pooka with a chip on his massive shoulders.

Ruairi could visit her in broad daylight. He didn't have a murderous mother waiting to torture her. He could do as he damn well pleased, while I was stuck rotting away in that feckin' castle with nothing and no one.

What if Aveen ended up like Polly McGill, falling in love with the bastard and bearing his child?

She couldn't love him.

She was supposed to love *me*.

What the hell was I supposed to do now? I should've gone inside and reminded her what we had. I should've gotten the dagger and killed the Queen in her sleep. I should've killed the dog grinning at me.

The nerve of this fecker. Aveen bore *my* mark. He knew the rules. She was *mine*. He didn't deserve her. No one did.

I tightened my hold on the dagger.

I needed to kill someone.

I needed to kill *him*.

Feck it.

I buried the blade into his muscular thigh.

A deep, feral growl erupted from Ruairi's throat. His eyes glowed brighter as his lips twisted into a sneer. What was that supposed to do? Scare me? How pathetic would I be if I shied away from a pup with sharp teeth?

Suddenly, he blew out a harsh breath, fixed his snarl into a lopsided grin, withdrew my dagger, and let it fall to the grass. "I'll be sure to tell Aveen ye said hello."

Maybe she'd come outside and give out to me for stabbing Ruairi. Maybe she'd stab me back. Hell, at this stage, I didn't care, I only wanted to hear her voice.

Then again, if she walked out that door, I wouldn't have the strength to hold back. I'd be on my knees, begging for another chance.

I collected my dagger and muttered, "Don't bother," before stumbling toward the field to retrieve my pack. No sense sitting here in the freezing cold, waiting to see what time the pooka finally left.

Praying he didn't stay all night.

4

TADHG

My arse hurt, my head ached, and if I didn't get a slice of Eava's strawberry-rhubarb pie soon, someone was going to meet the wrong end of a cursed dagger. Preferably a true immortal so I could steal his life force and use it to resurrect my wife.

Not that I had access to the dagger since my infernal brother refused to hand it over because he said I had "suicidal tendencies" and he "didn't want to deal with the Danú in my stead." Which was fair enough. Still, I had no plans to take my own life…today, at least. All I wanted was to put an end to waiting. To wondering what would happen when Keelynn returned in four weeks.

"How many more?" I asked our servant Oscar as I gently massaged my temples. That final glass of púitín last night had been a mistake, and I couldn't even blame Ruairi because he'd already been passed out on the settee.

"Two, Prince Tadhg."

Only two more. The moment they stepped out of this room, I'd be able to take off this stuffy waistcoat, evanesce to the tower where Keelynn slept, and shift the entire pie all for myself.

A familiar orange-haired witch entered the great room. I hadn't spoken to Anwen since the night my darling brother had sentenced her to death for stealing from the humans. Where were

27

her little ones? She usually had at least one of her brood hanging from her skirts.

I scrubbed my clammy palms down my breeches and sat up a little straighter. "Anwen."

The hair coming loose from her chignon fluttered against her cheeks when she bobbed her head. "Prince Tadhg."

"What can I help you with today?"

Her gaze darted to Oscar before returning to the throne. "I'm afraid it is a delicate matter. Would it be possible to speak to ye in private?"

Oscar shuffled closer to where I sat, resting a hairy hand on the top of my throne.

I'd learned my lesson about being alone with women while cursed. I had a wife now—albeit a dead one. The last thing I wanted was to screw up again and give Keelynn more reasons to despise me. "Oscar won't be leaving."

A fierce blush raced up Anwen's neck to her jaw. Her gaze dropped to her slippers. "I...um...I'm in need of rations. I've been unwell these past few months and unable to work. My eldest is in the shop morning, noon, and night, and—"

"There's no need to explain yourself. Go around the back to the kitchens and knock on the door. Eava will fix you up with whatever you need."

She went to say something more, but then her gaze caught on Oscar, and her mouth snapped shut. She bobbed half a curtsey, thanked me, and hurried back out into the hallway.

One down. One to go.

I could practically hear the pie calling my name.

When a man walked in bunching a flat cap between his hairy hands, the tension in my stomach eased. Although I'd seen this grogoch delivering apples to the castle, I couldn't recall his name.

"Seaney," Oscar greeted with a smile and a tip of his own cap.

The newcomer nodded to his fellow grogoch and then to me. "Oscar. Prince Tadhg."

"What can I do for you, Seaney?" I asked.

His slightly protruding jaw rolled back and forth as he mulled over his response. "I'm supposed to pay taxes, ya see. But my entire crop has been struck down with a blight."

Grogochs were brilliant farmers. For an entire crop to die wasn't unheard of, but for a grogoch's crop to die, that was something else entirely. "What sort of blight?"

"It's hard to explain. Be best if ye come and see fer yerself."

Oscar offered to tag along, which was a relief since I knew next to nothing about apples except they tasted good in a pie. On the way out, we ran into Ruairi by the fountain.

"Where are ye off to?" he asked, lifting a quizzical brow at our small party.

How did he always look so refreshed after a night's drinking? So feckin' unfair.

Seaney answered so I didn't have to. "The southern fields."

For some reason, that made Ruairi frown. He braced his hands on his hips and turned back to me. "Before ye go, might I have a word?"

As if I'd turn down my best mate. I told the lads to wait beyond the wards. With my magic bound, I wasn't sure I'd be able to make it there and back on my own power alone.

Ruairi glanced around the empty courtyard before coming so close, the tips of his boots hit mine and I could smell last night's drink on his breath. Maybe he wasn't so unaffected after all.

He'd been drinking like a feckin' fish. When I'd asked if anything was wrong, he'd snorted and told me to pass the bottle.

"I need yer help," Ruairi whispered.

So there was something wrong. I feckin' knew it. "Does it require you to be this close to me for long?"

A chuckle rumbled in his throat. "Unfortunately, it does. I'm working on a secret project and can't be having anyone in the castle hearing about it." He shot a pointed look toward Rían's darkened window.

So he wanted to keep this "secret project" from my brother, then. As intrigued as I was, the last secret project I'd helped with left me buck naked in a briar patch. Not exactly where you want to spend a hungover Sunday morning.

"This won't be like the last time. Ye can even keep yer breeches on," Ruairi said, as if reading my mind.

After all he'd done for me over the centuries, it was the least I could do. Oscar and Seaney watched us from beyond the wards. "Come with me to the fields, and then I'll help however I can." That's what Fridays were for. Helping.

If anyone asked me to lift a finger tomorrow, I was going to tell them to feck off.

Outside the wards, the four of us joined hands. Oscar's cracked, dry fingers wrapped around mine. I lent some magic to the cause but mostly let Seaney steer us where we were meant to go.

The world went dark, and my stomach plummeted. When I opened my eyes and saw a bunch of blackened trees with sagging, gnarled branches, it bottomed clean out.

Seaney's entire orchard looked as if someone had lit the field on fire, leaving only charred remains. The blackness didn't stop at the roots either. It seemed to seep into the ground, turning the grass the color of ink. Bodies of birds and tiny rodents lay prone, their little legs pointing toward the sky next to hundreds of blackened apples.

Ruairi let out a low whistle through his teeth while Oscar bent to run his fingers through the bone-dry soil. When I poked the bark on the nearest tree, my finger sank into the tree's spongy flesh. A foul-smelling red sap oozed down my hand.

The trees weren't just dead, they were rotten all the way through.

From where he knelt, Oscar's gaze lifted to mine. One look at his face told me everything I needed to know: This was bad. Really bad.

"What could possibly cause this?" I asked.

Oscar pushed to his feet and scrubbed a hand along his wiry

red beard. "Looks like it might be poison of some sort. But to know for sure, we'd need to find the source of the blight."

The blackened earth stretched from the orchard into the forest beyond. I had a sinking feeling I knew exactly where it had originated. And who was responsible.

My theory was confirmed when we traced the blight back to the Black River and found the land on Tearman's bank as devastated as the Black Forest's shore.

This had to be the Queen's doing.

To what end? If the blight had spread on Airren's side of the Forest, I'd understand her motives. But why would she attack the people she'd always claimed to want to save?

Only one person could answer that question, and I wasn't about to speak with the Queen all by myself with my magic so feckin' low.

First things first. I needed to ensure Seaney's safety. Not that he'd be foolish enough to consume the blackened fruit, but there was no telling what this blight might do if it reached his cottage. Or beyond.

Focus on the task at hand. Maybe he'd incensed the Queen somehow and she had a vendetta against him.

I turned to Seaney, finding a grave expression that surely matched my own. "Have you had any interactions with the Queen?"

He appeared taken aback by my question. "Not a one, sire. I swear it. Never even met the witch."

Feck it anyway. The only thing left to do until we learned more was to get him away from this place. "Who else lives in your cottage?"

"Just my wife and me."

"We'll need to shift your home away from this mess." *We.* I almost laughed. I wouldn't be shifting dinner, let alone a feckin' cottage. "I'll send my brother this afternoon." He could shift a hundred cottages. Hopefully, it wouldn't come to that.

"And the taxes?" Seaney asked, his face losing all color at the mention of my brother.

"You can't pay them if you have no crop. Come to the castle if you find yourself in need of rations."

"Thank ye, my prince."

He really shouldn't have thanked me yet. Not until I figured out how to stop the blight from spreading.

I told Seaney to explain the plan to his wife and asked Oscar to retrieve my brother. The two of them evanesced, leaving Ruairi and I alone.

The stress of all this shite only made my headache worse. I could've really used a drink, but that would have to wait. "You still need my help?" I asked the stone-faced pooka.

He nodded, transfixed by the blackened earth. I held out my hand, and together, we evanesced to a stone well surrounded by a lush forest. It took me a moment to place where we were: the portal near Hollowshade.

"This has to do with *her*?" I knew better than to say Aveen's name when there was no telling who would overhear. If anything happened to Aveen, I would never forgive myself.

With a brusque nod, Ruairi brought me deeper into the woods, to where Aveen paced between trees, the skirts of her plain gray gown dragging on rocks and twigs.

When she saw us, she rushed over, her face flushed and eyes bright. "What took you so long?" Her eyes widened as her gaze bounced between us. "Something's happened. What's wrong?"

Since I couldn't lie and had no intention of inciting panic, I nudged Ruairi with my elbow.

He stepped forward to lay a reassuring hand on Aveen's shoulder. Oh, my brother would not have liked that one bit. Not that I'd be telling him how friendly the two of them appeared.

"Nothing," Ruairi assured her with a gentle squeeze. "Just dealing with some rotten trees."

She patted his hand, a smile gracing her lips. Then she turned back toward me. "How is he?"

"Don't know. Haven't seen him in ages." The castle had been so peaceful. Granted, I had a lot more shite to do, but that couldn't be helped.

Her brows came together. "You haven't thought to check on your own brother?"

"If he wants to sulk, it's no concern of mine." When I felt down, all Rían seemed to do was annoy me. I feckin' hated it. I figured I'd be the bigger man and leave him the hell alone.

Her eyes narrowed.

Aveen didn't look at all like her sister, but there was something in her glare that reminded me of my wife.

I missed Keelynn so feckin' much.

According to Ruairi, Rían hadn't seen Aveen in months. He must've been missing her too. Maybe I should've shown him a bit more sympathy. "I'll check on him when I get back." And he'd probably kill me for it. "Happy?"

Sighing, her shoulders seemed to sink. "No. But it'll have to be enough for now. I don't understand why he hasn't even tried to see me."

Ruairi removed his hand from Aveen's shoulder and took a retreating step. "That may be my fault."

Aveen turned that glare on the pooka, and he actually shrank back.

"A while ago, I ran into Rían outside yer cottage and may have let him believe the two of us were more than friends."

"You *what?*" she shrieked.

Ruairi held up his hands as if trying to calm a wild beast. "He's the most jealous lad I've ever met, and ye were so sad, I thought it'd give him a kick up the hole to stop sulking about."

Aveen's hand balled into a fist, and she punched Ruairi in the bicep.

"Feckin' hell, human." He winced and rubbed his arm as if it actually hurt.

"Is this the secret project?" I asked, gesturing toward Aveen. "Trying to get the two of them back together?" As far as I was concerned, Aveen was far better off without Rían. Not that anyone asked me.

Aveen gave Ruairi one final baleful glare before letting a resigned sigh steal the tension from her shoulders. "I need to learn to evanesce."

That was all? "Think of where you want to go, and your magic will take you there."

A twig snapped beneath her boot when she stomped. "That's exactly what Ruairi said, and I've tried a thousand times, but it doesn't work."

"Then try again."

A determined scowl fell over her features as she braced her feet between the scattered stones and closed her eyes.

"Think about somewhere special to you. Somewhere you felt safe." The more emotion tied to a place, the easier it was to get there, especially when you were first starting out. "Feel the heat in your chest?" She nodded. "Good. Call it forth. Tell it where you want to go."

A smile tugged at Aveen's lips. She drew in a deep breath and...nothing happened.

Her eyes flashed open, disappointment swirling in the icy blue depths. "See! It doesn't bloody work."

What had I missed? I folded my arms over my chest and ran through the steps in my mind. "Don't worry. We'll figure it out."

I studied my brother's closed door, seriously considering my life choices. I wanted to help Aveen, really I did. But mostly I wanted to help myself get into Keelynn's good graces by making her sister happy. And if that meant stepping into the lion's den, then so be it.

With a deep breath, I turned the knob and pushed the door, only to meet resistance. Not from a lock or a ward but from a heap of empty wine bottles discarded across the floor. Feckin' hell.

It was worse than I thought. I mean, I'd known he was up here drinking but hadn't thought it was this bad. Even I hadn't drunk this much.

I braced my shoulder against the door and shoved. Glass clinked, but the barrier moved enough for me to squeeze through the gap without spilling the tray Eava had given me.

I found my brother sitting at his desk, staring out the window like he hadn't noticed me. "I like what you've done with the place. Very cozy."

Slowly, he turned, his narrowed eyes finding mine.

Even after Leesha's death, he hadn't looked this broken. Had I ever seen him without a cravat? I was shocked his neck could hold his head up without one.

"Don't you have maidens to ravish?" he muttered.

The retort on my tongue would've only made matters worse, so I swallowed it down deep. "I brought you dinner." According to Eava, he hadn't let her in his room for three weeks. That was her fault for asking for permission instead of forgiveness.

Rían yanked the tray from my grasp and slammed it onto the desk, rattling the dishes and cutlery on top. "Is that all, Your Highness?"

Normally, it would have been. But since I'd promised Aveen… "You look like shite."

He snagged the fork and speared a roast potato, no doubt pretending it was my head. Instead of eating the thing, he smeared it around in the gravy over and over again. "Thank you, Your Majesty. I do so thrive on your compliments."

He's hurting.

Be patient.

If you kill him, he'll only kill you back.

"What's wrong with your face?" The facial hair reminded me of our father. Probably not the best thing to say aloud considering Rían had despised the man.

"I ask myself the same thing every time I look at you," he muttered around a mouthful.

I snagged a potato for myself. Before I could slip the greasy morsel between my lips, Rían shifted it right out of my hand and stuffed it into his mouth as well.

Not fair. I hadn't had my dinner yet either. "I'm hungry."

He stabbed a carrot. "Then get your own dinner and leave me alone."

He would be so lucky. I stuffed my hands into my pockets and eased onto the corner of the desk. *Hold on.* Was that a stain on my brother's shirt? This was worse than I thought. "So, how's life?"

"Funny you should ask me that considering you're ten seconds from losing yours."

Better get to the point, then.

I understood what Ruairi had been trying to do by letting Rían believe he and Aveen were a couple. To be honest, I was shocked it hadn't worked better. Clearly Rían had no intention of going to Aveen. I wasn't averse to helping her learn how to use her magic, but there was only one person strong enough and smart enough to get her to this castle.

And he was sitting right next to me, shoveling steak into his mouth.

For Keelynn, I would risk my brother's wrath.

"They're not together, you know. Your one and Ruairi."

He slammed down the fork and collected the bottle from the corner of the desk. "I don't give a shite who she fucks," he muttered before taking a swig.

And another.

And another.

"I'll be sure to tell her that when I see her tomorrow."

His pulsing jaw didn't scare me as much as the dead look in his eyes as he tilted the bottle toward me. "Don't tell her a feckin' thing. Why are you seeing her, anyway? If the Queen finds out—"

"The Queen is too busy poisoning the land to worry about my comings and goings. Besides, I'm taking precautions. You could do the same, you know." If he wanted to see Aveen, he could. Unlike me, stuck talking to my wife's corpse until she came back.

He slammed the bottle onto the desk. "If I ever come to you for advice, you have my permission to kill me."

"You're not the only person in this castle feeling miserable."

He eased back on the chair, chewing slowly as he studied me. His throat bobbed when he swallowed. "Are you trying to bond with me?" His eyes widened. "Holy shit. That's what this is, isn't it." He glanced around behind me. "Where is it?"

"Where's what?"

"Your olive branch."

"Feck off."

"Shall we cry on each other's shoulders? You can wipe away my tears and I'll wipe away yours. Wait! I know! Why don't we plait each other's hair and swap corsets?"

I shoved away from the desk and started for the door. "At least I'm trying."

"How about instead of trying to 'help' me, you try going two days without getting absolutely scuttered?" he shouted at my back.

My brother's clothes may have looked worse for wear, but he was just as much of a stubborn bastard as ever.

5

AVEEN

Ruairi stomped in a circle, something I'd seen him do every time he got irritated. Which seemed to happen at least twice a day. "Yer wrong. It's more a tingle than a burn."

"I think I know what evanescing feels like," Tadhg countered with a hard shove against the pooka's chest. "I've been doing it since I was ten."

Ruairi shoved him back, straight into a bloody tree. If they didn't stop bickering, this poor forest wasn't going to survive another training session.

"Well, I've been doing it since I was nine, so that makes me the expert."

"Bollocks. No one can evanesce that young."

Ruairi folded his thick arms across his chest. "I could."

I stood back and watched my two trainers spat while Phil crunched on a carrot. Despite Tadhg and Ruairi's "help," I still hadn't been able to wield magic. Tadhg suggested that my human blood may have had something to do with the blockage, but if that were true, surely I wouldn't have been able to return from the dead.

There had to be some other reason, and we would never figure it out if the two of them didn't stop arguing. I'd tried evanescing on my own, evanescing holding one of their hands, holding both of their hands. Nothing worked.

"Does it really matter who learned first?" The question earned me a matching pair of scowls. Here we were, another day wasted, and I was no closer to learning how to evanesce. No closer to seeing my sister when she came back from Tadhg's curse in seven days. *Seven.*

My suggestion to bring Keelynn's body to the cottage so she could wake up there had been shot down immediately. I was all out of ideas and quickly running out of time.

Tadhg and Ruairi went back to bickering like children. I closed my eyes and did my best to tune out their cursing. My lungs expanded as I drew in a deep breath, focusing on the latent heat in my heart, willing it to expand through my chest.

Fire sparked in my veins. Nothing to be excited about since I'd gotten this far before. My blood zinged the same way it did every time Rían touched me.

I missed him so bloody much. All those wicked smiles. The crisp cinnamon scent of his magic clinging to his starched shirts. The decadent tang of cherry tarts on his lips the first night we spent together.

A different sort of heat flooded my body, pooling between my thighs as my head began to spin. *Not* the way I wanted to feel with two irritating men standing so close. "When you're finished, I'll be over there," I said, gesturing to a gap in the trees where sunlight streamed through. If I was destined to fail, I may as well do so while basking in the sun's warmth. The yearning in my core grew with each step. By the time I reached the patch of grass, my magic hummed in my chest.

With my instructors otherwise occupied, I sank onto the soft earth and tipped my face up to the sky. If Rían were here, I knew exactly what we'd be doing to ease this frustration. I dragged a hand along my neck, wishing it belonged to a wicked fae prince.

He was harsh breaths. Sinful whispers. Slow, trailing kisses. Lingering touches igniting bare skin. The way he would touch me... The fire in his fingertips would build on this latent heat like it had that night in his townhouse when we'd first made love.

Every time I'd tried to evanesce before, I'd focused on getting to the castle in Tearmann. But in this moment, with delicious pressure building low in my stomach and tingling my spine, my mind drifted to a different place. A small living room overflowing with fuchsia. Golden plates and a tray of cherry tarts. A man whose body I longed to feel against my own. A prince who could set fire to my blood and make me revel in the flames.

My rushing heartbeat filled my ears. In this moment, if I could've gone anywhere on this island, I would have gone back to that townhouse, back to that night where I discovered how Rían could make me burn.

The world around me fell away. The ground under me no longer felt soft but hard and unyielding.

My eyes fluttered open, settling on a ceiling with a crystal chandelier hanging high above. To my right, I found an empty hearth surrounded by marble.

I was no longer in a forest but in the middle of a small living room. In Rían's bloody townhouse. In bloody Graystones. Laughter bubbled up inside my chest.

I'd done it! I'd actually—

Oh, no.

I'd done it.

Panic doused the fire in my blood, and I screwed my eyes shut. I tried as hard as I could to hold on to the heat, but my magic evaporated, stealing my elation with it.

Think of the sounds of chirping birds.

Think of the smell of the soil.

Think of the way the grass prickled your hands.

The rush, the fall, never came. Again and again, I tried. Each time I opened my eyes, I found myself staring into a barren fireplace in an empty townhouse. At least, I *hoped* it was empty. What if the staff were still here? What if someone found me?

I crawled to the settee and curled up behind it, listening for signs of life. What was I supposed to do now? I couldn't very well go outside and have someone recognize me when I'd died over a year ago. My heart pounded against my ribs. Where had all the air gone? I gulped breath after breath, but the pressure in my chest refused to ease.

I squeezed my eyes shut and massaged my temples, willing my racing heart to slow. The air was all around me, right where it had always been. I needed to calm down. Keep a level head. Focus.

I needed a disguise.

Keelynn had lived here when she'd been married to Rían.

I meant *Edward*. Keelynn had been married to Edward DeWarn, the faux Vellanian Ambassador, not my Rían.

My Rían. Was he even mine anymore?

When I told him to leave, I thought he'd last a week, maybe two. But months had come and gone, and he hadn't given in to jealousy or temptation. Perhaps the thought of being with me no longer tempted him. Perhaps he finally realized I wasn't worth all the hassle and had found someone else to occupy his time. Someone the Queen would approve of. Someone he could love without constant threat.

Tadhg and Ruairi would've told me if he had moved on. Wouldn't they? They'd been going behind Rían's back to help me train; their loyalty was clearly with me.

Wasn't it?

Such disheartening thoughts would do me no favors right now, so I shoved them aside. First, a disguise, and then a plan to return to Hollowshade. I crept out from behind the settee, through the parlor, and into the empty hallway. The stairs creaked as I tiptoed up to the bedrooms to search for something to wear. Behind the first door, cinnamon-laced air tickled my tongue. This must've been Rían's room. The fine waistcoats in the armoire confirmed it.

Down the hall, I found a room filled with dresses from when I'd gone shopping for my trousseau and purchased gowns for Keelynn instead. There wasn't a hope of me fitting into her dresses, but I did find a soft green velvet cloak that should do the trick.

I draped the cloak around my shoulders and tucked my hair beneath the fur-lined hood. If I kept my head down, maybe I'd make it out of town. And then what? Hollowshade was on the other side of the bloody country. Getting there would take weeks, and I had no money to hire a horse or pay for lodging along the way.

Talk about a disaster.

I stalked toward the window, searching desperately for a way out of my predicament. A handful of men and women lingered in the square. Thankfully, no bodies hung from the gallows today. My gaze strayed to the sign swinging over the shop next door. *That's it.*

Dame Meranda had gotten a message to Rían once before. If there was one person in this town I could rely on for help, it was her.

I descended the stairs and crossed through the hallway to the kitchen's back door, emerging into a garden the size of a postage stamp, overgrown with thistles and weeds. I slipped down the alley and up the stairs to Meranda's shop. The bell over the door welcomed me with a joyful jingle. To my dismay, four other women milled around inside.

Sinking deeper into the cloak, I bowed my head and pretended to consider the ivory muslin on a nearby table. Behind the counter, Meranda wrapped a stack of garments in brown paper before slipping them into a bag. Slowly, I made my way through the cluttered tables and dress forms to the changing area at the back. Each time a customer left, the bell chimed.

One.

Two.

Three.

Four.

I was about to turn when the icy kiss of a sharp blade pressed against my throat.

"Tell me yer name, witch, or I'll cut ye from ear to ear," Meranda hissed against my temple.

"A-Aveen Bannon," I choked, my heart in my throat.

The pressure eased a fraction before dropping entirely. Meranda caught my shoulders and twirled me toward her. Her eyes widened as she peered beneath my hood. "Bloody hell, woman." Her arms came around me in a fierce hug, setting me off-kilter. "I thought for certain ye were a witch."

"No. Just me."

"What're ye doing here?"

Although I trusted Meranda, I wasn't sure I should tell her this secret. Not that I thought she would betray me on purpose, but if word got back to the Queen, it would not end well for me. "I came because I need to speak to Rían, and I have no way of getting word to him."

Meranda's lips pursed.

"I know you're busy, and I hate to impose, but this is extremely important. Would you mind helping me once more?"

"'Tisn't an imposition at all, milady. I'll get him here. Ye have my word." With a flick of her wrist, the sign on the door flipped to *Closed*, and the bolt scraped into place. A moment later, my friend evanesced, leaving me standing in the middle of her shop.

Instead of staying where anyone looking through the windows could see me, I drew my hood and hurried back toward the staircase leading to Meranda's apartments. The thought of seeing Rían again made my stomach flutter. I knew better than to get my hopes up that our reunion would end with him coming back to me, but couldn't help myself.

We'd spent too long apart. If he helped me get to Keelynn first, then I would be willing to leave Airren with him so we could start a new life elsewhere.

I would miss my sister fiercely, but perhaps someday I would have enough control over my magic to visit her. I could take all necessary precautions, even wear a glamour if Rían wished.

43

The door to the rear entrance blew open, startling me out of my musings.

Nervous butterflies took flight in my stomach when a man stepped into the shadowed doorway. Finally. *Finally.*

A relieved smile tugged at my lips as I lifted my hands and threw back my hood. Rían wasn't going to be very impressed with me evanescing, but I'd take his wrath over his absence any day.

The man emerged from the shadows, and my breath caught in my throat. He smelled not of cinnamon but the salty perfume of the sea.

This couldn't be happening. My eyes must've been playing tricks on me. That's what this was. A trick of the shadows. My body refused to budge, leaving me frozen like a fool, staring at a face I hadn't seen in years.

A man whose stubble had scraped against my neck, my chest, my bare thighs. My fingers had tangled in the windswept golden curls atop his head. I'd stared into those liquid chocolate eyes and planned a future that wasn't meant to be.

Heavy breaths and stolen kisses. Black sails and whispered lies.

"Aveen? Is it really you?" The sound of his voice drove any remaining doubt from my mind that my past had come back to haunt me.

Captain Caden Merriweather had returned.

6

RÍAN

My dagger waited beside me on top of a mound of unwashed clothes that reeked of blood and sweat. There must have been a mouse or two scurrying around here somewhere. At night, I heard them nibbling on the crumbs that had fallen from the bits of food I forced myself to eat.

Just enough to keep me alive so I could die again.

I'd shifted rope to tie around my neck and hung myself from the beams on the ceiling. I'd carved my wrists and let myself bleed out. Even managed to slit my own throat once. Stabbed myself in the heart so many times, the scar on my chest had gone hard. Unfortunately, no matter how painful the death, I always came back.

My life was a desolate wasteland without end, all because I'd let her slip away.

Tadhg burst through the door, his scowl not faltering like it had the last time he came in and saw the state of my room. I probably should've been embarrassed by the bottles piling up and the mountain of dirty clothes, but if anyone understood the way I felt, it was Tadhg.

His eyes widened when they flashed to where I sat on the floor, surrounded by the evidence of my failings. "Feckin' hell, Rían. When was the last time you ate a decent meal?"

Probably the day he'd come in and tried to steal my potatoes. How long ago was that now? I couldn't even remember. "I do not appreciate your feigned concern." All I wanted was to be left to my misery. Was that really so much to ask?

"We will deal with this"—he spun his hand around the room —"when we get back. But first, I need your help."

He could take his request and shove it up his arse. I had no plans to leave this castle for the next decade at least. "Find someone else." Someone with the will to live.

His expression hardened. "We lost Aveen."

Hold on a minute. Did he say they'd *lost Aveen*? He did. He feckin' did. I rocketed to my feet, catching myself on the bedpost when the floor tilted. "What do you mean you *lost* her?" She was a woman, not a feckin' cravat.

Cursing, he raked his fingers through his dark hair. "Ruairi and I have been trying to teach her to evanesce, but she hasn't been able to go anywhere. Today, she vanished right out of the forest."

Please. People didn't vanish into thin air. Unless… "Someone must've taken her." *The Queen…*

He braced his hands on his hips with a scowl. "If someone else had been there, Ruairi would've scented them."

There was only one other explanation. "She figured out how to evanesce."

"That's what I've been trying to tell you."

If Aveen had been having trouble evanescing, getting back would be nearly impossible—especially if she panicked. She could literally be *anywhere* on this cursed island. What if she'd ended up back in Gaul and someone recognized her from the trial? What if she'd landed in Graystones where she was presumed dead? What if she'd ended up in some random shite town and could never get back home?

Shit. She could be in the feckin' Black Forest right now. The Queen could have her in the castle.

She could be dead.

I kicked the bottles aside on my way to the armoire. "What business do you have teaching her anything about magic?" He'd been cursed so long, he probably couldn't even remember what true power felt like.

"Some of us aren't happy ignoring a woman in need."

"She doesn't need to learn to evanesce." She needed to stay put in that cottage where I'd left her so that she could be safe. I dragged the lone shirt from its hanger and threw it over my head. What had once been fitted now gaped around my chest and midsection.

"Yes, well, she's determined to be with Keelynn when she wakes."

I whirled, pinning him with my darkest glare. "Have you lost your feckin' mind? Aveen can't come here." The Queen would find her then, and I would have wasted months without her instead of stealing every moment of her free time for myself. All of this would have been for naught.

Tadhg shrugged like he didn't care. If she were his human, he'd be singing a different tune.

I dashed my hands through my hair. The walls, the ceiling, the floor...all of it closed in on me. I was being smothered, buried alive. No escape. My fingers and toes started going numb, my body determined to shut down while my heart raged in my chest. "What instructions did you give her?" I choked. "Your exact words. Leave nothing out."

Tadhg's pained wince left my stomach sinking with dread. "We've been working with her for months. I don't really remember specifics."

Of course he didn't. That would have been to feckin' simple. "Go back to the forest and tell that worthless dog to wait there in case she returns. Then find Eava, ask her to scry."

With a nod, Tadhg evanesced.

I shoved the hem of my shirt into the waistband of my breeches and tightened my belt. And then I evanesced as well, through the wards, straight to the gates, back to the place I'd grown up but had never called home.

A pile of emaciated bodies had been stacked by the gates. My heart thrashed wildly as I searched the gaunt faces for one I recognized. Not here. She wasn't here. My relief ended when a woman's screams pierced the air. I sliced my palm and let the blood drip into the lock keeping the high gates closed, and...

Nothing happened.

Why hadn't it worked? For as long as I could remember, my blood had let me pass through the castle wards. But that was before I'd betrayed the Queen. I had to get inside. I had to save Aveen.

"Mother! Mother!" The iron gates shuddered when I kicked them. "*Mother!*" If she didn't show up in the next two seconds, I would—

The Queen's smooth voice crooned from the black castle's front steps. "Must you always be so dramatic?" Her blackened veins seemed more pronounced beneath her translucent skin. But what caught my eye was how *young* she looked. *Feckin' hell.* She looked no older than me. How many lives had she taken to regain such youth?

It doesn't matter. Only one thing mattered, and I realized too late that I couldn't come right out and ask if she had Aveen because then she'd know my love was alive and...

I dragged at my collar. What was with this feckin' shirt? Was it trying to choke me?

The Queen's mouth pinched as her gaze swept from my too-long hair to my dull boots riddled with scuffs. "What has happened to you?"

As if she didn't already know. "This is your fault. *You* did this. *You* took her from me." Tears burned my feckin' eyes, and if there was one thing the Queen hated more than dirt, it was tears.

48

"You should place blame where blame is due. Your human stole from me. She had to pay for her crime."

Truth. But true *when?* Did she believe Aveen had died on the cliffs, or was my love's body in that castle right now?

"Honestly, Rían. I thought I taught you better. Look at you, throwing yourself away over some girl who met her end months ago. I am ashamed to call you my son."

Truth after truth after truth.

The Queen thought Aveen was gone.

Finally, the confirmation I needed. "I am no more your son than you are my mother," I said. And with that, I evanesced back to the castle.

Where else would Aveen have gone? Somewhere familiar. Somewhere she knew well. Somewhere like...*Graystones.* I could start at her father's estate and work my way out from there. I'd scour this entire island if I had to.

When I reached the Bannon estate, a heady sense of nostalgia clung to the cold, damp air. The last time I'd been here was the day I had married Keelynn. Talk about dreadful.

I checked Aveen's room first. The thick layer of dust told me no one had been in here in a very long time. The rest of the estate seemed quiet. No horses in the stables. No servants mucking about.

I threw on a glamour. When I knocked on the front door, Lord Bannon himself answered, more silver threaded through his dark hair and mustache than when I'd last seen him. His stomach looked rounder and his face flabbier as well.

His eyes narrowed into slits as he scoured me from head to toe. "Who the hell are you?"

Was that any way to treat a wealthy visitor? And to think, someone so brilliant as Aveen had been sired by this man. "Sir Walter Rich, a friend of Lady Aveen's. Apologies for calling in unannounced, but I recently returned from the continent and was hoping to see her."

"What is it with men calling to my door today?" he muttered

under his breath. "I'll tell you the same thing I told the last gentleman. My daughter Aveen is dead."

The bitter sting of his truth hit me square in the face.

If Aveen had evanesced here, he would know she wasn't dead. Then again, I doubted she would have made herself known to him after all he had put her through.

I thanked the bastard when all I really wanted was to bury my blade in his belly and watch him bleed out on the marble floor.

Where the hell was Aveen?

7

AVEEN

"IT'S GOING TO HURT, ISN'T IT?" OH, GOD. I WAS BABBLING, BUT I *couldn't help it. There was no way something that size would fit in my body without excruciating pain. Why did women do this? As far as I could tell, there wasn't anything in it for us.*

Caden's calloused palm grazed my cheek as he slowly tilted my head so my wide eyes could meet his steady gaze. "We don't need to do anything, Angel. I'm more than content to spend the night kissing these lips." His thumb pressed against my mouth, swollen from his heady kisses.

I loved kissing him too, but I wanted to do more. I'd already given him my heart, and tonight I had decided to give him my body as well. "No. I want you."

"I want you too." He adjusted himself in his loose trousers. "Clearly," he chuckled. "But there's no rush."

How could he say that when his ship sailed with the morning tide? The sea was such a dangerous place. What if something terrible happened and he ended up swallowed by the depths? I would never know what it was like to truly be loved by this man who had swept me off my feet when I least expected it. What a travesty that would be.

I wanted to do this on my own terms, with a man I had chosen for myself, not some awful lord my father had picked.

My newfound resolve spurred me onward, and I slipped my hand inside his loose trousers. Instead of letting his size scare me, I reveled in the way his breathing caught and the soft curse that escaped his lips as his hips bucked forward, driving himself deeper into my grasp.

"I love you, Aveen," he murmured, adjusting his position where he hovered above me so he could untie the laces on my stay.

"I love you, Caden." Cold air prickled my bare skin as he peeled the fabric away, exposing my breasts. My cheeks heated with embarrassment until his head lowered and his lips locked around one pebbled tip. A different sort of heat bloomed in my core and between my thighs. My grip on his rigid length tightened as his hips edged forward and drew back again and again.

He braced his weight on one elbow and laced together the fingers of our free hands.

"Come with me tomorrow," he murmured, lavishing attention on my other breast. Candlelight glinted off my nipple, damp from his salacious ministrations.

My back arched, pushing more of my aching flesh into his greedy mouth. Such a tempting offer, especially when he flicked his tongue like that. My toes curled in my stockings.

"I can't," I breathed. I couldn't leave Keelynn all alone with Father.

His hand squeezed tighter, as if loath to ever let me go. "When I am finished this run, I swear to come back for you." His eyes lifted to mine. "In return, I want you to promise me that you will leave with me aboard my ship."

He would return this summer. That would give me time to spend with Keelynn and make sure she would be all right without me. I wouldn't be able to tell her the truth, at least not yet. There was no sense worrying her until Caden sailed back into port. Once she met him, she would surely understand my burning desire to be with him forever.

"I promise."

Joy sparked in his dark eyes. His boyish grin sent heat pumping through my veins. He let go of my hand to dance his fingertips down to where my skirt had ridden up my thighs. And when they slipped beneath the fabric, I wasn't afraid.

Caden stumbled forward, stretching a hand toward me as if I were some specter when he was the one pale as a bloody ghost. "Your father told me you were dead."

At the mention of the man who had essentially sold me to pay off his bad debts, my heart stopped beating. "You spoke to my father?" Lord Bannon hadn't known about my history with the handsome captain. And if he had known, he never would've approved.

Caden nodded, his hand falling to his side. "Aye. I told you I would."

He had said that. He'd also promised to come back for me by the end of summer.

"Four years ago." I'd gone to the market every day, searching the port and the horizon for a ship with black sails. "I waited, but you never came back." He'd told me he loved me, used my body for his own pleasure, and then left me as if I meant nothing.

He ran a hand down his neck, the bronzed tone slowly returning to his sun-kissed skin. "Because I've spent the last four years in a Vellanian prison. The only thing that kept me alive was knowing the moment I escaped, I would come running back to you."

Questions filled my mind but never left my lips because the answers didn't matter. What I had felt for him had been fleeting. I loved someone else now.

Caden caught my hand, bringing my knuckles to his full lips. No fire burned. No nerves tingled. He may as well have been a stranger.

"Gods, I've missed you." His hoarse words feathered against my cheek. "Now that I've returned, you and I can marry. I'll take you away from this place—to my home in Iodale, just as I promised."

Hold on a moment. He thought he could sweep in here and we'd pick up right where we left off? Even if I'd still had feelings for the man, such expectations were insane. We barely knew one another. The entire foundation of our relationship—if one could even call it that—was built on one night of shared passion.

"Stop." Tears flooded my eyes. Not for myself but for how he must have suffered in that prison. And I was about to inflict even more pain on his heart. I closed my eyes, unable to look at his features when they crumpled. "Please stop. I can't—"

A loud crack rang through the air. Caden's body slumped to the ground, his head at a wrong angle as he stared at the wall through unblinking eyes.

Rían stood over him, his blue eyes glowing like hellfire.

"What did you do?" I breathed.

Rían's brow furrowed. "Killed the bastard attacking you."

"He wasn't attacking me!" My knees cracked off the floorboards as I knelt to check Caden's pulse. *Please don't be dead. Please, please, please don't be dead.*

His chest no longer rose and fell. His heart no longer beat.

"You actually killed him…" Caden hadn't deserved to die. He had done nothing wrong.

"He had you pinned against the wall. You were begging him to stop," Rían ground out, his hands flexing and eyes bleeding to black.

My head dropped into my trembling hands. How could he *kill* him?

What was I saying? This was Rían. Had I expected a rational reaction? For him to ask questions first and snap necks later?

Tears trailed warmth down my cold cheeks. I might not have loved Caden, but I didn't wish the man dead. And after suffering in prison all this time…

Rían's palms cupped my face, his thumbs smoothing away my tears. "Where did he hurt you?"

I shook my head, trying and failing to stop these bloody tears from spilling free. "He didn't hurt me."

"Then why were you crying and telling him to stop?"

I turned away, scrubbing my cheeks with my sleeves. "Because he and I have a history." At least he'd been given a painless death.

If Rían had found out who Caden was *before* he'd killed him, there was no doubt in my mind that Rían would've ensured the captain's demise was anything but quick.

From the corner of my eye, I saw Rían's eyes expand. "He's the one, isn't he? The one you gave yourself to."

I could only nod, a fresh wave of mist clouding my vision as Rían began to pace in the cramped stairwell, his breathing growing more ragged with each passing second. The air vibrated; the hair on the back of my neck lifted as if lightning were about to strike. "Do you still love him?"

His sharp question stretched between us, piercing the tense air. "*What?*"

He scowled down at me, his eyes black pits and the veins in his neck pulsing. "Do you still love him?"

He couldn't be serious. How could I love Caden when I loved the murderous wretch standing right in front of me? "Yes. I love him so much that I've completely forgotten about you. Is that what you want to hear? It's what you wanted, isn't it? For me to move on and find happiness with someone else."

He scrubbed a hand over his pinched face. "You think this is what I *want?*"

"I haven't seen you in months. I don't know what you want anymore."

Rían sucked in a breath, his mouth hanging loose. His gaze dropped to where the tip of a blade protruded from his chest. Deep red bloomed across his white shirt.

He fell to his knees, tipping forward onto the floor with a quiet curse before falling silent.

Caden stood at his back, a sword dripping blood on his worn brown boots, only he wasn't the same Caden from a few moments ago. A vicious gash sliced across his left eye. Silver scars ringed his wrists, broader and thicker than my own. Shadows lived in the pits of his gaunt cheeks beneath his stubble. Scars shaped like the letter "P" had been carved into the skin of his muscular forearms.

A pirate's brand.

Pointed ears peeked from beneath his shaggy curls.

Not just a pirate.

A *fae* pirate.

"You're not human," I whispered.

A lock of hair fell across his brow when he shook his head. "I am sorry for the deception, my angel, but you must understand why I couldn't tell you."

I understood, all right. If I'd known, I wouldn't have been brave enough to give myself to him. He hadn't told me the truth because he'd been dead set on getting under my skirts, no matter the consequences.

Caden returned his sword to its scabbard, not bothering to clean Rían's blood from the blade. "You are even more beautiful than I remember." His reverent whisper sent chills down my spine as he stepped froward to brush one of my curls from my sticky cheeks.

I turned my face away, the familiar sting of betrayal cutting to my core. "You need to leave."

His chin jerked back as if I'd struck him. After all he'd done, I really should have. "Angel, if you'll only let me explain—"

"You had your chance to explain, but you chose to lie." Another selfish man wanting to take and take without giving an ounce in return.

He stuffed his hands into his pockets, his broad shoulders rising and falling with his weary sigh. "I'm sorry, but if you can find it in your heart to forgive me—"

He expected me to forgive him? Based on what? Trust? *Love?*

All he'd given me were broken promises and a bed of lies. "Swallow your apology just as you swallowed your truth." I was done listening and done with him. I knelt beside Rían, lifting his head onto my lap and pressing my palm to his still warm cheek. "If you're here when Rían returns, he will make you suffer."

"Rían?" Caden's good eye flicked to the body in my lap. "As in... *Shit...*" He retreated toward the back door. "The two of you are...Gods, Aveen. You cannot be serious. He's a monster."

"Yes, well. I'm clearly a terrible judge of character."

Rían might have been a monster, but he was *my* monster.

And when the prince returned from death, there was no doubt in my mind that he would make Caden pay for crossing him.

8

RÍAN

SNIPPETS FROM THE LAST FEW HOURS FLICKERED THROUGH MY mind. Seeing the Queen. Speaking with Aveen's father. Going back to the castle only to find Meranda waiting by the gates with a message from my human. I hadn't hesitated, evanescing directly to Meranda's shop in Graystones. The sounds of Aveen's pleading voice had sent me into such a panic, I'd been convinced the Queen had somehow found her.

But when I'd rounded the corner and saw a man pinning my human to the wall, I'd snapped his neck like he deserved.

My eyes flashed open, finding a beautiful face darkened by shadows only a breath away. So stunning, even through her tears. If anything, the depth of emotion in her eyes made her even more so. Like an endless well I could drink from for the rest of my days. To feel so acutely and to express those feelings without reservation. How could I do anything but marvel at this woman?

The back door banged, startling me out of my reverie. A harsh reminder that when I'd died, the two of us hadn't been alone. I searched for the man who'd stabbed me in the back, but he wasn't in the narrow stairwell.

Neither was the one who'd attacked Aveen.

Then I remembered: He'd been her lover.

All those tears… Were they for him or for me?

I eased upright, my chest still burning from the bastard's iron blade. Aveen said my name, but I'd already lumbered to my feet to check the back alley for signs of my attacker. "Where did the feckin' coward run off to?"

Aveen's lips rolled together. "Calm down."

Like hell I would. I needed answers and wouldn't leave this room until I got them. "Where's the body?" I demanded.

She winced. "I told him to go away."

She told a body to go away? That didn't make sense. Unless… "He's a true immortal." The man I'd killed—her *lover*—had been one of us. I readied my blade. This time, I wouldn't be caught unawares. His life was forfeit the moment he touched what belonged to me. "Where is he?"

"I don't know."

I inhaled her bitter truth. "What is his name?"

"I don't know," she repeated.

Beautiful liar… "Tell me his name this instant, or so help me—"

"So help you *what*? What are you going to do to me?" She rolled her eyes and shook her head the way Eava used to when we were children in need of scolding. "Honestly, Rían, I think you've lost your bloody mind."

I had lost my mind. Over *her*. And now her former lover was back, and she was upset over me killing him. She shouldn't have been upset. She shouldn't have cared at all.

"His name, Aveen."

Her sigh of irritation turned into a glower.

Fine. She didn't want to tell me? I'd find out another way. There had to be at least one other person in this forsaken town who knew him. I stalked out of the stairwell and into Meranda's shop.

My interest in this bastard wasn't solely borne of jealousy. If the bastard knew the Queen, he could tell the witch that Aveen was alive, and we'd be right back where we were six months ago.

"Rían! Get back here—"

As if I'd listen to her when she was covering for him. Meranda stood behind the counter, arms crossed and frown menacing. Not sure who she thought she'd scare. My mother was the Phantom Queen. Menacing frowns were like smiles around the Black Forest.

"There was a man here. Blond hair. Pirate's brand. Scar across his eye. Who is he?"

"Don't tell him!" Aveen twisted the back of my shirt in a pitiful attempt to drag me back.

Meranda's chin lifted as her gaze met Aveen's. "I'm not going to."

What was it with these obstinate women banding together? I pinned Meranda's feet to the floor with magic so she couldn't escape. She may have been a witch, but she wasn't a true immortal. One careful swipe of my blade and she'd be relegated to the underworld with every other person who had crossed me. "Do you want to try again, or will I carve out your heart and send it to the Queen?"

Aveen's fist slammed into my spine. "Rían! Let her go!"

I would—as soon as one of them told me what I needed to know. "His name, Meranda."

"He's not going to kill you. I would never allow it."

Did Aveen not realize the lengths I would go to keep her safe? If that meant killing a woman I'd almost consider a friend, then so be it. What was another stain on a black soul? "This witch is interfering with an official investigation. I'm well within my rights to take her life."

The witch's jaw popped in irritation. "His name is Caden Merriweather. He's a...a captain. Of a ship."

"And how do you know the dear *captain*?"

"He's a distant cousin."

Truth.

"That wasn't so hard, now, was it?" I sent my dagger away and collected a tailored blue shirt from one of the hangers on the rack. "I'm buying this." I couldn't very well be wandering around with Aveen in a blood-soaked shirt with gaping holes in it, could I? I shifted coins to the desk before taking Aveen's hand and dragging her toward the door.

"Come on. I'll get you home." Once I'd regained my strength, I would deal with her beloved captain. Feckin' prick. The nerve, showing his face again after all these years, thinking he could waltz right in and steal Aveen away.

If Meranda hadn't gotten the message to me in time, he might have done just that. And I would've spent the rest of my days searching this island, believing the worst had happened to her. Not even the best scryer would've been able to find her the moment she set foot aboard the ship, and without possessing merrow or selkie blood, her magic would've been useless at sea.

How close I'd come to losing her…*again.*

My teeth ground so hard, my jaw ached.

Aveen tugged loose, her eyes sparking with icy fire. "I'm not going anywhere with you."

"You'd rather let them discover you've returned from the dead and find yourself dangling from the gallows? Fine." If she wanted to be foolish, who was I to stop her? "Meranda?" I called, unfastening the buttons on my shirt to trade it for the blue one. "Can you shift Aveen's body to the cottage once she's dead?"

Aveen shouldered past me on the way to the alley, but not before I caught her taking a good long look at my bare chest. "You are insufferable."

"And you are infuriating." I trailed after her, fastening buttons while keeping my gaze on the angry set of her shoulders and not the way her hips swayed with each stomp. Mostly. When we reached the alley, I held out my hand once more. Although she scowled, she laced her fingers with mine. Her harsh intake of breath reminded me of the sounds she used to make when I would ease inside her. The fire between us still burned as strong as ever. Had she felt this with her pirate?

"Call your magic forth," I gritted out.

"I don't know how," she shot back.

She must know something considering we were all the way in feckin' Graystones and not Hollowshade. "How did you do it before?"

Her cheeks flushed. "I don't know."

Little liar. I pulled her close, entranced by the shards of deeper blue running through her light eyes. Before she could protest, I stamped my mouth to hers. She melted. Then, as if she remembered she no longer cared for me, she jerked away. The flat of her palm met my cheek with a loud *slap*.

Anger. Rage. Lust. All powerful emotions and perfect catalysts for accessing one's magic. I grabbed her hand and told her again to call on her magic, feeling the heat rise almost immediately. Her lips fell open, and we were gone. Falling through nothing until we reached the portal in Hollowshade.

Aveen let me go and started down the hill.

"You're welcome!" I called after her.

She whirled, narrowed eyes alight with murderous intent. I almost wished she would stab me and give me a respite from this nothingness. "You think I'd thank you for abandoning me?"

Now, hold on one feckin' minute… "I abandoned you? You're the one who kicked me out."

She dragged on her curls, her eyes snapping with frost. "Because you lost your mind!"

"Would you blame me?"

The sound of flapping wings lifted around us as a bunch of birds took off through the trees. Aveen blew out a harsh breath. "No, Rían. I don't blame you. I blame *her*."

And just like that, my anger blew away in the autumn breeze.

I knew how overbearing I'd become, but I hadn't been able to stop myself. Aveen was all that mattered to me. Keeping her safe. Keeping her for myself. And in doing so, I'd driven her away.

"Have you been able to shift anything since that night?" I asked, wanting more than anything to spend a few more moments in her light before returning to the darkness where I belonged.

With a huff, she shoved her silken curls back from her flushed face. "I shifted Ruairi's coat a few months back, but nothing since."

Feckin' Ruairi. Stepping in like a knight in shining armor when I'd left. Must have been nice to be so feckin' gallant.

If she hadn't been able to shift, then how the hell had she evanesced all the way across the island? "Is your magic warm or cold? Does it fizzle and flash beneath your skin or swell like the tide? Does it seem to be ready and waiting, or do you have to fight to call it forth?"

She scrubbed her hands down her cloak. Green, not blue. Had Tadhg given it to her to irritate me? I wouldn't put it past the gowl.

"It's...um...it's warm?" She tucked a strand of her hair behind her ear. "I know this may sound foolish, but it feels like it's blooming. Like a flower. Unfurling, stretching, warming me from the inside out."

Aveen's magic would manifest itself as a flower. If I wasn't feeling so feckin' lost, I would've smiled. "That doesn't sound foolish at all." It sounded beautiful, like her. "Can you call it at will?"

"Sometimes."

"When?"

"Mostly when I'm angry."

"Are you angry often?"

Her eyes flashed. "Only when I think of you."

Do you think of me often, little viper? "Is that the only time you can call for it?"

Her cheeks flooded with pink as she shook her head. "When I'm angry, it's hard to focus. And when I'm upset or scared, it's nearly impossible. But when I'm..." Her words trailed off.

From the way her flush deepened, I had a feeling I knew exactly what she wouldn't say. "Aroused?"

She glanced away.

I had seen every inch—kissed every inch—of her body, and yet she still blushed when she spoke of such things. "Your magic is tied to your emotions. That's not necessarily a bad thing. There's a way to fix that."

For the first time since we'd been reunited, hope sparked in her eyes. "Tell me how."

I didn't want her practicing magic, but she clearly had no intention of heeding my warnings. Tadhg and Ruairi had proven themselves absolutely useless—surprise, surprise. With them left to handle her education, she'd probably end up evanescing to the feckin' Forest.

A plan began to form in the back of my mind. One that would make her hate me more than she already did. But at this stage, I had nothing left to lose. "Give me your hand."

She did so without hesitation, her warm, small fingers slipping against mine.

"Close your eyes."

Her lashes fluttered shut, and I allowed mine to do the same as I tried to recall the correct spell. With the words in my mind, I called on my magic and whispered in the ancient tongue, ignoring Aveen's sharp intake of breath as the spell took hold.

Reluctantly, I let her go. "How do you feel?"

She held her hands up to her face, turning them over as she studied them. "Strange." Her gaze flicked to mine. "What did you do?"

"Cast a spell to keep your emotions from controlling your magic." The blatant lie tasted like bile on my tongue.

She checked her hands once more. "What now?"

I stepped back, putting distance between us so that I would have the strength to let her go. "Now you return to your cottage and try not to get into any more trouble."

"No." Her head shook. She tried to reach for me, but I was already gone.

Those at the docks in Graystones spoke of a ship whose sails would change from black to white depending on the captain's whims. According to every feckin' record I'd been pouring over for the last two days, Captain Caden Merriweather didn't exist. Meaning either he hadn't been born in Tearmann or Airren, or he was using a false name. I'd gone back to Meranda's, but the witch was nowhere to be found. So I sent word to Shona, a selkie I didn't despise nearly as much as the others of her kind, asking for her to come to the castle. She knew these seas and the men who sailed them better than the merrow themselves. If anyone could uncover the truth about this Caden fellow, it would be Shona.

The only problem was that her wife was about to welcome her fifth child into the world and had "more important" things to do. You'd think by the fifth one, it wouldn't be some big production.

The pirate wasn't a rotting corpse, so I assumed he was a true immortal. Which meant he had magic. If he truly was able to change the color of his sails on a whim, then his magic presumably worked at sea. Put me on a dingy in the middle of a pond and I wouldn't be able drum up a feckin' spark. Meaning he must possess merrow or selkie blood.

Ruairi popped his head into the study. When his gaze met mine, his golden eyes narrowed into slits.

Maybe if I ignored him, he would go away.

"What did ye do to Aveen? She can't feel her magic."

Good. At least I didn't have to worry about her reaching Tearmann until I'd found some way to destroy the Queen. "I don't know what you're going on about."

"That's total bollocks, and we both know it."

I pushed away from the desk and gave the pooka a smile. "Maybe she just needs a better teacher."

His nostrils flared. "Yer some bastard."

"That is common knowledge, yes."

"She'll figure it out."

Not without help. But that was neither here nor there. I shrugged. "If you say so."

With that, I returned to my room and shifted a bottle.

9

TADHG

THE BLIGHT HAD SPREAD, CONSUMING TWELVE ACRES OF LAND bordering the Forest and killing everything in its path. Animals, trees, crops. Two colonies of faeries had been displaced from the trees they'd called home for centuries, and we'd relocated ten families to Tearmann's western coast.

What were we going to do when there was no place left to go but into the merrow-riddled sea?

Rían rubbed the back of his neck as he glared down at the twisted black trees that, up until two days ago, had been lush and green. Although I'd never admit it, I was glad to have him out of his room. The castle had been all too quiet and congenial without his irritating presence.

Two sheep that must've wandered onto the blackened grass lay lifeless next to the fencepost, their mouths painted black from whatever poison infected the earth. The other day, the Franklin family had lost twelve head of cattle.

"It's moving too fast," Rían said.

"I know." At this rate, the curse would reach the castle before Yule. Rían may be able to relocate the structure, but could I ask it of him? He'd already used so much magic helping the others. If

Keelynn broke my curse, then maybe my latent power would allow me to do more than delegate.

Such pointless, fanciful thoughts.

I'd spent the last year yearning for her while she'd been asleep, my love only growing. When Keelynn woke tomorrow, she'd feel the same as she had when I'd killed her. When she'd found those bodies in the castle.

Angry. Horrified. Betrayed.

But that was a problem for tomorrow. This blight needed to be dealt with today. Oscar had taken samples of soil to one of his friends who studied such things in hopes that she could unravel whatever poison the Queen had used. So far, she hadn't had any luck.

I could think of only one way to put an end to this. "We need to meet with the Queen."

Rían's shoulders stiffened, and his head swung toward me. "*You* can meet with the Queen. I like my heart right where it is."

I understood his reluctance, really, I did. But after what had happened the last time the Queen had called over to the castle, the witch wouldn't be foolish enough to meet with us if Rían wasn't present the entire time.

"We could ask her to make a vow not to harm anyone within the castle walls before we let her through the wards." At least that would give us some peace of mind.

He shifted on his feet, his gaze dropping to where the toes of his boots met the blackened ground. "Do you really think she'd make such a vow? You may as well cut out your heart yourself and serve it to her on a feckin' platter."

His mother may be an evil, merciless witch, but she also claimed to care about the Danú. Although I didn't approve of her methods, she had been nothing if not consistent in that. Never attacking humans beyond the borders of the Forest. Enacting penalties that were perfectly legal according to the treaty with Vellana. As far as I could tell, she had never broken a law. I doubted that she would attack us so brazenly.

"What other options do we have? If we don't stop this, all our land will be dead." And we didn't have enough rations to support a quarter of our population, let alone everyone. "Our people will starve or be forced to move to Airren or abroad." The number of Danú being killed on this island had doubled in the last few months. There were trials every day—even Sundays. Just this morning, I'd had to watch two leprechauns, a half-witch, and a wingless faerie strung up in Rosemire. The humans were angrier than ever, culling their land of "monsters."

People who had lived peacefully and remained hidden for centuries had been exposed and executed.

Rían picked at a piece of lint that dared to make its way onto his black waistcoat. "They're your people, not mine."

Anger boiled in my gut, bubbling violently enough to break through the surface. "Enough of that shite. You may have everyone else fooled, but not me. I know you care about them." Every time he returned from an execution, I could see the distress in his empty eyes. "Wouldn't it be easier to have a simple conversation instead of wasting magic relocating every feckin' cottage in the country?"

He couldn't argue with the truth. And from the scowl Rían wore, he knew it.

He bobbed his head once, his hands fisted at his sides. "When?"

"I'll send a letter to the Forest today."

"And if she denies your request?"

I hadn't a feckin' clue. We'd tried creating wards around some crops a few weeks back, but the curse had consumed the plants all the same. Short of abandoning our land, I didn't know how else to make this go away.

I gave his stiff shoulder a nudge. "Then I'm sure you'll figure something out."

We followed the singed edge of the blight to make sure no one would be caught in its path for the next few days. Over a knoll, down into the valley, and around a bend, the song of the waves growing more pronounced with each step.

I kicked a pebble along with the toe of my boot, trying to figure out why things felt so awkward between us. I never thought I'd say this, but I missed my murderous brother. This melancholy one was so dull.

"How are the magic lessons going?" he asked suddenly.

I'd been spending a decent amount of time tutoring Aveen this week, but she hadn't been able to call on her magic at all.

"Why don't you see for yourself?"

His hands flexed at his sides. "No."

"She could use your help." Keelynn would be so disappointed to come back and not have her sister nearby.

"This conversation is over," he announced, picking up his pace.

As if I'd allow him to dismiss me so easily. "You could be teaching her to save herself." At least then he wouldn't have to worry about Aveen being helpless in a fight. If Keelynn had magic, I'd be teaching her every trick in the book.

"You'll be the one needing saved if you don't stop harping on. She's staying put."

Our footsteps were lost to the pulse of waves and caw of black and white birds darting high above. A woman in a billowing black cloak stood at the top of the next hill, a basket swinging from her pale hands.

Rían caught my arm, his fingers digging into my bicep. "Do you see that?" he whispered.

"You mean the woman?" Why wouldn't I see her? She was right there.

He dragged his free hand across his eyes, the color melting from his face. "So I'm not mad. There's a woman on that hill."

"I can't agree with the first part, but there is, indeed, a woman on the next hill."

Rían let out a string of vicious curses, tugging and dragging on his hair. *Not mad, my arse.*

"You there!" I shouted, waving toward the woman.

Rían dropped to the ground and curled into a ball in the long, swaying grass. "Stop that," he hissed. "Don't let her see me."

Too late. The woman was already twisting toward us. Before I could call out a second time, she evanesced. I waited for her to appear closer, but she never did.

"She's gone." Odd. Almost as odd as my brother covered in dirt as he parted the tall grass to peer through. It was official. He had lost his mind.

When he confirmed she was indeed gone, Rían shot to his feet, his eyes unfocused and hazy. "You need to move Keelynn to the cottage before she wakes. Especially if the Queen is to come to the castle. If she's in the castle, there's no telling what will happen."

I couldn't send Keelynn away. I needed her here so I could spend every waking moment convincing her to fall in love with me. Was that selfish? Yes. But I'd never claimed to be selfless.

"She's not going anywhere." If Keelynn decided to leave me, I wouldn't stop her. At least, I'd try not to. She wouldn't want to leave though...would she?

Rían's brows inched toward the hair falling across his forehead. "And when you tell her what's happened while she was gone?"

"She will forgive me."

"You sure about that?"

No. That was the problem. But I would tell her the truth of this hellish year and let her decide for herself. And if she still chose me, I would spend the rest of my days proving that I was worthy of her forgiveness. Of her love.

Not the rest of my days...

The rest of *hers*.

Keelynn was still human. Still had a finite number of days to draw breath before crossing over to the afterlife for the rest of eternity.

An eternity I would have to spend without her.

Love may be strong enough to break a curse, but love was a curse its own right.

Especially when it ended.

By the time we reached the castle, I was more than ready for a drink and a nap. However, those plans fell by the wayside when we found a group of Danú crowding the courtyard. Oscar stood at the entrance to the castle, trying unsuccessfully to convince them to return on Friday.

"What do they want now?" I muttered.

"They're your beloved people," Rían said with a smirk. "Why don't you ask?"

Seeing no way to avoid the situation, I used what little magic I had left to evanesce next to Oscar. The poor man looked so relieved, I thought he'd burst into tears. When Rían appeared next to me, the murmuring stopped.

"To what do we owe the pleasure of your visit?" I asked, directing my question toward one of the pooka at the front of the horde. His black hair had been plaited into tiny braids that reached past his bare, bronzed shoulders.

"We want to know how you're plannin' on stopping the blight," he replied, golden eyes narrowed.

If he wanted to live to see the next sunrise, he'd want to get rid of that snarky tone. I didn't answer to this man or any of the others. I was their ruler, their sovereign. They answered to me. Still, I knew better than to return disrespect with more disrespect.

"The blight is coming from the Black Forest. My brother and I will be reaching out to the Queen for assistance."

"And if she refuses?" a feminine voice shouted from near the back.

If she refuses, we may be shite out of luck.

"I am certain your Queen has her people's best interests at heart," Rían said, saving me from having to respond.

Good thing one of us could still lie.

The plan seemed to appease the mob for now. At this stage, easing their panic was the best we could hope for. As the crowd began to turn away, a collective gasp lifted from the rear. Those gathered parted, allowing Ruairi through their ranks.

Only Ruairi wasn't alone.

In his arms, he held a woman wearing a blood-drenched gown, whose limp arms and legs swayed with each step. Golden curls peeked from beneath the hood of a gray cloak.

My blood ran cold.

Aveen.

A whimper broke from Rían's throat before he took off toward Ruairi. When he tried to take Aveen's body, Ruairi shouldered past him, up the stairs and into the castle.

I expected to find a murderous gleam in my brother's eyes as he raced past.

Instead, all I saw was hopelessness.

10

RÍAN

THE QUEEN MUST'VE FOUND HER. I'D BEEN OFF WITH MY BROTHER dealing with pointless problems with no solutions while the one person in this world who mattered to me had been cut down. Her heart. I had to check her heart. I lunged, but Rúairi planted his boot against my thigh, knocking me back.

"If you don't let me pass, so help me—"

"Swallow yer baseless threats, fool. I've no time for them."

He thought my threats were baseless, did he? I'd show him once and for all how little his life mattered. I withdrew my dagger, but it vanished. Tadhg stood in the doorway, dagger in hand, glowering at us both. "Attacking him isn't going to help."

It would help me.

His head swung toward the pooka. "What happened, Ruairi?"

The dog laid Aveen onto the settee, and I was about to shift her back to the cottage where she belonged when he withdrew a folded piece of parchment from his back pocket. He tried to pass the page to my brother, but I stole it for myself. My hands shook as I unfolded the crinkled page and stared down at my love's delicate handwriting.

Bring me to the castle so that I may see Keelynn.
Don't let Rian find out or he'll send me away

A war raged within me, between Aveen's request, my own selfish desires, and what I knew in my worthless heart was right. Aveen wanted to be here. I wanted her here. But being here was too dangerous. Then again, leaving her to her own devices had been dangerous as well.

"Aveen asked me to meet her at the cottage at half four," Ruairi explained to Tadhg, his back to me as if he didn't think I would bury a blade in his spine. If he had refused her request, none of us would be in this predicament. "Kept saying not to be late. When I arrived, I found her in the middle of a blood-soaked bed, a dagger lying next to her and fresh wounds on her wrists."

Feckin' hell. This *woman.* Killing herself so she could make it back in time for her sister to return. No sense of self-preservation whatsoever. I should've been happy. After all, she wouldn't have been with me if her head was screwed on right. Knowing she would willingly put herself in danger to spend time with her irritating sister made me want to stab my former wife and put us all out of our misery.

Only, I'd hurt Aveen enough.

And when she returned from the underworld, the process would take twice as long because of the spell I'd used to bind her magic. Once she came back to her body, I could undo the binding, but while she was dead, her magic was dead as well. My love would be in excruciating pain because of my inability to protect her.

When I tried to shift Aveen up to her room, nothing happened. When I tried to approach her body, an invisible force blocked my path. My feckin' brother smiled his last smile.

He thought he could keep me from going to her? "Drop the ward."

Tadhg's infuriating smile only grew. "Not until she wakes."

"We both know you only have enough magic to keep it up for another five minutes at best." I could be patient. Bide my time.

Ruairi stepped right through the ward and folded his arms over his chest, scowling down at me as if he had the right to be near her and I didn't.

"Give her to me." My voice cracked. I didn't care if I sounded weak. I didn't care about anything but Aveen. I needed to hold her one more time. To ensure the pooka's story checked out. To check her for the Queen's scar.

"I want your word that you will not send Aveen away from the castle." Tadhg's infuriating tone rang with authority. "She died so she could see Keelynn. You will not make it for naught."

Although my teeth gritted together, I managed a curt, "Fine." I would have to figure out another way to keep her safe until she could return to Hollowshade.

The barrier keeping me from Aveen vanished. The pooka stepped out of the way, allowing me to slip my hands beneath my love's cold body and cradle her limp form against my chest. I evanesced straight to her room before anyone could stop me. She felt impossibly light. Impossibly small. Impossibly fragile.

"What were you thinking, you loon?" I muttered, settling her on the bed and using magic to change her into one of the clean shifts from the armoire.

Tadhg had been right all along.

I'd spent the last year worrying and breaking my back trying to keep her safe when I should have been teaching her how to escape.

I shifted a bowl of water and a cloth to clean the dried blood from her wounds, already pink and bubbled. What if her bound magic didn't bring her back? The last time could've been a fluke.

An hour of pacing and cursing and hoping and praying, finally, blessedly, ended when Aveen took a harsh, shuddering breath. I sank onto the mattress, assuring her she wasn't alone as she suffered through the agony of returning from true death.

My fingertips brushed the matted curls stuck to her temples

until her eyelids peeled open. Those eyes. How I'd missed their glare.

I caressed her cheek, willing my warmth to seep into her bones. "I cannot believe you killed yourself to get here."

Her tongue darted out to lick her lips, stirring desire that had been buried beneath so many fears. "What other choice did I have?" she croaked.

"You should've stayed where you're safe."

Her eyes hardened. "Unlike you, I want to be with the people I love. I had to be here for Keelynn."

Knowing this woman, if I forced her to leave, she'd only come right back. Meaning I needed to find a way to keep her safe while she was here. "I will let you stay on one condition: you must promise to stay in your room."

"I will do as I please," she countered.

As much as I loved this woman, stubborn Aveen was quickly becoming my least favorite.

Unfortunately for her, I was more stubborn. "There are plenty of free cells in the dungeon. And I hear the oubliette is exceptionally dark and dank this time of year. Those are your choices, Aveen."

"No."

I sat back, studying the obstinate lift to her chin. "What do you mean, no?"

"I mean, you have forced me into a bargain for the last time. However, since I am not a fool and I understand your worries are not without merit, I will keep to the castle *on one condition.*"

This ought to be brilliant. "Go on, then. Name your terms."

"You must teach me to evanesce."

A logical request, and one I wouldn't have minded granting *if* circumstances were different. I'd be a hell of a lot more careful teaching her than Tadhg or Ruairi. However, evanescing was a difficult skill to master, and even with practice, she could end up somewhere besides her desired destination. Not a risk I was willing to take. Still, I agreed because I'd been bargaining for centuries and knew exactly how to swing this one in my favor.

"And you must teach me how to glamour myself," she added.

"That's two demands."

Her lips curled into a vicious smile. "How about we make it three? *When* I can glamour myself, you will let me roam without restrictions."

And risk her glamour slipping and the Queen finding out her true identity? Not a hope. I held out my hand before she could add any more "terms." Her smile turned smug as her palm slipped into mine. I almost felt bad for what I was about to do.

I called on my magic to bind us to our bargain. Speaking of binding... I closed my eyes and muttered a spell. Heat swelled in my palms. Aveen's harsh intake of breath fanned against my cheek.

She tore out of my grip. "I can feel my magic." Her fingers flexed as she stared at them. "I couldn't before, but now I can, clear as day." Her eyes lifted to mine, rife with accusation. "You did something to me, didn't you?"

I twirled one of her loose curls around my finger, relishing each silky strand. "I've missed you, little viper." Her fire. Her passion. Her rage.

She knocked my hand away. "I asked you a question, Rían."

Clearly, she wasn't going to let this drop. I supposed there was no point in lying. The more she hated me, the better. "Yes. Fine. I did something. But it was only to keep you safe."

Her hands balled into fists. "I swear, if you say the word 'safe' one more time, I am going to scream."

She wanted to scream, did she? How the hell did she think I felt? "You evanesced across the feckin' island without knowing how to get back. What was I supposed to do? Let you accidentally end up in the Forest?"

"Rían Joseph O'Clereigh. What. Did. You. Do?"

"I bound your magic."

A dark cloud descended over her petite features.

My fingers itched to smooth the tiny wrinkles between her gathered brows. The devastation in her eyes left my heart in tatters. I'd known this would happen, that this decision would drive her away, and yet I'd done it anyway.

Her head dropped, her golden curls falling forward to curtain her face. "You know, I thought getting your heart back meant you would be in control of your own life. Instead, you're still letting the Queen pull the strings."

"I'm sorry." What other choice did I have? To indulge in my own selfish desires? We both saw how that had worked out the first time.

Her shoulders stiffened. What had I expected? Forgiveness? A man like me knew better than to hope for that after making all these mistakes.

"When is our first lesson?" Aveen asked, looking not at me but through me.

"Not today, anyway. I'm far too busy." I needed to strengthen the wards before heading to an execution in Swiftfell. "Maybe I'll find the time tomorrow or the following day." We'd struck our bargain and without a time constraint; technically, I could go centuries without having to lift a finger.

If I glamoured her myself and hauled her fine arse outside the wards in a day or two, she'd be mad enough for her magic to swell. Then it was only a matter of directing that magic into evanescing back to Hollowshade. She got to see her sister, and I got to put her back where she belonged. Everyone won.

"You promised to teach me!" The flush to her cheeks and rapid rise and fall of her chest made her look positively delectable. I really deserved some sort of medal for resisting Aveen in such a fiery state. She'd probably rake the skin off my back with those nails of hers. Maybe she'd punish me with her teeth.

"How about I teach you about bargains instead?" I shifted an old tome from the study that my reprobate father had slammed down in front of me when I was only a boy. "I think you'll find chapter four positively riveting." I tossed the book onto the bed.

"Building Better Bargains," Aveen murmured, reading the title aloud. She flipped through the yellowed pages to chapter four. "Time constraints?" Her eyes flew to mine. "You bastard."

I held up my hands in surrender. "You made the bargain, Aveen. I simply agreed. Once you've read the book cover to cover, I'll consider discussing glamours."

She released a frustrated groan as I turned and started for the door. Something whizzed past my head. I smiled to myself as I bent to collect the book. "Here. You dropped this."

She yanked the covers to her chin and turned over, giving me her back.

"I'll leave it on the nightstand so you can have a look when you're feeling better."

"I despise you."

A lie never tasted as sweet. "I missed you too." More than she would ever know.

With that, I evanesced to the kitchens, where I found Eava dragging a wooden spoon around the edges of a mixing bowl. Buns and cakes and biscuits crowded the countertop. She must have been preparing for Keelynn's return tomorrow.

Waste of dessert if you asked me.

When Eava saw me, she set the bowl aside. "Why do ye look as if someone left an iron too long on yer favorite silk waistcoat?"

"My human is back." And I was trying my best to bear in mind that this was not a reason for celebration.

"In the castle?" When I nodded, her face brightened. "That is brilliant news. Isn't it?"

Brilliant news until the Queen found out.

Eava's hands landed on her wide hips, dusting the dark material with flour. *"Isn't it?"*

"You and I both know it's not safe here."

"Little Rían, ye cannot control this world and everyone in it."

I didn't want to control the whole world. Only the parts that could hurt the woman I loved.

"Come now, my boy. What's done is done. Fretting won't

make it any better. Ye look as if yer wastin' away to nothin'." She pulled out one of the stools at the high table and gave the top a pat. "How about ye sit down, and I'll make ye something special too? Perhaps a fresh batch of tarts?"

"I don't want any tarts." I grabbed an apple from a bowl in the sink instead. Water droplets cascaded down the red flesh toward my fingertips. "But maybe you could make a batch for her."

Nothing numbed the sting of betrayal quite like a good pastry.

11

TADHG

Rían shifted his stance in front of me, resting his ear against the door.

I couldn't wait any longer. I just couldn't. "Well?" I gave his arm a poke. "What's she saying?"

"Quiet. I'm trying to hear." His brow furrowed in concentration. A few moments passed before his lips quirked into a smile. "She said something about...wishing she was still married to Edward."

I shoved the chuckling bastard aside and pressed my own ear to Keelynn's door.

"How is that possible?" *Keelynn's voice.* My heart stumbled. She was back. Thank the heavens and the stars and whoever made them. My love had finally returned to me. "He was dead," she said. "I killed him."

"Rían brought him back with the dagger," Aveen explained in a soft, soothing tone. "And then Tadhg kissed you."

That fateful day with Fiadh felt like a million years ago.

Why the hell had I let Aveen convince me to let her be in the room when Keelynn woke instead of being there myself?

This isn't about you.

This is about Keelynn and what she wants.

What if she wanted to move to Hollowshade with Aveen? That wouldn't be the end of the world. If I conserved my magic, I could evanesce there any day of the week. But what if she decided while she was away that she no longer cared for me? Worse, what if she found someone else she cared for more? After what I'd done, I could hardly blame her for wanting someone better than me.

Keelynn gasped. "Are you saying I've been gone for an entire year?"

Was that pain in her voice? I should go to her. I grabbed for the doorknob. Rían smacked my hand away. The bastard.

"You said you'd give Aveen time," he chided.

Five minutes should have been more than enough time for Aveen to explain what had happened.

Somehow, I gathered patience I didn't even realize I possessed until Aveen had finished speaking.

Enough was enough. I was going in.

Before I could try for the knob, Rían stepped in front of me. "They're done," I told him. "Listen for yourself. They're not saying anything."

He pressed his ear to the door for a moment before easing the barrier aside.

This was it. The moment of truth.

Forgiveness or eternal misery. Two possible fates hinging on one woman's whims.

"I see our guest has returned to us," Rían said from the doorway, blocking me with his body. I could have evanesced but didn't want to startle the poor woman. What if I gave her a heart attack from fright and she died for real? I could always kiss her again but honestly didn't think I could survive another year without her.

"It's about damn time," Aveen said, a smile in her voice.

Rían bowed like an eejit. "Good to see you looking so well after your stay in the underworld, Lady Keelynn."

I wanted to *see* her, and I was this feckin' close to killing everyone to get some time alone with my soulmate. Rían shot me a withering glare before turning back to the women. "Aveen, I've held him off for as long as I can. If you want to keep the castle intact, I'd suggest you catch up with your sister at dinner."

I knocked Rían aside and had every intention of bowling over anyone else who got in my way, but then I saw Keelynn and my body turned to stone. Glossy chocolate waves fell over her pale, slender shoulders. With Aveen hugging her, I couldn't see her face. All I wanted was to see her face. For her eyes to give me answers to questions my cursed mouth didn't want to utter.

When I cleared my throat, Aveen finally shifted out of the way, her hands falling as she released Keelynn.

How I'd missed the spark in those steely gray eyes. The world that had seemed so dark only yesterday now brightened. Like spring finally emerging from the frozen confines of an eternal winter.

Aveen whispered something that sounded an awful lot like, "good luck" and gave me a watery smile on her way out, following my brother down the hallway toward the staircase. The two of them had issues of their own to sort out. Hopefully sooner rather than later, because Rían had become even more of a miserable bastard.

I closed the door, wishing there was some way to close off the butterflies crowding my chest as well. So much had happened this year, between Aveen and the Queen and my feckin' curse, I didn't know where to begin.

My tongue swelled so thick, I could barely swallow. *Speak, you gowl.* "I see you're alive again."

Keelynn's lips flattened. "Yes. I'm alive again."

Why did this feel so feckin' difficult? I loved this woman, having a conversation with her should not have been this difficult.

I needed to say something better. Something poignant. "Death isn't a very pleasant experience, is it?"

"No. It's not."

"Can you walk yet?" *Another winning line from the Prince of Seduc-*

tion himself. It was a miracle I'd won this woman over in the first place.

"No."

"Right. Um . . . Well . . ." *Just say it.* "You'd think I'd be ready for this. I've had a feckin' eternity to prepare." For some reason, all the speeches I'd written in my head fell short of what I truly wanted to say to her. *I love you. Please forgive me. If you take me back, I will never let you down again.* "Right, so. First and foremost, I would like to apologize. I should have revealed who I was the moment we met and let you run the cursed dagger through my black heart outside the Green Serpent."

Since I'd met Keelynn, her life had gone from bad to worse.

"If I'd accepted my sentence, Fiadh wouldn't have tried to kill you twice, and you wouldn't have been forced to marry me, and you could've gotten Aveen back right away and . . ." Padraig wouldn't be gone. She wouldn't be in Tearmann. Robert wouldn't have assaulted her in Gaul. The list of offenses went on and on. "I'm so sorry."

She flattened her palms over her quilt-covered thighs, her expression softening. "Tadhg, I'm the one who's sorry. If I hadn't made that bargain with Fiadh, none of this would've happened."

"If you hadn't made that bargain, we never would've met. And that is the one part of this mess that I do not regret." Before Keelynn, I'd been living half a life, searching for freedom and fulfilment in places where no such happiness could be found. Even if she told me she never wanted to see me again, I would forever be grateful for the few fleeting moments of joy her presence had brought me.

Her head dropped, but not before I caught a glimpse of silver tears lining her thick lashes. "How can you say that after I killed you?" she whispered.

She could kill me a thousand times over, and I still wouldn't regret it. "I killed you too, so I suppose that makes us even."

A small smile tugged at her lips but vanished just as quickly, making me wonder if it was even there. "What do we do now?" she asked.

"That's up to you." She'd been told what to do her entire life. If she wanted me, I was hers. If she didn't...

I'd still be hers but from afar.

She nodded as if to herself before raising her piercing gaze to mine. "If you wouldn't mind me staying a week or so, until all my faculties have returned and I've had a chance to catch up with Aveen, then I will leave."

"Is that what you want?" I forced past the swelling lump in my throat.

"Y—" She licked her lips and tried a second time. "Y—" She sighed and her shoulders curled in on themselves. "No. It's not what I want."

Talk about relief. I swiped my clammy palms down my breeches. *Here goes nothing.* "Then stay with me."

Luxurious waves spilled over her shoulders when her head tilted. "How can you stand being near me after all that's happened?"

"Because I love you."

Her gaze fell to the emerald ring on my little finger. "Liar."

I removed the small band and threw the thing onto the mattress. It belonged to her now, after all. "I love you, Keelynn." Always would. My heart was hers, even if she didn't want it.

Her tongue darted out, leaving her lips pink and glistening. "Even after all I've done, you still love me?"

"Desperately." And without reservation.

I sank onto the mattress, reaching out for my soulmate. When we touched, our hands buzzed. I'd missed this feeling. Missed her more than she could ever fathom. "I know you don't love me," I said, "but I think I love you enough for the both of us."

A small wrinkle appeared between her eyebrows as she stared up at me, blinking slowly as if still processing my words. But words meant nothing without action. I would prove myself worthy of her, if only she'd let me.

"I love you," she whispered.

The air around us thickened.

Hold on. Did she say she loved me? "How can you lie?" That should have been impossible.

The corners of her lips lifted into the most breathtaking smile as she stared down at the emerald ring still lying on the bed.

"Keelynn, look at me. How did you break the—"

She jerked forward, her lips finding mine. When I tried to pull away, she pressed closer, catching the back of my neck and refusing to let me save her from myself. Not another year. I wouldn't survive it. I wouldn't—

Her lips…

They didn't sigh or fall away or turn cold and black. They remained warm and tender and moving against mine. The thousands of thoughts swirling through my mind fell silent when her tongue swept into my mouth, hot and needy, replacing confusion with burning desire.

I lost my fingers in her hair, holding onto the only woman I'd ever loved, the knowledge that she loved me—*ME!*—in return seeping into my pores like sunlight on a summer's day. Despite all my faults and all my sins, this woman had found something in me worth loving.

The cursed chains binding my magic fell away; lightning flooded my veins. My body moved of its own volition, pressing Keelynn into the mattress, needing more of her. We kissed until our breaths came in ragged gasps, our chests rising and falling in time.

"Did it work?" she gasped through swollen lips. Pink, not black. And oh so perfect.

My fingertips skimmed her pulse, racing and strong. "You seem to be alive, but I could be dreaming." And if I was, I hoped to never wake. This room, this bed, was where I wanted to stay for eternity.

Smiling up at me, Keelynn brushed my hair back from my face. "Lie to me."

If she wanted a lie, I'd tell the biggest one of all. "I hate you," I whispered, sampling the warm skin of her throat.

She adjusted her grip on my neck, shifting and parting her thighs so I could settle between them. "Again."

My heart may have swelled with love, but the other parts of me swelled with need. I nudged my hips against hers, relishing the way her soft gasp tickled my throat. "I have been so happy without you. I never want to marry you again. I have absolutely no desire to lift up your skirts and sink between your thighs."

I was about to ask if her faculties had returned when she tugged my shirt free and reached for my belt.

Her lips curled even as her eyelids lowered. "I hate you too."

"Show me how much, Maiden Death."

Her cool hand slid into my breeches, finding me hard and ready, stroking so slowly, I was sure to make an absolute mockery of myself if I didn't get it together. I bunched her skirts around her waist and tugged her undergarments down her smooth thighs. The magic burning my fingertips was nothing compared to her dripping heat. I kissed her for every day she'd been gone, working another finger inside as she moaned against my mouth. My cock nearly leapt out of my breeches at the sound. I could wait a little longer. You know what couldn't wait, though?

I tugged down the front of her shift, baring her breasts and teasing the pebbled tips with my tongue.

"Tadhg…"

My name on her lips had to be the most beautiful sound ever heard. I curled my fingers at the same time as my thumb pressed the bundle of nerves at the apex of her thighs. Her back arched, thrusting her breasts further into my mouth. No shame, no regret, nothing but love and warmth and magic. I urged more power into my hand, revelling in her whimpers as I worked my fingers and tongue, tying all her glorious threads into knots.

Her grip on my cock tightened and then fell away when she began coming apart around my hand. I dragged my breeches down my hips and eased into her pulsing sheath, the final waves of her release nearly bringing me to the edge of my own.

I had been waiting for this day for far too long to let this pass quickly.

She turned boneless beneath me, her pale cheeks glowing and eyes full of warmth. "I love you."

Those three words sent tension ratcheting up my spine. Each thrust shoved her closer to the headboard, until she was forced to lift her hands to keep her head from slamming against it.

"More," she moaned.

I'd give her more. I'd give her everything. I'd take her to the top of this cliff once more and fall over the edge still clinging to her.

I lifted one of her long, shapely legs over my shoulder so I could drive myself into her tight body until she stopped begging and started whimpering. I found that spot that drove her wild and teased her until we were both crying out for one another and clinging to the glittering edge of bliss.

My lips grazed the inside of her knee as we rediscovered each other. The sound of our bodies meeting over and over again pounded in time with my galloping heart until spots speckled at the edge of my vision. Pleasure ripped through me, spilling into the deepest recesses of her.

Next time, I'd take my time. Next time, I'd show some semblance of control. Next time...

I collapsed onto the mattress beside Keelynn and drew her into my arms, her head finding its home on my chest. Toying with the ends of her hair, I allowed myself to revel in this love I thought I'd never find. The world outside this room was falling to pieces, and yet I couldn't stop smiling.

My finger slipped beneath her pointed chin, urging her eyes to mine. "I have missed you, not only for the last year, but for my whole life." I drew in a shaky breath. Now for the part I'd truly been dreading. "I'm afraid there's something I must tell you. While you were gone, I—"

Her palm pressed against my lips, stopping my confession. "What happened while I was gone doesn't matter. What matters is that you and I are together now."

What had I done to deserve such a good woman? Not a damn thing. "You should marry me. Again," I added with a chuckle. "But this time, I don't want to wed in secret. I want the world to know we've found each other. That because of you, I am finally free."

Keelynn's eyes widened, and the corner of her lips lifted. "A real wedding?"

I nodded, willing to give her the world if she kept smiling at me like that. "As big or as small as you'd like. Whatever you want, name it, and it will be yours. Flowers, candles, cakes, jugglers—"

"Jugglers?" she laughed. "I'm almost afraid to ask what sort of weddings you've been to."

"None as glorious as the one I want to give you. If you'll have me, that is."

Her fingers slid across my stubbled jaw, drawing me in for a slow, deep kiss. "I'll have you, my prince. Now and forevermore."

12

KEELYNN

As I meandered up the winding staircase, trailing my fingertips along the smooth gray stones, I couldn't believe *this* was my life. *This* was my home. How many other hands had done the same in this ancient place? Had any of them been humans?

At the landing, I turned right, still getting used to the size of this beautiful castle. The other day, I'd accidentally taken a wrong turn and ended up in an attic filled with broken furniture coated in a thick layer of dust.

At least I hadn't stumbled upon any more bodies.

A smile had lived on my face ever since I'd returned a week ago. My sister was alive, and so was I, and together we were planning the most glorious wedding.

Sometimes my mind would wander to the last wedding we'd planned together—the one for Aveen and Robert. Any time those depressing thoughts dared to appear, I would squash them like ants under my heels. This was truly the most joyous time of my entire life.

Marrying not only the man I loved but a handsome prince as well.

The stuff of storybooks, fairy tales, and mythical legends.

Yes, I'd married him twice before, but this time felt different.

This wouldn't be under the veil of night or guise of saving my life. This ceremony meant standing in front of the world and Tadhg's people, declaring our love for one another.

Tadhg had been incredibly supportive of all my ideas for our wedding. We would be married in the great hall and invite everyone he knew. I'd been working with Eava on the menu and most importantly—at least according to Tadhg—the cake. Four tiers of amaretto and vanilla deliciousness slathered in butter-cream frosting. The samples Eava had made were perfection.

"Aveen?" I rapped my knuckles against her door. "Aveen, are you there?" I had been so nervous about how Aveen and Tadhg would get on given how protective she'd been of me. But they'd had plenty of time while I was cursed to sort out their differences. The same could not be said for herself and Rían.

Every time I asked about their relationship, her smile fell away. So I'd stopped asking. Still, I saw the way she glanced at him when he walked by, her eyes filled with such longing. And the way he stared at her over dinner when she wasn't paying him attention was borderline obscene.

I did not approve of the two of them together. Not in the slightest. Rían was an ass at the best of times. Still, she deserved to be happy, and she supported my relationship with Tadhg. I needed to do the same for her.

Her soft voice reached me a moment later. "Come in."

My sister sat at a desk in front of the window, scribbling in a notebook, sunlight falling like a golden crown atop her head.

"You're still in your shift." Didn't she realize the time? The vendors would arrive at any moment.

The tip of the pen scratched against the page with each hurried stroke. "I'm afraid I cannot come with you today."

"But we're to pick out the flowers." Flowers were her area of expertise, not mine. "And the seamstress is to measure me for my gown." I didn't want to choose a gown without my sister there to offer her opinions as well.

She set the ink pen down with force, and her head fell into her hands. "I know. I'm sorry. But I promised Rían I would stay out of sight."

I should've known this had something to do with him. If he thought he was going to keep my sister out of this, he had another thing coming. "What happened between the two of you?"

"Nothing."

Did I look as if I'd been born yesterday? "Stop that this instant. You were the martyr once before, and I refuse to let it happen again. Your happiness matters just as much as mine." If not more considering how much she'd sacrificed for me. "Now, tell me what's wrong so that we might come up with a solution."

Aveen's eyes fluttered closed as she eased back in her chair and let her head fall in defeat. "I'm not the one being the martyr. He is."

Rían didn't strike me as the martyr type. But I kept that to myself and gave her shoulder an encouraging squeeze.

"He's terrified that his mother is going to find out she didn't kill me and rip out my heart."

Ah, yes. *That.* Now that I knew Rían's mother was the Phantom Queen, I could see the resemblance. Not only did they share the same shade of mahogany hair, they were both awful. "And you're not afraid of that happening?" I asked.

"Of course I'm afraid. I'd be a fool if I wasn't. But I'm going to be afraid whether we're together or not. She has stolen so much from him, and every day we spend apart, she wins."

"I'm still having trouble wrapping my head around the two of you together."

"He's not what he seems."

"I should hope not. Because he seems like an arrogant prick."

Aveen let out a small chuckle. "All right. Perhaps he is exactly what he seems. But he's not that way with me." Her eyes lifted to mine, so full of affection, my heart broke for her. "I love him, Keelynn. And I know that he loves me. But it's like, in letting the Queen keep us apart, he's saying our love doesn't matter."

"Then you need to talk some sense into him." Perhaps I could help her. She'd sacrificed so much to ensure I ended up with the man I'd wanted to be with, the least I could do was try.

Although she hummed a non-committal response, her expression faltered as she collected her notebook and held it toward me. "Here's what I think you should order for your bouquet. I know you love hydrangeas, but a few pops of color would be nice as well."

I took the notebook and scanned the list. Some of the flowers I knew, others were foreign to me. Either way, I trusted my sister's judgement, on this especially. "And for your bouquet? Should it be the same but a bit smaller or would you like something different?"

She glanced away. "I don't need a bouquet."

"Of course you do. Your hands will look silly empty." On second thought… "I suppose you could carry a candle like they did at Cousin Regina's wedding, but since the ceremony is being held during the day, it doesn't really make sense."

Her lower lip wobbled when she spoke. "I don't think Rían will let me go to the wedding."

The notebook slipped from my fingers, clattering to the ground. Rían wouldn't *let* her? This decision had nothing to do with that stuck-up pig.

"He cannot keep you from my wedding." Rían and I would need to have a little chat, now, wouldn't we?

I wrapped my sister in a hug, holding her close. Tears pricked my eyes, but I refused to let them fall as I silently vowed to make this right.

When I let her go, she reminded me to bring the notebook. I left her room feeling a little heavier, and by the time I reached the bottom of the staircase, my limbs felt downright leaden. A handful of Danú mingled inside the great room. The moment I stepped through the door, their quiet conversations fell silent.

My hands itched to scrub at my skirts or wring behind my back, but showing nervousness would only make me look weak. And without possessing magic, I was already at a disadvantage. So I steeled my shoulders and offered them a confident smile. "Hello.

94

I am Keelynn Bannon, Tadhg's fiancée. I appreciate the time you all took to come in today. Hopefully, we can get this wedding planned without too much hassle."

No one spoke. Not even a word of greeting. They kept staring, their expressions cold and unimpressed as I continued to the small table Tadhg had shifted in front of the dais. I took the chair closest to the thrones and waved the first man forward.

His brow furrowed, the wrinkles so deep, you could have hidden a penny in them.

I set Aveen's notebook to the side and laced my fingers together atop the table. When I asked his name, he grumbled, "Arnold."

The florist. Perfect. "Nice to meet you, Arnold. Prince Tadhg tells me your flowers are the most beautiful in all of Tearmann."

His lips tugged into a reluctant smile. "In Airren as well, milady."

That title felt like yet another barrier between us. "Just Keelynn, please."

He shuffled a bit closer to the table, his gaze dropping to the notebook containing Aveen's list. As I read the flowers aloud, he jotted everything down in a notebook of his own, bobbing his head with each choice, as if he approved.

Once I finished, I asked him to make a smaller one for my bridesmaid. Aveen would be there, whether Rían approved or not.

Arnold stuffed his notebook into his breast pocket and gave it a pat. "Fine choices, milady—I mean Keelynn. These'll make the most stunning bouquet. Just you wait and see."

"I have no doubt. If you need anything more from me, please do not hesitate to come by. Thank you again, Arnold."

With another bob of his head, the grogoch turned on his heel and left.

The next two meetings didn't go nearly as well. Loads of talking on my end, and very little interaction from the musicians and caterers. And they both refused to call me Keelynn despite me asking them three times to drop the formal title. Eava had offered to cook for the event, but I wanted her to enjoy herself as well, not spend the day slaving away over a hot stove.

The last person happened to be a seamstress Tadhg had recommended. He had offered to speak to Dame Meranda, our favorite dressmaker from Graystones, but I wanted to give work to the locals wherever possible as a sign of goodwill.

The white-haired woman named Melody came into the hall carrying a small carpet bag. Her own olive-green gown cinched tight around her tiny waist and flowed like a waterfall down her curvy hips.

"Your dress is lovely."

Melody's skirts rustled when she fluffed them. "Thank you, milady. I made it myself."

Brilliant. I had a feeling I was going to love whatever she created for me.

From her bag, she withdrew a measuring tape and a bolt of black fabric.

"There's no need to measure me. I've written all my information down for you." I withdrew a folded piece of paper from my skirt pocket. I'd been the same size for years.

"If it's all the same to you, milady, I'd just as soon take them myself."

Waste of time, if you asked me, but since she seemed insistent, I gave in without an argument. Best to save my fight for my brother-in-law.

Melody gestured to the dais. "Stand up there on the first step and tell me what sort of style you're lookin' for in a dress."

I did as I was told, keeping my legs slightly spread so Melody could measure my inseam and then holding out my arms so she could measure them as well. "Something simple. Off the shoulder, perhaps?" My breasts weren't very large, so I thought that style would give the illusion of a little more in the front.

"Would you be wanting a train?"

"I don't think so." Extra material would only end up getting trampled on.

I watched Melody jot figures down in her notepad. The number she wrote for my waist was two inches larger than my normal measurement. And my chest was an inch too small. "Are you sure those are correct?" I asked, gesturing toward the open page.

She snapped the notebook closed and stuffed it back into her bag. "Absolutely."

I wasn't so sure, but there would be multiple fittings before the actual wedding, and if something was wrong, it would be up to her to fix it.

Tadhg appeared in the doorway, a smile spread across his sinful lips as he leaned against the doorframe. Lips I had spent the better part of this morning getting reacquainted with.

Melody whirled toward where he stood. "Goodness, is that you Tadhg?" she said, all breathless and throaty.

What was with that tone?

He barely spared her a glance, his emerald eyes locking with mine. "I hope you're taking care of my fiancée, Melody."

"The best of care for you, Tadhg."

Feeling silly standing here while the seamstress ogled my prince, I let my arms fall to my sides. "Is that all you need, Melody?"

She blinked at me as if she'd forgotten I was standing right beside her. Who could blame the woman? Tadhg did look rather distracting in his slightly wrinkled white shirt and unbuttoned vest. Like he'd thrown it on as an afterthought. I couldn't wait to strip him out of it.

"Yes, milady." She dropped her things back into her bag and looped the strap around her shoulder. "I'll have something for you to try by the end of next week."

That seemed a little late considering the wedding was in four weeks, but I didn't want to add extra pressure on the woman, so I thanked her and said that would be perfect.

"All go well?" Tadhg asked when she left.

"Overall." There was only one tiny little detail I needed to sort out to make this wedding perfect. "Have you seen your brother around?"

His brows lifted. "I believe he's in the study. Why?"

"I need to discuss something with him."

Tadgh offered to go in my stead, but this was between me and my former husband. "Thank, you but I'd like to speak with him privately."

Tadhg's head tilted, and he looked as if he wanted to protest. Instead, he blew out a breath. "If he gives you any grief, let me know."

I could handle one surly prince. I pressed my lips to Tadhg's, tasting sweet almonds there. "Were you eating Eava's cake samples?"

"Of course not."

"Liar."

He grinned before taking control of my mouth once more, his tongue sweeping against mine. "Come to the bedroom when you're finished," he murmured against my lips.

My stomach tightened with anticipation. "I'm sure you have more important things to do."

His lips tugged up. "Nothing is more important than you." He swatted my backside and vanished, presumably to the room we'd been sharing since I returned.

I found Tadhg's ignorant brother poring over a stack of books at Tadhg's desk.

He glanced up when he saw me, then promptly looked back at the text in front of him.

I dragged one of the stiff chairs next to the bookcase toward the desk, the legs scraping loudly across the uneven stones. Once I reached the desk, I sank onto the chair and folded my hands in my lap. He still hadn't acknowledged me.

I cleared my throat. Still nothing. *Ignorant ass…* "I don't like you very much."

Sighing loudly enough to wake the dead, he turned to the next page in the book. "It should come as no surprise to you that the feeling is quite mutual."

And here I'd thought we had nothing in common. "For some reason that I absolutely cannot fathom, Aveen loves you."

Another sigh. Another page flip. "She'll get over it."

"She won't. But that is neither here nor there." No sense arguing when I knew I was right. "I've come to tell you that I expect her presence at the wedding."

Sigh. Flip. "No."

My hands balled into fists. *Churlish pig.* "Do you want me to get Tadhg involved? Because I will."

Rían's eyes lifted from the page. A smile curled the corners of his lips. "Is that supposed to scare me?"

"It should. Tadhg's curse is broken, his magic unbound, and he is your sovereign." At that, Rían flinched. "So, I'll ask you one more time to stop trying to control my sister and let her come to my bloody wedding."

"I'm not—" His mouth snapped shut. Through his teeth, he said, "I'm not trying to control her. I am trying to keep her safe. Surely that's something even a featherhead like you can understand."

He could sling insults all he wanted. That wouldn't deter me. "And surely someone as dense as you can see that making decisions for my sister instead of allowing her to make her own is the exact same thing our father did. Shall I remind you how that turned out?"

His eyes narrowed into slits.

"Father wanted her to marry Robert Trench, and she died to avoid that. You tried to keep her from returning to Tearmann, and yet she is right upstairs. She will find a way around this bargain of yours, and it could very well end up putting her in the danger you have been trying so desperately to avoid. You need to help her."

The book slammed shut, and his hands landed on the desk

with a loud *slap*. "Where do you get off, ordering me around, human?"

Don't take the bait. Don't do it.

I may have been human, but he was being ridiculous. "She *will* be at my wedding."

His lips twisted into a sneer.

I plowed on even though I imagined he was probably plotting my death at this very moment. "And since I, too, am concerned with her safety, I would like you to help her learn how to glamour herself."

"If you were truly concerned, you'd tell her to skip the whole feckin' thing." He shoved to his feet, stalking around the desk and jabbing his finger in my face. "Just so we're clear, *if* I decide to do this, I'm not doing it for you. I'm doing this for her."

"Thank you, Rían. You are most kind."

My arms snapped to my sides, and a rope appeared out of thin air, wrapping around my torso and binding me to the chair so tightly, I could barely breathe.

"Joke's on you," I laughed. "I wasn't planning on leaving."

A piece of cloth stretched across my mouth.

That miserable pig. I glowered at Rían's back as he sauntered out of the room and let the door fall closed behind him. If I had that cursed dagger, I'd have used it on him myself. The nerve, tying me up in here.

Now I had to wait until someone found me, or try to get to the hallway myself. Thankfully, he hadn't tied my feet together. I managed to ease forward enough that the chair rocked and I was able to stand, the chair bound to my back like a turtle's shell. I wobbled toward the door but quickly realized I wouldn't be able to twist the knob.

Bloody Rían. Why must he ruin everything he touched?

I slammed the chair onto the stones and kicked my boot against the door. Once. Twice. A third time.

The door flew open, and Tadhg waited on the other side, his

smile slipping into a scowl when he saw me. With a flick of his wrist, the bonds vanished. "Who did this to you?"

"Who do you think?" I stood on unsteady legs and straightened my skirt. Next time I saw that man, I was going to kick him in the shin.

"You are off limits. Rían should know that."

"Yes, well, Rían doesn't care." Selfish codfish. How could someone as good and kind as Aveen love someone as twisted and wretched as him?

Tadhg's head tilted, sending an unruly dark curl tumbling across his forehead. "Rían's problem was never that he didn't care," he said softly. "It was that he cared too much."

13

TADHG

As I slipped my clammy hands into the pockets of my breeches, one thought swirled through my mind: I should've brought Rían. People loved nothing more than a juicy bit of gossip, and if this didn't go as planned, it'd definitely get around. Yet the idea of having to rely on my brother's power after mine had been returned galled me to no end. I'd leaned on him for far too long. It was time to stand on my own two feet.

So here I stood, on the edge of yet another blackened field, staring at three houses far larger than I remembered. A young lad leapt down the stoop of the first, crafted of gray limestone. They'd added a conservatory since I'd last been here. Looked feckin' heavy.

When the young pooka saw me, he grinned, flashing a pair of elongated fangs far too large for his thin face. "Mammy! The prince is here!" he shouted back into the house. He continued to an abandoned skipping rope next to a broken hoop.

Oh, to be a child without a care in the world.

Right, so. No more waiting. Time to do this.

I withdrew my hands and gave them a good shake. Everything would be fine.

A slender woman appeared in the doorway, her long raven

hair lifting on the breeze. Her gaze caught mine, and her brow grew more furrowed the longer she stared at me. "May I help ye, sir?"

Sir? Awfully formal coming from a woman I'd known for ages. Her husband and Ruairi were related in some way or another—don't ask me how. Pooka family trees were more tangled than a blackberry thicket. "I've come to relocate your cottage."

At that, she startled. "Where's the prince?"

The boy jumping rope in the front lawn paused his skipping. "Mam! Yer talkin' to him."

She lifted a hand to shield her eyes from the blazing afternoon sun. "Tadhg?" Her eyes widened. "By heavens, it is you. What're ye doing wearin' a glamour?"

I wasn't wearing a—*wait*. This was the first proper outing I'd taken since my curse had been broken. No wonder none of the women in the courtyard had so much as waved to me. They didn't recognize me without my curse. How handy was that?

"It's a long story," I said, because it was. Most people knew I had been cursed in one way or another, but very few knew the extent of what Fiadh had done to me. The last thing I wanted was to get into it when there was so much to be done. "Will you clear the house so I can move it?"

She bunched her skirts in her fists, lifting them as she stepped daintily around the toys littering the lawn. "The place is empty. Joel brought the little one to his mam's on the coast to keep her from wandering."

My stomach sank. The youngest O'Brien boy had wandered into the blight and was found two days later, dead as the earth beneath him. "Will I shift your place to the coast as well?"

"If it's all the same to ye, I'd rather not live next to my mother-in-law." When her son laughed, she gave his shoulder a good whack. "And if ye tell yer father that, ye'll be without dessert for a month."

We'd bought a few fields from an ancient grogoch on the northern tip of Tearmann, so that was where I'd put them instead. Shifting something this large took not only a great deal of magic, but a great deal of control—something I'd always lacked even at the best of times.

"I know just the place," I said, passing through the gates to press both my palms against the sun-warmed house. The gritty stones scraped my fingertips as I walked ten paces down the side. Another twelve around the conservatory and back to where the kitchen window overlooked an overgrown garden tinged with black. Back around the side where the bedrooms were located and across the front.

"What's he doin'?" the little lad whispered.

"Quiet. Don't distract him."

I couldn't help but smile. "It's all right." If anything, a bit of distraction eased some of the pressure building in my chest. "Although you should probably stand back, just in case." Once they were clear, I evanesced to where Rían had relocated the other homes. Organized in neat rows, with not nearly as much land and space as there used to be. Not all the Danú were like pooka and enjoyed living in tight communities. Given that we didn't have an infinite amount of land to work with, everyone had to make some sacrifices.

I closed my eyes and called on my power. When I was cursed and tried to shift something, I could feel my magic drain like water in a sink with no stopper. *Focus. You're not cursed anymore.*

Now the power kept flowing, a rushing tide without end.

I pictured that warm structure, full of life and stones fused together for centuries. Windowpanes reflecting the sunlight. A chimney and a blue-gray door. I called on the fire within me...and flicked my wrist. When I opened my eyes, an empty patch of land greeted me.

Darkness rose up, threatening to swallow me whole.

What was I missing? I'd be damned before I asked Rían to help. I shifted a flask and took a drink. Liquor burned down my throat to my empty belly.

What was the point of being free when you could do nothing

with your freedom? May as well be cursed for eternity if I couldn't even help a couple of families. I swiped at my sweaty brow. *You can do this.*

I stuffed my flask into my pocket, closed my eyes once more, and called on my magic. Sparks coursed through my veins.

The house. I needed the house right here, all in one piece.

Something tugged on my magic like a fish nibbling on some bait at the end of a fishing hook. The tug grew stronger, no longer a fish but a shark, heavy and fighting every step of the way. Sweat rolled down my brow and the back of my neck.

That shark became a feckin' whale, heavier than anything I'd ever felt before. With a flick of my wrist, the weight vanished.

The house stood in front of me, conservatory and all.

A smile broke across my face.

This time, when I withdrew my flask, I raised it to the sky in a silent toast and took a victorious sip. Time to shift two more.

What a glorious day. What a glorious sunset, painting the sky in pinks and oranges. Orange really was such a lovely color. Didn't get enough credit, if you asked me.

And look at my castle. So impressive on that hillside. Imposing as well. How lucky was I to call such a spectacular place home?

Not even the sight of my darling brother stalking toward me with a scowl on his face could dampen this wonderful day.

"Good evening, Rían. Beautiful sunset, isn't it?"

He didn't even turn around to check. Too bad, really. He was missing out. "Where've you been?"

"Everywhere." And I wasn't even tired.

"Good to know you've time to gallivant while your people suffer. Did you forget that the blight reached Saoirse and Joel?"

His lack of faith—while warranted—stung. "I shifted their houses first thing this morning."

Rían halted at the bottom step. "By yourself?"

"That's right."

He breathed in my words, testing for a lie. He'd find none here. Not on this perfect day. "How many did you move?" he asked.

"Four."

He didn't say anything more, but he didn't have to. I could tell from the sour look on his face that he was impressed. I threw the heavy door aside, letting light stream into the murky foyer. As lovely as this place was, it could really do with more windows. Big ones. Huge panes of glass so we could watch the sunsets.

Aveen appeared in the hallway leading to the kitchens. When she saw me, she startled. I glanced past her, but there was no sign of my darling fiancée. "Have you seen Keelynn?"

Her gaze bounced between Rían and I, her brow furrowing. "I'm sorry. Who are you?"

Rían snorted. "That's Tadhg."

The wrinkle between her eyebrows deepened as she studied me. "Why is he wearing a glamour?"

"He's not." Rían's scowl returned. "How did he look to you before?"

Her lips pursed as her gaze swept from my head to my boots, making me feel like a cow gone to market. "Stronger."

Excuse me? I gave my biceps a squeeze. They weren't as large as Ruairí's, sure, but I was plenty strong in my own right. Keelynn liked my arms just fine, thank you very much.

"His face is thinner as well."

She really needed to work on her adjectives. My face wasn't *thin*, it was chiseled.

"His hair always looked blond."

It was my turn to snort. Aveen would've seen me as her ideal man. And my brother may have been a lot of things, but blond he was not. Rían's lips pulled down into a frown.

I clapped him on the shoulder. "Don't worry, brother. You can always dye your hair."

He smacked my hand away. "Feck off."

"Ignore him," Aveen said with a slight flush to her cheeks. "I love your hair just as it is."

Hold on. If I looked different to Aveen, did I appear different to Keelynn as well? Did she still find me as attractive as she always had?

I evanesced into my bedroom. Sure enough, I found my fiancée tying the last of her laces. When she saw me, her lips lifted into a coy little smile. My teeth scraped my lower lip as I considered how to word this question. Better to say it straight out, I supposed. "How do I look to you?"

She blinked those long lashes framing serious gray eyes. "Pardon?"

I pointed to my "thin" face. "My face. How has it changed?"

Her lips pursed. "Are you feeling all right?"

"Answer the question. Please." I didn't give a toss if I was no longer attractive to any other woman except this one. She hadn't seemed startled or confused when she saw me, but she'd been with me when the curse broke. Was she trying to spare my feelings? If she told me how she used to see me, I could live under a glamour.

"Tadhg. You look the same as you always have. Straight nose. The perfect amount of stubble. These pointed ears that hear everything, even words I don't say. Sinful mouth that I cannot stop kissing." Her lips grazed mine, still such a tantalizing sensation, to feel this sort of connection without the fear of having her keel over afterward.

That was true love. Seeing a person for who they truly were and loving them anyway.

This called for a celebration. And I had just the thing. With a flick of my wrist, a basket appeared on the end of the bed, filled with goodies I'd gathered after shifting the cottages.

Keelynn let out a delighted squeal and lifted the lid. "What's in this?"

"Presents."

"More than one?" She withdrew a pink and white pastry box. "Peach cobbler?"

I nodded. "From a bakery in Oakton."

"You went to Oakton?" She laid the box onto the bed. "I thought you were shifting cottages?"

"I did that too."

"You had enough magic for both?" She pulled out another box, this one blue as a robin's egg.

"I did. And that's pear and almond tart with berry compote from Longshadow." My mouth started to water when I smelled what was inside.

Her eyes expanded. "That's a long way away from Oakton."

I caught her by the hips right when she reached for yet another delicious treat. "I'm not sure if you've heard, but I am quite powerful now that my curses have been broken."

Her smile was more stunning than any sunset. "Oh, I've heard." Her gaze returned to that basket. "Are these from—"

"Graystones," I finished, plucking one of the sugarplums from the box. "I remember you saying you used to eat them when you were little."

She withdrew four more boxes and arched a quizzical brow.

"Rhubarb pie from Burnsley, salted caramel fudge from Achad, shortbread biscuits from Swiftfell, and spice cake from Windwick."

"You've been a very busy prince."

And yet I'd never felt more energized. "I've been all over this country and all I could think about was returning home to you."

"So you're not too tired?"

My teeth grazed the slender column of her throat. "Too tired to strip you out of this dress and have you for dessert?" I grinned against the goosebumps erupting over her skin. "Never."

14

AVEEN

How foolish I'd been to believe I could bend Rían to my will through bargaining. I supposed I should have been grateful that he didn't send me directly back to Hollowshade.

Although, from the way his shoulders stiffened and jaw ticked each time I entered a room, perhaps that would have been better. He never smiled anymore. I felt no longing or desire rolling from his rigid frame, only anger and fear.

As much as I loved the tiny cottage he'd given me, I didn't want to return to that empty house. Not when everyone I loved was in Tearmann, fighting for their land and the Danú people. I had magic, dammit. I should have been able to help them in some way.

Instead, I got to slink around and stew.

We were broken, and with him keeping this distance, I didn't know how to fix us. I'd gone to his room almost every night, ready to throw myself at him, but each night I had talked myself off that ledge. He wouldn't appreciate how pathetic I had become.

I curled onto my side and watched the sun sink below the gray stone wall. Keelynn hadn't been back to tell me how her meetings went today. Maybe that was for the best. Seeing her joy only made my own melancholy harder to bear.

I hated that my own happiness was so wrapped up in someone else. Someone unreliable and unpredictable and downright maddening.

A knock sounded at the door. Probably Eava come to bring me some tea. I'd told her not to wait on me, yet she persisted. I sat up and pinned on a smile, back to pretending once more. "Come in."

Rían, not Eava stepped inside, his eyes guarded as he drank me in. How handsome he looked in his black attire. How deliciously villainous.

His deep voice sent chills down my spine. "Get up."

As if I would do what he said simply because he used a commanding tone. I settled back against my pillows and folded my arms. I would get up when I was good and ready and not a moment before. "I'd rather not."

His eyes made one unmistakable pass down the thin white shift I wore before returning to mine. "I said, get out of the bed."

"Lose the tone and I'll consider it."

He squeezed the back of his neck, the veins in his forehead bulging. "If your arse isn't off that mattress in the next three seconds, I'm not teaching you to glamour yourself."

I could ignore the tone this once. Hope sparked in my chest as I kicked the covers to the side and stepped out of the bed. Then I remembered that the last time he'd promised to help, he'd bound my magic. If he thought he could do so a second time, he had another thing coming.

Rían's jaw pulsed when his gaze landed on the silky hem that didn't quite reach my knees. "Where did you get that shift?"

"I don't see how that's any of your business."

The harsh breath he expelled through his nose sounded a lot like victory for me. "Fine. Don't tell me."

Fine. I wouldn't. "What do I need to do?"

"First, you need to get dressed."

His eyes tracked my hand as I smoothed my palm down my silk-clad waist. "But this is so comfortable."

With a flick of his wrist, I was no longer in the shift but in a dowdy blue dress big enough to fit two of me. As if I wanted to wear *his* color. I lifted the thing over my head and let it fall to the ground. In the back of my armoire, I found one of the dresses I used to garden in and pulled that on instead.

Sufficiently covered, I offered the irritating prince a mocking curtsey. "I am dressed, Your Highness. What shall I do next? I am but your humble servant."

Although he crossed his arms over his chest and scowled, I could have sworn I caught a smile playing on the edge of his lips. "Now who has a tone?"

He was so bloody obnoxious. It was a wonder I loved the man at all.

He held up a finger, and all I could think about was biting it off. That'd teach him not to point it in my face. "Before I teach you a thing, know this: I will not release you from our bargain until you can hold a glamour through a feckin' hurricane. If you can't, I will chain you up until the wedding is over."

I wouldn't put it past him to do it either. "How do I know you're not lying? That you're not going to bind my magic again?"

He shrugged like he didn't care either way. "You're going to have to trust me."

What difference did it make if he did bind my magic? If I could learn to glamour myself, there was a chance he would release me from this infernal bargain. Otherwise, I could be stuck hiding in this castle for the rest of my days.

My magic began to hum when he stepped nearer. This would work. It had to. I refused to watch my sister marry Tadhg from the other side of a window. I wanted to be right by her side, where I belonged. Where I should have been all along.

"We'll work on your body first, and then your face," Rían said. "You'll want to alter your most recognizable features. Maybe go with smaller breasts and leaner hips. Think of someone with those attributes."

Almost everyone from my circle back in Graystones had

smaller breasts and leaner bloody hips. I thought of Lady Luisa Miller. I'd always been jealous of her statuesque frame. "I have someone."

"Good. Take my hand." My palm slid against his; heat flared from the contact, and my heart began to thump harder in my chest. "Now close your eyes."

I cast him a wary glance. "Don't bind my magic."

His mouth flattened. "I won't."

His smooth voice fell over me, telling me how to weave a simple glamour. I followed his instructions to the letter, drawing on his magic more than my own. My skin warmed and then cinched tight, as if my entire body had been corseted. Even my arms felt stiff. *Bloody hell.* Talk about uncomfortable. How did he wear one of these so often?

"Good. Very good. When you open your eyes, don't lose sight of that feeling. Remain focused."

I could do this. For Keelynn. For myself. For this man so terrified of his mother taking me away that he kept this distance between us. When my eyes opened, I met my own face in the mirror. But my frame appeared reed-thin. Heavens above, I'd never been this slim, even as a child.

Rían moved around me, presumably inspecting my glamour. I held out my hands, no longer tanned but pale as milk. I'd done it. I'd actually done it.

He stepped closer, his legs brushing my skirts.

"You need to stay focused."

"I am *focused.*" Delicious heat licked up my spine as he moved so close, his muscular thighs pressed against the backs of mine. What would it feel like to have him touch me while I was someone else?

"Are you sure?" His eyes tangled with mine in the mirror.

"Yes." I was more than sure. I was certain.

Rían eased forward...

His soft breath tickled against the shell of my ear. Desire

bloomed in my belly; heat pooled between my thighs. Magic burned through my blood, and the glamour I wore vanished.

Inky black invaded Rían's narrowed eyes. "I thought you said you were focused, Aveen."

"It's a little hard to focus with you standing so close, *Rían*."

Those black eyes locked with mine through the reflection, full of dark desire. "I could fuck you sideways looking like a feckin' leprechaun. I will not release you from our bargain until you have the same level of control."

My entire body flushed with heat. This man and his filthy mouth would be the death of me.

"Do it again," he commanded. "And this time, do not let it fall."

Three days ago, all I had wanted was for Rían to help me. Now, I couldn't wait for him to go away. We'd spent another day stuck in this room. Another day still practicing glamours. With all Rían's instructions and threats, I could barely think straight. And I thought he'd been unbearable that morning he made me go for a run with a hangover. I'd take that Rían any day over this one.

He paced between the mirror and the bed, his hands flexing at his sides. "All it takes is one human realizing you're using a glamour to report you. The soldiers know to be fast. They'll chain you in iron first and ask questions later. Do you wish to die more times than necessary?"

When would he get it through his thick skull that reciting the potential consequences repeatedly wasn't helping?

"Well? Do you?"

My nails dug into my palms as my hands tightened into fists. If I were a violent woman, I would've jabbed them straight into his bloody eyes. But he'd probably have liked that. "Of course not! I am trying my best."

He gestured toward me with a careless wave. "Your best isn't good enough. Now, do it again."

Nothing was ever good enough for the prince of perfection. No wonder the Danú despised him. "I'm tired. I need a break." Tomorrow I could disappoint him anew.

I dropped onto the end of the bed with a heavy sigh.

Rían caught my arm and dragged me upright once more. "You can have a break once you're finished making a fool of yourself with these pathetic things you call glamours."

I'd show him pathetic.

Creating a full glamour wasn't a problem. Even Rían had seemed impressed when he first saw the face I'd stolen from my cousin, Lady Regina. I was still blond, but instead of curls, my hair was straight as straw. My face appeared less round, while my body looked a lot like Keelynn's, thin and willowy and perfect. I still couldn't figure out how to make myself taller. Every time I tried, it felt as if I were walking on twigs instead of my legs. Instead, I remained my normal height. Which was unfortunate because I would've loved nothing more than to look down my nose at Rían when he was being an ass.

As instructed, I pulled my glamour.

"Now hold it." Rían didn't poke or shove me as he'd done earlier. He did something far worse.

He leaned forward and let his lips graze my jaw.

I sucked in a breath, relishing the pressure of his soft mouth. The sparks were there but subdued, the barrier of the glamour keeping him too far away from me.

"Hold it," he murmured, his fingertip tracing the scalloped neckline on my gray dress. Without warning, he tugged the material and peered beneath.

I waited with bated breath for him to touch me, to quench this fire burning a path across my aching breasts.

"Dammit, Aveen. Where are your nipples?"

My what? I glanced down to where he still held my dress out from my skin. Sure enough, my glamoured breasts were there, small and perky, but missing something important. "I highly doubt the Queen or anyone else will be checking my body for nipples."

"That's not the point." He let me go with a curse and resumed his pacing along the dent he'd worn in my rug. "You need to think of everything."

We'd been practicing for days, and I was still barely able to hold a simple glamour for more than an hour. "This is so unfair. I shouldn't have to hide who I am."

He glanced sidelong at me.

What was I complaining about? Rían knew exactly what this was like. The man had lived most of his life beneath a bloody glamour.

He ran a hand through his hair and sighed. "No, you shouldn't. But you do. Try again."

I was sick and tired of trying and failing. "I want to see you do it."

In a blink, Rían was no longer himself but Ruairi, from his shoulder-sweeping raven hair to the length of his canines, he looked exactly like the pooka. Everything except his eyes.

I wonder... I reached for the buttons on his white shirt.

Rían shirked back, his broad shoulders curling in on themselves. "What are you doing?"

"You checked my chest, it's only fair that I get to check yours as well."

Although a muscle in his jaw worked, he didn't stop me from unbuttoning his shirt, revealing a toned chest dusted with dark hair, a taut abdomen, and a line of hair that disappeared into the waistband of his low-slung breeches. He had nipples too. Not that I'd seen Ruairi's to be able to assess for accuracy.

Moving on...

A wicked thought sprang to my mind, and I found myself stepping closer. My hand fell to the buckle of Rían's belt.

His fingers wrapped in a death grip around my wrist. "What the hell do you think you're doing?"

"I distinctly remember you saying that you could fuck me sideways while glamoured. I want you to prove it."

"That's enough."

I smiled at him. "All talk."

"I could if I wanted to. But I don't."

"Liar." I could see the yearning in his eyes. He wanted this just as much as I did.

Rían's eyes darkened to an almost desperate hue. "I'll not touch you with someone else's hands. Kiss you with someone else's mouth. Fuck you with—" He clamped his mouth so hard his jaw pulsed.

"Then drop the glamour and do all of those things as yourself." Perhaps I should've been embarrassed, throwing myself at him like this. But I didn't care. It had been far too long since he'd touched me. Since he'd loved me.

Rían's glamour vanished, leaving a prince whose gaze locked on my lips.

One kiss.

We could stop there.

One kiss to remind me what it felt like to be his.

Rían peeled my hands from his body as if he could no longer stand my touch. When he spoke, his voice came out cold and emotionless. "When I see you again, I expect you to be able to hold your glamour."

When he saw me again? He couldn't leave *now*. "Rían, please—"

"Wear it every day from the moment you wake until you go to sleep. Do not let it fall."

And then he vanished, leaving me there to burn alone.

15

KEELYNN

Songbirds flitted through the air, dancing high above us. Despite his size, Ruairi's footsteps were almost silent compared to my own.

He glanced sidelong at me, his golden eyes sparkling in the sunlight. "I can carry those if ye'd like," he said, gesturing to the red wicker basket in my arms.

"Would you mind? It is awfully heavy." I handed Ruairi the basket laden with mince pies that Eava and Aveen had baked earlier this morning. This time of year always made me think of snow-dusted fields and barren trees. Pine garlands and shuddering candles. Cold, red noses and thick scarves wrapped around your chin.

None of that existed in Tearmann. Every day in this land ruled by magic felt like a balmy summer's kiss.

Still, a mince pie would be delicious no matter the season.

Ruairi's elbow nudged against my arm. "Ye seemed to have settled in well at the castle."

There hadn't been much settling required. I'd moved straight into Tadhg's chambers, and Aveen slept only down the hall like she had at home. Ruairi was always good for a laugh, and Eava was an absolute delight. Rían was still making everyone miserable, but at least he'd been helping Aveen with her magic. Although lately, he'd insisted on teaching her in the middle of the great hall with at least one other person present. Not sure what that was about. When I'd asked Aveen, she'd claimed it didn't matter. I'd done my best to prod for an honest answer, but my darling sister remained as tight-lipped as ever. Would she ever learn to lean on me the way I'd always leaned on her?

I frowned up at the wispy white clouds high above. "I'm finding my way." Overall, life inside the castle was better than I'd expected.

Life outside those wards, however, left something to be desired.

Back in Graystones, I'd rarely left our estate, and that sheltered life had turned me into a fearful, ignorant woman. I was determined not to let the pattern continue and slip into the same habits here. So I went into the courtyard every day, introducing myself to the famers bringing crops to fill our stores. Although a handful had been welcoming, most of the Danú regarded me with understandable wariness. A few had glowered with outright disdain, but I refused to let them taint my view of this beautiful place.

Two men leading a donkey up the hill stopped to stare as we passed. When Ruairi tipped his head, the men mirrored the greeting. I waved, but neither waved back.

Rude.

I dared a glance over my shoulder, only to find the men still watching us. An unwelcome, heavy feeling settled in my stomach. Hopefully that wasn't some sort of bad omen for today's mission.

A tiny cottage the color of peonies came into view, one that hadn't been there two days ago. Tillie Thatcher was one of the many who had been displaced by the terrible blight. I found the small woman bent over some gardening tool, sweat glistening on her brow and a patch of tilled earth beneath her mucky boots. Dirt smeared the apron she wore over her brown cotton dress.

I offered our newest neighbor a friendly smile. "Good morning, Ms. Thatcher."

Her unkempt brows slammed down over dark eyes.

"My name is Keelynn—"

The woman's fist twisted on the tool's handle. "I know who ye are. Another one of the prince's many whores."

My molars ground together. Did she not notice the emerald engagement ring I wore? "I wanted to see how you were faring on your new plot. And to give you this." I flipped the checked cloth from the top of the basket and withdrew one of the pie boxes.

She stared down at the box as if it were covered in worms.

I didn't have time to stand here all day waiting for her to accept my gift. Melody would be at the castle in a few hours for my first fitting.

"Eava made it," Ruairi said with a tight smile, his sharp canine teeth on full display.

The woman's creased lips lifted into a genuine smile. "Thank ye, Ruairi. Ye always were a good boy." She dropped her tool, took the pie, thanked him again, and retreated into her tiny house.

"Am I invisible or something?" I muttered, smoothing a hand down the cinched waist of my forest-green day dress.

Ruairi's giant hand landed on my shoulder and squeezed gently. "Give them time to warm up to ye. Most of these people have spent their entire lives being distrustful of humans."

Hadn't I felt the same way about the Danú not so long ago? Dismissed Danú beggars on the street. Been fearful and mistrusting of their motives. Set out to murder their prince.

The day I discovered the truth about my beloved Padraig, everything changed.

Tears pricked the backs of my eyes when I thought of my coachman. He'd loved me as a father despite my ignorance. And learning he'd been fae all along hadn't dulled my affection for him.

Trust wasn't earned in a day.

This was only the first step in a process. I refused to be disheartened.

We continued to the next cottage, one with tiny clothes flapping on the line.

When I went to open the gate, Ruairi remained on the other side, grimacing at the house. "Maybe we should give this one a miss."

I glanced back at the cottage's faded front door. Nothing seemed amiss. Sure, the grass could do with trimming, but other than that, the place looked warm and inviting. "Why is that?"

His brow furrowed for a moment, and then his broad shoulders lifted in a shrug. "Anwen hasn't been displaced."

My purpose wasn't only to help those who were displaced. I also wanted to get to know our neighbors. Perhaps find a friend or an ally among them. And I couldn't do that if I showed favoritism. "We'll visit all the houses," I said, walking straight down the gravel path to knock on the door.

Ruairi sidled up next to me, looking less than impressed.

A baby's high-pitched wail erupted from inside the cottage. A woman answered, the frizzy strands of her tangerine-colored hair plastered to her flushed cheeks.

"Morning, Anwen," Ruairi blurted. "We brought mince pies from Eava." He withdrew a pie and practically shoved the box at the poor woman.

She seemed too busy studying me to notice. Unlike the last woman, I felt no contempt, only curiosity. She tipped her head toward me but directed her question at my companion. "Who's this?"

Again, the pooka responded for me. "Lady Keelynn Bannon."

We needed to chat about him using my title when introducing me. I wasn't a Lady here. "Just Keelynn is fine." I held out my hand.

Anwen's dainty hand slid against mine in a tentative shake. "That's Tadhg's ring yer wearing."

"Yes, it is." About time someone noticed. "We are to be wed in two weeks' time."

"*Married?*" Her eyes scorched a path down and up my body. "To a feckin' human?"

Heat bloomed up my throat. So much for making friends.

Thankfully, I was saved from having to respond when a young girl appeared behind Anwen, her orange hair reaching nearly to her waist. "Mammy! Brogan's roarin' again."

Anwen waved her away. "Give him the bottle. I'll be there in a minute."

The girl was too busy staring up at me to listen. "Who's she?"

"I said, take care of yer brother, child," Anwen snapped.

The girl's face fell before she twisted back toward the hall.

"How many little ones do you have?" I asked, desperate to break the tension in the air.

Anwen braced her hands on her hips. "Four."

I reached into the basket and took out another box to add to the one Ruairi still held. "Here. Take an extra pie so you have enough for the small ones." The sooner we ran out, the sooner we'd be able to return to the castle.

Anwen accepted the boxes from Ruairi with a mumbled thanks and closed the door in my face.

Ruairi refused to meet my questioning gaze as we ambled toward the next house belonging to a grumpy, stone-faced grogoch. "Ye will have to excuse Anwen. Herself and Tadgh—"

"I gathered as much." I wasn't foolish. I'd known the cursed life my fiancé had led would come back to haunt me someday.

We visited ten more Danú, seven residents and three displaced, their receptions each as chilly as the one before. In time, they would learn that I wasn't like the humans who persecuted them. At least, not anymore.

I approached the final house with a heavy heart. Ruairi suggested keeping the pie for ourselves, and as good as that idea sounded, I needed to see this mission through. I might not have made a connection with any of the people this day, but at least I'd made a start. To leave this pie in the basket felt a lot like failure.

So I steeled my shoulders and knocked.

The stooped woman who answered had more wrinkles than not and a pair of spectacles perched on the end of her slightly hooked nose. When she saw me, she startled.

"My name is Keelynn, and I've come from the castle with a gift." I handed over the pie.

The woman lifted the lid and inhaled deeply. "Thank ye. It smells delicious." Her crinkled lips fell into a frown. "Not sure I need a whole one, though. It's just me in this big, drafty place."

At least her refusal had been polite. I was about to take back the box when the strangest thing happened. The woman opened the door wider and invited us to join her.

Perhaps I hadn't heard her correctly. Best to be sure, just in case. "You want me to come inside?"

"If ye have the time. I just put the kettle on."

"But…you don't know me."

Her wispy gray eyebrows came together. "Aren't ye the human who killed that wicked witch who cursed our prince?"

Ruairi let out a gruff chuckle.

All right. Perhaps she *did* know me. "Yes. I am."

"That's what I thought. Get yerself in here for a nice spot of tea and tell me all about it." Her soft brown eyes lifted to my escort. "And bring yer handsome friend as well."

The woman's name was Nettie May, and it turned out she was a witch as well. She didn't bat an eyelash at my humanity or my engagement to the prince, only offered a heartfelt congratulations to us both. We stayed for as long as we could, chatting about her life in Tearmann and laughing like old friends. In spite of all the cold shoulders and glowers today, I left her house feeling as if I'd finally done something right.

That was until we passed Anwen's cottage on the way back to the castle and found a murder of crows collecting by the front gate, picking at a feast of mince pies.

Ruairi tried to make excuses, saying maybe they'd gone off, but we both knew that was a lie. After all, we'd eaten more than our fair share of Eava's pie at Nettie's house. The heaviness in my heart returned tenfold. By the time we reached the castle's warded gates, all I wanted was to curl up in bed and cry.

Instead, I got to stand in the great hall and try on my wedding dress.

Melody nodded in greeting as I closed the door behind me. A swath of ivory silk hung over the back of Tadhg's throne.

"I apologize for keeping you waiting." I started unfastening the buttons on the front of my dress until the garment pooled at my feet. "Will I keep my shift on or remove it as well?"

Melody barely spared me a glance from where she dragged pins and shears from her carpet bag. "Take it off if you don't mind. That way we have a better idea of size."

I stood in my corset and knickers in the middle of the drafty hall. As Melody helped me into the gown, I had a sinking feeling this was not going to go well. Not only did the dress look nothing like I'd imagined, it looked as if a child had sewn the seams.

"This doesn't come off my shoulders."

Melody fluffed the lace at my throat. "I thought a high neckline would better suit your slender neck."

If I'd wanted a high neckline, I would've asked for one. "And the ruffles?"

She tugged and dragged the fabric over my backside, nearly taking my knickers with her. "To give the illusion of hips. You're thin as a post."

I resisted the urge to say that Tadhg loved me despite being "thin as a post."

As I suspected from the measurements she'd written down weeks ago, the material gaped over my waist, pinched my chest, and fit so tight over my arse that it'd rip clean in two if I tried to sit down.

I didn't need a mirror to know I looked awful.

Melody hummed while she pinned the bottom hem short enough that you could see the laces on my boots. "I'd really like the skirt longer."

Something sharp jabbed my ankle. "Nonsense. This is the

perfect length," she countered. When she stood once more and took a step back to admire the atrocious gown, saying how perfect it was, something inside me snapped.

"It's not perfect, Melody. It's hideous." The poofy sleeves made crossing my arms impossible, so I settled my hands on my hips instead, mostly to prove that, despite being "thin as a post" I did, in fact, own a pair of hips. "You haven't listened to a word I've said since the moment we hired you. I will not wear this dress."

Melody tossed her long white locks over her shoulders with an exasperated huff. "What am I supposed to do with it? The fabric alone is worth a small fortune, and I have been working all week on this when I could've been doing something important."

She could throw the monstrosity into a fire for all I cared. "Let me know how much it cost and I will reimburse you for your time."

"I have never been treated so poorly. I demand to speak to the prince."

"You don't get to speak to my fiancé. You get to speak to me."

Her face turned red as a tomato. She ripped her bag off the ground, tossed in the pins and shears, and stomped for the door.

The nerve of that wretched woman. The wedding was in fourteen days, and now I had nothing to wear. I'd married Tadhg once in a blood-drenched gown, he wouldn't care. But I did. I wanted to look well for him. For him to be proud of me standing at his side in front of his people.

His people who despised me.

I reached for the buttons at the back of the dress but couldn't unfasten them.

After the day I'd had, I needed a bloody drink.

I stalked out of the room and down the hallway to the parlor.

When I threw myself onto the settee, a terrible ripping sound echoed through the air. Without looking, I knew my arse was hanging clean out of the back. *Bloody Melody*. I tilted the bottle of wine left on the coffee table into an empty glass. It wasn't until I heard a quiet curse from the wingback that I realized I wasn't alone. Rían shrank lower in his chair, looking as if he wanted to crawl inside the pages of the book in his lap.

When he caught me scowling at him, his own eyes widened, sweeping down the monstrosity clinging to my body. "What the hell are you wearing?"

I picked up the corner of my ruffled skirt and let it fall. "My wedding dress. Isn't it beautiful?"

"Looks like a child sewed it together."

I took an angry sip of wine and forced myself to swallow the revolting liquid. "Yes, well, it appears as though the seamstress your brother suggested is a fraud."

"Who did he hire?"

"Melody."

Rían sniggered.

My head fell back against the settee. "Everyone in this bloody kingdom despises me."

"And?"

Leave it to this ass to not understand basic manners. "And most people would try to make me feel better."

"Your feelings are none of my concern. Why do you care what they think, anyway?"

"Unlike you, I do not wish for everyone to hate me."

At that, he sneered. "What did you expect? You're a human who has stolen the most eligible man in Tearmann. Women have been salivating over my brother for centuries and yet he has never settled down. Now he's married you, what? Twelve times?"

Rían knew exactly how many times we'd been married. "Twice."

"Exactly."

I understood jealousy. After all, hadn't I been jealous of the person I loved most in this world, my very own sister? But jealousy served no purpose other than to destroy and make enemies where there were none. "How do I make them like me?"

"You're asking the wrong person for advice. Go find Ruairi. For some unknown reason, everyone seems to like him."

Everyone *did* like Ruairi. I had hoped having him accompany me outside the castle would let people see that I was kind and caring and worth getting to know. Instead, my efforts appeared to have had the opposite effect.

Rían flipped to the next page in his book, seeming to put me and this conversation out of his mind. I sipped the terrible wine in silence, falling deeper and deeper into despair. It wasn't as if I could leave, unless I wanted him to get an eyeful of my knickers.

Rían muttered, "You could try to find something useful to do that will convince these halfwits that you aren't entirely a waste of breath."

Bloody hell...

Had I just gotten good advice from Rían?

What would be useful to these people? I'd been raised to be a rich man's wife. Besides playing piano forte and sewing the odd needlework, I could plan a parties and throw balls. None of those skills seemed relevant here. At least Aveen had her gardening. What did I have to offer them?

The ones I'd visited today appeared to live simple lives. Food and shelter were their priority, not the colors of their gowns or the style of their hair. They worked hard for what little they had while I'd been handed everything. Even if I wanted to get a job, I wouldn't know where to start.

A job.

That's it.

I'd been raised to be a rich man's wife. And that meant hiring household staff, giving people jobs. Tadhg hadn't kept much staff in the castle while he was cursed, but now that he was free, perhaps we could help the community by hiring a few maids and footmen.

"I'd like to hire a maid."

Rían rolled his eyes and flipped to the next page. "So hire one."

I would, except I didn't know the first thing about how to go about it here. "Will you help me?"

"What do I know about maids?"

I set my glass down and glared across the space at my former husband. "I seem to recall you being very close with our maids at the townhouse, so I imagine you know a great deal."

He dragged his narrowed eyes to mine. "That was low."

I couldn't help my grin. "I'll take that as a yes."

16

RÍAN

W<small>HEN MY EX-WIFE AND SOON-TO-BE SISTER-IN-LAW</small> (FOR THE hundredth time) suggested hiring a maid, I probably should've deterred her to save Keelynn the heartache. However, since I was miserable, I saw no reason that everyone else in this castle shouldn't be miserable as well. Besides, why did this irritating, useless human get to flit around this castle planning her wedding while I spent every waking moment trying to keep her sister safe? Why did my drunken wastrel of a brother get to spend his nights in his soulmate's bed and days playing the hero to those affected by the blight while I slept alone, destined to watch Danú get killed for crimes they didn't commit?

So many times I'd been on the verge of throwing caution to the wind and giving in to love. A few days ago, I'd gone to the gardens and found Aveen in dress cut so low, I'd been this close to dragging her straight to the dungeon. That afternoon, I acciden-tally walked in on her having a bath in the middle of the feckin' day.

This morning, I'd run into Aveen on the staircase, her cheeks flushed and hair around her face and neck damp. I'd been trans-fixed by a single drop of bath water still clinging to her skin, rolling down the smooth column of her neck to the hollow at her throat. How I longed to trace its path with the tip of my tongue.

I scrubbed my hazy eyes and forced myself to swallow past the lump in my throat.

The Queen could arrive at any moment.

Although she still hadn't responded to Tadhg's request for a meeting, it was only a matter of time before she did.

I had to keep reminding myself of the danger we were in. If the Queen recognized Aveen's scent wrapped around me, surely she'd learn the truth.

I couldn't let that happen. The best thing for everyone was to keep Aveen at arm's length. Misery was my only companion.

So that's why I agreed to help Keelynn hire a ladies' maid.

I leaned on the window's low ledge, one boot on the floor, the other propped against the wall, studying the woman sitting across the desk from Keelynn. At least twenty more waited in the hallway outside. Most I recognized, but some—the younger ones—I didn't.

Having all these unknowns milling about felt like a weight pressing against my chest, smothering me slowly. Every single person who entered this castle could be a potential risk to Aveen's security. Which was why the condition of my help was that I was the one to vet each new employee.

Keelynn's hands clasped primly on top of the notebook she'd asked to borrow as she smiled across at the red-nosed clurichaun. "As I'm sure you're aware, I'm looking to hire a ladies' maid for after the wedding. What experience do you have, Mrs. Fletcher?"

Mrs. Fletcher's broad shoulders deflated. "I was a ladies' maid fer the Bellington family in Rosemire fer ten years before they let me go fer usin' a glamour."

Keelynn sucked in a breath. "That's awful."

Considering the humans could have sent her to prison, being fired really wasn't so terrible.

Mrs. Fletcher's lips flattened as she stared down her slightly crooked nose at Keelynn. If she'd looked at Aveen with such disdain, I would've had something to say. But since this happened to be the irritating Bannon, I kept my mouth shut.

Keelynn glanced over her shoulder at me.

I nodded. Not even a hint of a lie.

She twisted back toward Mrs. Fletcher, her smile widening. "It sounds as if you have excellent experience and would be perfect for the job." Her hands fell from the table to twist together in her lap. "However, I do have one question that is of a sensitive nature." Color crept along the high neckline of her sage-green gown, all the way to her cheekbones. "I would like to know if you've ever had relations with my fiancé."

Ms. Fletcher's mouth popped open, but no words emerged. When they did, I had to hide my smile behind my hand. "Well, ye see, it was a long, long time ago. And I...um...I've been married since. Ancient history. I doubt the prince even knows my name anymore."

Beneath the desk, Keelynn's hands balled into fists. "Thank you, Mrs. Fletcher. I will let you know once we decide." She dismissed the woman and asked her to send in the next person.

I tapped my fingers to my lips, doing my best not to laugh. "Next time, maybe you should lead with that question."

Keelynn whipped toward me. "The first thing I say to these women can't be 'have you slept with my husband?'"

"You'd save yourself—and me—a lot of time."

The next woman came in. When she saw me, her cheeks pinkened. I wasn't sure if Tadhg had slept with this one, but I had. Keelynn conducted the same interview and then sent her away as well.

Another woman came in, her hands gnarled and skin paper-thin. I cleared my throat and shook my head. Keelynn still went about her questions but skipped the one about Tadhg. The moment the woman left, Keelynn's head dropped into her hands. "Don't tell me Tadhg slept with her too?"

"Afraid so. That was Darcy O'Brien. She was wearing a glamour." I'd recognize those fawn-brown eyes anywhere.

The next three lied straight to Keelynn's face, saying they hadn't slept with my brother. Lucky I was a supernatural lie-detector.

Keelynn slumped in the chair, her dark waves spilling over the back cushion. "I give up."

Better to face the reality of my brother's curses now than after she'd tied herself to him a third time. Maybe she'd realize this was a terrible mistake and leave for Hollowshade. Then Aveen wouldn't insist on staying in Tearmann.

A slender woman with a round face and bright yellow eyes slipped through the door. Her long, raven plait swung at her back.

Keelynn sat up and leaned forward on her elbows. "What's your name?"

"Millie Ward, milady."

The Wards hailed from the western coast of Tearmann, near the ruins of the ancient castle first used by my father's ancestors. Unfortunately, I didn't know much about the family beyond the fact that they paid their taxes each year without fail.

The chair creaked beneath Keelynn as she shifted on the seat. "How old are you, Millie?"

When Millie wrenched her hands in front of her, I noticed a black tattoo encircling the ring finger on her left land.

"Seventeen, milady."

Keelynn must've noticed the mark as well. "And you're married?"

She nodded. "Four weeks next Sunday. Never worked as a lady's maid before, but I'm a fast learner."

"Have you ever met either prince?"

The girl's eyes flashed to me briefly before returning to Keelynn. "Neither one, milady."

Keelynn's brows lifted as she glanced at me. I nodded.

Keelynn let out a loud sigh. "You're hired."

Thank feck. I was nearly asleep with my eyes open.

Millie looked at Keelynn with such reverence, you'd swear the human had hung the stars herself. After a torrent of heartfelt thanks, Millie skipped out the door with a giggle. Just what this castle needed. More giggles. If the blight weren't consuming our land, I'd have found somewhere else to live. Somewhere empty and dark, like my mood.

The door creaked open, and a woman with short cropped black hair slipped into the room on silent, bare feet.

Keelynn waved her off. "I'm afraid you're too late. We've already hired someone."

Shona quirked a questioning brow at me.

I launched to my feet and gave the back of Keelynn's chair a shake. "Up and out, princess. She's not here for you. She's here for me." It was about damn time the selkie showed up. I almost forgot I'd asked her to come.

For once, Keelynn minded her own business and left without a word.

Shona settled on the chair across from me, her legs crossed at the ankles beneath her rust-colored muslin dress. "To what do I owe this request?"

No sense mincing words and wasting both our time. "I need information about a pirate."

If my words surprised her, she didn't let it show. "I don't have much to do with pirates now that Wills and I have settled on Syren Isle. We're too busy with the children."

Ah, yes. The children. How could I forget? The reason she made me wait weeks for her to visit. I should ask about them, some menial question about their wellbeing and about her wife as well. But I didn't because I didn't give a shite about any of them. "He's fae," I said instead.

She eased forward, her expression darkening as she rested her forearms on the desk. "Well, that certainly narrows it down. His name?"

"Merriweather." Stupid name, that. *Merriweather*. You'd think an immortal pirate would have the good sense to change his surname to something less jovial.

"Caden Merriweather?" she breathed.

A thrill danced down my spine. *Finally.* "So you have heard of him."

Her head bobbed. "Aye. He's a smuggler, mostly. Doesn't attack ships unless provoked. Never heard of him losing a battle though. Cunning. Handsome."

Please. He wasn't that handsome. His face had been average at best. "If I needed to find him, where would I look?"

For some reason, the corners of her lips lifted as she stared down at her hands. "The rogue is from the fae lands in Iodale, but I've heard he spends most of his time at sea."

Wasn't that feckin' brilliant? If he stayed on the water, I'd have no way to get to him. Even if I did manage to board his ship, my magic would be useless after a few minutes, and catching the pirate unawares a second time would be nearly impossible, especially if I couldn't maintain a glamour. "What's his lineage?"

"Fae mam, merrow da."

That explained his ability to wield magic over the water. One didn't hear of many fae mating with the male merrow—they were notoriously hideous. If only the pirate had inherited his father's looks. Then Aveen wouldn't have set foot near the bastard.

Shona's long nail clinked against the decanter on the corner of the desk. I probably should've offered her a drink but really didn't feel like entertaining her longer than necessary. "Is there any particular reason you're inquiring after Captain Merriweather?" she asked.

As if I'd tell her. "That'll be all, Shona."

Her eyes flared but she quickly hid her irritation behind a tight smile. "Always a pleasure, Prince Rían."

The lie made me smile as I watched her saunter out of the room.

So Caden Merriweather was part merrow. Too bad I'd murdered my only connection to the merrow. They probably wouldn't take very kindly if I came calling again. At least with Aveen here at the castle, I could keep an eye out for any pirates who might come sniffing around.

I believed Aveen when she said she loved me. Could taste the truth in her words. But there was something about first love that burrowed into your soul.

I collected the decanter and poured myself a glass of whiskey. When I took a sip, the warm, smooth liquid burned my throat all the way down. Easing back in the chair, I studied the map of Tearmann stretched across the desk where Tadhg had been marking the progress of the blight since it began.

What were we going to do if the Queen refused to stop the blight and the entire country became infected? We could expand into Airren, but having so many Danú relocate all at once would surely draw notice. The trials hadn't stopped, they'd increased in number. Even with Tadhg and Ruairi attending, there still weren't enough of us to cover the farces.

Our future looked bleaker than ever before.

Bitterness coursed through my veins with every beat of my damned heart. All I wanted was to be happy like everyone else.

To be with the woman I loved.

And yet here I sat, drinking and drowning and cursing the Queen.

As if I'd spoken my desires aloud, Aveen stepped into the office. Candlelight played on her soft features, making her glow like the light she was.

Whiskey. I needed more whiskey. I took another deep gulp.

How could one person be so feckin' beautiful?

My body ached with such acute need, I felt as if I would burst through my very skin. Teaching Aveen to harness her magic over the last few weeks had been torture, and there was no end in sight.

Once she mastered a glamour, she'd need to learn how to evanesce properly without ending up somewhere she didn't want to be. And then there were other lessons as well, like shifting and simple spells. We'd be in each other's lives for the foreseeable future, and I was at my breaking point. The other day, she'd dropped a hair pin, and when she'd bent over to retrieve it, I'd nearly grabbed her by the waist and begged her to let me have her once more.

Aveen moved slowly, as if unsure. I hated myself for making this confident woman feel as if she wasn't worth the risk. She continued to where I sat, bringing along a rose-scented breeze to torture me some more. She sank onto the desk, covering Tearmann's western coast with her silken dressing gown.

"You look weary," she said in a voice as smooth as honey as she toyed with the silk tie cinched around her waist.

The Queen. Remember the Queen.

"I am fine." I'd been tortured plenty of times before and survived. That was all this was. Another form of torture. Delicious, sensuous torture.

Instead of pressing the issue, she twisted so she could see the map beneath her. "How far has the blight spread?"

Her dressing gown fell open, revealing another layer of silk beneath that I recognized from our first day working on glamours.

My fingertips brushed the silk at her knee. "I'd show you, but this is in the way."

Her clear blue eyes held mine. "Then move it."

The Queen. The Queen. The Queen.

If I touched her now, I wouldn't be able to stop. Instead, I said, "It's reached well above the midlands."

She shifted, a smile playing on the edge of her full lips. "Show me where."

Sweat beaded on my brow. My composure slipped a little more with each unsteady breath that escaped my lungs. I wasn't strong enough to resist her.

I tapped a spot on the bottom of the map near the compass rose and followed the road to that line of silk. "There's a road right along here."

Her knees spread wider.

Feck. "And if you follow it north, there's…"

"There's what?" she asked in a whisper, her robe slipping off one slender shoulder, taking my sanity with it.

My heart skidded to a halt. "There's trouble." So much feckin' trouble.

"I see." Her knees widened a fraction more. "And are you powerful enough to deal with the trouble?"

I wasn't powerful. I was weak. So feckin' weak.

My nails bit into Aveen's soft thighs. Funny. I didn't remember putting my hands there.

Since they were, I might as well enjoy the way her supple skin erupted with gooseflesh beneath my touch as I dragged them higher, to the swell of her hips.

This was dangerous. I really shouldn't let my thumb fall to the damp silk between her thighs. I *really* shouldn't. But then I did, and the whimper that fell from her parted lips was my undoing.

I pressed and stroked the hard nub hidden between her folds. "A problem like this isn't about power."

Her hips tilted ever so slightly as she leaned back on her elbows, her robe falling fully open. "Is it not?"

My hand shook as I tugged her knickers aside to find her body beneath glistening with arousal. My thumb grazed her slickness, pressing gently against that perfect spot.

Her head fell back, and a sigh escaped her lips.

"No," I whispered, calling heat to my hand as I worked her in slow, steady circles. "It's about skill…and persistence."

She ground herself against me, forcing my fingers deeper.

This was reckless. Foolish. *Inevitable.*

I'd have to take drastic measures to ensure the Queen didn't find out that I'd been with anyone, but feck it all if this didn't feel like stealing joy.

Aveen whimpered my name when I slid a finger inside. Cried out when I added a second. How had I resisted this temptation for so long?

My swollen cock ached against the buttons on my breeches, straining for release.

"I need more," Aveen begged. "Please, Rían. Please."

I couldn't deny her any longer. "Feet on the floor and turn around."

She did as I commanded, bracing her hands on the map, her arse pressing into me as she bent over the desk.

The voice of reason screamed in my mind, telling me to put an end to this, but the soft, needy moans coming from her throat sealed our fate. I tore off the robe and lifted her nightgown until the silk pooled around her waist. My knees nearly gave out as I slid her knickers down her thighs. While I was down here, I figured I may as well make use of myself. I slid my tongue up her seam, feeling her jerk forward. How had I gone so long without the taste of her? The feel of her. Those feckin' sounds of want. Of need.

I spread her wider, needing more than a taste. Needing to devour. To consume her the way she consumed me. When I flicked my tongue, she moaned, "Right there."

Right there was where I stayed, working in sharp strokes, building a rhythm, drinking every drop. I freed myself and stroked my aching cock, searching for release.

If we were going down, we'd go down together. And we'd go down in flames.

"Rían...I need you."

Not as much as I need you.

I clambered to my feet and nudged the head of my cock against her dripping heat. "I've missed you so feckin' much," I confessed, urging my hips forward and catching her hair to drag her back against me. Her body welcomed mine, hugging tight, her backside the perfect fit against my hips. When I started to thrust, she took each punishing hit with whimpers for more. The months I'd spent without her fell to nothing, squandered so that we could find this fleeting bliss.

"Tell me you love me."

"I love you," she gasped.

She loved me. Not Caden feckin' Merriweather. Only me.

I freed her breast, cupping the soft mound while stroking and teasing the turgid peak with my thumb. "Tell me you're mine." My hand slid to her throat, applying the lightest pressure, just enough so I could feel her swallow against my palm.

Her plush lips curved into a smile. "All yours."

I drank in her truth and urged her back to the desk. Her smile grew even as I gripped the swell of her hips and pinned her in place. Candles rattled and books fell to the floor each time my hips bucked forward.

"Promise me I'm the only one."

"You are. Forever."

Tension ratcheted up my spine.

When she cried out, and I felt her muscles seize, I chased my own release. Lightning burst at the edge of my vision but I pulled out at the last possible second, spilling onto her glorious ass. I fell forward, bracing my hands on either side of the crooked map.

When my heart finally began to slow, I gathered the curls that had fallen across her flushed face. "You did that on purpose."

"Whatever do you mean?" she murmured.

I gave her backside a good smack. She yelped a laugh. And feck it all, did that pale skin look even more delicious with my handprint branded upon it. "You know exactly what I mean." I shifted a cloth to clean us both. Guilt tugged at my core, but I refused to let it settle. Not yet.

Aveen righted herself and pressed a whispering kiss to my lips. "Who would've thought such a powerful prince could be undone by a few scraps of silk?"

The flimsy garments may have aided, but the woman who wore them held all the power. I fell back on the chair and pulled her on top of me, determined to revel in bliss instead of letting reality steal my happiness once more. "What am I going to do with you?"

Her laughter warmed my cold soul like a bonfire in the dead of winter. "Bending me over the desk was a good start."

I held her close, breathing her in, praying we hadn't just made the biggest mistake of our lives.

17

TADHG

Heavy pounding roused me from a deep, dreamless sleep. I always slept better with Keelynn by my side. Probably because we wore each other out so thoroughly. I blinked up at the canopy, her soft snores tickling my cheek.

There it was again. A heavy fist against wood, not inside the castle. Too much of an echo.

Keelynn flew upright next to me, dark, riotous waves dancing over her bare breasts. "What's that?" she asked, her voice thick with exhaustion.

"I'm sure it's nothing. Go back to sleep." Good thing I could lie now. No one came to the castle in the middle of the night unless something terrible had happened. Still, I saw no reason to worry her unnecessarily. If we were under attack, the person hardly would've knocked to announce his presence. Probably had something to do with that feckin' blight. Yesterday, I'd spent the entire day shifting cottages and cattle to a patch of land on the west coast far too small to handle the number of livestock the farmer and his family kept.

Keelynnn fell back to the pillow without another word and dragged the coverlet up to her neck.

I rolled out of bed, stuffed my legs into the breeches Keelynn had tossed aside last night, and grabbed a shirt from my armoire. Once all the important bits were covered, I evanesced to the entry hall right as the person pounded again. Rían appeared beside me, his hair looking as perfect as ever, while I imagined I looked like I'd slept in a field.

Neither of us said anything as he reached for the latch and drew the door open.

My mate Lorcan fell into the hallway, his hands and face stained black. The acrid stench of smoke clung to his blackened, torn shirt.

I caught him by the shoulders to help him stand. "What's happened?"

His golden eyes narrowed as he gasped for breath. "Humans. They torched the feckin' bar."

Lorcan and his wife Deirdre owned The Arches bar in Gaul, a rare establishment that welcomed both humans and Danú with open arms. And...*shit*.

They lived right above the place. My heart slammed against my ribcage. "Is Deirdre—?"

He dragged a singed sleeve across his mouth. "She's alive."

Rían shoved my shoulder. "What are you waiting for? Let's go." He flicked his wrist, and a pair of boots appeared on my feet. My body moved of its own volition, following Lorcan into the night. Our footfalls echoed off the stone walls as we sprinted for the gates. We cleared the wards, gripped each other's hands, and evanesced to an alley around the corner from the bar.

Shouts boomed from the street beyond; people darted this way and that, filling the air with curses and cries. Lorcan led the way, shoving past groups of people standing idly by, like this was some sort of theatrical performance for their morbid entertainment.

Smoke clung to the damp, salty air like a heavy fog, burning my eyes. The street where the Arches once stood looked like it had been struck by cannon fire. Not only was the main building gone, but the homes on either side had been reduced to rubble as well. Men in heavy wool coats bellowed from farther down the street, passing buckets of water to try and put out what remained of the orange flames licking at the starlit night.

Lorcan gripped his head in his hands; flames glinted in his tear-filled eyes. "It's gone, lad. It's all gone."

I would've called on my magic to help except there was nothing more to be done. No amount of magic could bring the Arches back. "What happened?"

He dragged his arm beneath his eyes, catching the tears spilling down his sunken cheeks. "Deirdre and I were asleep when I thought I smelled smoke. By the time I got up, the entire ground floor had been consumed."

That made no sense. Pooka had an unrivaled sense of smell. Surely Lorcan should've smelled the smoke well before it had done this much damage.

Rían smacked my hip and nodded toward the crowd growing larger by the second.

I twisted away from my friend, searching for whatever had caught my brother's attention. Before I could ask, my brother was pushing through the humans. I squeezed between two sobbing women in their nightgowns and skirted past another in a mop cap with a screeching baby clutched to her breast.

Rían started to run, which didn't bode well for whomever he chased since he'd always been a fast fecker. He darted down a skinny side street next to a blue and white tea house. By the time I caught up, he had a man on the ground, lying face-down in a puddle. A second man dragged himself along the ground by his elbows, his limp legs bent at wrong angles scraping the cobblestones.

"Have you lost your mind? You can't just go around killing humans." Tensions would be high enough in the aftermath of the fire. The last thing we needed was a bunch of humans feeling justified in committing more atrocities.

Rían's teeth gleamed in the lamplight when he looked up from the body. "Not even the ones who started the fire?"

I glanced between the two men, searching for whatever my

brother saw that had incriminated them. They wore the same dark breeches as practically every other man around. Sure, their white shirts were stained with soot, but so were everyone else's who'd been helping to put out the fire. "How do you know they did it?"

Rían blew out a heavy sigh, like my question was really putting him out. "When I set things on fire, I like to make sure whatever it was actually burns. Otherwise, what's the point?"

"Yes, but you're a psychopath."

Shrugging, he gestured toward the men with his dagger. "These two seemed shifty. I asked if they did it, and they said no."

And with Rían's ability to taste lies, he would've known the truth. If only such swift justice could help Lorcan and the others who had lost everything. "Get rid of the bodies before anyone—"

Sharp pain shot up my leg. The man from the puddle sneered up at me from the ground, a dagger in his clenched fist. The bastard had stabbed me.

I kicked his blade aside, my magic already knitting my skin back together as I knelt and shifted a dagger of my own. In one swipe, I'd carved a smile across his throat.

Only...no blood escaped the wound.

What in the fresh hell?

I could see the inside of his esophagus. How was he still trying to grab my boot?

Rían squatted next to the man. When he swiped for Rían's leg, my brother crushed the man's hand beneath the heel of his boot. "He should be dead," Rían said matter-of-factly, still staring down at the thrashing, snarling man.

No one could survive such a wound—not even a true immortal. A sword appeared in Rían's hand. In one swing, he relieved the man of his head. The bastard finally fell still.

"Was he one of us?" The thought that one of the Danú would've attacked one of our own like this made me sick to my stomach.

"Let's find out." Rían kicked him over and pressed a hand to the dead man's chest. I held my breath, listening to my brother's harsh inhale. "Strange..." His hand fell aside as he studied the headless body. "There's no life force. Not even a spark. Even humans have *something*."

I didn't even know that was possible. "If he's not human, and he's not Danú, what is he?"

"Good feckin' question." He reached for the man's head, and the bodies vanished.

I shot to my feet, searching the shadows for some sign of the corpses. "Did you do that?"

Rían shot me a baleful glare. "Yes. I shifted away the only evidence we had."

Sarcastic prick. "A simple 'no' would suffice."

Together, we searched the night for signs of who could have shifted the bodies. The silent shadows stared back, keeping their secrets close. Someone had used these *things* to attack the Danú. Someone with enough magic to be able to shift them away afterward.

Meaning humans hadn't committed this crime. It had been one of us. But who?

A discussion for later, when we returned to the castle.

Rían and I made our way back to Lorcan. With the pooka at least a head taller than the rest of the crowd, he was easy to spot. I didn't want to mention the mystery surrounding the culprits without first discussing with Rían. His mouth clamped shut, so I assumed he felt the same.

Still, I had to give the lad *something*. I settled a hand on Lorcan's slumped shoulder, my gut twisting with regret. "Rían caught the men responsible. They won't be a problem anymore."

Lorcan nodded, his lips pressing flat as he lifted his head toward the sky. "Why would someone do this? We weren't hurting anyone. Had our best year yet—more human customers than ever." He dashed his hands through his short black hair. "Saints above...what are we supposed to do now?"

"You could consider returning to Tearmann." Humans may

not have committed this crime, but our people in Airren were dying in droves. I'd asked Lorcan to come before, but he'd never agreed because of the bar. Now there was nothing holding him back.

"And leave Deirdre behind?" Lorcan shook his head. "I'll not be crossing the Forest unless my wife can come with me."

"You can request an audience with the Queen."

Rían rolled his eyes. We both knew the Queen probably wouldn't allow it, but it couldn't hurt to ask. Maybe Lorcan would catch her on a good day and she'd be feeling gracious. Then again, if she found out he was only half-pooka, she'd deny him on his heritage alone.

Lorcan just shook his head.

What remained of the colorful cushions Deirdre had bought for their living area peeked from between broken bricks and blackened logs. Deirdre had been so excited about those damn cushions. "Do you have somewhere safe to stay until then?"

He wiped a hand down his face, smearing soot across his brow and cheek. "Deirdre can go back to her family, I suppose."

I arched a brow. "Just Deirdre?"

Lorcan winced. "I'm not welcome there."

The two of them had been married for years and yet her family still hadn't accepted him? What a load of bollocks. Lorcan was a better man than any human I'd ever met. They were lucky to have him as a son-in-law.

"I'm friendly with the owner of the Red Bear," he murmured, still deep in thought. "He might be willing to rent us a room until we can get back on our feet."

I shifted two purses full of gold from our treasury and handed them to my friend. At first he refused, but when I pointed out how many nights he'd housed, fed, and watered me for free, he agreed the gold would more than settle my tab.

A pink dawn broke over the seaside town as Rían and I made our way to a quiet alley to evanesce back to Tearmann.

We needed to find a way to bring our people home, but there

was no way the ones with human partners would leave. Which left us with one option. "We need to find a way to get humans across the Forest without involving the Queen."

Rían's harsh breath lifted like white smoke into the crisp air. "If we can't stop the blight, we won't have a home."

How had I forgotten that feckin' blight?

We weren't preparing for a war.

We were in the middle of one.

18

RÍAN

The Phantom Queen had impeccable timing. She couldn't have come to see us before I'd given in, oh no. That would've been too convenient. She had to wait until I'd decided to steal back my joy to send a letter saying she would arrive the following day. The tight turnaround came as no surprise. She probably thought giving us very little time to prepare would make it less likely we'd double-cross her again.

It hadn't taken much to convince Tadhg to send Keelynn with Aveen to Ruairi's. Aveen didn't put up a fight either.

Watching my love leave the castle wearing her glamour left my heart in my throat.

I studied the letter from the Black Forest, the few simple words giving nothing away. The witch held our fates in the palm of her cursed hands, and all she had to say was, *I will arrive at half past four tomorrow.*

The first word was by far the largest. After all, she believed she was more important than anyone else. And the way she looped her letters? Entirely unnecessary. This wasn't a feckin' wedding invitation. Why did she always have to be so formal? So pretentious?

I balled the note in my fist and called fire to my palm. Flames engulfed the yellowed parchment, and I threw the thing into the fireplace's empty grate.

I tugged on the bottom of my waistcoat, ridding the black silk of any remaining creases. Ruairi loosed a song-suffering sigh, watching me from his wingback with a stoic expression.

"Are you certain you can't tell?" I asked, hating having to rely on him for something so vital.

Ruairi rolled his eyes and shoved his sleeves to his elbows, no doubt ready to deck me. "Fecks' sake, lad, I said I couldn't smell her."

The pooka was pissier than usual today. Seeing him scowl was a nice break from all his irritating grins.

After my moment of weakness in the study with Aveen, I'd bathed, killed myself, and bathed again. Between death and the pound of soap I'd used in the bath, I smelled like I'd slept in a vat of potpourri. But my senses weren't nearly as acute as the dog's. If he said he couldn't scent Aveen anywhere near me, that had to be good enough.

Nothing I could do about it now, and it wasn't as if I could leave. The Queen wouldn't set foot in this castle if I wasn't here as well.

Tadhg popped his head into the parlor to tell us it was time. We made our way out to the castle gates to wait. The long grass on the other side of the wards swayed and rocked, but no breeze reached us here. Would there ever be a time when we could live without the need for wards? I thought of Aveen's glamour and the ones I'd hidden behind for most of my life. Would we ever be truly safe?

The Queen arrived, six shadow guards following close behind, short swords crossed at their backs and masks concealing their features. The old witch barely acknowledged me, looking straight at Tadhg with her lips slightly parted in surprise, presumably at his appearance.

My brother had made a rare effort, his clothes starched and pressed, his borrowed waistcoat and cravat buttoned and tied to perfection. For once, he looked like a prince instead of a disaster.

Her black gaze darted to me before returning to my brother. "I do hope this isn't another ruse to steal from me."

Tadhg's hair fell over his forehead when he shook his head. "I can assure you that it's not."

Her shoulders rose and fell with a deep breath as she searched for his lie. Her lips pursed, and she nodded.

Stepping aside, Tadhg gestured toward the castle. "Come inside, there is something urgent we must discuss." The guards followed, their boots not making a sound on the gravel, as if they weren't marching in time. Phantoms, much like their master's favorite moniker.

To my surprise, the Queen sidled up to me. "You look awful," she murmured.

What was she on about? My clothes were immaculate, my boots polished to a shine. Eava had trimmed my hair, and I'd shaved. Leave it to the Queen to still find fault in perfection.

"Is that useless witch not feeding you?" she pressed.

I may have lost a little weight over the last year, and could have really done with a trip to the tailor, but I hadn't had the time —or the inclination.

"Save your false concern." She hadn't been worried about my wellbeing when she'd starved me for a week after I'd spilled a goblet of blood on the carpet. Why start now?

Her narrowed eyes roamed over my face. "I'm relieved to see this loss has hardened you. You always were too soft. I heard you even issued a royal pardon to a thieving witch."

Only because Aveen had made me realize the value in mercy. Pardoning Anwen for stealing fabric had been the right choice, even if the Queen would never see it that way.

I tamped down my irritation. All that mattered was that the Queen still believed Aveen was dead. And from the way she referred to her death as a "loss," I assumed our ruse was working.

"You know how eager I've always been to please you, *Mother*," I drawled, hoping she choked on the sweetness of my lie.

Although she said no more, her lips flattened as she swept into the dining room and took her seat at the head of the table. Tadhg shifted a bottle of blood, but she refused a glass, saying she was a busy woman and had no time for drinks and idle conversation.

Brilliant. Neither did we.

Tadhg flattened his hands atop the table and drew in a deep breath. "Right, so. I suppose we'll get down to business then. We have a problem. A blight is tainting the land, killing animals and crops. We've had to relocate thirty families and three faerie colonies."

The Queen's impassive expression gave nothing away. "How unfortunate."

"It seems as if the Forest is spreading," he went on.

Her face may as well have been a stone sculpture for all it moved. "I see."

Tadhg looked the Queen dead in the eye, his own eyes swirling with black shadows. "It needs to stop."

A surprisingly diplomatic approach all things considered. If I didn't know better, I would've called the warmth in my chest pride.

The Queen's dark eyebrows lifted toward her gleaming onyx crown. "What do you expect me to do about it?"

The witch had been alive for millennia and knew how to phrase her responses to keep from incriminating herself. If we had any hope of gleaning a genuine reaction, we needed to unsettle her. Force her to be decisive with a lie or the truth. Either one would work at this stage.

I leaned back in my chair as if I didn't care either way. No sense letting her know how invested I really felt. "We know you're the one behind the blight."

Slowly, she turned, glowering down her straight nose at me. "That is an awfully serious accusation, *son*."

Why attack her own people, the ones she always fought so

hard to "protect"? She never did anything without reason. There was always some strategy or ulterior motive. What would happen if all of Tearmann went black? Our people would be forced to relocate to Airren or flee the island altogether, catching ships to the fae lands in Iodale or the continent. Passage was expensive, so the former would be most likely.

An influx of Danú in Airren would make the Airren authorities uneasy, and tensions were already at an all-time high.

The Queen had always been vocal about what our father had conceded in the treaty. She'd never hidden the fact that she wanted to cull the island of humans and redraw the lines on the map to what they had been before the war.

Hold on.

Could that be why she was doing this? Now that I thought about it, I really should've seen this sooner. I was some eejit.

"You're trying to start a war."

Her lips twitched.

Feckin' hell. I was right. The Queen was trying to start a feckin' war with the humans.

"That is absurd," she clipped.

The air turned sweet. Absurd or not, I'd caught her out in a lie. "You're trying to force their hand," I said, her plan becoming clearer with each passing second. The fire at the Arches? I'd bet my cufflinks that had been her as well. "You're trying to get them to attack us first." The Airren authorities would see an influx of Danú as an imminent threat. They'd been building up their military presence for years. If Airren attacked, we would be forced to retaliate, or else the Danú would revolt against Tadhg's rule.

Hell, with his engagement to a human, his people were already on the verge of revolt.

Tadhg's hands balled into fists where they rested on the tabletop. "You know we cannot hope to win against a trained army with iron weapons. You would be leading our people to slaughter."

The Queen's thin lips twisted in a mocking smile. "You have

missed your chance to respond to this crisis. I will handle the issue how I see fit. Now, if you'll excuse me, I'll be going." She rose and smoothed down her dress, the veins in her hands as black as the feathers sewn into her skirts. "Oh, Rían. I almost forgot to give you your birthday present."

If she thought I'd accept a gift from her, she had another thing coming. "I want nothing from you."

Her teeth gleamed in the candlelight when she smiled. "I think you'll want this." She clicked her fingers at the guards. The dining room door creaked open. In stepped a woman with the hood of her black cloak pulled, concealing her features. She lifted her hands and eased back the hood.

Fiery curls spilled out.

The woman smiled a smile I'd kissed on far too many occasions. "Rían?"

My heart stopped beating.

The air evacuated my lungs.

My head began to spin and thump.

I knew her voice as clearly as I knew my own.

I stared dumbfounded at the woman standing an arm's reach away. It couldn't be. *Freckles across her nose.* It couldn't. *Moss-green eyes.* An excellent glamour, that's what it was. A trick of magic. Another feckin' mirage.

I stumbled to my feet, sending the chair clattering to the stones.

The woman's brilliant smile left my stomach sinking to my toes as she rushed forward and draped her long, slender arms around my neck. "Oh, how I've missed you, my love."

She smelled like bonfire smoke and pine, like all those times she'd fallen asleep in front of the fireplace with a book on her lap. How was this possible?

Leesha pulled away, her fingertips grazing my neck, making the hair stand on end. "Your mother has been most kind, giving me refuge in her castle until you could return for me."

The Queen? *Kind?* Now I knew she wasn't real. I caught her

wrists and forced her away from me so I could see her face more clearly. "Who are you?"

The young woman's brow furrowed as her lips turned down at the corners. Lips the same shade of pink as her flushed cheeks. "Who am I? Rían, it's me. Leesha."

No. That couldn't be. It wasn't possible. "You're dead. I saw you die."

She blinked, a quick sweep of her thick, dark lashes. "I'm not dead, silly." Her laugh was as throaty and sensual as I remembered. "I'm right here."

The Queen moved next to the woman who couldn't possibly be alive, snaking an arm around her shoulder, drawing her close. "I kept her safe just for you."

This wasn't happening. No one could bring back the dead, not even the Phantom Queen.

My pulse screamed in my skull as I tried to wrap my head around what the hell was happening.

Leesha was *here*.

Leesha was *alive*.

The Queen toyed with one of Leesha's soft curls, smiling as if she were caring, downright *matronly*. "Leesha, my dearest girl, from this day forward, I give you permission to cross the Forest whenever you wish."

Leesha beamed at her before dipping into a low curtesy. "Thank you, my Queen. You are most kind."

The Queen wasn't *kind*. She was an evil, vindictive witch.

What sort of twisted game was she playing?

The Queen urged Leesha toward me. My body stiffened as my former lover looped her arm through mine and squeezed my bicep, the picture of giddy excitement. This couldn't be happening. This could *not* be happening. The way she clung to my arm felt wrong—so feckin' wrong.

This *had* to be a glamour, except...her eyes.

Two centuries had passed since I'd seen this woman, and yet I recognized every fleck in their mossy depths.

Leesha smiled up at me as if... *feckin' hell...* as if she didn't realize she'd been gone for hundreds of years. "I don't know what you were so afraid of. Your mother is lovely."

Words failed me. Tadhg appeared to have been rendered mute as well, staring dumbfounded at the woman clinging to me. What was I supposed to do now?

The Queen's pat on my shoulder was the closest thing to affection she'd ever shown. "Happy birthday, Rían." With a flick of her wrist, she and her guards vanished.

My ears rang so loud, I couldn't hear a blessed thing. Tadhg and I remained paralyzed, like we'd been frozen in this moment for all of eternity.

"I am so excited to finally be here," Leesha said, her words ringing in my ears. "It feels as if I haven't seen you in forever. Is Eava about? I do hope she made a large cake. I am starving."

How could I answer any of her questions when I had so many of my own?

Where had the Queen been keeping Leesha? I had moved out of the castle the day she'd stolen Leesha's heart, but surely I would've realized if she had been living there this whole time. And Leesha was human, yet it looked as if she hadn't aged a bit since that fateful day. What sort of dark magic had the Queen used to keep her alive? To keep her from becoming one of the many rotting corpses left in piles along the southern gates?

She hadn't been alive, though. I'd watched my mother tear the heart from her chest. She mustn't have a heart.

My hands trembled as I tugged at the top of Leesha's dress, exposing the swell of her breast.

"Rían," she giggled, her cheeks flushing when she knocked my hand away and pulled her dress back in place. "Your brother is right there."

The scar. She had one across her chest, just like mine.

The Queen *had* taken her heart. That part hadn't been a dream.

I unhooked her arm from mine and told her that I needed to

speak with my brother in private. Leesha kissed my cheek and skipped out the door as if she hadn't a worry in the world.

"What's the plan?" Tadhg asked.

I couldn't even wrap my head around the last few minutes. How the hell could I come up with a feckin' plan?

"Rían?"

My eyes began to sting, and my vision blurred. "What am I going to do?" When Aveen found out, she would be devastated. We'd just found our way back to each other and now this?

Tadhg's teeth scraped his bottom lip, his gaze flashing to the darkened hallway before returning to where I stood. "You tell Aveen the truth."

The woman I loved is back from the dead. Oh! Did I mention that she thinks we're still together?

How the hell was I supposed to tell her that? I needed time to figure this out. Some peace and quiet and clarity.

I found Leesha in the kitchens chatting with a pale-faced Eava. When the witch saw me, her black eyes widened. I didn't know what to say, so I said nothing. Instead, I caught Leesha's hand and evanesced with her up to my room.

Giggling, she started unlacing the top of her dress. "Couldn't even let me have cake first, eh? I suppose we'll just have to eat an extra slice after."

"Leesha. Leave your clothes on."

Her hands fell to her sides, but her smirk remained. "Oh? This is to be quick, is it? I suppose it is your birthday, so..." She lifted her skirts, exposing long legs, milky skin, and a pair of blue lace undergarments that barely covered her arse.

"Pull those back down." I dragged her skirt back where it belonged. I couldn't have her flashing me her knickers every chance she got.

Concern glinted in her eyes. "What's wrong, my love?"

My face burned as I twisted away. *Everything.* Everything was wrong.

"Rían? Aren't you going to look at me?" The floorboards creaked when she stepped closer.

How could I look at her when my brain couldn't process any of this?

"I can't do this." I rushed for the door, clinging to the cold knob like a lifeline. Before I could escape into the hallway, someone knocked.

And then I heard Aveen call my name.

19

AVEEN

KEELYNN CLOSED THE DRAWER OF SILVER CUTLERY AND OPENED the cabinet below to find it full of crystal goblets and hand-embroidered serviettes. "Who would've thought Ruairi had such fine taste?" she said, moving on to the next.

I appreciated her attempt to distract me but couldn't focus on the fine home Ruairi owned or his impressive collection of fancy silver candlesticks. Not when Rían was meeting with that evil witch. According to the ticking grandfather clock on the wall near the fireplace, the Queen should've been at the castle by now.

What if this was a trap? What if she attacked and stole all their hearts?

Voicing my fears would only throw Keelynn into a tailspin as well, so I swallowed them down where they rotted like poison in my gut.

Keelynn peered out of the parlor and into the hallway toward the mahogany staircase. "I wonder what's upstairs?"

"Bedrooms, I imagine." Was this the sort of blinding fear Rían had lived with over the last year? I never should have been so hard on him. Perhaps we would have been better off getting on a boat and sailing away from this place. Tomorrow. We could all leave tomorrow.

"Come on." Keelynn poked my arm. "Aren't you the least bit curious?"

Perhaps the movement would do me good. It wasn't as if I could save any of them if the Queen decided to steal their hearts. Having magic I could barely wield made me about as useful as a spoon at a steak dinner.

Keelynn grabbed one of the silver candlesticks, and together we crept up the stairs. The tiny flame shuddered and turned to smoke.

Keelynn cursed.

I called heat to my palm the way Rían had shown me, letting the flame dance on my fingers before relighting the wick.

Orange light played across Keelynn's sharp features as her lips tugged into a frown. "Have I told you how jealous I am that you have magic?"

"Once or twice." We didn't discuss it much, though; the reality of my lifespan was too hard to contemplate when my sister remained human. I wasn't sure how I'd cope with watching her grow old and gray while I remained the same. How I would survive when she was no more. Although no one else had brought it up either, I'd seen the tension in Tadhg's shoulders when he'd looked at my sister, the innate sadness.

How cruel of fate, to pair a true immortal with a human soulmate.

Keelynn twisted away, but not before I caught the glisten of tears in her eyes. "Wonder what's in here?" she said, turning the knob on the closest door. On the other side, we found a bedchamber fit for a queen. The gold leaf headboard resembled a cresting wave. Blue damask wallpaper with the same pattern continued over the gold-tasseled drapes.

Keelynn lifted the candle higher, banishing the shadows to the recesses of the space. "I did not expect this."

Nor had I. I loved Ruairi, but he seemed more the type to live in a cave than in a fine house. Even our own estate in Graystones had shown signs of wear and tear. This place was immaculate.

Not one chip in the crown molding, fresh candles in the crystal chandeliers and wall sconces. As fine as any lord or lady's house back in Airren.

The next bedroom across the hall was as grand as the first, decorated in soft violets and pale yellows.

The third door led to a bathing chamber with a claw-foot tub big enough for both Keelynn and me. Rich wooden paneling on the walls concealed compartments with soaps and shampoos, fluffy towels, and thick dressing gowns.

By the time I exited the bathing chamber, Keelynn already had her head inside the next room. She glanced back, her eyes sparkling. "This one must be his."

Guilt tugged at my stomach. This seemed like an unnecessary invasion of privacy. Ruairi had offered his home as a refuge from the Queen, and here we were, snooping around like children searching for Yule gifts.

Before I could voice my concern, Keelynn disappeared inside. I reluctantly followed. Not to snoop but to keep her from getting into trouble. Not sure what sort of trouble we'd find in a pooka's empty bedchamber, but it was best to be prepared.

The gigantic four-poster bed boasted a thick velvet canopy. His fireplace had been set with kindling and fresh logs, waiting to be lit. The space had an adjoining bathing chamber, smaller but still as fine as the first.

Keelynn threw open the armoire, revealing serviceable white shirts, plain breeches, and a handful of waistcoats. Giggling, she withdrew one of the shirts and held it against her chest. "Good gracious. I think both of us could fit into one of these."

I clutched my skirts with clammy palms. We really shouldn't have been in here. "Probably. Now put it back."

She rolled her eyes, and her lips pursed into a pout that used to sway me when we were younger. "You're no fun tonight."

"This is very different from the last time I found two women in my bedchamber," Ruairi's deep voice rumbled from the hallway.

Keelynn squeaked and shoved the shirt back into the armoire, missing the rail entirely, before slamming the doors closed. The pooka standing in the doorway watched her panic with a wry smile.

He didn't know Keelynn as well as he knew me, and while I couldn't imagine him getting too upset, I wouldn't want his ire directed at her. I stepped in front of my sister and offered him a chagrined smile. "I was curious. I'm sorry."

Shrugging, Ruairi pushed himself off the doorframe. "I've nothing to hide except a few too many cobwebs and some dirty laundry in the hamper."

What was he on about? I hadn't seen even on cobweb. "Is everything all right at the castle?" I asked, wringing my hands.

His golden eyes seemed to flare at my question. "More or less."

"What does that mean?"

"It means everyone still has their hearts." He held open the door, and we exited with bowed heads, caught with our hands in the proverbial cookie jar.

I wanted to go back to the castle right away and make sure Rían was all right, but Keelynn didn't seem to be in a hurry. When we reached the parlor and found two thick slices of double-layer chocolate cake sitting on the coffee table, some of my anxiety abated.

Keelynn and I threw ourselves onto the settee and reached for the cakes. Ruairi retrieved two silver forks and held them out to us, his smile broadening to a grin.

I'd always been partial to chocolate cake, but what Eava did with chocolate felt sinful on my tongue. So fluffy and yet so moist. And the icing. My head fell back against the cushion as I savored each delicious morsel. If I were to die tomorrow, this would be a glorious last meal.

"Well? Tell us what happened," Keelynn said around a bite, the fork still in her mouth. "What did the Queen say? Is she going to help us?"

"Ye can ask the lads tomorrow."

The bite perched on the end of my fork fell back onto the plate, spilling crumbs onto my skirts. "Tomorrow? You want us to stay here tonight?" I couldn't stay here. I needed to get back to Rían.

Ruairi's long, blunt fingers drummed against the arm of his wingback chair. "Is my home not good enough for ye?"

"No, no. It's not that. Your home is beautiful. But I would like to return to the castle."

His fingers drummed harder. "The lads both agreed it would be best if ye stayed here."

Keelynn set her cake aside. "Why?"

Ruairi glanced toward the crackling fire licking up the brick fireplace. "I'll not lie to ye."

Something went wrong. *Dammit.* Here I was, eating chocolate cake when Rían could need my help.

Ruairi's fang scraped his lower lip. "Which is why I'm not going to say any more on the topic. Ye can ask Rían and Tadhg tomorrow."

I didn't realize how badly I was shaking until Keelynn's hand fell to mine. "Tell us why we can't go back tonight," she said.

"The Queen gave the prince an unexpected gift for his birthday, and he is… dealing with it."

Gift? *Birthday?* "Today is Rían's birthday?" Why hadn't he told me? And the Queen had scheduled this meeting on the very same day. That witch.

I set my plate on the coffee table and stood on unsteady legs. "I'm going back to the castle."

Keelynn shoved to her feet. "If she's going home, then so am I."

I collected our cloaks, handing Keelynn hers before throwing mine over my shoulders. Ruairi's weak protests fell on deaf ears. One way or another, I was going back to that castle tonight.

"Are you going to give us a lift, or will we make our own way?"

With a heavy sigh, Ruairi stomped outside and held open the

door until we were all standing in his front garden. One blinding flash later, he'd shifted into his equine form.

I slipped my boot into the saddle's stirrup, caught the horn, and settled myself atop the beautiful leather saddle, then offered my sister a hand up. Once she settled behind me, I gave his sides a nudge with my heels. Ruairi took off at a trot.

I nudged him once more, but he barely picked up his pace. "Would you mind going a little bit faster? We're in a bit of a hurry."

His ears twitched and head bobbed. A soft snort lifted into the air, and he took off like a shot.

The stars winking down at us through silver eyes blurred. The steady pounding of Ruairi's hooves tearing across the open fields helped me focus my breathing. I couldn't see very far in front of us, but Ruairi didn't seem to have the same problem as he ate up the distance between his home and the castle. In no time at all, we were standing outside the gates.

Keelynn dismounted first and waited for me to do the same.

Another flash, and Ruairi stood at our backs, a rare frown on his lips.

Together, we breached the wards and continued into the castle. Voices drifted from down the hallway, toward the kitchens. We found Tadhg hunched over a gigantic plate of cake and Eava chiding him for eating his feelings.

When they saw us and exchanged worried looks, my stomach sank even lower. This was Rían's birthday, he should've been the one gorging on cake, not his brother.

I braced my hands on my hips. "Where is he?"

Tadhg rocketed to his feet, knocking the stool to the ground. "I think you should wait until morning to—"

Eava's hand fell on Tadhg's shoulder, and his mouth snapped shut. "He's upstairs, child," she said in her soothing tone.

I turned and ran, my heart hammering as I sprinted up the stairs, barely slowing by the time I reached Rían's floor. I wanted to barge straight in. Kick down the door and hold the man I loved. But Tadhg and Eava had been wary for a reason.

So instead of charging ahead, I inhaled a deep breath, swiped my clammy palms down my skirts, and knocked. "Rían?"

"Who is that?" a voice asked.

A *feminine* voice I didn't recognize. I threw on a glamour, just in case.

"No one." Rían clipped. "I'm wrecked. I'll...um...I'll see you in the morning."

No one? What did he mean I was "no one"?

The door eased open, and Rían slipped through the gap, closing it right behind him so I couldn't get a peek inside. He looked strung tighter than a bloody bowstring, his smile forced and the skin beneath his eyes shadowed. "What are you doing here? I thought you were staying at Ruairi's."

"Seeing as it's your *birthday*, I thought you'd like to celebrate with me."

His eyes shuttered. "Aveen—"

The door flew open. A young woman with wavy hair the color of glowing embers stood on the other side. Impossibly dark lashes fringed a pair of deep-set green eyes. "Rían, can you help me with my—" The woman startled when she saw me. Her pale hand reached for Rían's arm, her fingers encircling his wrist directly above my blue ribbon he still wore. "Who is this?"

Rían's mouth opened and closed but no words emerged.

He had had another bloody woman in his bedchamber, and she wanted to know who I was? "My name is—"

"Rose," Rían cut in. "This is my friend Rose."

His *friend*? Hold on one bloody minute...

The woman smiled. "It's lovely to meet you, Rose. I'm Leesha. Rían's fiancée."

Leesha? As in...Rían's first love? The woman the Queen had stolen from him centuries ago who was supposed to be dead? She didn't look dead to me. Not only was she alive, she was here, in his castle. In his *room*. Clinging to his arm as if the two of them were—

I screwed my eyes shut and pinched my arm, praying all of this was some sort of terrible dream. When I opened them again, nothing had changed.

Rían was still there, and Leesha...her arms were wrapped around one of his, her cheek pressed to his shoulder.

Rían stepped forward, freeing himself from the woman's embrace and holding his palms out to me. "Please don't. Please."

Don't what? Panic? Curse? Cry? Scream at the top of my lungs? I retreated a step, then another, needing space and...and air. I needed air. There was never any air in this bloody castle.

I heard Rían mumble to Leesha that he would be back. His footsteps rang out as they closed the distance between us until his fingers circled my wrist and I was forced into a room that smelled of dust and mildew.

"Leesha? *Leesha?*" I gasped, the name burning my tongue. "As in, the woman you love?"

Rían's eyes shuttered. Another barrier between us. "Hear me out—"

How could I hear him out when none of this made any bloody sense? "You said your mother killed her."

He raked his fingers through his hair, his eyes hollow, haunted. "She did. At least, I thought she did." His quiet curse lifted toward the dark ceiling. "I should've known better. That she'd been playing me for a feckin' fool." He shook his head, his shoulders deflating. "She took Leesha's heart just as she took mine."

The Queen had used a spell to keep control over Rían for centuries. Had she been doing the same to Leesha?

He pressed the heels of his palms to his eyes, his proud shoulders rounding as if he could curl in on himself and become invisible. "All this time," he muttered. "She must've been in that castle all this time."

"But she's human." Shouldn't her body be dead by now?

His hands dropped, open and empty at his sides. "I know. I

can't explain it. But she's here. And she's a-a-*choo*." Cursing, Rían shifted a handkerchief and rubbed his nose. "She's alive. And she thinks it's my—*achoo*—birthday."

"It *is* your birthday."

Dark hair fell across his brow when he shook his head. "No, I mean she thinks it's my birthday two centuries ago. As far as I can tell, she believes no time has passed. She doesn't even—*achoo*. *Dammit*. She doesn't remember the Queen taking her heart."

Then she still wanted to be with him. Did that mean...

Did *he* want to be with *her*?

I shook my head against the foolish notion. He couldn't want her. He and I were soulmates, a perfect match in every way. Right? That was what he had been saying since the day we met. Could he have been wrong?

One long look at his conflicted expression was all the confirmation I needed. He did love her. *Oh god...* Rían still loved her. Where did that leave me besides alone?

I tried to step around him, but he moved as well, blocking the exit.

"Don't run from me. Please, don't run."

"What else do you expect?" I couldn't sit here and stay silent while he doted over his *fiancée*. When had he proposed to her, anyway? He'd failed to mention that juicy little morsel.

"I don't know, Aveen. But I need you to stay. Stay and tell me what to do."

"It's *Rose*, remember?"

Devastation swam in his bloodshot eyes. "I'm sorry for that, but I'm worried she may expose your presence to the Queen."

"So, what? Am I to disguise myself inside the castle as well?" He couldn't expect such a thing. If he wanted to be with Leesha, he could do so elsewhere. Build *her* a bloody cottage by the seaside.

"That would probably be best," he said with a resolute nod. "When you're not in your rooms, anyway."

My hands fisted at my sides. He wanted me to hide myself? Fine. I would hide my face, my form, and my heart. Heaven knew he'd trampled on it enough. "You want me to tell you what to do, Rían? Tell Leesha the truth." *Tell her the truth and choose me.*

He paused for far too long before responding. "I will. I just need a little time. She still thinks her parents are in the cottage. She doesn't know about her sister...that I...that I was the one who killed her."

His arms came around me, pulling me close. I found no comfort in his familiar cinnamon scent or the feel of him holding tight.

"I'm so sorry," he whispered once more before letting go.

I watched him walk away from me, ease open the door, and slip into the hallway to knock on his own door. Leesha answered, tugging him down for a kiss. He turned his face away at the last moment, his eyes locking with mine while another woman's lips grazed his cheek.

"Is Rose one of Tadhg's women?" Leesha asked.

The door fell closed, muffling Rían's response.

I drifted toward the staircase, finding Keelynn waiting on the landing. Tears streamed down her cheeks when she collected me in a fierce hug. "I'm so sorry, sister. Tell me how to help you."

My mouth remained closed. I'd finally gotten Rían back only to lose him all over again.

Nothing could make this better.

Nothing at all.

20

RÍAN

I'D HEARD PEOPLE SAY THAT YOU SHOULDN'T GO SEARCHING FOR answers at the bottom of a bottle. Yet here I sat, intent on proving them wrong. My fingers gripped the neck a little tighter so I could bring the wine to my lips. This shite really tasted awful.

Tadhg lounged across the settee, an eager spectator to my misery.

I swiped my lips with my sleeve like a barbarian. How far I'd fallen. "She's up to something."

Tadhg's glass stilled halfway to his mouth. "Who? *Rose?*" With that snarky tone, I expected a smirk, but his mouth remained flat.

Aveen must've told Keelynn what had happened earlier tonight. Since that shrew couldn't keep her trap shut, she'd obviously informed my brother of how dismally I'd handled the situation with Leesha. I'd had to feign a headache to get out of spending the night with her.

What would my excuse be tomorrow?

Now that my head had cleared and I could think straight—

I took another sip of faerie wine.

Somewhat straight.

I downed another fiery gulp. The only bit of warmth in my body at the moment. "Not Rose. The Queen." I recognized this situation for what it was: another one of the evil witch's plots. Just like the blight. Bringing Leesha back from the dead meant she would have eyes and ears in this castle. "Leesha's not a birthday gift. She's a feckin' spy."

Tadhg started nodding emphatically, splashing drink onto his breeches. "A spy. You're right. That's the only explanation that makes any sense."

Of course I was right.

Wasn't I? "But how do we know for certain?"

Tadhg tilted his glass toward me. "You could always ask her," he said, like it was some sort of great epiphany.

"Ask who? The Queen?" As if she'd do anything but laugh in my face. Besides, did I really want to risk losing my heart *again* to my mother?

"Not the Queen, you eejit. *Leesha.*"

I *could* ask Leesha. But there was only one problem. "I won't be able to smell a lie if she doesn't know she's a spy."

"You won't be able to smell anything but your own vomit if you don't stop drinking."

My stomach roiled. He had a point there. I set the bottle on the low table and fell back into my chair. It wouldn't hurt to ask Leesha a few questions, would it? It wasn't like I could avoid her forever. The sooner I sorted this out, the sooner I could put the whole situation behind me and move forward.

Now to figure out how to pry without Leesha getting suspicious. I needed a disguise. Thankfully, I was a master of disguises.

I glamoured myself as my favorite character to date: Lady Marissa. The unruly minx could say whatever she wanted, consequences be damned. When I "accidentally" ran into Leesha, she wouldn't suspect a thing. This would be perfect.

Tadgh glanced up from his own glass, his eyes widening.

"What do you think?" I shook out my black ringlet curls.

"I think that neckline makes look like a trollop," he murmured into his glass.

Trollop my arse. Tadhg was a feckin' trollop. "It does not. This is a classy neckline paired with a timeless silhouette.

He shrugged. "If you say so."

"You shouldn't be looking at my neckline anyway. You have a fiancée. Pervert."

"I doubt my fiancée will have an issue with me commenting on my brother's glamoured breasts."

"What's wrong with my breasts?" They looked brilliant from this angle.

"They're a bit large, aren't they?"

"I'll have you know, I have gotten more than a few lewd comments on these," I scoffed, clutching my chest. If he didn't have anything nice to say, he should've kept his opinions to himself. My skirts swished as I swept out of the room. What did he know, anyway?

The moment I set foot in the hallway, I heard Leesha's laughter drifting from the kitchens. Shouldn't she be in bed?

Memories of all the times I'd found her chatting with our kitchen witch flooded back. She'd spent almost as much time with Eava as she had with me. When I descended the stairs, a sight I never thought I'd see again greeted me: Leesha propped on one of the high stools, a cinnamon bun dangling from her fingertips and smile on her face. For once, Eava wasn't cooking. She sat on the other side of the table, returning the human's smile.

When Eava saw me, she did a double take. Her eyes widened, and she choked on whatever she'd been chewing.

Leesha glanced over her shoulder, a warm smile concealing her surprise. "Oh, hello."

"Hello." I glided over to the high counter. "I apologize for calling over this late, but I was visiting my brother down the road and wanted to call in on Lady Keelynn before returning home. Is she in?"

Eava's wispy brows jumped to her hairline. "She is. Will I fetch her?"

"That would be brilliant, thank you." I slipped onto the stool next to Leesha and held out my dainty hand. "I'm Marissa. What's your name?"

Leesha's cool fingers slipped into mine. "Leesha."

No spark burned between us. Was that because of my glamour or because of the Queen's hold on my former lover? Or was it because I hadn't known what true fire was until I met Aveen?

Aveen...

My stomach twisted. I'd gone to the spare room to speak with her only to falter when I heard her crying through the door. How could I offer words of comfort and promises when I hadn't a clue how to navigate this situation?

I smiled at the woman I once loved. "I haven't seen you here before, Leesha. Do you live close by?"

"My family protects the portal in the border cottage on the edge of the Forest." She scooted the tray of cinnamon buns closer to me. "Have one. They're delicious."

"I really shouldn't. They go right to my waistline." One wouldn't hurt though. I pulled apart the sticky treat and popped a bite between my lips. Eava truly worked miracles in this kitchen. "What brings you to the castle?"

"I'm visiting my fiancé, Prince Rían."

Had truth ever tasted this bitter?

"I didn't realize he was engaged. Congratulations."

She beamed. "Thank you."

"You are a brave woman. I have heard such wretched stories about his mother."

Leesha's expression softened as she bit off a tiny corner of bun with straight, white teeth. "I'll admit that I was terrified of her at first. I foolishly tried to cross the Forest without permission. Today was Rían's birthday, you see, and I desperately wanted to give him my present."

My heart stuttered. She got me a present?

Don't let her sway you. She's a spy.

Only...she didn't *look* like a spy.

I studied her clear, green eyes, the only hint of black in her wide pupil. If the Queen was controlling her, surely her dark influence would show somewhere. I licked my dry lips, the dessert in my hand forgotten. "What did you get him?"

With a quick glance around the kitchen, Leesha stuck her hand in the pocket of her skirts and withdrew a small package wrapped in a simple handkerchief. I set down the bun and wiped my sweaty hands on my skirts before taking the gift.

A pair of gold bar-link cufflinks.

"They belonged to my great-grandfather," she said.

I smoothed my thumb over the mother of pearl inlay. Leesha had never had a coin to her name and yet she'd wanted to give me a priceless family heirloom. "They're—" I cleared the lump from my throat. "They're beautiful."

"Maybe you should change out of that dress and put them on."

My head snapped up, meeting Leesha's smiling eyes. "You think I wouldn't recognize you beneath that glamour, Rían? I'd know those eyes anywhere."

Shit.

I dropped the glamour. Although the corset and dress were replaced with my usual shirt and breeches, the tightness around my chest remained, squeezing the breath out of me as Leesha leaned closer.

"Here. Let me." She turned over my free hand and plucked one cufflink from the handkerchief to slip through the buttonholes and fasten in place. "They look beautiful," she said proudly, tracing the pearlescent ovals. Her finger trailed down to Aveen's ribbon around my wrist.

I pulled out of her grasp, my heart in my throat, choking me.

She wasn't a spy.

Meaning the Queen had given her back to me for some other reason.

There was only one person who could tell me why.

I made some pathetic excuse about needing to run out for a

moment and bolted out the back door. Shit. Shit. *Shit.* Leesha was really sitting in the castle kitchens. My soulmate was crying upstairs.

And I didn't know what to do.

I ran for the gates, tripping over my own feet and out into the fresh air beyond the wards. Without a thought for my own safety, I evanesced to the Queen's castle in the Forest. When I shouted from the gates, she appeared almost immediately, her waist-length mahogany hair unbound and crown forgotten. Instead of one of her usual dresses, she wore a black feathered robe.

Without a word, she cut her own hand and let the blood drip into the lock. I drifted beyond the wards, my mind spinning with drink and memories.

"Would you like tea?" she asked, sweeping in front of me.

She was not offering me tea after upending my entire world. "No, I don't want tea. I want answers."

Her slender shoulders lifted and fell with a shrug. The end of her robe dragged up the stairs, along the marble floor to the parlor. No fire burned in the hearth. A single candle flickered on the table next to her chair.

She sank onto the chair and watched me pace in the darkness while trying to sort through my muddled thoughts.

"What game are you playing?" I demanded.

Her lips pursed. "I wasn't playing a game. I was reading. But if you'd like to play quadrille the way we used to, I suppose I could find the cards somewhere."

Had she completely lost her mind? "I don't want to play quadrille. I want to know why you brought Leesha to the castle."

She exhaled an exasperated sigh. "As I told you earlier, she is a birthday gift."

A gift, my arse. "She's a spy."

The corner of her lips lifted, like this was some sort of hilarious joke to her. "Why on earth would I want to spy on you?"

A non-answer. Big feckin' surprise. "You tell me. You're the one who sent a spy."

"She is your love, is she not?"

"Over two centuries ago!"

"You think me a monster..."

I didn't think. I knew. Had the scars on my body and my soul to prove it.

"...but this life is too long to be lived alone. You found love at too young an age and had many life lessons to learn before you were worthy of it."

Worthy of love? She couldn't be serious. Love, *true* love, didn't need to be earned. We didn't need to meet some sort of criteria to be worthy of it. Still, I tasted no lies in the air between us. Meaning she actually believed the shite she was spouting. "That wasn't your choice to make." It was mine, and she'd stolen it from me just like she'd stolen everything else.

"You are my son and my heir. I couldn't have you shirking your duty to your people to run off with some human."

"And now?"

If I didn't know better, I would've thought the spark in her eyes looked a lot like pride. "You are becoming the leader I always knew you'd be," she said, adjusting the tie at her waist. "And with your brother tying himself to that wretched girl, it is only a matter of time before the throne is yours."

She thought I wanted the feckin' throne? Talk about delusional. I wouldn't want to sit in Tadhg's place for anything. "You expect me to believe you truly want me to be happy? That you will permit me to tie myself to a human as well?"

She shrugged. "I like her."

I nearly choked on her truth. "You don't like anyone." Hell, she didn't even like me, and I was her own flesh and blood.

"Which makes it all the more surprising." She nodded at my hands. "I see she gave you your birthday gift as well."

I had the childish urge to stuff my hands inside my pockets. I didn't want her to taint any more of my memories.

I like her.

And yet she'd ripped out the woman's heart. "She doesn't remember you killing her."

Her arched brows lifted. "Did you want her to remember such a traumatic experience?"

I didn't want to hurt Leesha. But how was I to navigate this situation without telling her the truth? "How'd you do it? Keep her from deteriorating all these years."

"Come now, boy. You know I cannot divulge *all* my secrets."

My mother had finally given me the birthday gift I'd always wanted…and still managed to ruin my life.

21

TADHG

KEELYNN SANK ONTO THE THRONE BESIDE ME, HER HANDS wringing in her lap as she shifted her weight on the cushion I'd added only this morning. No sense in her being more uncomfortable than she already was.

"Are you sure this is all right?" she whispered, casting a worried glance my way.

That was one of the few perks of being in charge. If I said it was all right, then it was. And I'd already told her as much this morning over breakfast and again on our way into the great hall. But if she needed to hear it again, I'd repeat myself until my voice gave out.

"Of course it's all right."

She smoothed a hand along the chair's curved arm. "But this is Rían's throne."

"Rían isn't coming." I rarely felt sorry for my brother, but in this instance, I truly did. The Queen had once again found a way to destroy him. Not only him but Aveen as well. She certainly didn't deserve this.

Keelynn's shoulders fell even more. "I am no one—"

How could she believe such a thing after all she'd done for me? I squeezed her cool fingers until she stopped spouting nonsense. "You are to be my wife again soon enough. It's time my people learn to accept you as their princess."

Thus far, I hadn't been impressed with any of them. When Ruairí had updated me on what had happened with the mince pies, I nearly evanesced right down to those cottages and gave them a piece of my mind. I was their leader; I didn't need their permission to marry the woman I loved. But it wasn't my job to force people into loving Keelynn as much as I did.

If they chose not to, it was their loss.

They didn't have to like her, but they sure as hell owed her their respect.

Without Keelynn, I would've been cursed for all of eternity. Now I was free, the burdens I'd carried for so long nothing more than bad memories. Once again, power coursed through my veins.

All because of the strong, faithful woman sitting next to me.

After the wedding, Keelynn had plans to hire more Danú here at the castle, and I couldn't be happier. Maybe she'd find a few friends along the way as well.

I wasn't sure how this situation between Rían, Leesha, and Aveen was going to work out, and I couldn't see Aveen wanting to come around if Rían ended up choosing his long-lost love. Keelynn would be so lonely without her though.

What a feckin' disaster.

But it was a disaster for another day.

Keelynn sat back, her spine and shoulders straight as she gave me a nod and said she was ready. I gestured for Oscar to open the doors to the great hall, expecting people to pour in the way they always did. Instead, only two men stepped inside, both wearing matching scowls. The first took one look at my fiancée, turned, and walked out.

I gripped the arms of my throne to keep myself from launching after him and demanding he show her the respect she deserved. Not only as my soon-to-be wife but simply as a person.

The second man didn't leave, but if he didn't stop glaring at

Keelynn, he was going to lose his feckin' eyes. "So the rumors are true, then?" the man said, his voice gruff. "Yer to marry a human."

He spat the final word as if humanity were some sort of disease.

My people should've known better than to judge someone simply because of what they were. Wasn't that what the humans had done to us for so many years? And look at the shit storm we were in now.

A smile tugged at my lips even as the dark magic living in my veins itched to steal the life from his defiant eyes. "That's an odd way to offer congratulations."

The man seemed to startle. "Congratulations, my prince," he bit out, not an ounce of sincerity in his words.

Keelynn blinked rapidly. If that man made my fiancée cry, I was going to make an example out of him. It had been far too long since we'd had prisoners chained in the dungeon. Rían certainly wouldn't have any qualms over torturing a few people after what had happened last night.

"Was there anything else you needed, or did you just wish to meet my beautiful fiancée?"

He looked as if he wanted to give some snide response but seemed to hold himself back. A smart choice. "The ground near my cottage has gone black, rotting my cabbage and tomatoes. Not a plant has been spared by the blight. Thought ye might like to know, seein' as ye've been too busy to come 'round."

Thinly veiled insults were far easier to tolerate when they were directed at me. "You're not the only one suffering. See Eava around the back for a portion of rations. I will be around to shift your cottage this afternoon."

His hands flexed at his sides. "That land's been in my family fer generations. I'll not be leaving."

"Until we find a way to stop the blight, relocating those affected is our only option."

With a loud harrumph, he stomped past Oscar and into the

hallway. The slamming door echoed around the exposed beams. If people were going to be like this, I wasn't above canceling my Friday sessions. With the blight consuming more land every day, I had more important things to do than deal with these ungrateful wretches.

"I'm sorry," Keelynn murmured. Although her shoulders remained stiff, her eyes reminded me of rain clouds about to spill over.

Seeing her so forlorn left my chest breaking open. I reached for her hand once more to brush my thumb over her pale knuckles. "First, you've nothing to be sorry about. Second, once they get to know you and, more importantly, learn to trust you, they will love you as much as I do. If you recall, I didn't like you very much at first either."

A reluctant smile played at the corners of her lips. "That's only because I wanted to murder you."

The memory of our first encounter still made my stomach flutter. She'd truly despised me and yet she'd saved me in every way a man could be saved.

Rían strode in a moment later. When he saw Keelynn on his throne, his eyes widened. She made to rise, but I stopped her with a hand on her knee.

"Sorry I'm late," he said, shifting a chair from the dining room set to the other side of the dais.

Last I heard, he wasn't coming at all. "What are you doing here?"

"It's Friday, isn't it?" He ran a hand down his wrinkled waistcoat. Normally I would've made fun of him for the sorry state of his clothes, but considering all that had happened, he could use the break.

"Yes, but I didn't expect you to come today."

"I could do with the distraction." The way his hand shook as he raked his fingers through his hair undermined his confident tone. "Oscar, you may send in the next person."

With a nod, the old grogoch disappeared. Cormac, the pooka

with the braids, strolled in, two more broad-shouldered men trailing behind.

"We heard about what happened at The Arches," Cormac said when he reached the foot of the dais.

Icy dread twisted in my gut. It was only a matter of time before word got around. "What happened in Gaul was a terrible tragedy."

Their expressions darkened with their frowns. "Our brother lost everything," the one to the right said.

"And I have offered Lorcan and his wife funds to help rebuild." Lorcan had thanked me but had ultimately decided to take some time to consider the best options for his family. With Deirdre carrying his little one, I couldn't blame him. If only there were some way to get her across the Forest so the two of them could raise their child in peace. Then again, with this feckin' blight, I wasn't sure how long this peace would last.

"That's not good enough," Cormac growled. "You need to find the bastards responsible—"

"He did find them," Rían drawled from his chair, picking at his nails as if this conversation bored him to tears. "They have been dealt with."

The revelation seemed to take some of the wind out of the man's sails. But then his narrowed yellow eyes landed on Keelynn. His fangs flashed, but there was nothing friendly about his smile. "What of the blight?"

These questions were getting monotonous. Maybe I should make a sign and hang it on the gates. "Dealing with the blight is our top priority."

His sneer grew. "That's not what I hear."

Rían leaned forward and braced his elbows on his knees as he smiled at our visitors. Who knew a smile could be so feckin' unnerving?

"Is there anything else I can help you with?" I asked, more than ready to move them on.

"No, my *prince*. You've proven yourself as useless as ever." He left without so much as a bow or tip of his head.

"He's going to be trouble," Rían said under his breath. "Should I kill him?"

"If you killed everyone who is displeased with my rule, there'd be no one left—including you." I asked Oscar to send in the next visitor.

He returned a moment later with his flat cap bent between his hands. "There are no others, sire."

That couldn't be right. With the way the blight was spreading, surely there should be more. "Are you certain?"

He nodded.

Rían dropped his head into his hands. "I never thought I'd say this, but I kind of miss the old days."

So did I. Before this blight, all I had to do was collect taxes and settle the odd dispute between neighbors. Part of me wished someone would come in complaining about stolen chickens.

"Hello?" a soft voice called from the hallway. Anwen stepped through the door with a small bundle clutched to her chest. Unless she was here to apologize for being rude to Keelynn over the pies, she may as well turn right around.

The witch sauntered across the hall and didn't spare Keelynn so much as a glance as she sank into a curtsey at the foot of the dais.

"Anwen. What can we help you with?"

She straightened, shooting me a narrowed-eyed glare so full of hatred, I felt frost settling in my bones. "I have something that belongs to ye."

I leaned forward, trying to catch a glimpse of what she'd wrapped so carefully.

And then it made a noise.

Was that a...*baby*?

Anwen held the wriggling child toward me. My heart stalled. What game was she playing?

Rían's jaw hit the ground, but it wasn't his reaction I cared about. Keelynn had gone so still, like she wasn't even breathing, her knuckles white as bone and face equally as pale as she stared down at the small bundle.

"It's not...it can't be..." I couldn't bring myself to say the word *mine* because the moment I looked at the wriggling child, the truth was as clear as the pair of emerald-green eyes blinking up at me. The mop of chocolate-brown curls peeking from beneath the blanket didn't help either.

Shit...

Shit.

Slowly, Keelynn's head turned, her wide eyes glistening with tears.

I'd tried telling her what had happened while she'd been gone, but she'd insisted it didn't matter. I'd been in a bad place. I'd been drunk. I'd been *cursed.*

The baby let out a pitiful cry. Keelynn's hand flew to her quivering lips. I could feel her slipping through my trembling fingers, and there wasn't a feckin' thing I could do to keep her from drifting away.

22

KEELYNN

ANWEN THRUST THE CHILD AT TADHG'S CHEST, FORCING HIM TO take hold of the baby.

Not *the* baby.

His baby.

Tadhg had a child.

With someone else.

I'd woken up so bloody nervous about meeting with his people, anticipating disaster. But nothing could've prepared me for this sort of betrayal. My heartbeat, which had stopped the moment I realized the truth, thundered through my ears like I'd been dropped into a churning sea with no land in sight.

The baby couldn't be more than a few months old, meaning Tadhg had slept with this woman while I was dead.

He was cursed, a tiny voice whispered. *He couldn't say no.*

Had this woman taken advantage of him? Had he wanted to turn her down? Had he even tried? Bile roiled in my stomach.

I hated her.

Part of me hated Tadhg as well.

Hell, right now I even hated that tiny, innocent baby, and the child had done nothing wrong.

"I didn't...I can barely even remember..." Tadhg's mouth

opened and closed, but nothing he could say would make this any better or take away the vicious sting of reality. "Shit...I... *Shit*."

Logically, I knew this was no different than every other time he'd gone off with someone else. Except it was because the consequences of those other dalliances weren't starting to wail and thrash in his arms.

Anwen's chin lifted, her expression as unyielding as the stone walls around us. "I cannot bear the brunt of another babe. Brogan is yers. Ye can deal with him now." She didn't spare me so much as a look as she turned on her heel and sauntered away from her own bloody child.

I wanted to shout for her to come back, to take the screaming boy and hide him away forever so that I didn't have to face this catastrophe. So that I could go back to being blissfully happy like we had been last night.

"You have a child," I whispered, my words nearly lost to the boy's tearful cries.

Tadgh shook his head, his hair falling across his forehead. "No... no, I—"

"Clearly you do." Bloody hell. *Look at them*. They could've been twins.

Rían's nose wrinkled as he stared down at the wrinkly and impossibly small child in Tadgh's arms. "To be honest, I'm shocked you don't have a whole horde of whelps scratching at the door."

Tadgh shot him a look so full of hate, I knew he would've killed him if his hands weren't already occupied.

"Sire?" Oscar's voice cut through everything.

All of us looked up at the same time, to where the grogoch still stood at the door. He shifted on his feet, his flat cap mashed between his hands. "More folks are startin' to arrive."

Tadgh turned this way and that, the baby's swaddled body swinging to and fro as he searched for something. What? I hadn't a clue. He mustn't have either because he stopped and stared down at Oscar with his mouth pulled tight. "Tell them all to go away."

Oscar's eyes widened. "But, sire, it's Friday. And the blight—"

"I can't...I just...I can't deal with anything else right now. Send them home." Tadhg shot to his feet; the baby screeched even louder.

"I'll handle them," Rían said, gesturing toward Tadhg's son. "You both need to deal with *that*."

Tadhg held the baby out even farther, as if it were a puppy about to piddle on him. "How do I get it to stop crying?"

Rían's brows rose. "You're asking me for parenting advice?"

Tadhg looked as if he were about to cry. That made two of us. Three if you counted *his* baby.

Rían let out a low curse. "Find Leesha. She's always been good with children."

Nodding, Tadhg turned to me, his broken expression no doubt mirroring my own. "Will you at least allow me to explain? That is all I ask. Please."

I didn't want to be near him right now. I wanted my sister and silence and a bloody time machine. Still, I couldn't very well stay here with Rían and a bunch of strangers who already despised me. So I stood and followed my fiancé through the door behind the dais that led to the study.

As if we'd called for her, Leesha bolted into the room, a smile lighting her face. "Is that a baby I hear?" She skidded to a stop when she reached Tadhg, her smile growing as she peered down at the child. "Oh, look at how beautiful you are," she cooed. The child immediately quieted, blinking up at her through red-rimmed eyes. "Aren't you a handsome boy? Yes, you are." She rubbed his cheek with her finger, and the child turned his face toward her. "Yes, you are."

"Would you be able to watch him for a moment?" Tadhg asked, practically launching the boy at Leesha.

She cradled the babe against her chest as if he were the most precious thing in the whole entire world. "I would love to," she said, more to the baby than his father.

Bloody hell. Tadhg was a father.

That made me a *stepmother*. All the stories I'd read cast step-mothers as evil, wicked women. With the anger growing in my chest, I understood why.

Leesha's pale blue skirts swirled when she twisted toward the hallway. "Are you hungry, little one? Why don't we go down to the kitchens and see if we can find you some milk?"

While I had been raised to marry a rich man and bear his children, I didn't know the first thing about being a mother. My own mother had died when I was young, and I only had a few memories of her. Thank goodness Leesha was here.

A pang of guilt replaced the traitorous thought. I shouldn't be grateful to the woman who had come between my sister and the man she loved. And yet here I stood, grateful all the same.

Tadhg took my hand, and before I knew what was happening, we were standing in his bedroom, deafening silence stretching between us like a great chasm.

The moment I got my bearings, I yanked free, putting as much distance between us as I could. When he touched me, I could think of nothing but his betrayal, and my head needed to remain clear for this conversation.

Sinking onto the edge of his bed, Tadhg dropped his head into his hands. "I'm so sorry."

I could practically taste his sorrow in the air, but sometimes apologies weren't enough. Sometimes apologies were just useless words that filled the silence when there was nothing else to say. I gripped my hands in front of me and drew in a steadying breath. "You said that you took precautions while I was gone."

He scrubbed his hands down his thighs, his gaze pinned to the wooden floor. "And I did…after what happened with Anwen." He dragged a hand through the riotous curls atop his head. "I remember being up in the tower with you and having a little too much to drink. My brother had sentenced Anwen to death for stealing something from the humans…" His eyes narrowed as if searching the knots in the wooden floor for answers. "I can't recall what it was. But Aveen came and asked for my help. I didn't want to go, but I told her I would. My brother killed me for interfering."

As if I needed another reason to dislike Rían.

"When I came back," Tadhg went on, "I walked straight to Anwen's, like I promised. But my brother had already pardoned her." He fell silent, his shoulders lifting as he inhaled a ragged breath. When he raised his eyes to mine, the emerald pools glimmered with unshed tears. "Anwen and I have a history together, and she assumed I'd come over for a different reason. I tried to tell her that I wasn't there for that, but she wasn't interested in talking."

"What do you mean you *tried* to tell her?"

Tadhg, the bloody prince of seduction, actually blushed. "The witch likes to…play games. And if I hadn't just died and been weak as a babe——" He cursed. "Sorry. Weak as a…well, just weak, I might've been able to break the spells she used to keep me silent."

I didn't need to know what sort of games the witch liked to play. The fact that she liked to play them with the man I loved was enough of a revelation. "She took advantage of you," I said, reminding us both of the reality of this situation. If Tadhg hadn't been cursed, he would've been able to turn her down.

"Not on purpose." His brow furrowed. "At least, I don't think so."

Hearing that didn't make me hate the woman any less. Maybe this wasn't her fault. Maybe it was. Either way, the consequences remained the same. Where did this leave me? Where did this leave us?

I sank onto the mattress next to him. "I don't know what to do." It wasn't his fault. I knew that. But I didn't know how to cope or move past this. Hell, I didn't even know how I felt.

No. That wasn't true. I felt numb. Empty.

Like that tiny life had stolen my joy, leaving me devoid of emotion.

Tadhg's shoulder grazed mine as he shifted on the end of the bed. "I don't know what to do either. And I don't know the first thing about raising a feckin' child. I can barely keep myself alive some days."

He had a point. Running the country and dealing with the blight took up most of Tadhg's free time already. Would he be able to make time for his son? Perhaps I could hire someone to mind the baby. That was what most rich families in Airren would do. Hire a wet nurse or a nanny or a governess. Did they do the same in Tearmann? Would I be able to find one who hadn't slept with my bloody fiancé?

Perhaps Millie, the maid I'd hired for after the wedding, had some experience. Would she be able to start sooner?

Tadhg's teeth scraped across his lips. The way his shoulders curled in on themselves made him look like a lost little boy.

All I wanted was to run and hide and cry. Instead, I slid my fingers through his chocolate curls and drew his head down to my shoulder. "We will find our way through it."

A broken sob wrenched from his throat as his hands climbed my thighs to my waist, hugging me closer. "I won't blame you if you leave me."

"I'm not leaving." I'd chosen Tadhg, and he'd chosen me, for better or for worse. Yet, as we clung to each other, I wondered if we were strong enough to get through this together or if it would be what finally tore us apart.

23

AVEEN

Sunlight leaked through the leaded glass windows in the family room, warming my back. Part of me missed all the rain in Airren. A bit of miserable weather would have provided an excuse for my mood that didn't make me sound like a pathetic woman pining over a man.

Rían was either attending a trial or dealing with the Danú calling to the castle every other day, shifting cottages and livestock from one end of Tearmann to the other to help them escape the blight.

I spent what time I could with Keelynn as she and Tadhg wrestled with the sleepless reality of raising a child. With each passing day, the shadows beneath her eyes grew more pronounced, and I no longer saw her smile. Most of the wedding plans had already been put in place, which was a blessing, really, since my sister hadn't spoken of the event since the arrival of her stepson.

To be honest, I wasn't sure there would *be* a wedding on Saturday.

And then there was Leesha.

Brogan may have belonged to Tadhg, but from the way Leesha clung to the child, you'd swear she'd given birth to Tearmann's heir. But I didn't want to think about her anymore. About the way she hung on Rían's arm every time he walked into a room.

My teeth ground together. How much more time did he need to tell her the truth?

With everyone so busy, Ruairi had been helping me with my glamour. And by helping, I meant he'd been trying to distract me so that I'd let my magical disguise drop.

I glared down at the cards fanned in my hands, trying to remember the rules of this game that Ruairi had explained at least three times.

"I'll raise you one button and three marbles," I said, sliding my "tokens" toward the pot in the center of the low table where we'd once played snapdragon and laughed like fools.

Laughter no longer graced these rooms.

Only silence and tears remained.

Ruairi watched me with a furrowed brow, his own cards clasped in one massive hand. "Yer nose."

My hand flew to my face. *Dammit.* My nose did feel a good deal colder than the rest of me. The glamour must've slipped. With a bit of focus, I managed to fix it fairly quickly.

Smiling with his fangs on full display, Ruairi nodded in approval. "Yer getting better at it."

"Thank you." I wore my glamour all day, every day, imagining the magical layer as impenetrable armor between me and the world. Sometimes it worked. Most of the time, the pain still seeped in. "I was thinking we could go to the garden after lunch. You dig, I plant?" With so many Danú losing their homes and gardens, the castle's stores had grown dangerously low. I'd decided to turn my flower beds into vegetable patches. Rían hadn't bothered saying I wasn't allowed outside. He was obviously too busy spending all his free time with his first love to care about my safety anymore.

"Sounds like a plan." Ruairi matched my bet before laying down his cards.

I did the same, spreading them across the table. "I think three twos are good, right?"

Surprise flickered across his features. From the way Ruairí cursed, I knew I'd won.

I dragged my new buttons, cufflinks, and marbles across the table to add to the collection I'd amassed over the last few days. "You really do have the worst luck."

Ruairí's smile tightened. "Ye have no idea."

"Would you like to play another hand before we head out?"

With a sigh, he straightened the cards into a pile next to the few buttons he still owned. "I'd rather not lose again, but if ye really want to, I will."

"No, that's all right." I was bored of cards anyway. Everything bored me nowadays. Even gardening had lost its appeal.

Ruairí's fang dragged along his lip as he returned the cards to the box. "Would ye like to practice evanescing?"

"Why not?" It wasn't as if I had anything better to do. I still couldn't figure out how to evanesce by myself, but Ruairí was kind enough to lend me his magic. Yesterday, we'd made it to the tallest tower three times in a row.

We stood and faced each other. He offered me his hands, dwarfing my own. I closed my eyes as our connection began to heat with the magic passing between us. I pictured the garden, where the sun beat mercilessly through the wards. The air sticky and sweet with the perfume of flowers, grass, and dirt. The silence around us thickened like a warm fog.

"What the hell is going on?"

Rían's deep voice cut through the magical haze. I dropped Ruairí's hands, my face igniting when I realized Rían wasn't alone. Leesha stood at his side, Tadhg's child on her hip, making them look like the perfect little family.

Tears pricked the backs of my eyes, but I refused to let them see me cry. My tears were reserved for the bath, where the evidence could easily be washed away.

Leesha nudged Rían with her shoulder before gesturing

toward Ruairi and me. "See! I told you there were sparks between them."

Rían still hadn't taken his now-glowing eyes off Ruairi.

The pooka had gone unnaturally still.

"Ruairi and I are only friends," I explained, not that it was any of her business. "He's been helping me with my magic."

Leesha shook her head, swaying a bit as the baby's eyes drifted closed and his curly head fell to her breast. "I see the way that man looks at you. There is something more there. I have a sixth sense about these things."

I peered up at Ruairi, finding his lips pressed flat and bearded jaw flexed. He was my friend and occasional guard, nothing more. Not that he wasn't attractive. He was, in a rugged, masculine way, but I preferred my men more murderous prince than charming pooka. Although life would've been far easier if I didn't.

Leesha's smile widened to a grin. Why couldn't she have been haggard and old instead of slender and smiley and perfect and pleasant? "The two of you should join us for lunch."

Why did she have to be so bloody nice? No wonder Rían had fallen in love with her.

I had to constantly remind myself that none of this was Leesha's fault. She hadn't asked to have her heart ripped out or to be held captive by the Queen for centuries or to be brought back. In another life, perhaps the two of us could've been friends.

But in this life, I hated her.

And the last thing I wanted was to join them for lunch. "Ruairi and I were about to go into the garden." When I took Ruairi's hand again, Rían's eyes filled with black. The air began to vibrate, but instead of letting me go, Ruairi squeezed tighter. Knowing he was there for me despite the threat to his person made this situation a little bit easier to survive.

Leesha waved as if what I wanted was of no consequence, oblivious to the murderous glare in Rían's black eyes. "Nonsense. I insist you join us. Tadhg and Keelynn will be there as well. Eava has everything all set up in the dining room. It would be terrible to waste all that effort."

For Eava and Keelynn, I'd go. I peered up at Ruairi, half hoping he'd protest. "Is that all right?"

He shrugged. "I'll do whatever ye decide."

Leesha looked pleased as punch.

Rían, however, did not.

And part of me, the dark, wretched part, was glad. Let him be jealous of Ruairi. Let him see what it felt like to have me walking around with another man. Let him be miserable and hateful toward someone who didn't deserve any of it.

Leesha swept out of the room, gliding down the hallway and past the tapestries as if the castle belonged to her. When she curtsied at the Queen's tapestry, I bit back a snide remark. Did she not realize what the Queen had done to her own son? To Leesha herself? Why hadn't Rían at least told her that part? Wasn't she curious as to why there was a scar across her heart? Or had Rían made up some excuse that didn't involve his mother?

In the dining hall, the table had been set as if this were some sort of celebration instead of a regular old lunch. An emerald-green runner stretched the length of the table. Candles flickered from golden candelabras. Golden plates that reminded me of the first night Rían and I were together sat at each place setting.

I glanced up to find Rían watching me through wide black eyes.

Eava waited inside the door, snatching Brogan the moment Leesha crossed the threshold, cooing and bouncing the chubby little boy with a smile brightening her lined face. She caught me looking, and her eyes warmed with sympathy before she brought the baby away.

Keelynn and Tadhg were already seated at the heads of the table, as far from each other as they could get, neither of them speaking. Rían stopped next to me. His eyes had returned to their beautiful shade of blue. "Rose…"

He couldn't even say my name.

"Rían, come on." Leesha linked her arm through his and tugged him to the other side of the table. He followed without a word of protest, pulling out her chair for her as if she were incapable of doing it for herself.

Ruairi glanced between me and the chair, but before he could do something equally as infuriating and feed Leesha's narrative, I dragged out my own chair and plopped straight down.

Leesha kept the conversation flowing like a good little hostess while I shoveled bites of venison into my mouth. Tadhg looked as if he was asleep with his eyes open, and Keelynn wouldn't stop staring at me, her expression laced with concern.

Rían barely touched his plate, while Ruairi ate every bite of his green salad.

I'd been to some terrible dinner parties, but this one took the cake.

Leesha whispered something in Rían's ear that left his cheeks flushed. She traced the line of his jaw with her fingertip, her gaze so adoring, the food I'd eaten turned to ash in my gut.

I watched in horror as she eased forward and pressed her lips to his.

And while Rían didn't kiss her back, he didn't stop her either.

Had she been kissing him this entire time? *Oh god.* Had they been sharing the same bed? How far had he let this lie go?

My tears returned with a vengeance, and this time, there was no hope of stopping them.

I balled up my serviette and threw it on the table beside my untouched goblet of wine. I needed to get out of here before he saw me break. I clambered to my feet, hurrying toward the door and straight for the courtyard. Not even the sun's rays beating down on my brow could thaw the frost overtaking my heart.

"Where are you going?" Keelynn called from the castle steps, her serviette clutched in her pale hands.

I stopped and turned, hating myself for doing this to my sister. "I can't be here anymore," I choked, gasping for breath as I scrubbed at the tears painting my cheeks. "I'm so sorry. I feel as if I am abandoning you in your time of need."

She waved me off with her serviette. "Don't worry about me. I will be fine."

Her lie didn't sound very convincing. Yet I didn't have it in me to stay.

The only way to escape was the way I'd come in. I called magic to my palm, shifting one of the daggers from my cottage back in Hollowshade.

"What do ye need?" Ruairi called, jogging toward me. When he saw the blade in my hand, he froze.

I needed Rían to hold me close. To let me go. To do *something* besides asking me to stand by and do nothing.

Damn stubborn tears. I swiped my hands over my damp cheeks once more. "I need you to bring my body back to the cottage." The tip of the blade scraped below my sternum. I inhaled a deep breath and—

Rían appeared right in front of me, his shuttered eyes swirling with black. The dagger vanished right out of my hand.

"Give it back," I cried, hating that I sounded like a petulant child.

He shook his head, his voice catching. "You can't go."

Ruairi took my hand, drawing me back a step so he could wedge himself between Rían and me. Rían glowered at our connection. When he spoke, his words shook with rage. "Leave us, dog, or I will make you."

Ruairi didn't budge.

As much as I appreciated his willingness to put himself in danger on my behalf, I could fight my own battles. I pressed a hand to the pooka's back. When Ruairi glanced over his shoulder, I nodded. Only then did he move aside.

Rían reached for me, but I stumbled back. My heart broke a little more when he began to plead. "Please don't do this. Please don't leave me."

Was he serious right now? Don't leave *him*? After he'd left me to fend for myself while he swanned around with another bloody woman? "You left me first."

"I didn't go anywhere." He dragged on the front of his shirt, twisting the fabric in his white-knuckled grip. "I'm right feckin' here!"

If only that were true. He may have been within arm's reach, but he was farther away than he'd ever been. "Take my hand and bring me back to my cottage." At least then I could leave without having to die.

His expression hardened. "No."

"Why not? It's what you wanted, isn't it? For me to leave and never return." Stubborn bloody fae prince. Couldn't he see what he was doing to me? Didn't he care at all that I was becoming a shell of a person? Surely he, of all people, would understand wanting to be free of such torment. "I cannot be here with you. It's killing me."

Cursing, he raked a trembling hand through his mahogany hair. "I know. I know it is. And I'm sorry." His hands fell to his sides. "I'm just trying to figure all of this out. It's my fault she died. All of this is my fault."

It wasn't his fault. It was the Queen's.

And we were left drowning in the consequences.

"Do you still love her?" If he could say here and now that he no longer cared for Leesha, that all of this was purely out of obligation, then perhaps I could find the strength to stay.

Rían's face crumpled, but he said not a word.

His silence was all the confirmation I needed that the Queen had finally won.

Somehow, I managed to swallow past the lump in my throat. "Ruairi?" The pooka stepped away from the wall where he'd been leaning. "Bring me to Hollowshade."

Rían lunged, but he was too late.

I shifted the dagger right from his sheath and plunged it into my chest.

24

AVEEN

Returning from the Underworld gave me a different sort of pain to focus on than the unyielding agony seeping from the cracks in my broken heart. Eventually, the physical torment would subside, but I'd still feel as dead as the land devoured by blight back in Tearmann.

My tears soaked into the pillowcase as I listened to the wind and rain batter my tiny cottage. How could Rían have done this to me? After all I'd given up, all I'd sacrificed, he refused to tell me the one thing I needed to hear. At this stage, I wouldn't have even cared if it had been a lie. All I wanted was some sort of reassurance that his feelings for the woman he'd once loved were nothing compared to his feelings for me. Instead, he'd given me nothing.

Not a blessed thing.

The door creaked. When I managed to pry open my lashes, I found myself staring into a pair of rich brown eyes. I blinked. And blinked again. Ruairi's eyes weren't brown, they were gold. No matter how many times I blinked, I kept seeing a pirate captain perched on the edge of my bed instead of a friendly pooka.

"Aveen," Caden breathed, twisting the fabric of his billowy white shirt over his heart. "Gods, I thought you were gone forever."

The skin on my lips split with the slightest movement. "What are you doing here? How did you find me? Where's—" I stopped myself from saying Ruairi's name. Despite what we'd shared, I didn't know Caden Merriweather at all. The last thing I wanted was to put Ruairi in jeopardy. "Where is the man who brought me here?"

Caden collected a glass of water from the bedside table, gently eased me into a sitting position, and pressed the cold glass to my lips. I would've refused the pirate's help if I wasn't so thirsty. A sigh escaped as the first drops of icy water spilled through my lips onto my stiff tongue.

"Man?" he growled. "You mean the pooka carrying your lifeless body?"

I really shouldn't have been surprised Caden had seen Ruairi for what he was. My friend was too large for his own bloody good.

Caden jerked away the glass and slammed it on the bedside table, spilling water all over the wood. "First that bastard prince and now a damned pooka. Honestly, Aveen. Have you no sense of self-preservation?"

Apparently not, considering I had fallen for both a lying fae pirate and a wicked fae prince. "Where is he?"

Caden gave me a hard smile. "Detained."

What did that even mean? How powerful was Caden that he could best Ruairi? Technically, he'd beaten Rían as well, but stabbing the prince in the back could hardly be considered a victory. Caden settled me back onto the pillow. I wanted to shove him off my bed and demand answers. But all I could do was lie there like a slug until the feeling in my extremities returned. "If you hurt him, I swear, I'll... I'll..."

Curse Rían for not teaching me something useful to do with my magic, like how to incinerate people who annoyed me. Turning this bloody pirate to ash would've given me such satisfaction.

Caden plucked one of my curls from the pillowcase to wrap

around his fingers, clearly unbothered by my threating glare. "Are you going to finish that thought, my angel?"

I wasn't *his* angel. I wasn't his anything. This man left me behind. Made promises he couldn't keep. I wanted nothing to do with him. Not one blessed thing.

Magic surged through my veins, waiting at my fingertips for direction. If I'd known how to use it, he would have been in serious trouble. "I'll feed you to Prince Rían for tea."

That wiped the cocky look off his handsome face.

My eyes narrowed as my veins hummed with pent-up magic, begging for some sort of release. "Now, I'll ask you again, and this time, I expect a straight answer. What have you done to my friend?"

Caden drummed his fingers beside my knee. "There's no reason to fret. Your *friend* is alive...for now."

The fire inside me flared, giving me enough strength to press my hands into the mattress and slide myself against the headboard so I could look him dead in the eye. "You hurt him?"

"He'll survive."

"Caden!"

"I thought he killed you, Aveen! What was I supposed to do? Make him a cup of tea?" He dragged a hand down his neck, his face contorted with false concern. "Did you honestly expect me to believe him when he claimed you would return from the dead?"

I didn't *expect* anything because he wasn't supposed to be here! How had he found me, anyway? Had Meranda given away my location? Had he tortured her for it? If something happened to her as well...

I closed my eyes and pinched the bridge of my nose, praying for patience and a respite from murderous men. All I wanted was some peace and quiet. Was that too much to ask?

Caden bent down to peer beneath my bed. He dragged out the small trunk Rían had purchased a while back and then threw open the armoire. "Who is he to you? Another lover, perhaps?" A clean gray dress landed beside me, followed by a shift from my chest of drawers and a pair of thick wool stockings.

"That is none of your concern." I balled up the dress and tossed it back at him. I could pick out my own bloody clothes.

He dropped the dress into the trunk, dragged a second from the hanger, and threw that at me instead. "Of course it's my bloody concern! I love you, and—"

"Love?" I caught the fabric and launched it at his insufferable head. "Is that what this looks like to you?" How delusional was this man? Yes, I'd thought I loved him years ago. Before promises were broken. Before I experienced the joy and utter devastation of true love.

He threw that dress into the trunk and grabbed a third to shove into my arms. "Put this on."

"Don't tell me what to do." Where did these men get off, ordering me around? Did I have the word "pushover" tattooed on my bloody forehead?

His eyes began to glow, and I swore I heard his jaw creaking from beneath his stubble. How had I ever mistaken this man for a human? "Seeing you covered in your own blood makes me want to rip that pooka's head off. Now put on the blasted dress so that I don't murder your friend. And when you're finished, meet me in the living room. You and I have much to discuss." He stalked out of the room and slammed the door behind him, making the picture on the wall fall right into the open trunk.

As far as I was concerned, this discussion was over. But since I wasn't keen on Ruairi losing his head, I changed as quickly as I could with weak and wobbly limbs. Although the fresh scar at the base of my sternum had already turned silver, the skin around the wound still ached.

Caden waited on the sofa, one long arm draped over the back cushions and one booted foot thrown over his knee. "Sit." He patted the cushion beside him.

My entire body turned stiff as a plank. "I am not a dog."

His head fell back with his groan. "I am well aware of the toll it takes on one's body to return from the Underworld. Your legs must be aching. Please sit down so you don't fall over and crack your skull off the hearth and end up right back where you started."

I crossed to the sofa to sit as far from him as possible—not because he told me to but because I didn't want to leave Ruairi in whatever state he was currently in for longer than necessary.

Caden's dark eyes swept from the square neckline on the brown muslin I'd picked out myself to my bare toes peeking from beneath the long skirts. "It seems we have both been keeping secrets."

When we'd met, I'd had no secrets. Caden, on the other hand, had enough to fill the ocean.

"How are you alive?" he asked.

I would give him this answer only because I wanted him to understand that Ruairi posed no threat to me. "I am alive because I was resurrected with a true immortal's life force."

The color leached from his sun-kissed face. "You were truly dead?" When he reached for my hand resting on my lap, I flinched. Hurt flickered across his eyes before he dropped his hand and pressed back into the cushion. "Heavens above," he murmured. "When I left, I truly believed you would be safer on this island than with me. I can see now that I was wrong, and I'm sorry. I should've brought you aboard my ship when you asked."

I had only asked out of foolish desperation. At the time, all I could think about was being with Caden. In the end, his refusal had been a blessing. I would've never forgiven myself for leaving Keelynn behind, especially since it meant she would've ended up marrying Robert Trench to pay our father's bad debts.

Caden stuffed his hands into the pockets of his dark trousers. "How did you get mixed up with the bastard prince?"

"It doesn't matter." Rían still loved Leesha. Part of him loved me as well, I knew that. But I deserved someone who could give me more than half a heart.

"How can you say that after all we shared?" Caden shook his

head, his tone rife with disbelief. "Despite what you may think, I do love you."

"You lied to me, about everything. Why should I believe you about this?"

Cursing, he dragged a hand down the back of his neck. "I didn't lie about everything. I was born in Iodale, that part is true. Not in the capital, as I previously claimed, but in the fae lands. My stepfather was a merchant sailor. I inherited my ship from him. He and my mother used to sail together, but when she passed, he couldn't bear the thought of being on the water without her."

What a whimsical, romantic tale. One I may have actually believed if I didn't know better. "And your real father?"

"He was a merrow. My mother never told me his name, probably because he seduced her while wearing a glamour and tricked her into his bed."

"Sounds like it runs in the family."

The muscles in his jaw pulsed. "I hid my ears, Aveen. And my magic. Not because I didn't want to tell you but because this island is dangerous for Fae. I would have given you the truth before we married."

Another romantic story. Truth or lie, it didn't matter because when I looked at Caden Merriweather, all I saw was a handsome mistake.

I remembered the first time I'd caught sight of him outside the pub. The windswept hair, the sun-tanned skin, the mischievous smiles and glinting eyes, as if he'd had some deep, dark secret.

Turned out, he did.

My heart ached for the pain he must've suffered in the Vellanian prison. But the life I'd dreamed of with him was in the past. He was still as handsome—if anything, the new scars added to his rugged appeal—but I'd given my whole heart to another and knew I'd never get it back.

He stood, tugging the top of his trousers where they'd slipped down his trim hips. "Have all your faculties returned?"

I nodded.

"Excellent." He grabbed a leather jerkin from the back of one of the dining chairs and slipped his arms through the sleeves. "I'll give you some time to pack your things, but be quick. The tide will be turning soon, and I'd hate to waste yet another day on this cursed island."

He couldn't be serious. "I'm not going anywhere with you." In what world would I agree to run off with a man I barely knew?

I almost laughed.

Hadn't I been willing to do exactly that only a few years ago?

He fiddled with the collar of his shirt until it laid flat and then ran a hand through his unruly curls. "We had a bargain, you and me. Do you remember what we promised one another before I sailed away?"

Tendrils of icy dread slithered around my throat.

We had a bargain...

When I'd promised to join Caden on his ship, I hadn't known he was a bloody fae. I'd mistaken the flare of heat I felt when he'd held my hand as excitement. Had he truly bound me to my promise to leave?

A passage in the book Rían had given me about bargains sprang to mind. I hadn't wanted to read the thing, but since I'd had little else to entertain me, I'd scoured the text from cover to cover. The exact wording of a bargain could present any number of loopholes. The problem was, I couldn't recall the terms of our agreement. "What did I promise?"

The corner of his lips lifted into a crooked smile. "I promised to come back for you, and in return, you promised to leave Airren aboard my ship."

No.

I'd only been eighteen. I wasn't the same woman. I wasn't even human anymore. There must be some way out of this. *If I promised to leave Airren aboard the ship, then perhaps the moment we sailed away, I could leap into the water and swim to shore.* That was assuming I could get away from him long enough to escape. Perhaps I could appeal to his softer side, if it still existed after all these years. "Please, Caden. You cannot make me come with you."

He shoved his hands into his pockets and shrugged. "Cast me as your villain, it matters not. Come hell or high water, I vow here and now to save you from yourself."

What was it with these bloody men? I didn't need to be *saved*. I needed to be left alone. "If you make me do this, I will never forgive you."

His lips pursed as he considered, but the moment he opened his mouth, despair flooded my chest. "And I'll never forgive myself if I let you stay. Aveen, the man you're involved with is a monster. He judges without mercy, kills without a second thought." Caden gestured toward the white-capped waves beyond the window. "Tales of his terrible deeds have reached all the way to Iodale and beyond. He is the stuff of myths and legends, the monster creeping in the shadows, an instrument of the Phantom Queen."

Rían may have been all those things before, but he'd changed. "He doesn't even want me anymore," I said. "He's in love with someone else."

That gave him pause. "I saw the way he looked at you that day in Graystones."

"How? How did he look at me?" How pathetic and desperate did I sound? Searching for confirmation from my enemy.

Sighing, Caden shook his head and said, "The same way I do." He collected his tricorn hat from the hook beside the door.

He hadn't seen Rían with Leesha. Didn't understand their history.

I would find a way out of this. I would. But to do that, I'd need time to think.

Slowly, I rose, my legs unsteady beneath me as if we were already aboard his ship. "My sister is getting married. I cannot miss the wedding. Please, Caden. Give me that much. I am begging you. I love her more than anyone in this world. Let me celebrate with her, see her happy before I leave forever."

He settled his hat over his curls and blew out a breath, his brown eyes narrowing as he seemed to consider whether I was lying. "When is the wedding?"

"Saturday."

"I will come for you the day after—"

That was too soon. I needed more time. "Danú ceremonies last for days." I had no clue if that was true or not, but he didn't call me out on the lie. Some human weddings lasted entire weekends, so it wasn't unfathomable for a prince's wedding to last even longer.

His lips rolled together as he considered. "No. The Sunday after she is wed, I will be waiting for you at the port in Hollowshade." His expression hardened. "Do not try and test me, Aveen. I always get what I want."

That gave me a handful of days to come up with a plan.

"And my friend?" What had he done with poor Ruairi?

Caden's hand stilled on the doorknob. When he glanced back at me, his eyes sparkled with mischief. "Your friend is tied up in the shed."

25

RÍAN

I PACED FROM THE FIREPLACE TO THE SETTEE AND BACK AGAIN, every curse I knew flooding my mind. I couldn't leave, but how the hell was I supposed to stay?

"Are you sure you're all right?" Leesha asked from her perch on my chair, a glass of wine clasped in her slender fingers.

No. "I'm fine."

She smiled over the rim of her glass before taking a sip. "Then why are you wearing a hole in the floor?"

Because Ruairi had been gone for three feckin' hours. Even with Aveen's magic bound, returning hadn't taken her as long. Had something happened? What if the magic coursing through her veins ran out and she couldn't come back from the under-world? Had she considered the dangers before she killed herself?

The terror of watching her fall from those cliffs was nothing compared to the horror of seeing her take her own life so she could escape—not from a murderous witch but from me.

I couldn't even blame her. I was supposed to love her more than anyone else in this world, and yet when she'd asked about Leesha, I hadn't known what to say because I couldn't lie. Not to Aveen.

Do you still love her?

A Cursed Love

Such a simple question, and yet the answer was anything but. I'd wanted to say no, that I felt nothing for the woman I'd loved so long ago, but my soulmate deserved the truth.

And the truth…

The truth was complicated.

Where the hell was that feckin' dog? What if Leesha was right? What if their feelings for one another ran deeper? Was he there now, comforting her after I'd failed her so miserably? She wouldn't let him do that…would she?

Fuuu—

Leesha peered up at me through wide, worried eyes. "Rían?"

"I'll be back." I needed…a feckin' break. That's what I needed. This last year had been one disaster after another, punctuated by sparks of hope and love. Without Aveen, there could be none of the latter.

Leesha asked where I was going, but I couldn't answer because I didn't know myself. All I knew was that I had to get away. Footsteps sounded at my back, but I ducked into the nearest closet before she could follow.

"Get out," a deep voice hissed from the darkness.

I bit back my groan. So much for a feckin' break. I could have evanesced, but the effort of calling on my magic felt like too much at present. Everything felt like too much. "What are you doing in here?" I whispered back. Granted, I'd found my brother in stranger places before.

"What does it look like I'm doing? I'm hiding."

I inhaled a deep breath, finding no lie but a wealth of alcohol in the air. He smelled like a feckin' brewery. "Find somewhere else to hide."

"*You* find somewhere else to hide. I was here first."

"Keep your voice down." Was he trying to get us caught? He giggled, and that's when I knew… "You're drunk." Tadhg always did sound like a giddy wench when he was sozzled.

Despite the darkness, I could make out his silhouette and what looked like a flask in his hand. He brought the flask to his mouth and muttered, "Not yet, but I'm working on it."

The woman he loved was somewhere in this castle taking care of his child while he was in a closet drinking. This man was meant to save the Danú from extermination and he couldn't even handle a bit of bad news. "You need to man up." I was sick and tired of watching him throw himself away.

"Says the man who can't bring himself to tell a woman how he feels. Or, rather, how he *doesn't* feel."

"It's more complicated than that." Not that he would understand. "I don't even know why I'm talking to you about it. You're more of a disaster than I am."

"I'll have you know I give excellent advice."

A load of bollocks if I ever heard it. Who did he think he was, telling me what to do when he'd all but abandoned his child and his soulmate?

"I like Leesha," Tadhg said.

"Good for you."

"But Aveen..." A puff of alcohol breezed across my cheek. "She is the one for you. Did you see the way she stabbed herself to get away? That's true love, right there."

All right, that was enough advice for today. I reached for the handle and eased the door aside.

"Rían? What are you doing in there?"

Leesha. How the hell had she found me? That human had the nose of a feckin' bloodhound. "I was looking for something," I said.

From behind me, I heard Tadhg whisper, "Close the door."

Leesha's brow furrowed as she leaned past me to scour the darkness.

Keelynn marched around the corner, her hair a fright and her face pinched in irritation. My lips lifted. "Are you looking for Tadhg?" I assumed so from the murderous gleam in her steely eyes. When she nodded, I opened the door wider. "He's right inside."

Tadhg's quiet curse left a smile playing on my lips. Leesha's arm slipped through mine.

Keelynn folded her arms and glowered at my brother as he emerged from the closet, his dark hair sticking up at the back and his cheeks flushed. When he smiled his crooked smile, she huffed through her nose like a dragon ready to breathe fire. "Do I want to know why you were drinking in a closet with your brother?"

Was there anything better than watching one's brother be dressed down by a woman?

"I was only helping Rían." Tadhg turned that smile on me, and I knew I wouldn't like what he was going to say next. "He's struggling with a flaccid cock."

Rage burned up my neck, setting my cheeks aflame. *He did not just tell these women I had problems with my cock.*

"Is that true?" Leesha asked, her eyes brimming with concern.

Tadhg clapped a hand on my shoulder, setting me off balance. "No need to be ashamed, Little Rían. You see, he knows I've never had that problem, and that's why he came to me for advice."

I really missed the days when Tadhg couldn't lie. "Leave. *Now*," I ground through clenched teeth. He would pay for this when he least expected it, and I would relish every moment of his demise.

Keelynn took Tadhg by the hand and escorted him to the staircase while Leesha tugged me back toward the parlor.

Feck it all. I couldn't wait for this eternal day to end. "Has Ruairi returned?"

Her hair tickled my arm when she shook her head. "Not that I know of. Why?"

Because if he didn't show up in the next thirty seconds, I would pin him to the castle walls with a spear and peel his flesh from his bones. "I need to speak with him."

Her gaze fell to my breeches, and understanding brightened her eyes. "Because of your... problem?"

Tadhg was dead.

I couldn't even correct her because as mortifying as the lie was, it did give me an excuse not to sleep with her. I nodded.

A tall, dark figure appeared in the doorway. *Thank feck.* It was about damn time that pooka came back. My relief vanished when Ruairí stepped into the room.

His left eye was swollen shut, the skin around bruised black. Deep red blood trickled down his chin. More blood dripped from the broken skin of his bruised knuckles, splattering on his muddy boots.

Leesha gasped, and her hand flew to her mouth. "Good heavens."

I could do nothing but stare, my heart stalled in my chest. "Is she—?"

"*Rose* is fine," Ruairí said. His good eye flew to where Leesha clutched her hands to her chest before returning to me. "But you and I need to talk in private."

Leesha pressed a kiss to my cheek and gave my arm a reassuring squeeze before quitting the room.

I summoned a tost, drowning out the sounds of her footsteps in the hallway. "What the hell happened?"

"I brought Aveen's body to the cottage, settled her in bed…"

My hands balled into fists.

Do not murder him. Do not *murder him.*

"But when I went to collect water from the well, there was someone waiting."

"Who?"

"Don't know. Black hair, dark eyes. No whiskers. Tall, but not as tall as me. I asked if he needed help, thinking maybe he'd come to the wrong house by accident. The fecker hit me in the face and used magic to hogtie me in the damned shed."

"And you left Aveen there on her own?" Honestly, did no one on this cursed island have a lick of sense?

If the stranger had magic, he almost certainly would've been wearing a glamour when he encountered the pooka, so the description Ruairí had given was useless.

Although I'd deny it until my dying day, Ruairi was one of the strongest men I'd ever met. Even with the element of surprise, it would've taken an exorbitant amount of magic to subdue him. This mysterious stranger was either incredibly powerful…or desperate.

"Unlike ye, I respect a woman's wishes, and when she asked me to leave, I did."

I didn't care about Aveen's wishes when her wellbeing was at stake.

"She seemed genuinely shocked to find me in the shed and asked what had happened. Either she was lying about not seeing anyone else or the man never went inside."

"I don't give a shite whether she saw the man or not." Which wasn't entirely true, but the point was, "*You* saw him. He *attacked* you. And yet you left her alone in that cottage, unable to defend herself! I should tear out your feckin' gullet, you worthless piece of—"

"For feck's sake, lad. She's not alone."

"Who is there with her?"

"Meranda."

Not who I thought he'd say. I would've expected her crotchety neighbor Marcus, maybe. But not Meranda. "Why?"

His mammoth shoulders lifted and fell in a shrug. "Don't know. Didn't ask."

"You really are useless."

"And yer a fool."

My hand snapped out, catching his unbuttoned collar. "Say that again. I dare you." This dog's death had been a long time coming.

He bared his teeth like the animal he was, fangs flashing in the dim light. "Aveen loves ye, and yet yer here with another, acting like ye haven't got the most precious woman in the world pining fer ye. What're ye playin' at?"

My grip loosened, but only a fraction. "What am I supposed

to do? Cast Leesha aside as if she means nothing? All of this is my fault. If it weren't for my mother, we would be together."

Ruairi unhooked my fingers from his collar and shoved me back. My arse collided with the settee. "If it weren't for yer mother, she'd be dead."

That may be true, but—

"Do ye really think there's only one person out there for each of us? If ye had spent a life with Leesha, she would've succumbed to old age or some other human malady centuries ago. And yer immortal arse would still be right here, except maybe ye'd be a little less of a prick because the Queen never would've stolen yer heart."

I could barely get my mind around his words as he jabbed a thick finger at my chest.

"And yer doing that other woman no favors by giving her false love out of some sense of guilt." He straightened and shoved a hand through his disheveled hair. "Now, if ye will excuse me, I'll be heading home to change before going back to Hollowshade to keep an eye on *yer* soulmate while ye play house with someone else."

26

KEELYNN

ALTHOUGH I AGREED WITH AVEEN'S DECISION TO LEAVE, THAT didn't make me miss her any less. If I'd had magic, this wouldn't be an issue. I could pop by her cottage any time I wished. Since I didn't, I was stuck here, waiting to see if she would return for the wedding, selfishly hoping she didn't miss it. But the thought of my sister having to kill herself to do so... How could I expect that of her?

My heavy feet carried me down the stairs. I heard the rustle of skirts before I saw who owned them. Expecting Leesha, my heart sank when Millie walked into the foyer instead.

She offered me a hesitant smile. "I ran into Miss Eava yesterday, and she mentioned you might be wanting me to start before the wedding."

I searched her face for some sign of disapproval but found only soft kindness. My legs nearly collapsed with relief. I'd made the right decision in hiring this young woman to help me around the castle.

"I am so glad she did."

She brushed her raven hair back from her flushed face. "Thank the stars. I'd feel like a right eejit altogether if ye didn't want me here."

With Tadhg spiraling and my sister gone, this castle had become so desperately lonely. More than a maid, I needed someone to talk to. "Come, let me show you around." She followed me from one room to the next, glancing around with wonder. "You've seen the great room, of course. And the study." I swung open the door. Rían sat at the desk, scowling across the room at us. Behind me, Millie flinched. "Don't mind him," I whispered under my breath. "He's really not so bad."

Rían's eyes narrowed, but I closed the door before he could throw around one of his favorite insults or threats and scare my poor maid.

We slipped silently back through the great hall, into the hallway, and down to the kitchens.

"The world believes Tadhg rules this castle, but I can say with confidence that this place would crumble without Eava."

Eava waved at us with purple-stained fingers. Looked like we were to have blackberry pie for dessert. Tadhg would be delighted —assuming he could pull himself from the bottle long enough to join us.

Millie laughed and waved back, asking Eava about her day. While she chatted with our cook, I stole a sprig of grapes from the bowl of fruit displayed in the center of the high table. Eava's cooking, while glorious, wasn't very kind to my waistline.

Three grapes in, my stepson decided it would be the perfect moment to make his presence known.

Millie sucked in a breath, her head lifting at the sound of the little boy's cries. Her wide eyes met mine. "Ye've a babe in the castle?"

I nodded, hoping she didn't notice the blush creeping up my throat. "Tadgh's son. He's upstairs if you'd like to meet him."

"I'd love to." Millie trailed after me, out of the kitchens and back to the staircase. Brogan screeched louder. Where the hell was Tadhg or Leesha?

"So the little one is Prince Tadhg's, but not yours?" Millie asked.

I couldn't hold her curiosity against her. She was too young to realize the polite thing to do was to keep her questions to herself. Did she know about Tadhg's curses, or would she believe he had been unfaithful to me of his own accord? Part of me wanted to set the story straight, but this was Tadhg's tale to tell. I would keep his secrets as closely as I held my own.

"Not mine," I confirmed, content to leave it at that. "Have you any experience with children?" I asked, more than ready for a change in subject.

Her head bobbed, making her short fringe sway against her forehead. "Loads. I've seven brothers and sisters."

If she had that much experience, perhaps she'd be willing to share some tips. Thank heavens for small mercies. The moment I set foot in the room, Brogan's wails fell silent. He twisted his head to glare at me. I still felt so awkward picking him up from this position, and with his head so floppy, I wasn't sure I was giving him enough support. But when Millie didn't immediately reach for him, I had no other choice.

Let her judge me for my inexperience. I wouldn't learn if I didn't at least try. And with my darling fiancé missing more often than not, this responsibility fell to me. Brogan's thick lashes fluttered as he turned his head into my chest, wriggling like he wanted to escape my arms.

Millie leaned close, stroking Brogan's plump cheek with her fingertip. "See the way he nuzzles into you there? He's lookin' for food."

He wouldn't find anything there.

Tadhg did the same thing, but not because he was looking to eat. The thought made my face flush. The two of us hadn't shared a bed since Brogan came into our lives. I tried not to be resentful, but failed most of the time.

"Will I go down for a bottle?" Millie offered.

If I'd thought ahead, I would've asked Eava for one before we left the kitchens. "That would be wonderful. Thank you."

In a blink, she vanished.

I stared down at the little boy. Such a scowly little thing, just like his uncle. Perhaps he was Rían's son and not Tadhg's at all. I laughed to myself—it was either that or cry.

No, there was no denying whose son this was.

"Hello, Brogan. Do you remember me? I am your stepmother, Keelynn." The boy quieted, peering up at me through glassy green eyes. I hated the word "stepmother" and everything it entailed. As if the distinction was another barrier between us. We already had so many of those.

His lower lip jutted out and began to wobble.

"Oh, please don't cry. I'm sure this must be awful for you, and you must be missing your mother, but I am doing my best."

A throat cleared from behind me. Millie waited in the doorway with a bottle clutched against her chest. "I'm sorry. I didn't mean to eavesdrop."

"It's all right." If she remained in this castle long enough, she would likely hear far worse than my pathetic confession. When I offered her the child, she made no move to take him from me.

"I hope ye don't mind my asking," she said, "but how long have ye had him?"

"Not even a week." And yet, with the sleepless nights stretching into eternity, it felt like he'd been part of our lives for far longer.

"Here." Millie pressed the warm glass bottle into my hand. "I think ye should be the one to feed him."

"I don't know how." How mortifying to admit. I'd tried once, but he'd refused to take the bottle for me.

Millie gestured toward the wingback tucked beneath the window. "Sit down on that chair, and I'll grab a pillow to tuck beneath your arm. He looks like a strong lad and will get heavy after a while."

After a while? He was already heavy. I managed to sit without jostling Brogan too much. Millie stuffed a pillow beneath my arm where his head rested, taking away the child's weight altogether.

The moment the bottle's teat met his little mouth, he sucked greedily. *Just like your father.*

I couldn't help my smile.

Millie smiled down at us, and for the first time since Brogan arrived on our doorstep, I felt a little hope in my next breath.

"When he's about halfway through that bottle," she said, "I'll teach ye how to wind him."

I raised my eyes to hers. "Thank you."

Her golden eyes softened as she sank onto the rug next to me and wrapped her arms around her knees. "I have a stepmother."

"You do?"

She nodded. "Yes. And she loves us like we're her own flesh and blood. That's all ye really need to do, princess. Love the little lad and the rest will sort itself out."

TADHG

"She's going to leave me. Just you wait and see." I could practically hear Keelynn's footsteps as she walked out the door. See her silhouette fade into nothing. Feel my heart shattering into a million broken shards, slicing me from the inside out.

Ruairi shook his head, his eyes on the dark shadow spreading across the horizon. Not from the falling sun—no, that remained high in the sky. From that feckin' blight. "Would ye blame her? Ye haven't been sober since ye found out."

The flask in my hand shook when I raised it to my lips. "This is the only thing that makes it better."

His side-eye oozed judgement. "It's making things worse."

Who asked for his opinion, anyway? What did he know about love? Not a feckin' thing. "Do me a favor and keep your thoughts to yourself."

Fire ignited in his golden eyes, but like the friend he was, he let the subject drop. "Let's go."

I didn't want to go anywhere. I wanted to stand here in abject misery and let the wind sweep me into the gnashing sea. My next sip warmed my throat. The one after that made the grass go a tiny bit hazy.

Ruairi nudged me with his elbow. "Yer to shift the Canny's cottage."

The only thing I'd be shifting today was more puítin. "That's Monday."

"It *is* Monday."

That couldn't be right. Today was only Sunday.

I couldn't shift a cottage in this state. *Surprise, surprise.* I was going to let my people down *again.* I flopped onto the ground, willing the blight to take me away from this forsaken place. A rock jabbed my arse and another poked my spine. Why the hell was the sun so feckin' bright? Why were there never any clouds in the sky? If I asked nicely, would the land open up and swallow me whole?

The toe of Ruairi's boot jabbed my ribs. "Get up."

"Leave me be." Right here seemed as good a place as any to sleep off the alcohol swimming in my gut. At least it was quiet.

Ruairi squatted next to me, pity written all over his face. "I've followed ye fer centuries, Tadhg. But I'll not follow ye down this road again. Ye have a good woman and a son who both need ye. No more drink." He tried to pluck the flask from my hand, but I wouldn't let him.

He couldn't take away the only constant in my life. The companion that had brought me through more trials and tribulations than one could count. If Keelynn left me—who was I kidding? This wasn't a matter of *if* but *when.* Who wanted to go through life with a broken man? Fiadh had crushed my spirit and my soul, and what was worse—I'd let her. So here I was, the happiest I'd ever been, only to have that stolen from me too.

But of course, my best mate had to be a strong fecker who knew I was ticklish beneath the arms and used that knowledge against me.

The flask slipped from my grasp, but it didn't matter. As soon as his attention shifted elsewhere, I'd find something else to drink. It was better to sink to the bottom of a sea of alcohol than to waste my days swimming toward a surface that didn't exist.

27

RÍAN

THE DAY WE'D BEEN DREADING FOR MONTHS HAD ARRIVED. THE blight had finally reached the castle. Almost as if the moment Aveen's body had crumpled to the ground, all the life in this place had been snuffed out as well.

Do you still love her?

Days later, that question still haunted me.

I'd spent last night in Hollowshade, sitting on the hillside watching smoke puff from Aveen's chimney, trying to drum up the nerve to go inside and explain how I felt. The problem was, I didn't *know* how I felt from one minute to the next. I felt so many things all at once, it was difficult to sort through them all to see what hid at the very core.

"Will the wards keep out the curse?" Tadhg slurred, a half-empty bottle of puitín hanging from his fingers as he stared through the gate.

"I suppose we'll find out tomorrow or the next day." Our wards were ancient and strong, continually fed by my magic—and since his curse had broken, Tadhg's as well—but last year, the Queen had waltzed straight through as if they weren't even there.

I imagined the blight she'd created would do the same.

Tadhg's head tilted as he continued looking off into the blackened distance. "We should probably strengthen them just in case."

"Probably."

Instead, I lifted my glass, and he his bottle, and we both took burning gulps.

The fire in my throat was nothing compared to the anguish in my heart. Last night, I'd seriously considered ripping the feckin' thing from my chest to rid myself of this emotion-fueled indecision. Life had been so much simpler without it.

Without warning, Tadhg stalked through the wards and dropped to his knees on the ground to press his free hand into the dirt. Although his hand lit with magic, blackness from the earth climbed his fingers, as if searching for the dark magic that lived within him. The same thing had happened to me each time I'd tried to force the blight away.

"It's not going to work," I told him.

Tadhg's hand jerked into the air, and the blackness dripped down his fingertips like ink, seeping back into the ground from whence it came. He stomped back to where I waited beneath the murder hole and took another pull from his flask. "Can I ask you something?"

"Only if it has nothing to do with women."

He gave a humorless chuckle. "Do you think Tearmann would be better off if we let the Queen take the throne?"

The Phantom Queen ruling all of Tearmann. Now *that* was a terrifying thought. I took another sip. "That depends on whether or not you value human lives over Danú."

He glanced sidelong at me, the darkness of the grass reflected in his wary eyes. "You truly believe she would kill them all?"

After seeing firsthand how much disdain she felt for them and being forced to kill so many myself, there really was no doubt. "If she had the means, yes. I do." To the Queen, the sins of the father were the sins of the son. No human was innocent of the crimes that had been committed against the Danú.

Tadgh's shoulders slumped as he gestured toward the distant

cliffs with his bottle. "Do you ever wish you could get on a ship and sail away?"

"I lived the first nineteen years of my life in a castle on a cliff at the heart of the Black Forest with a witch who used to whip me for not standing up straight. What do you think?"

The places I'd planned on going. I'd even had the guts to do it once. The night before my thirteenth birthday, I'd evanesced to South Port and bought myself a one-way ticket to Iodale. I barely made it out of the port before retching my guts up because of the ever-shifting sea. Ended up jumping overboard to drown myself. Thankfully, my body washed up on the shore, and the rest, as they said, was history.

"Rían?"

The sound of Leesha's too-sweet voice echoed around the courtyard. How many years had I spent wishing to hear her call my name?

She waved at us from the top step, sunlight dancing in her fiery tresses. "I've tea in the family room. Won't you join me?"

"I'll be there in a moment," I called over my shoulder.

Tadhg's bloodshot eyes narrowed as he studied me. "What are you going to do about her?"

"What are you going to do about your bastard?" I shot back.

There was a beat of silence, and then we both drained what remained of our drinks. What a sorry pair we were.

Eventually, I got up the nerve to go inside and found Leesha sitting on the settee, her hands clasped in her lap and a smile playing on her lips.

Do you still love her? Aveen's voice whispered from somewhere far away.

In a perfect world, the answer would have been no. But this world was far from perfect.

My feelings for Leesha all seemed to stem around guilt. I'd promised her so much, and if I didn't follow through, that made me a terrible person.

But I was terrible.

The man Leesha loved had been...not good, per se, but certainly better than the man I was today.

When I thought about my situation like that, the answer was so feckin' simple.

I couldn't tell this woman the truth because I didn't want to hurt her even though the lie was so much worse. With Aveen, I couldn't bear to lie. She knew everything there was to know about me, the wretchedness I was capable of, and loved me anyway.

Wasn't that the point of this life? To find someone who would love you despite all your faults?

Didn't Leesha deserve to find something true instead of a false love rooted in guilt?

The moment my arse hit the cushion, Leesha started rubbing my arm. Her hands weren't the ones I wanted on my body. Her smile didn't make my breath catch.

This needed to end today.

Leesha's brow furrowed as she watched me stand right back up. "My love?" She made to reach for my hand, but I took another step back. "Why are you acting so strangely?"

"Please don't call me that." I wasn't her love. Not anymore.

"What's wrong?" she asked, the note of panic in her tone impossible to ignore.

I'd already lost Leesha, healed, and moved on.

I couldn't lose Aveen as well.

"I'm sorry, Leesha. But I can't do this anymore." Aveen had said the same words the other evening, and I'd been an eejit for letting her go. Leesha's lips pressed flat as she reached for me once more.

"I do not feel the way I used to," I blurted.

Her hand stilled mid-air before falling open at her side. "I don't understand." Her deep green eyes darted back and forth, searching mine for something she would never find.

"I do not love you anymore."

"You don't . . . love me?" she repeated slowly, as if the words made no sense. Then her eyes widened, pinning me in place.

Leesha shot to her feet. Red splotches painted her freckled cheeks. *"You don't love me?"*

So much for letting her down easily. "Calm down and let me explain."

"You expect me to calm down? I gave myself to you!" she hissed.

"And I gave myself to you." We'd gone into this relationship together, our eyes and hearts wide open.

Her eyes glittered, and her head shook as if she could deny the truth in my words. "And that means *nothing?*"

"You don't understand—"

She needled my chest with her finger, glaring up at me as tears leaked from her eyes. "Oh, I understand perfectly. You are just like your philandering brother. All this time, you pretended as if you were different. You know what?" Huffing a mirthless chuckle, she collected her hair with short, jerking movements, tying the long, heavy strands back with a black ribbon. "I take it back. You're not like Tadhg. You're *worse.*"

I accepted each and every vicious word, letting them steal away some of my guilt. "I'm sorry."

"You're sorry, are you? For what? Being a lying bastard? You promised me forever!"

"That was two hundred years ago!"

Leesha's jaw dropped. She caught the edge of the mantle, her face as pale as the marble beneath her fingers.

"You've seen the scar on your chest." Her hand flew to her breast. "The Queen stole your heart. You have been dead for *centuries.* I mourned you for years. But eventually I had to…"

Her palm rubbed idle circles over her heart as her eyes slowly widened. I wasn't sure if it was a minute or an hour. All I knew was that it felt like forever before she said, "You've moved on, haven't you?"

I nodded.

Sniffling, Leesha wiped her sleeve beneath her eyes. "The woman who was here. She isn't Ruairí's, is she? She's yours."

She had been mine. But now, after everything, I wasn't so sure. "Yes." Feck it all, I hoped it wasn't a lie. "I'm truly sorry for the life that was stolen from us," I said, meaning every word. I would have given her a good life, a happy one. But as Ruairi had pointed out, her life would have ended long ago.

"Two *hundred* years," Leesha whispered, the words muffled by her trembling hand. "My family…"

She'd been here for days and had been making plans to visit those she'd left at the cottage, but I'd always managed to dissuade her. But not today. This was a day for truths.

"Your family is gone." I couldn't bring myself to tell her about what I'd been forced to do to her sister. I couldn't hurt her more than I already had. "You have distant relatives still living in the border cottage, but those you knew have long since passed. I am sorry. I have tried to find what I once felt, but there is nothing left." Nothing but fond memories and heartbreak.

"You say my family is gone, and now you're gone as well? What am I supposed to do?"

"You can stay here as long as you'd like."

"Don't you see?" Her broken sob made me feel every bit the villain I was. "Every time you walk into the room, I fall more in love with you. I cannot bear to be near you knowing you will never feel the same." Leesha's arms came around my shoulders. When she lifted onto her toes to press a soft kiss to my lips, I let her. She tasted of innocence and desire, but there was no fire. Not even a feckin' spark.

Her grip on my collar tightened. "You feel nothing?"

I shook my head. "I'm sorry, Leesha."

Nodding, she let me go and stepped away. "Then it's clear I need to leave."

"Where will you go?"

She offered me a watery smile. "Does it matter?"

It didn't. Once she left, I would not be seeking her out. This woman I'd known so well was now a stranger to me, and her life would be far better if I became a stranger to her as well.

I shouted for Eava, and the witch appeared a moment later. Her brow pulled in concern as she glanced between the two of us. "Can you see that Leesha gets wherever she wishes to go?"

Her eyes filled with understanding as she nodded. "I will of course, my boy."

As the woman I once loved turned and walked away, thoughts of another woman consumed my mind.

It was time to beg for forgiveness.

28

KEELYNN

No matter what I did, Brogan wouldn't stop crying. The poor little boy's eyes were so swollen, they barely opened. When they did, I swore he glared as if he blamed me for his mother abandoning him. He refused the bottle and even the crushed-up biscuit mixed with milk. I tried rocking him, singing to him—which, admittedly, would make anyone cry. I was at my wit's end, and once again Tadhg was nowhere to be found.

Rían stepped out of the study, but when he saw me standing at the foot of the stairs, he darted straight back inside. I couldn't blame him for hiding. I'd hide too if Tadhg hadn't left me to deal with Brogan on my own. After two full days at the castle, it was Millie's day off, and while I'd been happy to give her time with her own husband and family, I desperately needed assistance. Which was why I followed Rían into the study, finding him about to slip through the door to the great hall.

"Where is Leesha?" I wasn't supposed to befriend her out of loyalty to my sister, but at this stage, I'd have befriended Fiadh if she could return from the underworld and calm the child.

Rían's lips pursed as he scowled at Brogan thrashing in my arms. "She's gone."

"Gone where?"

Rían shrugged.

Wasn't that just bloody brilliant? I tried to sway my hips the way Millie had, but the movement only made Brogan more cross. "Have you seen your brother?"

"He's in the family room."

Back in the hallway, Ruairi waited with his back against the tapestries and one booted foot propped against the wall outside the family room. When I tried to enter, he slid in front of me. "Where might ye be going, human?"

Brogan stopped crying the moment Ruairi started speaking. Fat tears clung to his long, dark lashes, and his full lower lip trembled as he blinked up at the pooka. "I need to speak to Tadhg."

Ruairi stood up taller. "He's indisposed."

"I know I'm the only human of you lot"—a fact I was still not happy about—"but I swear, if you don't move by the time I count to three, I will tear every hair from your arm. One..."

Ruairi threw the door open in a flash; the wood slammed against the wall inside, sending Brogan into another fit.

I knew exactly how the little boy felt. "Thank you, Ruairi."

Instead of remaining in the hall, Ruairi padded quietly behind me.

I found my dearly betrothed surrounded by empty bottles, a glass cradled against his chest the way his son should have been. His eyes were closed, but his brow was furrowed, as if his dreams plagued him.

"Is he drunk again?" That or he was dead because no one should have been able to sleep through Brogan's racket.

"Afraid so," Ruairi murmured.

I should've run down to the kitchens to borrow a pot and wooden spoon and bang them right next to his ear.

But Tadhg would be of no help if he didn't sleep off whatever drink he'd consumed.

Drunk at noon on a Tuesday. We were to be married in four days. Would he be drunk for that too? I heaved Brogan to my other hip to give my right arm a break. "Do me a favor. When he wakes, don't let him have anything else."

Ruairi rolled his lips together as he stared down at the drunken prince. "I'd love to promise ye that, but if Tadhg wants drink, he'll find some."

What was I supposed to do? Tadhg had said he'd stayed off the drink for months while I was gone. I understood the stress of this fatherhood situation, but drinking himself under the table wouldn't make life any easier. If anything, trying to mind a child with a raging hangover would be worse.

Brogan's wails turned into soft whimpers, his eyes fluttering before drifting shut. I nearly shouted with excitement. He'd never fallen asleep for me. Not even once. And here he was, his chubby cheek pressed to my breast and mouth hanging slightly open, looking like a bloody angel.

He really was perfect, with his little chocolate curls and those lashes, still wet from his tears. The red splotches on his face eventually faded, leaving his skin milky pale.

As perfect as he was, he still belonged to someone else.

By the time I carried him up to his cot, my arms were ready to fall off. I eased his body onto the tiny mattress, holding my breath and praying his eyes remained closed. I considered throwing myself down for a snooze as well but decided it would be best to eat something first before my howling stomach woke the beast.

Back downstairs, the most delicious smell of roast meats and freshly baked bread wafted from the kitchen's open door. Eava hummed to herself as she chopped carrots for what looked an awful lot like beef stew.

Eava glanced over her shoulder and smiled. At first, her black eyes had reminded me of Fiadh and the Queen. But after only a few minutes in her company, it was clear this witch was nothing like them. "Finally got the babe down I see," she said, as warm and welcoming as the plate of hot cross buns sitting on the high table.

Finally was right. "It only took two hours." Yawning into my fist, I sank onto the closest stool. I wasn't sure what I wanted more: to lay my head down and pass out or to eat one of those buns. Eava made the decision for me when a plate appeared, two steaming, buttery buns on top. I thanked her, then thanked her again when I took the first bite. I'd only been alive a few weeks and already my dresses felt a little tighter. The food back in Graystones had been good but was nothing compared to Eava's masterpieces. And to think, this time last year I had been afraid to eat fae food.

Savoring each bite as I chewed gave my brain some time to process the last few days. I thought of those men who'd come to the hall on Friday, the ones who'd sneered and told Tadhg he was a fool for marrying me. My mind drifted to Anwen next. And finally, to her son. "Do you think it's possible for a baby to resent you?"

Eava heaved her chopping board to the edge of the pot on the stovetop and shoved the carrots straight in. "No, child. Although they can sense stress, even when they're wee babes."

Stressed didn't begin to cover how I felt. Maybe if I'd been there from the beginning, if I'd been the one to go through carrying him, seen his first smile, heard his first laugh, maybe I'd feel differently. But he wasn't mine.

He was Tadhg's and Anwen's.

A constant reminder of my husband's infidelity while I was in the Underworld.

He was cursed.

He wasn't your husband then.

He was cursed.

It wasn't the child's fault. Rationally, I knew that. But part of me still resented him for it. And that made me a horrible, awful person. It felt even more important to find a way to connect with Brogan so he didn't resent me as well.

Eava carried the chopping board and knife to the sink. "Where's Tadhg?"

Groaning, I stuffed another bite between my lips. "Passed out."

She gripped the edge of the counter and let out an exasperated sigh. "I love my boys, but sometimes they do things that don't make a lick of sense."

Tell me about it. What was it about men that made them so bloody daft?

"It feels like he's pushing me away." Avoiding me. Drinking morning, noon, and night. This wasn't the man I fell in love with. Even on our darkest days, he'd never been this bad. I could appreciate that he was struggling. I was struggling too. Why couldn't we lean on each other instead of letting this break us apart?

Eava turned, her expression grim as she crossed to where I picked at my food instead of eating any more. "The lad's convinced yer going to leave him over the babe. And he won't stop till ye do."

"I don't want to leave him." But I didn't know how I could stay like this either.

She pressed a wrinkled hand to her forehead, worry written in every line on her face. "This has happened twice before, him letting the darkness take over. He's the only one who can decide whether or not it wins."

I wanted to ask about the other times, but Eava continued speaking, replacing my questions with new ones. "I can't believe I'm sayin' this," she said, "but maybe the sooner he's proved right, the sooner he'll get his shite together. I love that lad like he's my own, but as long as he has someone else to lean on, that's what he'll do. With Leesha and Aveen gone, that leaves ye." Her eyes turned serious. "If ye were to go…"

Had she lost her mind? I couldn't leave Tadhg in this state. "He'll think I abandoned him."

"Sometimes the end justifies the means."

Eava's words haunted me all the way back to Brogan's room, where the little boy slept peacefully in his cot, looking so much like his father, my heart ached. Was Eava right? Would Tadhg be better off figuring this out on his own? If I left, how far was I willing to go?

If leaving gave us a chance, then that was what I'd do.

At the bottom of an armoire in one of the spare rooms, I found an old carpet bag and stuffed a handful of dresses, stockings, and undergarments inside. Only enough for a few days. I'd need money to pay for lodging as well. Was there an inn close by that hadn't been affected by the blight? I hadn't seen one during my walks with Ruairi. I'd ask Eava. She'd help me.

Tadhg appeared in the doorway, his cheeks sunken and sorrowful green eyes surrounded by dark bruises, reminding me of when he used to wear the enchanted kohl. When his gaze landed on the half-packed bag, the color drained from his face and his eyes snapped to mine. "Why are you packing a bag? Are you going somewhere?"

What was I supposed to say? That I didn't know? That I just needed to get away from all of this so that he could figure himself out?

He caught my hand, tugging me into him, craning his neck so we were eye level. "Look at me. Tell me what's in your head."

He didn't want to know. Still, he needed to see how serious this situation had become. That I refused to stand by and do nothing while he threw himself away. "I can't be here anymore."

His grip on my hand tightened. "I'm sorry. I know I've been..." His throat bobbed when he swallowed. "I'll do better. I promise. Please don't leave me. I'm so sorry."

When you heard those words so often over the same thing, they began to lose their meaning. "If you were sorry, you would stop destroying yourself."

His gaze dropped to the floor. "I'm not cut out for fatherhood."

"And yet you're a father all the same. Your son needs you." Not me. Not Millie. He needed his father.

Tadhg's hands fell to his sides, and he straightened. "And I need you."

I need you too. But I needed him trying to be better instead of trying to find an escape. "I can't watch you do this to yourself. I just…I can't."

His eyes shuttered, closing him off from me yet again. "This is about Anwen, isn't it?"

I couldn't say it wasn't because it was. At least part of it.

"You said it was fine," he ground out. "That you forgave me because it wasn't my fault."

I had said that and meant it. What had happened with Anwen hadn't been his fault. But this, the drinking, the distance he's kept between us, that was on him. "This"—I gestured to his drink-splattered shirt and stained breeches—"isn't fine."

"So you insist on throwing us away?"

"I'm not throwing anything away, Tadhg. I am trying every-thing in my power to save us. But every time I look at your child, I am overcome by jealousy and resentment over an inno-cent baby who has done nothing wrong. I am trying to work through these dark, treacherous emotions cleaving me apart in order to find my way back to you." I would have loved to drink myself into oblivion, but I'd had no time to wallow because I'd been taking care of Tadhg's son so he could drown. "I need a break."

His chin jerked back as if I'd slapped him. "A break from what?"

"From trying to fix someone who would rather be broken."

"So you'll cross the Forest, never to return. And when we wed, I can, what, visit you every other week?"

I stiffened. How could I have forgotten the bloody wedding?

He grasped my hands, holding tightly, as if he could keep me here by sheer force of will. "We are still to wed. Keelynn, look at me. Tell me you haven't changed your mind."

Tadhg let my fingers slip from his. He dragged a hand through his hair, his eyes haunted and hollow. "Feckin' hell. I have invited everyone I know, and you've changed your mind."

"I never said that." I wasn't backing out. Not yet. But I

couldn't marry him like this, not when I couldn't trust him to be sober at the bloody ceremony.

"You didn't need to. You can't even hold my gaze."

There was no point denying the truth. Seeing him like this broke me too. "I'm sorry, Tadhg."

He didn't bother saying it was all right. We both knew it wasn't. His breaths came in short, ragged gasps. "How long do you need? A day or two? A week?"

I wanted to ask him the same bloody question. "I don't know."

"Give me something, a fraying thread to cling to. Anything," he gasped.

"I love you. Is that enough?"

He shook his head. "Please, don't do this."

I left him there and escaped into the hall, my head and heart pounding in time. Weary legs carried me down the stairs, my mind so lost, I nearly collided with Ruairi at the bottom.

His massive hands fell atop my shoulders, keeping me from collapsing at his feet. "Where are ye off to in such a rush, human?"

I swiped at the tears bleeding down my cheeks. Why couldn't they have stayed away until I could be alone? "I need some-where…somewhere to g-go. I c-can't stay here."

A loud crash echoed down the staircase. What was Tadhg thinking? He was going to wake the—

Brogan's shrill screech cut through me like a scythe.

Ruairi held out his hand and said, "Come with me."

29

TADHG

Keelynn was gone. Well and truly gone.

She'd left me. Well and truly alone.

Brogan let out a pitiful whimper.

Not alone.

My son was with me, and the halls echoed with his screams. It sounded like Rían's dungeon in here.

Speaking of Rían, he hadn't returned since he'd gone to find Aveen. Ruairi was nowhere to be found. And when I evanesced to the kitchens, Eava was missing as well. She'd left a plate of food for me and a bottle of milk in warm water, along with a note that said she would be back tomorrow.

Tomorrow.

Although my stomach grumbled, I grabbed the bottle and evanesced back to the bedroom.

Brogan screeched louder than one of Ned's victims. Nothing wrong with the lad's lungs, that was for sure. My head thumped and vision swam. "Could you not do that? I've a headache brewing." He only cried harder. Maybe he was actually Rían's child since he clearly had a penchant for torture.

"Here." I handed him the bottle, but he was in such a strop, he wouldn't take it. His tiny fists clenched and swung, as if he'd box me in the ear if he could. *That makes two of us.*

I deserved a good boxing. If Rían were here, I'd let him kill me. Death would've been a welcome respite from all the crying.

"Brogan? You're going to have to calm down, lad." I reached into the cot to pat his head when it hit me.

The stench. Feckin' hell. I'd never smelled something as rotten, and I'd woken up beneath a pile of dead bodies on more than one occasion. Where had Keelynn said the nappies were? I dragged out every drawer in the room, finding nothing but miniature clothes. You know what? One of these tiny pants would have to do.

When I picked him up, he only roared louder. When I laid him on the bed, his legs kept pumping up and down, making it nearly impossible to catch his tiny ankles and get him undressed.

Bile singed the back of my throat, and my eyes stung.

This child wasn't well. That much was clear when I saw what he'd done to his nappy. No wonder he was so cross. If I'd done that, I'd be screaming too.

I shifted a bath because there was no way in hell I'd be able to get him clean enough without it. He only slipped beneath the water once, but I was there to catch him. When I saved him from drowning, the funniest thing happened. He *smiled* at me, water dripping down his face, as if he'd enjoyed the unexpected dousing.

Then he took a shite in the tub and that was the end of that.

With the nappies nowhere to be found, I made do with a washcloth and a few pins. The little lad didn't seem to care as he sucked his bottle dry, scowling over at me every so often. Why had I thought this would be so hard? You had to keep him clean and fed—same as Rían.

Brogan threw the bottle aside and let out a belch loud enough to rattle the feckin' window.

I couldn't have done it better myself.

By some miracle, I hadn't felt like touching a drink this whole time.

A record since Anwen had made her unexpected appearance. Shame warmed my face. I never should've let Keelynn take the brunt of this responsibility. I was some fool.

I picked Brogan up from where I'd propped him between two pillows. He felt too small and fragile in my hands, like the snow globe my mother used to own. One I'd accidentally dropped. I held Brogan a little tighter. When I tried to put him on my shoulder the way I'd seen Leesha do so effortlessly, he vomited down my back.

"Not the worst thing I've had on my shirt today," I muttered, changing us both for the third time.

This time, when I lifted him, I tucked a hand towel beneath his drooly chins to catch anything that might spew out. Down to the kitchens we went, and by the time I got there, the lad was asleep again, which was feckin' brilliant considering I was hungry enough to eat the whole vat of stew Eava had cooked—and I wasn't all that fond of meat.

I shifted a few cushions from the family room, arranging them into a bed on the floor using my boot. The moment I tried to lay Brogan down, his eyes popped open, a threat in those green depths. Any time I tried to move him from my right arm to my left, it happened again.

I stared down at my dish of stew, my mouth watering the way Brogan's always seemed to.

Using my left hand, I tried to stab the first carrot. It flew right off the plate and onto a cushion. I managed to get a prong on the second one, and that vegetable tasted of victory. Since I wasn't able to cut the beef, I stabbed the thick chunks and gnawed on them like an rabid animal.

At least no one was around to see how far I'd fallen.

Some red wine would go really well with this. I shifted a bottle only to realize I couldn't open it with a child in my arms, and since this was the first proper break I'd had all afternoon, I wasn't about to attempt putting him down.

Thankfully, Eava had left a jug of water next to the sink. I filled a glass and choked it down.

Brogan continued snoozing away, still snuggled tightly in the crook of my arm, his mouth hanging open the way Ruairi's did when he'd had too much drink and passed out sitting up.

Passing out sounded pretty good right now. That nap I'd taken earlier really hadn't done much to curb my exhaustion. I tiptoed to the family room and eased onto the settee, keeping Brogan toward the back so he didn't accidentally roll off. He was like a tiny hot water bottle, all cuddly and warm. My eyes drifted closed, the weight of the past few days finally catching up with me.

I'd figure out this fatherhood thing, and then I'd find a way to win back the woman I loved.

As I listened to Brogan's even breathing, my own slowed to match. Blessed sleep tugged at the corner of my consciousness…

Until Brogan let out a bone-chilling howl right in my feckin' ear.

My eyes snapped open, burning with tiredness. Somehow, I found the strength to force myself upright. Brogan wriggled as if he were uncomfortable, so I put him down. He didn't like that one bit, alternating between screaming and gasping for air.

I tried everything: a bottle, a rattle, picking him up, putting him down, bouncing him on my hip, rocking him back and forth until I nearly fell asleep standing up, but nothing worked.

That's when I smelled another round of shite.

It was going to be a long night.

A warm breeze skated down the back of my neck as I stood outside Anwen's house clutching Brogan to my chest. Eava hadn't returned this morning as she'd promised, and neither had my brother.

All it took was one long, sleepless night to prove that leaving the baby with me had been the wrong choice. The witch had already raised three children—or was it four? I couldn't remember. Either way, Anwen was far better suited to this parenting lark. That was why I'd bundled Brogan in one of Rían's thick wool jumpers and marched straight over to where Anwen's cottage had been relocated because of the blight.

Returning Brogan to his mother would be best for everyone involved.

Even knowing that, my heart ached when I raised my hand to knock. I didn't have what it took to keep this boy alive. All he did was cry. He didn't even like me. He must miss his mother.

But the thought of not seeing him again didn't sit well with me either. Maybe we could work out some sort of arrangement where I took him a few days and she had him as well. That was fair, wasn't it?

I forced myself to rap my knuckle against the wood.

When no one answered, I knocked harder. How had Anwen raised all her children in such a tiny home? I'd need to find her something bigger, someplace closer to the castle.

Actually, that wouldn't work either because we'd need to relocate the castle because of that damn blight.

Besides, how would Keelynn feel about having my former lover living so close? That wasn't fair to her, was it? Assuming she still wanted to be with me after I sorted this out. *Dammit.* Every time I thought I had a solution to my problems, another one arose.

Where the hell was Anwen?

I knocked a third time before walking around to one of the smudged windows to peer inside.

There wasn't a piece of furniture in the entire room.

My stomach sank as I hurried back to the door to try the knob. Unlocked. The ratty sofa, the coffee table, the mirror that used to hang above the dining table—all of it had disappeared. My footsteps echoed around the hollow living area.

Anwen and her children were gone. There wasn't so much as

a note saying where they went or if they ever planned on returning. She'd abandoned her child with me.

As if he'd heard my thoughts, Brogan's lower lip began to tremble, and his eyes flooded with tears.

I knew exactly how he felt.

Back at the castle, I found a stack of letters waiting on my desk, most of them invitations to the wedding that had been returned unopened. A wedding I wasn't sure would still go ahead. There were two letters from old friends who said they wouldn't be able to make it due to prior engagements, and one that said something far worse.

Too many have been lost to the humans.
I cannot support your decision to tie yourself to one.

When Brogan began to cry, so did I.

30

AVEEN

Weeds. God love them, they refused to give up. Every time I ripped one out, another two seemed to pop up in its place. It was infuriating. Then again, everything infuriated me. I used to be placid and docile and accepting of my fate. Or at least I'd pretended to be. And then I'd met a fae prince who made me dare to want more from life and love.

My trowel stabbed into the rich topsoil beneath the dormant climbing roses. I worked the handle, leveraging the small dandelion until its roots cracked and gave. I added it to the pile of thistles and weeds to be burned and then started on the next.

Doing this sort of work usually helped to clear my mind.

Not today. Today, the betrayals cut too deep, a scythe clearing everything in its wake. Caden holding me to a vow I didn't realize I'd made, and Rían choosing another love over me. Since I could do nothing about the latter, I tried to focus on the former.

Leaving my sister behind with so much turmoil in her own life would break my heart, but remaining here, in this cottage Rían had built for me, surrounded by memories of our time together would break me as well.

I could leave with Caden and see what happened. I was going to be unhappy no matter where I ended up, so I may as well see some sights while I was at it. Someday I would find my way back home. It wasn't as if I didn't have the time. Being a true immortal meant I had nothing but.

Phil plucked the dandelion from the pile and gnawed on the stem with crooked, brown teeth. A rare ray of sunlight glinted off the drool coating his tiny white beard. Perhaps he'd eat all the weeds and I wouldn't have to bother with a fire.

With the weeds cleared, I used my hand rake to scrape wet leaves from the bed and add them to a tin bucket. From the corner of my eye, I saw a man with hair the same color as my goat strolling up the lane, clutching a brown paper sack.

He didn't look familiar, so I paid him no mind.

Until he stopped to lean on the gate and said, "Nice day, isn't it?"

As a woman living on her own, I knew to be wary of strangers. Luckily, my prince had stashed a meat cleaver in with my gardening tools. Not that I planned on chopping anyone up today. Unless Caden returned. Then I might have to make an exception.

Phil looked up, and his head tilted, the mouthful of weeds rolling with each chew.

I brushed back the hair sticking to my forehead and offered the man a polite smile. "It is that." For Airren, anyway. No doubt the sun was shining in Tearmann.

From his pocket, he withdrew a shiny red apple and held it out to my goat. Phil dropped the weeds in a flash and trotted over to the stranger to steal the fruit for himself. Instead of continuing on his way, the man kept watching me.

Couldn't he see that I was elbow-deep in dirt and leaves? I hardly had time for a friendly chat. That was what I got for smiling and pretending. The next man to interrupt me would get the scowl he deserved. I blew out a breath. "Is there something I can help you with, sir?"

"Nah. I'm just trying to figure out if you'd rather stab me with your shovel or cleaver."

My hand flew to shield my eyes from the brightening day. Sure enough, the stranger had familiar cerulean eyes. Phil jumped when I shoved to my feet and started for the cottage. The nerve of him, showing up here after what he'd put me through. My shattered heart couldn't handle any more. "I have nothing to say to you."

The gate's hinges creaked; footsteps pounded behind me. A hand grabbed the doorknob before I could. I whirled, finding myself wedged between a firm chest, that mysterious paper sack, and an unforgiving door.

I should've shifted that cleaver and driven the blasted thing into his gullet, give him another nasty scar to remember me by.

Too bad I still loved him.

His face became his own, from the tiny scar across his nose to the squareness of his jaw and point of his chin. Eyes I'd drowned in searched mine. "You may have nothing to say to me, but I have plenty to say to you."

My elbows rammed into his chest when I crossed my arms. Maybe I'd be chopping someone up today after all.

His voice dropped, leaving the hairs on my neck standing on end. "Before you left, you asked if I still love Leesha."

I shook my head against the words curling around my throat, tightening like a noose. *I still love Leesha. I still love Leesha. I still love Leesha.* "I can't do this." I couldn't stand here and listen to him say words meant for me and me alone.

He adjusted his hold on the sack, freeing one hand to caress my cheek. How pitiful of me to want to lean into his touch. "Please. Let me get this out."

I rolled my lips together to keep from saying what I really wanted.

"You asked me if I still love Leesha. I didn't know how to answer then, but now I do." His throat bobbed when he swallowed. "The answer is yes. I still love her."

He came all the way here to crush my broken heart beneath

241

the heel of his boot? Why couldn't he leave me be? At least give me some time to get over him.

Oh, who was I kidding? He was it for me. The be-all, end-all. I would never find another love like him.

His thumb grazed my chin, applying the slightest pressure, urging my gaze to his. "I love her with the heart of a nineteen-year-old boy who had never known kindness or compassion. Who was naïve and young and hopeful."

His hand slipped around the nape of my neck as he eased his forehead against mine. It wasn't until the soft fan of his words caressed my damp cheeks that I realized I was crying. "But I love you, Aveen, with the heart of a man who has lived for centuries in the dark. A part of me will always love her, but the rest of me is yours."

My fingers wrapped around his collar, leaving brown stains on the white material. "I really should hate you."

The corner of his lips lifted. Those dimples of his flashed. "Think of all the effort that would take. Why don't you love me forever instead?"

I would love him forever no matter what. Although we didn't *have* forever, did we? After the wedding, I would be gone. I couldn't bring myself to tell him the truth about my bargain with Caden and ruin this joyous reunion. There was no telling how he would react.

What if he changed his mind? Sure, he loved me now, but what if he realized Leesha was who he truly wanted? Rían leaned forward. Before his mouth could capture mine, that paper sack knocked against my stomach, and my curiosity won out over the lust clouding my mind. "What's in the bag?"

"What bag?" he asked, his tongue sweeping his lips, his gaze transfixed on my mouth.

I tapped the package. He blinked down at it as if only now noticing its presence. "Oh, right. I brought you a peace offering." He pressed the gift into my arms.

I loosed the twine tied around the top and withdrew...a small blue pot of dirt. "You got me dirt?" Definitely not what I had expected, especially from someone who loathed dirt.

"Your favorite," he said with a crooked smile. "And if you water your dirt and give it sunlight, maybe you'll find another surprise."

I hugged the pot to my chest, loving it even more. Not just dirt… "You got me a flower?"

His finger traced along the beveled edge of the pot. "I considered purchasing a bouquet from the market, but those flowers would die, and you deserve something as alive as you make me feel. So I spoke to Oscar, and he told me how to plant this so it should bloom come spring."

"It's perfect. You know how much I love dirt."

He took the pot and set it on the stoop. When he stood back up, he finally closed the distance between us. "Almost as much as you love me," he murmured, his lips grazing mine as if memorizing their shape with his own.

"Almost as much," I agreed, slipping my hands around the back of his neck and pressing my body to his. Perhaps I shouldn't have forgiven him so easily, but I was going to forgive him eventually, and today seemed as good a day as any. We needed to steal this precious moment before yet another dark cloud rained on our happiness.

His molten tongue set fire to my own with each scintillating stroke. Our kiss was a greeting. A reminder. A promise.

The doorknob rattled as Rían fumbled for the handle and pushed the barrier aside. We stumbled into the dim living area, both of us refusing to break our connection. I wanted to breathe him in, to take his essence into my body and lock it away for when we were forced to part.

The door slammed closed. The possessive way his fingers dug into my hips left my heartbeat quickening.

I held out a hand, needing to clear up a few things before I fell back down this slippery slope. "Tell me this: Are you going to give me up because of the Queen?"

His grip on me tightened as he kneaded my skin. "Never again."

"Are you going to try to control me and tell me what to do?"

He smirked, his eyes blazing with desire. "Only when we're naked."

My hand dropped, and his mouth crashed to mine, taking everything I had to give and more with each swipe of his carnal tongue. My arms and legs twined around him like vines, clinging and climbing. My fingers lost themselves in his thick strands of mahogany hair.

My back met the kitchen table, and I didn't bother pointing out that there was a bed only a few steps down the hall. Not when going there would waste precious seconds.

"I'm sorry it took me so long to find my way back to you." His fingertips extended toward the swell of my breast, his thumb sweeping across the scar he'd given me our first night together before finding my pebbled nipples straining beneath my wool dress. "Are you certain you don't wish to be angry with me?"

I unfastened the buttons of his shirt with steady hands. "I'm still angry. But my anger will never outweigh my desire for you."

Uncertainty flickered through his darkening eyes. "Do you promise?"

"I swear."

His right hand came around my throat, smoothing up to cup my jaw. He lifted so we were eye to eye and spoke the words I'd longed to hear. "I love you, angry Aveen."

His left hand fanned out across my hip, catching the material of my skirts. "Are you fond of this dress?"

"Not very."

"Thank feck." He shifted his dagger and sliced away the buttons. The wool slid down my hips and onto the floor. He drew the shoulders of my shift down until it, too, pooled around my boots while I worked to free him from his breeches.

His fingertip traced the scar below my breast from where I'd taken my own life. "I will never forgive myself for the pain I've caused you."

A smile tugged at my lips as I brought his hand to my stomach. "I know one way you could make it up to me."

His fingers delved between my thighs, sinking deep only to withdraw and tease my center, leaving me drenched in my need for him. My body became his to mold and tease, to wind around his skillful hands, rocking, seeking friction, and begging for more.

He anchored his hands around my waist, lifting me onto the table with ease. "Will I take you here?"

I couldn't handle any more teasing and taunting. "Yes. Take me now." My legs locked around his trim hips, dragging his length against where I burned. When he finally sank into me, our ragged exhales mixed together. He captured the aching peak of my breast between his lips, stroking and skimming with his tongue, matching each powerful rock of his hips. The table slid closer to the wall with each pounding thrust until it could go no farther. One hand closed around my throat, gripping tightly enough to leave me gasping for air, while the other slid between our bodies to flick and toy with the bundle of nerves at the apex of my thighs.

My frantic, frenzied hands kneaded his toned shoulders and arms, caught and held his firm backside. Our bodies collided, answering the other's call, heating and setting our blood alight until starlight burst behind my eyes, more vibrant than the most colorful sunset. Pleasure ripped through me, pulsing with each rapid hammer of my heart until Rían collapsed forward, his chest melting against mine and our hearts beating perfectly in time.

I reveled in this moment, knowing that it couldn't last forever but allowing myself to wish for forever anyway.

I toyed with the ends of Rían's hair, wrapping them around my fingers before letting them fall only to find another strand, my body soft as butter left in the sun. "So she's no longer with Tadhg in the castle?"

Rían shook his head where it rested against my chest. "She's with the dog."

Keelynn would be safe with Ruairi. Still, she must've been hurt fiercely to have left Tadhg so close to the wedding. "I must go and see her."

Rían's head lifted, a muscle in his jaw ticking as he stared down at me. I braced myself for the inevitable argument. But then he closed his eyes and let out a weary sigh. "Will you wear a glamour?"

A hopeful smile lifted my lips. "You're letting me go?"

"What other options do I have? I certainly don't want to see you stab yourself ever again."

He was letting me go! I stamped a kiss to his lips to take away some of the sting when I shoved him off me. "I'll have to go outside so I can use my magic."

"Aren't you forgetting something?" His gaze swept down my naked form.

I propped a hand on my hip, struggling to ignore the fire in his hungry gaze. "I'm certain Ruairi wouldn't mind," I teased.

The fire turned to smoke. "I do not find that amusing."

"Lighten up, grumpy Rían. I feel nothing for him besides friendship."

He inhaled deeply, as if desperate to ensure there was no lie. "He'd probably make you happier," he said with a frown.

I kissed his worries away. "Not possible."

We dressed and traversed the field to Hollowshade's portal. Before I could call on my glamour, Rían leaned forward and pressed a kiss to the top of each of my breasts and whispered, "I will miss you, but I will see you soon."

He was so bloody irresistible when he was being ridiculous. With a bit of magic, my chest went nearly flat, although I could still feel the heaviness of my breasts, like they were being squeezed into a too-tight corset and gown.

Rían gripped my hand, and heat swelled.

I pulled my fingers from his. "Do you think I could try on my own?"

He heaved a sigh and looked at me from beneath his lashes. "You are determined to test me today, aren't you?"

"Please?"

He stroked the hollow of my throat, sending desire coursing through me anew. "Close your eyes."

With a little focus, I managed to call on my own magic. Blackness came over me, and I fell into nothing for a split second before Ruairi's house came into view. Rían appeared a split second later. I launched myself at him, squeezing tight. "I did it!"

"You did." His dimples flashed. He dragged a finger along my smiling lips. "How I've missed you, happy Aveen."

Reluctantly, I let him go. Rían unlatched and opened the gate set between two low stone walls.

I stepped through, taking in the cheerful garden and steep, sloping roof. "I still cannot believe Ruairi lives here."

"Because it's so small?"

"It's not small."

Rían snorted. "It's not as big as my castle."

Probably best not to point out that, technically, the castle belonged to his brother. When we reached the doorway, Rían let go of my hand only to draw me into a tight hug. "I will return for you in an hour."

"Can you make it two?" I didn't want to rush Keelynn.

"Fine."

I poked a finger into his dimple. "Look at you. Apologizing and compromising all in the same day. Miracles do happen."

He didn't smile or laugh as I'd hoped. "This heart makes me too soft."

I pressed a kiss to his cheek and whispered, "I don't recall you being too soft an hour ago."

Chuckling, he grazed a final kiss to my lips before pulling away. "I will see you in two hours. And if anyone you don't know shows up," he said, withdrawing his dagger and handing it to me, "kill them."

Knowing better than to protest, I took the dagger. Rían evanesced, but I assumed he hadn't gone far because I could still feel the heat of his gaze as I raised my fist and knocked against the wood.

The door swung open, and Keelynn appeared, her eyes red-rimmed and cheeks flushed and splotchy. When she saw me standing there, her brow furrowed. "May I help you?"

It took a moment to remember the full glamour I wore. "It's me, Keelynn."

Understanding lit in her eyes and her lower lip began to tremble. When she launched forward and collapsed in my arms, I wasn't sure two hours would be enough time to sort this out.

31

KEELYNN

"WE DON'T NEED MEN," AVEEN ANNOUNCED FROM THE SOFA, HER shoulders thrown back and spine stiff, a warrior prepared for battle. All she needed was some armor.

I nodded in agreement. "You're right." What good were they, anyway? Always causing problems. We would be far better off on our own. "We don't need men, we need cake." I wanted to say wine, but alcohol had caused this mess. It felt important that I remained in solidarity with my estranged fiancé while he struggled with his addiction. I'd even gone so far as having water with my dinner each night. Not nearly as satisfying, but at least it didn't give me a headache in the mornings.

Aveen clapped her hands beneath her chin. "Oh, yes. Cake is exactly what we need."

There was only one problem. "Do you know how to bake a cake?"

"Yes." Her mouth tugged down at the corners. "Sort of. I've baked one with Eava before, and I think I remember."

"I want to bake with Eava." I'd always heard the way to a man's heart was through his stomach. For Tadhg, that meant anything and everything with loads and loads of sugar. He'd be so impressed if I brought him a blackberry pie made entirely by me.

It had only been two days since I left and already I missed him so bloody much.

Aveen gave my knees a squeeze. "When you get back to the castle, you will."

Assuming I made it back to the castle. If only I had her optimism.

My sister stood and caught both of my hands, hoisting me to my feet. "Come on. Let's bake our blues away."

Ruairi's kitchen was surprisingly well stocked for a bachelor living on his own. Not that I had much to compare it to considering I'd gone down to the kitchen in our father's estate exactly once, never went in to the townhouse kitchens, and visited Eava only a handful of times.

Aveen opened cupboard after cupboard, dragging out ingredients and setting them on the butcher block counter. Flour, eggs, sugar, butter, salt, milk, something called yeast powder...

The man even had a vial of vanilla that smelled good enough to drink.

Aveen went in search of a mixing bowl, leaving me with the cannisters. "How much of each?"

"Three cups of flour, I remember that much," she threw over her shoulder from where she balanced atop a tiny footstool. "And four eggs."

"Let me do the eggs." I plucked one from the basket and turned it over in my hand before adding it to the bowl.

Aveen's laughter echoed through the kitchen. "You need to crack it first."

Warmth spread down my cheeks and throat. "I knew that." I hadn't. How did one crack an egg? When I ate poached eggs, I typically used a spoon. I banged the hard shell against the wooden counter, and the orange yolk spilled everywhere, covering my hands and the counter in slime.

"Not like that," Aveen chuckled. "Like this." She collected another egg and tapped it against the edge of the bowl. A small crack appeared, and when she broke the thing down the middle, the innards spilled out on top of the dry ingredients she'd already added to the bowl.

When I tried, bits of shell fell in as well. Why was this so bloody difficult?

The other two she cracked with ease. "It takes practice," she assured me.

I didn't want to be helpless if I ended up on my own. I wanted to be self-sufficient, like Aveen. She'd told me all about her adorable cottage on the coast. Perhaps we could live there together if I never made it back to the castle. I grabbed a tea towel from beneath the sink to clean my hands. "Do you think Eava would teach me to cook even if Tadhg and I don't end up together?"

Aveen glanced sidelong at me before handing over a wooden spoon. "Is that the way you're leaning?"

I mixed slowly to keep from slopping milk and eggs all over my dress. "I love Tadhg, but I cannot be with him if he does not have a tight leash on his demons." I understood his struggle. Look at what had happened after Aveen's engagement to Robert had been announced and she'd been cursed. I'd numbed my own pain with drink then as well. But it wasn't just the two of us anymore. We both had to be stronger than we were before.

"That's fair enough."

Was it, though? Tadhg been leaning on alcohol for far longer than me. How much change could I really expect from him? Would he be angry at me for abandoning him in his time of need?

I handed Aveen the bowl of batter. She scraped the edges and bottom with her spoon, releasing the pockets of flour that had been stuck.

With my hands braced against the edge of the counter, I stared out the window into the fading day. If I turned my head just so, I could see my reflection staring back. Darkness spread beneath my eyes like bruises. My hair looked a fright, all tangled and matted. Who did I have to impress? No one. "Love can be such a burden sometimes." There was something to be said for remaining unattached. Spinsters never had to worry about anyone but themselves.

Aveen set the spoon aside and leaned a hip against the counter. "True, but it can be freeing as well." She tapped me on the nose the way she used to when we were younger. "I was so worried about you falling for the infamous Gancanagh, but Tadhg's love shines in his eyes when he looks at you. How he speaks to you and about you when you aren't in the room. You should've seen how broken he was while you were cursed. And look at all that your love has done for Tadhg, saving him from his curses too."

Ah, yes. Tadhg's curses. The reason we were in this mess in the first place. He was never the villain I'd always believed, simply a man who had made mistakes and paid dearly for them. If Robert had been a witch, I probably would've ended up with a curse or two as well.

Even though I'd forgiven Tadhg for what had happened with Anwen, bitterness still festered in my heart. Who was to say he hadn't given in because part of him had wanted her too? How could I hope to keep a man like Tadhg satisfied when I lost my youth and he remained forever handsome? Would he still want me when my face became wrinkly and my skin sagged off my arthritic bones?

Only time would tell, and I wasn't sure I could stand to wait.

Aveen smoothed a hand down my arm. "Keelynn? Are you all right?"

A false smile was all I had to offer. "I'm tired. I haven't been sleeping well."

Her eyes softened. "It's difficult going back to an empty bed when you're used to having someone beside you."

I didn't want to talk about men anymore. Tonight was for the two of us. "How about we bake this cake and eat every last bite?"

With a grin, Aveen set a silver cake tin next to the batter and said, "That sounds like a good plan."

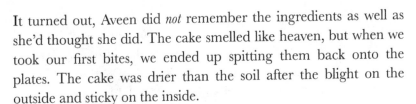

It turned out, Aveen did *not* remember the ingredients as well as she'd thought she did. The cake smelled like heaven, but when we took our first bites, we ended up spitting them back onto the plates. The cake was drier than the soil after the blight on the outside and sticky on the inside.

Groaning, Aveen frowned down at what remained of the gigantic slice she'd cut for herself. "I'm so hungry, I'm considering a second bite."

"You couldn't pay me to eat another one. There's some fruit in the basket." Personally, I'd had enough fruit to last me the year. All Ruairi had in this place were fruit and veg and ingredients to bake terrible cakes.

"I don't want fruit. I want something sweet—or savory." She fell back onto the cushion. "I miss Eava." The tall grandfather clock let out a low, thrumming *gong*, marking the hour. Another day nearly gone. "I'm surprised Rían hasn't shown up yet."

As if he'd heard her all the way in the castle, the front door flew open, and Rían waltzed right through, his black attire making him look like a shadow. My smitten sister sighed like a swooning youth. If I wasn't so happy for her, I would've rolled my eyes.

Rían's nose lifted in the air. "Something smells good."

"I baked a cake," Aveen said with a glint in her eye, nudging her plate toward him.

Rían picked up her fork and sliced a bit off the end. We both watched with tight lips as he took a bite...and choked. "Do you love it?" Aveen asked, batting her lashes.

"It's...um..." By some miracle, he managed to swallow the dry chunk.

I couldn't take it anymore. The poor man looked positively green. Laughter bubbled in my throat. Aveen joined me, falling forward and clutching her stomach as tears spilled through her lashes. "It's vile," she managed between gasps.

Rían's scowl only made me laugh harder. "And you didn't think to tell me that *before* I ate some?"

"I'm sorry."

"No you're not." He tugged one of her curls with a gruff chuckle. "I was going to give you some of the leftover tart I hid from my brother, but after that little trick, you get nothing."

Despite my melancholy, my smile remained. "Don't punish me for my sister's mistakes."

A pie plate appeared in his hands, and my mouth immediately began to water. Aveen went to swipe for it, but Rían yanked it back and handed it to me instead. After all he'd done, I didn't want to like him, but he wasn't nearly as bad when he was being sweet to Aveen and feeding me.

I thanked him and retrieved our forks from the abandoned cake plates, handing one to Aveen. We both dug into the gooey center and moaned when sweet cinnamon and apples hit our tongues. So bloody good.

Ruairi appeared in the doorway, his golden gaze landing on the abandoned cake. "Oh, cake."

None of us said a word.

"Happy now?" Rían asked from beside the fireplace.

Aveen rubbed her stomach and nodded. "Immensely."

"Shall we head back to the castle?"

More than anything, I wished to be going with them. To climb those long, winding stairs and huddle beneath the covers next to Tadhg's warm body. Fill my lungs with the sweet, almondy scent of his magic.

Not only did I miss Tadhg, I missed Brogan as well. The way he would hold my finger as he angrily slurped at his bottle. The thick sweep of his lashes against his cheek when he finally succumbed to sleep.

Aveen shot me a sidelong glance. "I'd like to stay with my sister tonight. For old time's sake."

Rían's mouth flattened. Hell, his entire expression did. "You're not staying here on your own."

"Ruairi will be here. It is his house, after all."

I nodded my agreement. I liked Ruairi and appreciated his calming presence. And he wasn't hard on the eyes either. We'd technically been living together for two days, but I barely saw him. I wasn't sure if that was on purpose or if he was usually this absent. Seemed a shame to have such a fine house so empty.

"Why does he get to stay and not me?" Rían grumbled.

"Because he is a gentleman and won't try to invade my bed."

Ruairi pressed back into his worn wingback, his fingers drumming against the scrolled arms. "Hear that, Little Rían? I am a gentleman."

Rían snorted. "If you're a gentleman, then I'm a feckin' swan."

Aveen patted Rían's waistcoat. "Go home. I'll be back first thing in the morning."

His teeth ground together, but he got up and started for the door with only a few mild curses.

"I love you," Aveen shouted with her hands cupping her mouth to project her voice.

"Love you too," Rían grumbled back before slipping out the door.

Ruairi took one glance at my sister and me and pushed to his feet. "Right, so. I'll be heading upstairs. Help yerself to whatever's in the kitchen, but maybe leave the baking to Eava." He smoothed his hands down his leather-clad thighs, straightening his breeches.

"Oh no you don't." Aveen clicked her fingers and pointed back to his chair. "You're going to sit right there and tell us news from the castle. How is Tadhg?"

The pooka dropped back down with a huff. "Managing." Ruairi's eyes darted to me. "Missing ye."

"And the drink?" Aveen asked.

"Not a drop as far as I can tell. Hasn't had the time. With Millie gone as well, he's been the only one around to take care of the little lad."

I let out a breath I didn't realize I'd been holding. Tadhg was doing better, thank heavens for that. Would he continue to improve, or was this only a temporary fix, like a tiny bandage over a gaping, festering wound?

"Thank you, Ruairi."

"Yer welcome, human."

Aveen laced her fingers with mine, once again tugging me to my feet. "Come, sister. It's time for bed." To Ruairi, she said, "Thank you for letting us stay here."

The pooka's expression softened into something almost whimsical as he watched Aveen direct me toward the staircase. "It's not a bother at all. Kinda nice having a bit of life about the place. Sleep well."

She followed me up and into the room I'd been staying in since arriving. The crackling fire cast the space in a warm, orange glow. "Are you staying here as well?" I assumed so since she'd started stripping down to her shift.

She flipped the sheets down. "If that's all right."

It was more than all right. The nights were too bloody long and lonely. If I wasn't so determined to help Tadhg face his demons, I would've caved that first night and begged Ruairi to bring me back to the castle.

I slid in next to Aveen, and she patted her chest, whispering, "Head here," as I knew she would. I couldn't help my tearful smile as I eased my head down and snuggled into her soft, comforting embrace. Her heart beat a steady rhythm beneath my ear.

"I've missed you." Those months I had believed her dead had been the worst of my life. Being married to Rían hadn't helped either.

She squeezed me tighter. "I've missed you too, sister."

"Can you promise me one thing? That no matter what

happens, we will still make time for this." I could get through anything as long as Aveen remained by my side.

"I promise," she murmured.

My lashes drifted closed, and I let the dreams flirting at the edge of my mind consume me.

Dreams of a green dress, snow-white flowers, and an emerald-eyed prince waiting for me at the end of a long, petal-strewn aisle.

32

TADHG

You don't need a drink.

You want a drink.

There's a difference.

At least, that was what I'd been telling myself every single time I felt like shifting a feckin' bottle or flask. Even when Keelynn was cursed, life hadn't felt this dire. Probably because she hadn't chosen to be apart from me. Fate and Fiadh had taken her away back then. Now, my own weakness had driven her from my side.

My fingers caught on tangled strands when I dragged my trembling hands through my hair. I usually didn't mind stains on my clothes, but this morning they smelled particularly foul, courtesy of my son. I stripped down and shifted a bath in front of the empty fireplace. The tense muscles in my body slowly uncoiled as the steaming water closed over me.

If Keelynn were here, I'd have invited her to join me.

I sank until the water lapped at my earlobes, then slid deeper still, holding my breath as I slipped beneath the surface. Surrounded by blessed silence, I thought of all I'd been given: forgiveness, freedom, love…and all I had lost. My lungs began to burn for air, and yet I felt no need to rise up and claim a breath.

Since I couldn't drown myself with drink, maybe I'd drown myself in this tub instead.

Except I couldn't risk taking too long coming back and leaving Brogan here on his own.

Reluctantly, I pushed to the surface. Droplets cascaded into my eyes, and I shoved my sopping hair back from my forehead. Even my bones felt tired, as if exhaustion had burrowed into my marrow. My head fell back against the smooth porcelain. When my eyes closed, I could do nothing to stop them.

How could I have hoped to hold a woman like Keelynn when I couldn't hold my own shite together? Why would any woman want to tie herself to a man without control over his own body? Who had failed to keep his people safe time and again? I might not have been burdened by my own curses any longer, but my land continued to suffer. And here I was lying around, doing nothing about the blight that surrounded the castle on all sides.

I'd tried everything I could think of, but that didn't mean I should give up.

And ever since Anwen had handed over my son, that was what I'd done.

Those pooka who had questioned my priorities had been right. Not about my relationship with Keelynn but about my own shortcomings. I should've dedicated myself to stopping this blight instead of spiraling into darkness.

I rose from the water and shifted a towel. Once I dressed, I popped into Brogan's room to ensure he still slumbered. He looked so peaceful, angelic even, lying on the small mattress inside the white cot. So tiny and helpless. So innocent.

The thought of my son growing up in such a dangerous world left my soul aching. My own childhood, while riddled with plenty of trouble, had been a happy one. I'd had a mother who loved me. My father had been a bit of a bastard, but he'd been there for me when I needed him. I'd had Ruairi and Rían... A smile found my lips. The mischief the three of us used to get into.

If I didn't find some way to stop this blight, Brogan may never know that kind of peace.

I wanted to make Tearmann the sanctuary it once was, not only for my son but for all the Danú—and the humans they loved. But I couldn't do any of that from inside the safety of these walls.

It was time—beyond time—to fix this. To stop at nothing until every section of blackened earth had been banished back to the Forest from whence it came.

I evanesced down to the courtyard and crossed beneath the warded gates. I couldn't go far in case my son needed me, but I had to try *something*. For what felt like the hundredth time, I knelt next to the blackened ground and pressed both hands to the dry earth. My palms began to warm as I called on my magic.

The more magic I sent, the darker the soil became, as if the shadows living inside me were bleeding into the ground. My arms began to tremble, and yet I did not falter.

Eava's soft voice drifted to my ears. "Yer giving too much."

Clearly not. The blight hadn't moved back so much as a feckin' inch. It had burrowed beneath me, outlining my legs and feet where I knelt. The more magic I sent, the farther it spread.

Let anyone who passed see that I was willing to give it all to save this land. Every last drop of magic in my veins. And when I died, I would return only to do the same.

A hand landed on my shoulder. "Ye've too much darkness in ye," Eava said. "We all do."

I tore my hands from the earth, my body shuddering and vision swimming. "Then how do we stop it?"

Her crinkled lips pursed as she gazed out over our dying land. "Not sure we can."

Brogan's tiny fists battered the air like he wanted to fight the entire world. I understood the sentiment. After spending all afternoon holed up inside my bedroom with the little lad, I *had* to escape.

Since I couldn't leave the castle, the family room had to do. I'd nearly turned around when I found Rían draped across his chair by the fireplace, staring down at a book. But even my infernal brother's company seemed preferable to my own.

Rían flipped the page with such force, I was shocked he didn't tear the thing clean out. "Does that child ever shut up?"

"No. Just like his Uncle Rían."

My brother rolled his eyes, casting a wary glance in my direction. "What does it want?"

First off, referring to my *son* as "it" made me want to strangle him. But since I didn't want to subject my boy to violence at such an early age, I settled for pulling on my hair until my scalp ached. How the hell did you get a child to stop crying? I'd changed his nappy, given him his bottle. He'd napped and played around with the rattle Eava had left for him this afternoon before disappearing again.

What else was there? "Don't you think that if I knew I would've given it to him by now?"

All the wailing muted Rían's response. "I'm not entirely sure. You've always been a bit of a masochist." He checked his pocket watch, which looked suspiciously like the pocket watch I'd stolen from Robert Trench, before sighing and pushing to his feet. Instead of leaving the room, he folded his arms over his chest and glowered down at my son where he flapped his arms and kicked his legs like a chicken trying to fly. That look had cowed more than a few full-grown men, and yet Brogan didn't seem to care.

"Maybe it doesn't like you," Rían said matter-of-factly.

"*He*, not *it*. And I'm his father. Of course he likes me."

"You sure about that? I didn't like our father."

Maybe he had a point. This baby hadn't known me from the beginning—he'd never gotten the chance considering Anwen had kept his existence a secret. Not that I could blame her. Still, if I'd known the child was mine, maybe we could've bonded earlier instead of me trying to play catch-up with an angry little devil.

"Here." I thrust Brogan into my brother's unsuspecting arms.

Rían yipped like a dog whose tail had been stomped on, the child bobbling against his chest. "What're you—I'm not going to —*dammit*, Tadhg. Take it back." He swung my son toward me.

"Shhhhhh." I pressed my fingers to my lips. For the first time in *hours*, Brogan had stopped crying. He blinked up at my brother through wide, watery eyes, his lips wobbling as if he were about to screech at any moment. But he didn't make a peep.

"It stopped," Rían mouthed, still holding the boy awkwardly out from his own chest.

I took one backward step toward the settee, and then another. Rían's expression turned stormy as he watched my retreat. "All I need is one hour," I whispered. One blessed hour to close my eyes and switch off my brain without having to listen for Brogan's cries. "Please. I haven't slept since she…" Tears blurred my vision, choking me. "Since she left. I just need an hour." After that, maybe I'd be able to think of a solution to this blight.

Although Rían groaned, he didn't attempt to give the child back. Instead, he scanned the room, his gaze landing on the rug. With his elbow, he knocked one of the throw pillows onto the ground.

"I'll just put it down," he murmured to himself. The moment the boy's head met the pillow, he let loose. Rían cursed and grabbed him back off the pillow. The boy instantly quieted.

"Come on, Rían. It'll be easy." I sank onto the sofa, my eyes already drifting closed. "Just treat him like your favorite waist-coat," I muttered, letting sleep steer me toward darkness. I thought my brother said something about too many wrinkles, but I was too far gone to respond.

Sun peeked from between the curtains. Birdsong and silence greeted me as I pushed myself upright. There was no sign of Rían or Brogan. I felt like a new man as I stretched my stiff arms over my head. What time was it? I shifted my pocket watch back from my thieving brother. Half five? Had I really slept for eight hours?

I kicked off the blanket someone had draped over me, my body stiff as a feckin' board as I stumbled toward the door, eventually finding my brother in the study, his back to the doorway as he selected a book from one of the shelves. No sign of Brogan anywhere. Had he forgotten he was to mind the child? Had he pawned my son off on someone else? What if something happened to him?

"Rían—"

"Quiet!" he hissed, twisting to glower at me.

I scrubbed my eyes once. Twice. Three times.

No matter how many times I blinked, the sight in front of me remained unchanged.

My brother had fashioned some sort of sling across his chest and was wearing my son while Brogan snoozed away, his face scrunched up where it pressed against Rían's shirt.

"What are you doing?" I whispered.

He glanced down at Brogan as if he'd forgotten the child was literally attached to him. "You did say to treat him like my favorite waistcoat."

"I didn't mean for you to wear the boy."

Shrugging, he carried the book over to the desk. "Hagan likes it."

"Who the hell is Hagan?"

"Do you know what Brogan means in the ancient tongue? Badger. Do you really want your son to be named Badger for the rest of his life? It makes him sound like a gowl."

Of course I didn't want my child to be named after one of the most terrible of all woodland creatures. Still, "You cannot rename my child without consulting me—his *father*."

"He likes it. Don't you, Hagan?"

By heavens, the boy smiled a sleepy smile. *At my brother.*

"What did you need?" Rían asked, as if I were interrupting some important business meeting.

"I...ah...nothing. Thank you. For today."

He shrugged and flipped open the book in his hands. "You owe me."

He probably expected me to jump down his throat and remind him who was in charge in this land. Instead, I did something that surprised us both. I agreed.

"I do," I said. "And for more than this. For everything you've done since...well, since forever, really." Tearmann would've fallen long before this if it weren't for my brother.

"Yes, yes. I am better than you. I am wonderful. I am great."

The urge to kill him returned with a vengeance, putting the world to rights once again.

Now all I needed was my soulmate by my side and for this damned blight to retreat, and my life would be complete.

33

KEELYNN

BEING ALONE THIS WEEK HAD TAUGHT ME A LOT.

Mostly that I hated being alone.

It wasn't that I minded my own company. I was used to it after having been married to "Edward". Rather, if I were given the option, I'd spend my time with those I loved. And despite all his faults and failings, I still loved Tadhg. At this stage, I even missed Rían's snarky comments and irritating smirk.

Aveen had promised to visit again this afternoon, to keep me occupied so I didn't dwell on the fact that my third wedding to Tadhg was tomorrow. Assuming he got himself together in time for the ceremony.

When I went downstairs, I found not my sister but the man I'd been pining over, waiting in the living room. Had he always been this handsome?

The spark had returned to his mischievous eyes. His hungry gaze took me in like a man too long in the desert stumbling upon an oasis.

His dark green breeches slipped down his trim hips when he stood and offered a tentative smile. "Hello."

I pressed my hands to my fluttering stomach. Even his voice sounded deeper, richer. "Hello."

"How are you?"

Miserable and lonely. "I am well. And you?"

His shoulders fell. "I miss you."

I missed him too, dreadfully, but this plan wouldn't work if he knew how close I was to my breaking point. "Would you like some tea?" I asked instead, turning toward the kitchen.

"No, thank you. I can't stay long. We've asked some guests to the castle to help us try to find a way to stop the blight."

That was brilliant news. Why did it make me feel so sad? "It sounds like you're quite busy."

"Not busy enough to keep me from missing you." The sigh that left him sounded of longing and regret. "I'm so sorry, Keelynn."

I knew he was sorry. His remorse had never been the problem. The way he dealt with it, drowning himself or avoiding the issues altogether, that was the real problem.

"I think..." His Adam's apple bobbed above the silver scars encircling his throat. "No, I *know* I took advantage of you, cast all my problems on your shoulders so I didn't have to deal with them. You were right in forcing me to face the consequences of my actions on my own.

"I've been so selfish for so long that having someone else to take care of—someone who cannot care for himself—has been a revelation. One I cannot possibly deal with while drunk or hungover." His gaze flicked up to mine, overflowing with emotion. "I haven't had a drink since you left me."

Although I'd been asking Ruairi for updates, to hear Tadhg hadn't had a drop of alcohol from the man himself gave me some hope that we would both come out of this stronger than before.

"I didn't leave you, Tadhg." I may not have been at the castle physically, but he held my heart no matter where I went. I felt like only half a person when he wasn't near. Even if we weren't together, I would always be his. "I need you to know that I will never mind you leaning on me. When your burdens feel heavy, that's what I'm here for. But to cast them all on my shoulders and treat me like a pack mule cannot happen again."

"I know. I want to do the same for you, to be strong enough to not only deal with my own problems but to help with yours as well."

He'd spent the beginning of our relationship doing just that, saving me at every turn, ensuring my safety, bringing me right where I needed to be.

A good week finding himself didn't mean he would be cured of this need to drown his sorrows. After so many years giving in, denying himself would be a constant struggle. One I didn't want him to suffer through alone.

He stepped forward and reached for my hand slowly, as if waiting for me to pull away. I couldn't if I'd tried. His warm fingers clasped mine, tangling us together. My love for him sparked like tinder in my heart.

"Come back to me," he whispered.

Such simple words, and yet the request was anything but. I wanted to say yes, to leap into his arms and return to our life together in that castle, to my family borne not of blood but through fate. But before that could happen, I needed to make sure this wasn't a temporary fix. That Tadhg truly had turned a corner because I couldn't bear to see him slip into darkness over and over again.

His son deserved better and so did I.

Somehow I found the strength to pull away. I clasped my hands behind my back to keep myself from reaching for him once more. "Not yet."

His eyes widened. "But the wedding is tomorrow."

"I know."

Tadhg's breath fanned against my cheek when his soft lips grazed my temple. "I will wait for you," he said. "For a day, for a month, for a year. Whenever you're ready to come back to me, I will be there."

I'm ready now. Take me with you.

My boots remained planted on the worn floorboards as Tadhg drifted toward the door, his shoulders slumped and head bowed.

I almost stepped forward, almost called him back. Except I needed to be certain this change ran deeper than the surface. That Tadhg could handle the disappointment without shirking his responsibilities to his son and his people. I would be at the wedding tomorrow…I only prayed Tadhg would be sober when I arrived.

I fisted the ivory lace of my skirts. If Tadhg could have seen this wretched gown, he'd probably change his mind about marrying me again.

The hinges on the front door whined when it swung open. Aveen stepped in from the sunny day, but when her gaze landed on me, her smile vanished. "Keelynn, you look…"

"Hideous. I know, it's awful." I stood from the sofa and clasped my trembling hands in front of me.

So much for salvaging this monstrosity. I wasn't even sure why I'd asked her to bring it from the castle. No one should ever wear this many ruffles. No one.

"How is Tadhg?" I asked, desperate for good news.

Aveen closed the gap between us to fluff the ruffles over my shoulders. "He's quiet tonight."

"And the drink?"

She circled me slowly, her brow furrowing as she studied the tiered skirt that sat wider than any hoop I'd ever seen. "The lads are drinking away, but as of the moment I left, Tadhg hadn't joined them."

Air puffed from beneath my skirt when I collapsed back onto the sofa, relief spilling through my chest. "Any luck with the blight?"

Aveen's curls bounced when she shook her head. "They've

tried everything, but death continues to spread. Tadhg and Rían relocated another ten homes."

Why couldn't the bloody Queen keep to herself in the Black Forest instead of being so dead set on hurting her own people? The humans I could understand. But as far as I knew, Aveen and I were the only humans in Tearmann—and my sister had magic now, so technically she was more Danú than not.

Aveen considered the sofa, but with my skirts taking up the entirety of the empty cushions, she sat on Ruairi's striped wing-back instead. "Enough about that bloody blight. What are you going to do tomorrow?"

"I still want to marry him. Is that mad?" I searched her face for signs of disappointment, but her neutral expression gave nothing away.

"Who am I to say? Yesterday, Rían murdered four people." Her shoulders lifted and fell in a casual shrug, as if we were discussing the flowers in her garden. "Marry him, Keelynn. And if it doesn't work out, we can ask Rían to kill him too."

True. There were some perks to marrying a true immortal, I supposed.

The front door swung open, startling us both. Rían stepped inside and ran a hand through his hair. "Who am I murdering?" he asked.

I swore Aveen's eyes lit up as she took in his impeccable black breeches paired with a black waistcoat and black shirt. "Your brother if he hurts my sister," she said.

"Gladly." He smirked down at her, but when his gaze swung toward me, his eyes narrowed. He gestured to my dress. "Why are you wearing that atrocious thing?"

I ran my hand down the undulating waves of fabric over my legs, but they refused to stay down. "This 'atrocious thing' is supposed to be my wedding gown."

"It's even worse than I remember." He clicked his fingers. "Stand up and let me have a look at you."

I pushed to my feet and twirled.

"Look how it bags at the waist." He tugged at the fabric above my hips. "And it's far too tight across your chest. And those sleeves. With your silhouette, you really should be wearing something off the shoulder."

I couldn't believe I was about to say this aloud, but desperate times called for desperate measures. "Do you think you could help me?"

Part of me expected him to laugh in my face or make some snide comment about coming to him for assistance. But there was no laughing, only another sweep of his cerulean gaze from my poofy sleeves to my flouncy skirts.

"I'm good at a lot of things—just ask your sister," Rían threw over his shoulder with a wink at Aveen. A deep blush crept up her throat, and she hid her smile behind her hand. "But sewing is not one of them. Fortunately, I know someone who should be able to help."

34

TADHG

"There must be something wrong with yer eyes, lad." Ruairi beat his fist against his bare chest hard enough to leave a red mark on his bronzed skin. "That's all muscle."

Rían snorted, his fingers deftly fastening the buttons of his crisp white shirt. "Keep telling yourself that, dog. Maybe go easy on the cake today. Otherwise, you won't be able to fit into your breeches."

"The only reason my breeches wouldn't fit is if my cock gets any bigger."

"Must be quite impressive since you have so many women pining after your prick," Rían drawled. "They're practically lining up at the gates for a ride."

While I appreciated the distraction their squabbling provided, the last thing I wanted was for them to whip out their cocks and shift a measuring stick. I'd seen enough of both men without their breeches to last a lifetime. There was only one person I wanted to see naked today and it wasn't either one of these eejits. "If the two of you could save your pissing contests for tomorrow, that would be brilliant."

They both turned on me.

Rían's vicious smile fell into a frown as he glanced down at my attire. "Where is your cravat?"

He knew I hated those feckin' things. "In the fire where it belongs."

"You gowl. That cost me a small fortune." He huffed a breath. "You know what? Never mind. I knew you'd ruin this, so I bought you two." With a flick of his wrist, another cravat appeared in his hand. He stepped forward to tie the emerald-green noose around my neck in some fancy knot that made it impossible to swallow.

"It's too tight."

"It's not."

"It is." I tried to slip a finger between the material and my poor throat but couldn't. "See? It's choking me."

Rían's hand shot out, gripping my gullet until my face started to burn. "*This* is choking you." He let me go with a shake of his head and no sympathy whatsoever as I gagged and gasped. "This," he said, flattening the end of the cravat, "is fashion. And if you even think of throwing this one in the fire, you're going in with it."

As if he'd be willing to ruin the custom suit he'd hand-picked over a cravat.

Ruairi and Rían wore black, while I wore a deep, forest green to match the emeralds in my crown. I still hadn't gotten used to wearing the thing, but since this wedding would be my last, I figured I may as well go all out.

With another flick of Rían's wrist, my coat appeared over his forearm. "Put this on."

Eava waltzed in without so much as a knock. When she saw us, her hands flew to her mouth, and she let out a choked gasp. Tears glittered in her black eyes. "Look at my boys. Aren't ye all so handsome?" A basket appeared in her hand, smelling suspiciously like chocolate. The angel always knew what I needed even before I did.

I gestured toward the basket. "Is that for me?"

She nodded. "A little something to get ye through. Yer all wastin' away to nothing."

Ruairi shoved Rían so hard, he fell into the bedpost. "Ha. See. I told ye I'm fitter than ever."

Although Rían glared, he righted himself without any of his usual murderous threats. "Please." He smoothed the longer hair at the top of his head back into place. "She's only trying to fatten you up so she can keep you all to herself."

Chuckling, Eava withdrew a chocolate biscuit from the basket and held it out to my brother. "Yer the one who needs fattening. Yer practically skin and bones."

With a roll of his eyes, Rían took a biscuit and bit into it. I grabbed three, and when those were finished, I shifted a fourth. Eava added one more to my pocket with a wink before leaving us to finish.

Ruairi sank onto the end of the bed to pull on his boots. "What time are the ladies arriving?"

"Two." Assuming Keelynn decided to come. Part of me felt silly for going through all this trouble for an event that may not happen, but I'd promised to wait for her and I intended to keep that promise. I'd wear this suit every single day until Keelynn came back to me. Although I might conveniently misplace the cravat.

When a screech erupted from the next room, I darted between Ruairi and Rían and out into the hall to peek around the corner into Hagan's chambers. My son scowled at the door from his cot. The moment I stepped inside, his little mouth lifted into the brightest smile.

And just like that, all those sleepless nights were forgotten.

Hagan wasn't concerned with my bleak past or blackened soul. All that mattered to him was the fact that I was there when he needed me.

"There's my nephew." Rían shouldered past me, and damn it all if Hagan's smile didn't grow. He wasn't supposed to like his uncle more than he liked me. A towel appeared over my brother's shoulder as he scooped up my son, pressed a kiss to the dark curls matted on his head, and then turned and handed him to me with a scrunched nose. "He smells like shite."

Maybe we needed to call a physician. My son defecated more than any other living thing I had ever met. A towel appeared on my shoulder as well, presumably to catch the spittle the little lad liked to spew every so often. I brought him over to the changing table, but before I could remove his nappy, my brother caught my arm.

"What do you think you're doing?" he snapped.

"Changing his nappy." It wasn't as if Rían had offered to do it.

"You can't change him in this." He tugged the bottom of my coat. "I don't have spares."

"I think I can change my son without getting shite on my clothes."

"I have seen that child shoot a stream of piss across a feckin' room. The coat and waistcoat come off."

Knowing it would be less of a headache to give in, I slipped out of both. Rían also made me remove the cravat because the spare had reduced to ash. "Happy?"

He pursed his lips at my shirt.

"The shirt stays on," I insisted before he could tell me to take it off too. All those buttons were more hassle than they were worth.

Rían backed all the way to the window with my new clothes and gestured toward my cooing son. "Proceed."

Did he really have to stay here to supervise? Talk about obnoxious. I unpinned the corners of Hagan's nappy, which had *used* to be white. Definitely needed to call a doctor. Shite should *not* be this color. As soon as the cool air hit his bare skin, a yellow stream shot toward me. I threw the towel over him, but it was too late. Wetness seeped into my shirt.

Rían bent over, clutching his stomach, his harsh cackle echoing off the low ceiling.

My quiet curse only made him laugh harder. "Has anyone ever told you that you laugh like an old hag?"

Hagan cooed and kicked, his tiny pink tongue darting around his lips. "I've a feeling you'll be making a fool of me every chance you get," I whispered, patting his unruly curls while I waited for him to finish his business.

Once I had my son in a clean nappy and vest, Rían traded me for a fresh shirt and the rest of my clothes. This time, when I dressed, my hands trembled, like they knew the first time had only been for practice.

Time to see if I was to spend the night alone or with my new wife.

A single cello played a haunting tune for a great room full of empty white chairs.

Actually, that wasn't fair of me to say. The room wasn't entirely empty. Eava and Oscar, Millie and her husband Martin, Ruairi, and my brother were here. As was my mate Lorcan. Unfortunately, the Queen had denied his request to cross the Forest with his wife, due any day now with their first child, so he was on his own.

At least there weren't many around to witness my utter humiliation as I stood on the dais beneath the arbor Oscar had built, waiting for my bride.

Aveen had been gone since dawn, and at first, I'd taken her absence as a good sign, assuming she was busy helping Keelynn get ready for the wedding. Now I wondered if maybe she'd spent the entire morning trying to convince Keelynn to come and been unsuccessful.

I could have evanesced to Ruairi's house to put myself out of this misery, but on the off-chance Keelynn did show up, she'd be devastated to find no one waiting for her. So that's what I did instead. I waited like I'd promised, in front of my family and the few select friends willing to put their own prejudice aside and support my choice to marry the woman I loved.

"You're sweating," Rían whispered from beneath the arbor, green and gold ribbons dangling from his pocket. "Worried she won't show?"

Of course I was feckin' worried. "Not in the least."

His smile grew. *Dammit.* Someday I would remember not to lie to him.

Movement from the end of the aisle drew my gaze toward a beautiful woman with golden curls spilling across the shoulders of her blue gown. Although Aveen didn't look like herself because of the glamour, the confident way she moved revealed her for who she was. The fact that she wore a smile settled some of my unease. She wouldn't be smiling if Keelynn had decided not to come.

My brother remained transfixed as he watched his disguised soulmate walk down the aisle, never blinking. When this celebration ended and we found a way to end this blight, I would make it my mission to help him defeat his mother so that neither of them had to hide. After all he'd done for me over the centuries, it was the least I could do.

I avoided looking at the empty chairs next to Eava and behind Lorcan. My people disapproving of my marriage didn't bother me nearly as much as the fact that my friends, those who knew me the best, didn't believe I deserved to be happy as well.

Those I'd known my entire life had shown their true colors. The next time they came to me for help, I'd tell them exactly where they could go.

The music changed, slowing in tempo. The few who were present rose to their feet, turning toward the hall's entrance, where the most breathtaking woman stood, not wearing ivory lace as expected but swathed in emerald-green silk.

A silent claim. A promise.

My heart kicked up at the sight of her. I'd said it before and I would say it until my dying day: I would make her proud to be my wife and I would not let her down again. Keelynn Bannon had saved me in more ways than I could count. From my curses. From myself.

I wanted to be worthy of her forgiveness. Of her love.

I blinked back my tears, not wanting to miss a second as Keelynn started down the aisle, a smile on her lips and her gray eyes pinned to mine. Her long, soft waves swayed with each step, held back at her temples by emerald clasps. The emerald necklace at her throat looked vaguely familiar.

"Is she wearing—?"

"Your mother's necklace?" Rían murmured. "I figured you wouldn't mind."

Mind? The fact that he'd gone through the trouble of digging the thing out of the warded treasury made my heart swell. Who would've expected my brother to be such a sympathetic fool?

When Keelynn finally reached me, I couldn't catch my breath. The snow-white blooms in her bouquet of hydrangeas trembled as she handed the flowers to her sister before placing her hands in mine.

Rían performed the ceremony—our third marriage to one another.

Time and again, this woman had chosen me, despite all my faults and failures. Once again, she had forgiven me my transgressions. For however long we had, we would remain at each other's sides.

"Prince Tadhg O'Clereigh of Tearmann, do you take this woman to be your wife, to hold and to cherish in this life and beyond?"

"I do."

Rían withdrew his dagger; the shiny blade reflected Keelynn's wide eyes.

"The prince has requested a blood oath," my brother explained. "If there are any objections, make them known now."

Keelynn's brow furrowed as she searched my face for answers.

"Our bond will remain for eternity," I whispered to her. "Nothing, not even death, will separate us. But if you'd prefer a simple handfasting instead—" Not many Danú ceremonies included a blood oath nowadays, for obvious reasons.

She didn't even blink as she held out her hand. Rían cut our palms and bound our hands with ribbons of gold and green. Blood dripped between us, magic from my palm finding its way to hers, healing both our wounds.

When the ceremony finished, everyone present laughed and cheered. Even Hagan let out a high-pitched shriek from where he bounced on Eava's hip.

"Is it everything you'd dreamed it would be?" I asked my bride.

Keelynn shook her head. "It's so much better because it's with you." Her gaze flicked toward our guests. "And because it's with them."

She was right. Who needed the support of a nation when you could have the support of the best people you knew?

35

RÍAN

HAGAN SMILED A DREAMY SMILE THAT USUALLY PRECEDED A terrible smell. Hopefully his shite remained inside the nappy instead of on my waistcoat like last time. Good thing I'd bought two for myself. When I looked up from the chair, I found Aveen staring at me, slack-jawed and wide-eyed, as if I'd just decapitated her best friend.

With such a small crowd present, she'd been able to drop her glamour. The sight of that silk gown hugging her curves made my heart slam against my ribs.

I shifted on the seat, my blood warming beneath the weight of her gaze. "What's wrong? Is my hair sticking up?" I'd told Eava the top was too long to lay right—not that the old bag of bones had listened. I smoothed a hand over my head just in case.

Aveen blinked and blinked, her brow slowly furrowing as her gaze dropped to the dozy bundle in my arms. "I distinctly remember you saying that you hated children."

"I do." Children were smelly and loud and asked the most irritating questions. The younger they were, the more obnoxious I found them. Unruly little waifs, always covered in something sticky and brown.

Aveen pointed at Hagan snuggled in my arms. "That's a child."

"This is not a child. This is my nephew." And as far as babies went, he was probably the most perfect one to ever exist. As if he knew I was speaking about him, he grinned, drool clinging precariously to his chubby chin. Definitely a shite coming.

The wooden chair to my right creaked as Aveen sank next to me and brushed a finger over Hagan's dimpled fist. He smiled at her too, which made me like him even more. My nephew had impeccable taste.

"And if you had a son?" Aveen asked, glancing up at me from beneath the curtain of her lashes.

If I had a child, presumably it would be with her. And since I loved her and loved myself, surely that meant I would care for any offspring we had as well. "I suppose I wouldn't throw myself from a cliff."

Aveen's mouth fell open. "You want children."

"I never said that." Having one and not loathing it was a far cry from wanting one. And there was the tiny issue of my mother to consider.

"May as well have."

"Now who's being ridiculous?"

She began to idly rub at her full bottom lip as her gaze traveled down the length of my body and back up again to tangle with mine. The woman didn't even need to touch me to ignite desire deep in my belly. All it took was one hungry look for me to leap to my feet and practically throw my nephew at my brother. Hagan bobbled and his eye popped open to glare at his father.

He may have started crying, but I didn't stick around to find out. I yanked Aveen up off the chair and straight out into the empty hallway and was about to evanesce when she launched herself at me, pinning me to the tapestry.

Her mouth found mine, frantic and starving, as we stumbled for the closest room—the closet where Tadhg used to keep his bodies. We bumped coffins as we continued devouring one another. She clawed at the hem of my shirt, tugging it free of my breeches and tearing at my belt like the world was ending.

Her teeth sank into my lip, and I tasted blood.

"Hungry, little viper?" I asked with a smile, licking the blood from my lips.

"Starving," she murmured. She nipped at my jaw and shoved my breeches down my thighs. Her tongue slid along her lips as she stared down at my aching length. The fire burning in her gaze matched the flames coursing through my veins as her fist came around my base.

I had just moved to free her breast when she dropped to her knees.

My stomach clenched and cock twitched. "Stand up," I rasped.

She shook her head, her eyes straying once more to my cock as she stroked. Then she leaned forward, her plush lips slightly parted as she took me into her velvety mouth.

"Aveen," I choked. How I managed to keep from thrusting into her, I'd never know. Her tongue swirled around the tip. When she took me deeper, I knew what true death felt like. The utter devastation of her mouth was something I would never come back from.

Her head bobbed and tongue flicked and *fffuck*.

I gathered her hair back from her face so I could watch her work. I'd been sucked off plenty of times before, but to see this woman on her knees for me was my undoing. I never wanted her to stop, but if she kept going, I wouldn't last.

I tugged the hair in my fist, and her eyes raised to mine. "Stand up." I couldn't wait any longer to have her. Her cheeks hollowed out, and she gave one final drag before rising.

My fingers slid along the length of her slender throat, capturing her jaw and bringing her lips to mine. "Wicked thing."

Her eyes glinted with a salacious gleam. "You've rubbed off on me."

I captured that wicked mouth with my own and hiked her

skirts up to her waist. When I drew her knickers aside, I found her dripping for me.

Her tongue lashed against mine, and she gripped my cock, urging me toward her center. I backed her against the wall, lifting her up and driving into her with one deep thrust.

"You know..." I murmured against her bobbing throat, grinding into her wet heat.

Her head fell back with her moan.

"The likelihood of true immortals conceiving is one in a thousand—"

"Don't care," she gasped, freeing her breasts and arching her back so I could taste the pebbled tips. Roses and desire.

Her heels dug into my ass as I continued rocking into her. So tight and wet. Sinfully so.

"Rían, I'm—"

Before she could get the words out, her body clamped down on mine, pulsing and drenching my cock in her pleasure. Three more thrusts, and I found my own. This woman drove me out of my mind. I couldn't get enough of her.

We righted ourselves, I helped with her dress while she handed me my discarded waistcoat. Already, I wanted her again, but my brother would likely lose his mind if we made him wait any longer for cake.

I sank onto the edge of a coffin and watched Aveen fiddle with the pieces of hair that had fallen around her face.

"You looked exquisite walking down that aisle today." I'd been transfixed, unable to take my eyes off her. "It made me wonder... what I mean to say is...would you ever consider..."

Her hands fell to her sides as she smiled down at me. "Consider what?"

For some reason, my palms started to sweat. I slid them down my breeches and pushed to standing. "Marrying me?"

Her body stiffened and smile faltered as she glanced around the shadowed room. "Are you proposing right now? In a closet of coffins?"

Always such a feisty thing. I caught her by the waist and pulled her into me. Her supple chest bumped mine, and she let out a throaty laugh. "I am simply inquiring as to what your answer would be if I were to do something so foolish as to want to tie myself to one woman for the rest of my days." I let my lips graze across the swell of her breast and my tongue trace over the scar I'd given her.

"Rían," she moaned, "don't try to distract me by—Rían!"

"Hmmm?"

"Look at me."

I swirled my tongue again. "I am."

"At my face, you fool." She clasped either side of my jaw and tried to force me to do her bidding.

I loved her face, but right now her breasts needed my attention more. After a final kiss, I straightened and looked into her eyes. She threaded her hands through my hair and pulled me until our foreheads touched.

"You want to marry me?" she whispered.

I'd never given marriage much thought, but after all the hulla-baloo over Tadhg's insistence on marrying Keelynn for a third time, perhaps there was some merit to the idea. Knowing this woman would be mine come hell or high water, that the two of us would be forever bound, had a great deal of appeal.

"The thought has crossed my mind, yes."

She blinked up at me, but no smile graced her pouty lips. Weren't women supposed to smile when a gallant prince proposed? Granted, this wasn't the most romantic setting. I prob-ably should've held my question until we were in the garden.

"I...um..." Her hands fell to her sides, and she took a retreating step toward the door. My stomach started to sink. "I don't know what to say."

How could she not know what to say? It was a fairly straight-forward feckin' question. A simple *yes* or *hell no* would have sufficed. "Then I guess I have your answer." Good thing I didn't go through the trouble of getting her a ring or dropping to one knee or any of that shite. The humiliation of begging for her hand only to stand up without it would've made me want to curl up and die.

"I'm sorry, Rían. I just—" She wrung her hands in front of her. "All my life, I've been treated as if my sole purpose was to find a husband. It's not that I don't love you, but I don't see why we need to exchange vows to be committed to each other."

I didn't need vows…but the more I thought about it, the more I *wanted* them. Clearly, she didn't feel the same. "Is it really that difficult for you to understand why I would want the woman I love to be bound to me in any and every way? Why I wouldn't want any offspring we may have to be bastards as well?" After so many years of hearing the derogatory name aimed at myself, you'd think I'd be used to it. And I was. But that did not mean I wanted my children to bear the same burdens.

"Rían…" she sighed.

I stalked toward the door, but before I twisted the handle and returned to the "joyous" celebration, I had to say one more thing. "I have never dreamed of marriage, never thought I'd find someone I'd want to be with for all of eternity, and yet if you would've asked me, do you know what I would've said?" She shook her head. "I would've said yes. Without hesitation. Because I am already yours, from my worthless heart to my blackened soul. I only wish you felt the same."

I left her there, but instead of continuing toward the excited chatter drifting from the dining room, I evanesced to the silence of my room. I couldn't blame such a good, kind woman for being hesitant to bind herself to a man like me. But that didn't make her refusal hurt any less.

36

TADHG

GOLDEN-BROWN CHICKEN AND STUFFING, CREAMED CORN, A colorful salad, an entire vat of mash dripping with butter, miniature tarts and cakes and pies still steaming from the ovens waited at the center of the long table in the dining room.

I had to wipe my mouth to keep from drooling all over my new waistcoat.

"Were you expecting to feed an army?" I asked the old witch swaying with Hagan on her hip.

Eava smiled her same old smile. "Figured it's better to be prepared than to let ye starve."

We'd be eating this for weeks. Not that I was complaining. Still, I had to keep in mind that I would be making love to my wife before the night was over, and I didn't think she'd appreciate me rutting on top of her with a paunch.

I rubbed at the black band encircling the ring finger on my left hand. "I suppose this'll put an end to my Saturday night proposals for a while."

Eava nodded toward where my brother was watching Aveen with such rapt attention, the world could have been on fire around him and he wouldn't have noticed. "I've a feeling I'll be down to only one suitor soon enough."

I counted myself fortunate that, despite the lack of support from the Danú, I had been able to marry the woman I loved. Not everyone was so lucky.

I lifted my goblet for a toast—the first of many, hopefully. Everyone in the room did the same. Everyone except my brother, that was. He was too busy rolling his eyes. Aveen kicked him in the shin. His curse echoed through the hallway, and he lifted his goblet, albeit with obvious reluctance.

I smiled down at my wife, feeling lighter and happier than ever before. The first time we'd married had been out of necessity. The second time had been out of lust. This time, love had brought us together. "To a love strong enough to break a curse, and the woman I don't deserve."

My friends—my family—repeated the toast with their goblets high before taking sips of their drinks. The grape juice in my glass left something to be desired, but at least it wasn't water.

Eava patted Rían's shoulder. "You're next, my boy."

My brother snorted and drank a little deeper. Aveen averted her gaze, her cheeks blushing bright pink.

Ruairi knocked his shoulder against the witch's. "Ye know what that means," he said with a smirk. "I'll have ye all to myself."

Eava tilted her goblet toward him, her black eyes alight and grin growing. "Ye want to marry me? Name the time and the place, lad. I'll even throw on a fancy new frock."

Everyone but Rían laughed. Not even his abject misery could bring me down today. We filled our plates amidst cheerful chatter, everyone talking at once. Every so often, Keelynn would glance over at me and smile, or I'd reach for her tattooed hand and squeeze her fingers. Who knew a heart could feel this full?

After this would come the real highlight of the evening: the cake. I may have already quietly cut myself a teeny slice from the very back and then hidden the gap behind a flower. Eava had caught me and clicked her tongue with false irritation but kept my secret.

As soon as we had our fill of dessert, I would be dragging my wife up to our room and locking her inside.

The door burst open, and Oscar fell into the room. His flat cap skidded across the stones. "Sire! Yer needed in the courtyard."

Rían and I jolted to our feet and raced after him, out of the dining hall, through the entryway, to the castle's front steps. We both stilled when we saw the crowd of men in the courtyard. There had to be at least fifty of them. The torches in their hands fought against the growing darkness as the sun sank below the horizon.

I heard footsteps behind me but didn't dare turn around.

"What's happening?" my wife whispered.

"I haven't a clue," Aveen whispered back.

The men at the front of the crowd seemed to look straight past Rían and me to the women at our backs, their mouths twisting into sinister smiles.

A cool hand slipped around my elbow. "Tadhg?"

I gave Keelynn's fingers a reassuring squeeze, hoping my voice didn't betray my anger. How dare these men ruin the most perfect evening. How dare they. "Stay inside, my love."

Rían remained stone-faced, his expression almost bored as the firelight glinted in his black eyes. "Tadhg's right. Both of you need to go to your rooms."

"We aren't children," Aveen hissed. I glanced over my shoulder to find her glamour thankfully back in place. Before my sister-in-law could give out any more, she and Keelynn vanished, and the heavy door slammed closed behind us.

"What'd you do with them?" I asked under my breath.

Rían's lips twitched. "Locked them in the tower."

"They won't be happy about it."

"Good. I like it when mine's angry."

I folded my arms across my chest, bracing for whatever shite these men had to share. I recognized Cormac at the very front. Troublemakers, the lot of them. "To what do we owe this unexpected pleasure?" I asked in the voice I reserved for making decrees and handing down judgements.

Cormac stalked forward, his bare chest rising and falling in irritation. "Did ye marry that human bitch?" he snarled.

The rest of his posse sniggered.

"If by 'that human bitch' you mean Princess Keelynn, then yes, I did. Have you come to offer your congratulations?" I asked, giving them a chance to change their tune before I destroyed every single one of them.

The pooka spat on the stairs, narrowly missing Rían's boots. My brother's lips twisted into a smile that sent shivers down my spine. So much for sparing the pooka's life. Hopefully the others wouldn't be as foolish. "Yer supposed to be our leader," the man growled. "And look at ye, tying yerself to one of *them* while we're fighting fer our lives against the ruin they brought."

What complete and utter shite. Did they truly believe humans had brought about this blight? "You are aware that humans do not possess magic and therefore cannot kill the land. What's happening outside these walls has nothing to do with the humans."

A squatty man with a wooden leg hobbled forward, the handle on his torch nearly as tall as he was. "That's just it, ye see. It's happenin' *outside* these walls." Embers drifted into the sky when he gestured toward the castle with his flame. "Yer safe in here, hiding away on yer throne while yer people are sufferin'."

Had they not seen my brother and I shifting cottage after cottage and tending to those who had been displaced? Had they not witnessed me pouring all my magic into the ground time and again until I could barely stand? Ungrateful wretches, that's what they were. At this stage, I wasn't even sure they'd be happy if I did manage to find a way to defeat this blight. Nothing I did would be good enough for them.

"I've said that we will help anyone who suffers," I explained, somehow managing to keep my voice steady despite the anger rising in my core.

"And when all our land is gone?" the pooka demanded with a roar, throwing his arms into the air, rallying those gathered behind him. "What then? The Queen has offered to intercede on our behalf. She's promised to cure the blight!"

I bet she feckin' did.

The blight would be easily remedied by the witch who created it.

The orange flames shuddered when the mob lifted their torches in a rousing cheer. Despite their cloaks and hoods, I managed to pick out a few faces I knew well. Men I had pardoned, some whose taxes had been forgiven, and one my brother had saved from execution in Airren. All it took was a little hardship to make them forget who had taken care of them over the last two centuries.

All it took was a wedding for them to rally against me.

"And what does the Queen want in return for her benevolence?" I asked.

The pooka sneered. "The Queen wants the heart of the human who has brought shame to our land."

The crowd seemed to shift and sway in unison as empty hands filled with swords and daggers and axes.

Did they honestly think I would hand over my wife? Even if Keelynn's death would save every single person on this island, I'd gladly sacrifice every last one of them for her.

"After all I've done for you, this is how you repay me?" Boiling rage flooded my chest. For centuries, I'd given these people everything. And now that my curse was broken, now that I'd finally found happiness, they wanted to steal it away? The nerve. The *gall.* "I'm giving you one chance to put down your weapons and return to your homes."

My warning reverberated off the stone walls. Not one person had the good sense to flee.

"Rían?" I met my brother's vicious grin. His eyebrows arched. I inhaled a deep breath and said, "Imprison them all."

Surprise flickered across his features. "Imprison?"

I nodded. We already had a rebellion on our hands and didn't need to make matters worse. As happy as it would have made me to impale every last one and hang their bodies from the castle walls, we were better than the Queen. These men would stand trial and face the consequences of their actions as was their right as citizens of Tearmann.

With a flick of Rían's wrist, their weapons vanished. Another flick, and those at the front fell to their knees, grabbing their throats, their faces turning a wicked shade of blue.

"Rían..."

He rolled his eyes at the warning in my tone but flicked his wrist once more. Every single person in the courtyard vanished, and I swore I could hear their wails from the dungeons.

His eyes met mine, returned to their lighter hue. "When will we schedule the trials?"

No sense rushing. We were quite busy, after all. "Next month?"

His grin flashed in the night. "Perfect."

37

AVEEN

My toes began to cramp as I teetered on the rickety step stool I'd found abandoned in the corner. "I can't see a blessed thing." Who installed the windows in this tower, anyway? Giants? I'd already tried evanescing out of the locked tower but to no avail. Meaning Rían must've warded the place. Leave it to him to never forget a loophole.

Keelynn's head fell back against the wall, her porcelain complexion rosy with irritation. "Then why do you keep looking?"

Good question. One I unfortunately didn't have an answer to. "Perhaps if I get on my hands and knees, you could climb on my back?" She was a good bit taller than me and might have been able to see down into the courtyard from her tippy toes.

Although she smiled, she didn't bother getting up. "Sit." She patted the stones beside her. "They will let us out when it's safe."

She had a point. It wasn't as if they would keep us locked up here forever. Although, after my conversation with Rían in the closet, perhaps he'd be happy not to have to face me for a day or two. I sank onto the hard stones and drew my knees to my chest, mirroring Keelynn's position.

Shouting erupted from the courtyard, followed by stark

silence. Keelynn's wide gray eyes flew to mine. "What do you think they wanted?" she asked.

"To give you a wedding gift, obviously."

Although she laughed, there was no mirth to the sound. Those men had bad news written all over their scowling faces. Perhaps it had been a good idea to send us away. Still, I hated sitting around like a bump on a bloody log.

I nudged my shoulder against Keelynn's. "How are you faring?"

She plucked a piece of hay from the bottom of her skirts and threw it aside. "I knew the night would end with me locked in a room but had assumed my darling husband would be locked inside with me."

Not exactly the visual I wanted in my mind right now. We needed to talk about something else.

"Rían asked me to marry him," I confessed in a voice barely above a whisper. And the disappointment on his face when I turned him down would live in my mind forever. While I meant what I'd said about my thoughts on marriage, the full truth was that I couldn't commit to anyone or anything while the bargain with Caden loomed over my head. I should've told him before. Now it was too late. Tomorrow morning, I would slip away and spend the rest of my days trying to get back to him.

Keelynn's eyes widened. "He did?"

Tears burned the backs of my eyes when I nodded. This should have been one of the happiest days of my life—my sister had gotten married, and the man I loved had proposed. Instead, I felt as empty and hollow as this tower.

"What did you say?"

I ran a finger beneath my eyes to clear some of the dampness. "I told him I couldn't."

"Because of his mother?"

I shook my head. A wrinkle formed between Keelynn's delicate eyebrows as she assessed me. I didn't want to ruin her day but had learned my lesson about leaving without saying goodbye. Once Tadhg returned, I had a feeling he wouldn't let his new wife out of his sight. They'd be holed up in his room for the rest of the night—and probably most of the morning as well.

"But you love him," she said.

If only our lives were that simple and love could be enough. More tears spilled free, rolling in warm streaks down my cheeks. Each time I scrubbed them with the heels of my hands, more tumbled out, taking their place. "I love him so much, it hurts."

Her arms came around me, and she pulled me close. "Then why did you turn him down?"

I buried my head in the crook of her neck, unable to bring myself to look her in the eye when I made my confession. "Because I made a mistake and cannot move forward until I have fixed it."

"We've all made mistakes, Aveen. Your life doesn't have to be perfect for you to find happiness."

Now for the part that would hurt the most. "I'm leaving."

She drew back, her face a mask of concern as she searched mine. "What do you mean you're leaving? Where are you going?"

"To Iodale."

"What's in Iodale?"

"Caden Merriweather."

"As in *the* Caden Merriweather? The man you—"

I squeezed her hand, keeping her from saying any more. I couldn't bear to hear her speak my mistakes aloud. "The very same."

"I don't understand. Are the two of you together?"

"God, no. I haven't thought about him since I met Rían. But when Caden returned to Airren, he found me and called in my bargain to leave the island with him." Holding me to promises I wasn't sure I'd ever meant to keep.

"He's fae?" she gasped.

All I could do was nod and hang my head.

Keelynn remained quiet for the longest time before taking me by the shoulders and turning me to face her. "This isn't the end of the world. We simply must find a loophole. What were the terms?"

"I promised to leave Airren with him, that much I remember." Her lips pressed flat with disapproval. What a terrible role model I had turned out to be. "But in my defense, I didn't know he was fae or that he would hold me to my promise. We sail from Hollowshade on the morning tide."

Her grip on my shoulders tightened. "How long ago did this happen?"

"He was at my cottage after I left here."

"How did he know where to find you?"

"Meranda. She arrived after he left and explained how he'd tricked her into giving him the information." As if I needed another reason to loathe the pirate.

Keelynn pressed a pale hand to her forehead. "Have you told anyone?"

I shook my head. "Not a soul."

"Of all the infernal, foolish things you've done, this one tops the list. We could have helped you get out of this, and yet you were determined to deal with everything on your own." Her hands balled to fists in her lap. "And you said you're supposed to meet him tomorrow?"

Nodding, I dropped my head into my hands. I'd wanted to tell her the truth the night I'd spent with her at Ruairi's, but she'd already been dealing with so much between the wedding, Tadgh's son, and leaving the castle, it didn't seem fair to burden her with my problems as well.

Keelynn braced her hands on the stones and rose to her feet. The silk of her gown caught the moonlight streaming through the high windows, making the material shimmer like a lake beneath a full moon. Before I could ask what she was doing, she pounded a fist against the door.

"Keelynn, stop."

She pummelled harder.

I stumbled to my feet. Even when I caught her arm, she

remained undeterred, using her other hand to slam against the barrier.

"You cannot tell anyone. Please. I don't want them to know."

The door swung open. Tadhg stood on the other side in a fresh shirt and black breeches.

When I tried to grab my sister's wrist, she yanked free. "Please, Keelynn…"

Tadhg frowned at us both. "I apologize for letting Rían lock you in the tower—"

Keelynn cut him off with a wave of her hand. "We have more pressing issues to deal with. Where are Rían and Ruairi?"

The two men appeared behind Tadhg. Rían's black eyes found mine and did not stray. My throat swelled, and my protests fell silent.

Keelynn was right. I should've told them the truth the moment Caden had returned to my life. We may not be bound by blood, but we were a family all the same. And family helped each other no matter what. Wouldn't I be furious if Keelynn had kept such a secret?

Keelynn braced her hands on her hips and leveled my prince with a narrowed-eyed glare. "Is there any way out of a bargain?"

His gaze flickered to her before returning to me. "That would depend what was promised."

Keelynn caught my wrist and dragged me forward. I stumbled into her, but instead of letting me go, she held tighter. I opened my mouth to explain, but no words emerged.

Keelynn's fingers squeezed mine. "Tell him."

Rían's brow furrowed. "Tell me what?"

"When Caden and I first met," I said, ignoring the way Rían winced when I said the pirate's name, "I promised him something. Now I have no choice but to leave Airren with him."

Rían's shadowed eyes began to glow. "Like hell you will."

"I'm afraid I don't have a choice."

"You do if I kill him."

Surprise, surprise. Rían wanted to murder someone. "He'll only come back." And I'd still be as bound to him as I was now.

A maniacal gleam flashed in his eyes. "Not if I use the dagger."

"You'd really rather waste your life ending his than find some other way out of this?"

His jaw worked as he considered. Silence stretched between us for far too long. He wasn't honestly considering this, was he? "Rían!"

"No. I don't want that," he muttered. With a vicious curse, he started pacing up and down the hallway.

"We must find another way out of this. Together," Keelynn announced. "Rían, you're the master at bargains and all that nonsense. Surely if you put your mind to it, you can find some way for my sister to escape."

He scrubbed a hand down the back of his neck. "How long do we have?"

"I'm meeting him tomorrow."

His jaw pulsed. Behind him, Ruairi muttered a curse.

I wrung my hands together, my chest so tight, I could barely breathe. "I'm sorry. I know that doesn't give us much time. He showed up when you were with Leesha—"

Rían stilled and his head snapped toward me. "I was never *with* Leesha."

"You know what I mean. I thought perhaps leaving wouldn't be so terrible. And by the time you and I made up, it was too late."

"I'll need to know exactly what you promised."

"I said I would leave Airren aboard his ship."

A strand of mahogany hair fell over his brow when his head tilted. "That's all?"

"I think so. But isn't that enough?"

"You gave him no time constraints? You didn't specify what was to happen once you left? Nothing more? Just that you would leave with him."

"Yes."

Rían glanced sidelong at Tadhg, who nodded. "Then you leave with him, and I will get you back."

That would've been well and good if Caden had planned on spiriting me away in a carriage. "I thought your magic didn't work on the water."

"I won't need magic. We'll do this the old-fashioned way. Your good friend Lady Marissa will accompany you onto the ship and then she'll relieve the good captain of his black heart."

"I do miss Lady Marissa."

Rían glamoured himself into the stunning, raven-haired woman, complete with bouncing curls and a heaving bosom. "Why, darling, how sweet of you to say," he drawled in Lady Marissa's honeyed voice.

"Will you be able to hold the glamour on the water?"

Rían picked at his manicured nails, the picture of nonchalance. "For a few minutes. But it won't take me that long to kill the bastard."

Knowing he'd be in jeopardy made me nervous. Caden claimed to care for me, but the same could not be said for Rían. Still, unless we came up with a better idea, this would have to work. And knowing I wouldn't be facing the pirate alone eased some of the pressure surrounding my heart and lungs.

Inhaling a steadying breath, I wiped my clammy palms down my skirts. "I guess I'd better get packed."

38

KEELYNN

"TELL ME, MY LOVE, WAS OUR WEDDING EVERYTHING YOU DREAMED it would be?" Tadhg's whispered words reverberated against my throat, his warm breath tickling the oversensitive skin.

I threaded my fingers through his dark hair, keeping him as close as our attire allowed. "It was certainly better than when I married your brother."

Tadhg's teeth caught my earlobe, making me cry out. "Not funny."

It was a little bit funny. But my laughter quickly died when my gaze snagged on the bouquet of flowers left at the corner of the dais. Flowers Aveen had given me when we finished getting ready. One of the many opportunities she'd had to tell me the truth about her agreement with Caden. If she hadn't wanted to sully our wedding day, she could've told me last week. When would she learn that she could lean on others for help? I'd relied on her for so much over the years. Did she not think me strong enough to handle the burdens? Did she not trust me?

Tadhg traced my lips. "What's this frown about?"

"I'm worried about my sister." My mind should have been consumed with more pleasant things, like my husband holding me close. The almond scent of his magic tickling my nose and tongue.

The warmth of his chest pressed against mine. Instead, all I could think about was Aveen.

Tadhg's callused hands smoothed along my bare shoulders to the sleeves clinging to my upper arms. His soft lips danced along my neck, his low hum vibrating against my skin. "You know, I've heard the best remedy for worry is a handsome distraction."

"Do you know where I can find one?"

His chuckle puffed warm air over my chest as his hands wandered to the silk at my waist. "Very funny."

"I thought so." A smile tugged at my lips until the question I'd been trying to avoid started to burn like acid on the back of my tongue. One I wasn't sure I wanted to know the answer to. It would be far easier living in a happy little bubble with my prince, pretending everything was right in the world even though that couldn't be further from the truth.

That was how I had lived my life back in Graystones, and it hadn't done me any favors. The Danú people deserved better than to have a leader content to bury her head in the sand. Like it or not, becoming a princess of Tearmann came with vast responsibilities.

Look at what silence had cost my sister.

I steeled my shoulders and drew in a fortifying breath. "What happened in the courtyard tonight?"

Tadhg glanced away, but not before I saw the flash of darkness in his eyes. "Some people did not support my decision to marry a human."

Nothing new there. Although to storm the castle the way they did—and on our wedding day, no less. That was unacceptable, not to mention disrespectful to their prince.

His stubbled jaw ticked. "Rían and I took care of them."

In his world, I knew exactly what that meant. "You killed them?"

He lifted my chin with his finger, urging me to meet his steady emerald gaze. "They're in the dungeon awaiting trial. But make no mistake, I will not hesitate to end any person who threatens you."

If anyone had threatened him, I would've done the very same. Not that I could have taken on an entire company of Danú and hoped to win. "What if there are more?" Once news of our marriage vows spreads, there were bound to be many people who would hate to see a human on Tearmann's throne.

"My beloved princess, tonight you are the only thing that matters. The world could burn for all I care. Tomorrow, we'll dance on the ashes." Tadhg cupped my jaw, bringing our mouths together for a slow, sensual kiss. Our tongues tangled and slid against each other.

Outside these walls and wards, the world was going to hell. But here in this throne room, beneath a veil of shadows and candlelight, in the arms of my husband, I'd never felt as safe.

When he pulled away, a whimper escaped. " I have a surprise for you."

I rolled my hips; his length swelled beneath me. "I think I'll like this surprise."

"Not that, minx. At least, not yet."

Nothing could be better than having him inside me. At least that was what I'd thought before a gleaming gold crown appeared in his hand, similar to the one Tadhg had worn during the ceremony.

I reached out to trace the emeralds dotting the delicate gilded twists and points. To think, only last year I had planned on killing this man, and here I sat, on his lap on a throne, being handed a crown.

"Do you like it?" he asked.

For a moment, I glimpsed the boy behind the man, sweet and a little unsure.

It was a bloody crown. What did he think?

"If you don't, we can always commission another."

"Don't you dare. I love it, Tadhg. But I don't deserve it." Who was I to accept such a gift? Perhaps once I'd proven myself—once I earned this throne...

"You are the woman who gave me back my life." A smile played at the corners of Tadhg's full lips as he shook his head. "This trinket isn't nearly enough." He clasped the crown between his hands and settled the piece upon my head with such reverence, my chest drew tight.

"Beautiful," he whispered, no longer looking at the gold and jewels but at me.

Beneath his heated gaze, I felt every bit the beauty he claimed to see. And with this crown, I felt powerful as well.

Tadhg's finger slipped beneath the flimsy strap on my gown, exposing my shoulder. "Now, as for that other surprise..." Soft lips grazed my collarbone. Waves of desire coursed through my bloodstream.

My head fell back, leaving my throat exposed to his wicked mouth. His tongue lapped and teeth nipped. My hips began to move steadily against his until I remembered where we were. We couldn't do this in the middle of the great hall...could we?

"Should we go upstairs? Someone may see us." Even as the words left my tongue, my back arched so he could slide the silk down my overheated skin to gather at my waist.

His teeth scraped his bottom lip as he stared down at my heaving chest. Darkness flooded his eyes, full of silent promise as his calloused hand closed around my breast. "Let the world watch me claim my wife." His head lowered, and his knowing tongue flicked over the peak of my breast. I cried out, unable to keep my own wantonness contained. An appreciative growl vibrated against my breast when I rocked my hips harder. The crown may have been beautiful, but this...this was the bliss we all searched for but rarely found.

Tadhg caught my waist and urged me to my feet. My dress floated to the floor, leaving me in nothing but knickers, a heavy emerald necklace, a crown, and a smile. Tadhg still had on all his clothes. That wouldn't do. I stepped between his spread knees, his desire for me quite apparent beneath his breeches. I eased forward and took my time unbuttoning his shirt, exposing his toned shoulders and the solid wall of his sun-kissed chest all the way down to his taut abdomen and the thin trail of dark hair disappearing beneath the waistband.

So perfect, as if carved from stone. And all mine.

His hips bucked when I cupped his bulging manhood, working him with slow strokes until all the green melted from his eyes.

Shadows tickled the backs of my legs, dragging up my calf to my knee like lazy fingers and eventually finding my core. My hand slipped off him, and I had to brace myself against his firm thighs to keep from collapsing.

All thoughts of patience fled my mind. He must've felt the same because we both lunged for each other, me tugging at his belt and Tadhg tearing my knickers clean off.

His mouth crashed against mine, and our tongues lashed and tangled, fighting for dominance. He dragged me onto his lap, my knees fell to either side of his hips, and with one thrust, he filled me so completely the breath left my body.

A dark curl fell across his brow when his head eased forward so he could swirl his tongue around my breasts. "Mmmm...even better than cake."

Tadhg and his cake. "High praise, indeed, coming from you."

The world drifted away, replaced by rocking bodies and thrusting hips. The carvings at the back of the throne bit into my hands as I gripped tightly, lifting and lowering until my legs began to tremble. Tadhg found that most perfect spot with his fingers, pressing and flicking and teasing in time with his tongue at my chest.

Glorious tension built in my core, gripping and tightening until I reached the precipice and tipped over. My body cradled his until he followed me into bliss.

His soft chuckle struck my very soul. He sounded so carefree. So happy.

"What's so funny?" I asked.

His fingertips dragged along my cheekbones to my jaw, as if memorizing my features. "I was thinking that this is the first time I've ever enjoyed sitting on this throne."

I laughed as well. How could I not? Every time I came into this room, I would be reminded of this very moment of bliss and shadows.

There was no telling what tomorrow would bring. All that mattered was that we faced it together.

39

RÍAN

THE SOUND OF MY FOOTSTEPS ACROSS THE STONES REFUSED TO drown out the worry pulsing through my mind. I should've been in bed, clinging to my human before she left me for another at dawn. Instead, I was in the family room, just me and my chaotic thoughts.

Aveen hadn't told me about her bargain with Caden because part of her had preferred escaping this island to dealing with losing me to Leesha. If it weren't for Keelynn's wedding, she could've been gone already. That was how close I'd come to losing her. No wonder she'd turned down my proposal. Those wounds were still too fresh in her mind. I'd been wrong to ask in the first place, and I absolutely shouldn't have been upset. After what I'd done to us over the last year, I didn't have a feckin' leg to stand on.

"Trouble sleeping?" Ruairi asked from the doorway, loitering in the shadows.

"No. I enjoy staying up all night pacing in front of a waning fire." What a stupid feckin' question.

He snorted and for some reason took my snarky tone as an invitation to come in, sink onto the settee, and pour himself a glass of puítin.

"I cannot believe she didn't tell me." And I wasn't sure why I'd said that aloud. It wasn't as if I wanted the mutt's opinion. Imagine how pathetic it'd be for me to ask a dog for advice.

"She's protecting her captain."

Wrong feckin' thing to say, beast. "I don't know why. Not only did that bastard leave her, he lied to her as well. And secretly bound her in a bargain."

He smiled into his glass before taking a sip. "That sounds awfully familiar."

"Watch it." The key difference between that captain and me was that Aveen knew me, inside and out. She never thought I was some knight in shining armor. "He and I are not the same."

He lifted a shoulder. "She still cares for him."

"She loves me." I'd tasted her truth time and again, holding my breath each time she'd said those words, waiting for them to stop being true.

He tilted his glass between his giant paws, his brow furrowing. "Doesn't mean she can't love him a little as well."

Did part of her want to go with Caden, not only to escape the pain I'd caused but to see if they could rekindle their romance? And if they had... My heart twisted at the thought. Would she have been happier with him than she was with me? Would she have accepted *his* proposal?

Ruairi finished the dregs in his glass and set it down on the coffee table to refill. "Do ye know what yer problem is?"

Wisdom from a pooka. How did I ever get so lucky? "I can't wait for you to tell me."

He leaned against the cushion and threw one arm over the back of the settee. "Ye work in absolutes. Haven't ye learned by now that the world isn't so black and white? There's plenty of gray in there too. Ye fell in love with more than one person. Why can't she?"

Because she was *my* soulmate. And yet I couldn't deny the truth in his words, no matter how much I wanted to. I'd loved Leesha—part of me still did. But Aveen held my heart, my soul. Did she feel the same about her captain?

Or would I arrive at the docks in Hollowshade only to have her look upon the freedom of the sea and change her mind? Could I really take that chance? I shifted a glass of my own and filled it to the brim, sinking onto the wingback across from where Ruairi lounged.

"She cannot go to him."

Slowly, he eased forward to rest his elbows on his knees. "Ye know better than anyone what it means to interfere with a bargain."

True, but Caden wasn't from Tearmann, so one could argue that our laws didn't necessarily apply to him. "If I can't kill the bastard before my magic wears off, he'll take her and never give her back." I should be able to end him before that happened, but where Aveen was concerned, I wasn't taking any chances. A plan began to form in my mind, one riddled with holes and potential pitfalls but that would not put the woman I loved in harm's way.

Ruairi's blunt nail *clinked* against his glass. "That's what I'd do if I were him."

I tried not to read too much into those words—otherwise, I'd no longer have an ally. "We can't let her go to Hollowshade."

"If she doesn't go, she can't fulfil the vow."

"All we need to do is *convince* the pirate that she's there and to release his hold on her."

His fang scraped along his lower lip.

"But in order to do that, I'll need help." And as much as I loathed the thought of asking this mutt for assistance, I couldn't think of a way around it. "I know you have qualms about not doing exactly what she wants—"

His golden eyes narrowed. "I've no qualms about this."

That'd be a first. "Why do I find that hard to believe?"

"The bastard tied me up and locked me in a shed. I don't want him near Aveen any more than ye."

I was fairly confident that I hated Caden a good deal more than Ruairi, but if he wanted to step down from his "live and let live" shite, who was I to deter him?

I tilted my glass toward him. "Aveen doesn't go to Hollowshade."

He tapped his glass against mine and said, "Agreed."

A vacant-eyed merrow with her breasts bared to the darkening sky bobbed at the front of the largest ship in Hollowshade's tiny port. The name *Merrow's Revenge* had been carved into the side of the hull.

I wasn't the least bit impressed. Who wanted to live on a dinghy, anyway?

"Are ye sure there's no other way?" Ruairi asked from the alley, giving the ship a wary glance.

"It's 'you' not 'ye.'" If he acted like the peasant he was, we'd never pull this off. "And yes, I'm certain." The wig I wore made my head itch. No matter how I adjusted the damn thing, it didn't help.

The pooka cursed and stepped out into the light. If it weren't for the golden eyes narrowed into a glare, it'd have been like looking into a mirror. Wincing, he slipped a finger beneath the impeccably tied cravat. "Don't fidget," I warned. A prince didn't fidget.

Peasants.

I slipped out next to him and took his fisted hand in mine. He scowled down at me. "Save your grumpiness for the captain," I murmured, tugging him toward the docks to where a bunch of smelly sailors loaded crates onto the ship. Captain Caden Merriweather stood at the helm, blond curls peeking from beneath a faded tricorn hat that belonged in the previous century.

When he saw us approach, he bounded down the stairs and over the side, skirting between men heaving sacks up the gangplank. His scuffed boots clipped with each stride up the dock to where Ruairi and I waited.

I had to keep my hands from balling into fists and knocking

the "good" captain's teeth down his throat when he grinned at me.

"You're really here," he breathed.

"You didn't give me much of a choice," I muttered in Aveen's voice, glancing away on the off chance that he noticed my eyes.

When he saw the pooka at my back, the two of them traded glares. "What's *he* doing here?" Merriweather ground out.

Water lapped at the posts keeping the wooden dock from floating away from the shore. I tightened my grip on Ruairi's glamour. "You didn't think I'd let my human come alone, did you?" the pooka said in my voice.

The rest of the crew stopped to stare. A few traded whispers. They all looked like they belonged in a prison. And this fool wanted to bring my soulmate aboard this rotting piece of wood and row it out to sea where merrow and selkie and sharks and who knew what else lurked beneath the depths?

Merriweather blew out a frustrated breath before stomping forward and offering his hand. "Come aboard, my angel."

Ruairi's fingers clasped my elbow, holding me back as we'd practiced. I clung to him, hoping the pirate attributed the stiffness of Ruairi's posture to the situation instead of the truth: that he was stuffed inside that glamour like a sausage.

"I want your word that once I leave, my vow has been fulfilled," I said with authority. "That when I escape, you won't make me come back."

His lips tilted into a crooked smile. "After a few days with me, you won't want to leave."

Arrogant prick. He'd been with Aveen once. He hardly knew what she liked, let alone what she wanted. And he obviously hadn't been *that* good considering she didn't want to be with him anymore.

"I need you to say it." I glanced up at Ruairi to appear uncertain, waiting for his nod before continuing. "And to remove your binding magic."

Caden extended his hand and waved me closer. "Come onto the ship, and I will do as you wish."

If this were real, Aveen would likely be loathe to let me go. Time to lean into the role. I threw my arms around the pooka's neck and smashed my lips to his. He didn't kiss me back—which was incredibly rude considering this was meant to be an epic goodbye. "I love you so much, Rían," I choked out, all weepy like she would've been.

When I pulled away, Ruairi looked mad enough to spit. He ground his teeth together and muttered, "I love you too."

He could've sounded a little more devastated. Not to worry. Our performance was almost through.

I drew the hood of my cloak over my head and stepped down onto the gangplank, letting the pirate take my hand and lead me onto the ship. My hold on my magic started to wane the moment my boots met the deck.

The whole thing tilted beneath my feet, as if it knew I shouldn't be here and was trying to throw me off. My stomach roiled. If I vomited, Ruairi would never let me hear the end of it. Caden caught my elbow, steadying me. I glanced away, back toward Ruairi. The whipping wind made my eyes water. *Perfect.*

I closed my eyes with a shuddering sob, really laying on the devastation Aveen would be feeling if she were the one here instead of me.

I thrust my hand toward the lowly pirate. "R-release me from our bargain." The tremor in my voice was perfect.

"Once the wind catches the sails."

"You promised to release me once I boarded the ship. I'm on the ship, our bargain is complete."

"You promised to leave Airren with me. Once we clear the port, I will give you what you desire."

Stubborn bastard was more cunning than he looked.

My skirts rippled in the breeze. Caden called for the plank to be removed and the anchor hoisted. A flurry of motion erupted on deck as the gears ground, lifting the heavy anchor. A few moments later, the sails were lowered.

If Ruairi kept looking at me like that, he was going to blow my feckin' cover. This wasn't exactly going to plan, but we would have to adapt.

I lifted my hand to the scowling pooka, feeling the magic holding his glamour in place slipping away. "Goodbye, Rían. I love you and will miss you every day until I return." Too much? Maybe. But seeing Merriweather's stiff shoulders and scowl was such a delight. Had he honestly thought he could waltz back into Aveen's life and drag her off to some foreign land and she'd be happy about it?

The pooka's lips pressed flat before he waved back and evanesced. With the connection broken, my magic swelled, but not nearly as much as it should have. *Feckin' water.*

Merriweather's fingers slipped around my elbow. "Come with me, my angel. Let me show you to our quarters."

It was awfully presumptuous to assume Aveen would want to share a room with him. Not that I could say that aloud until he released her.

I'd been in privies larger than the captain's "grand" quarters. If I weren't wearing a glamour, I would've had to duck to fit inside. The dear captain didn't have to bend at all. Short-arse prick with a chip on his shoulders, that's what he was. I couldn't wait to knock that chip right off.

"I cannot stay in here with you," I gasped. "It would be improper." Definitely something my human would've said.

"You have nothing to fear from me. I assure you that I intend to be the perfect gentleman."

Perfect gentleman, my arse. If that were true, he'd be giving Aveen this room and bunking with the other worms below deck. "You'll forgive me if I don't believe you."

I turned toward the circular window to stare out into the sea. How much longer was this going to take? "The bargain, Caden. You promised." My glamour slipped, and that was it. I couldn't get it back.

"Give me your hand."

Good thing I'd worn the gloves. Hopefully, by the time he realized he wasn't holding a woman's hand, it'd be too late.

He squeezed my fingers. "Lady Aveen Bannon, I release you from your vow."

I felt no magic, but then again, I hadn't expected to when I wasn't the one he'd bound in the first place. Still, the words had been spoken aloud; the magic would find my human and relieve her of any obligation to this monster.

"Look at me." The captain's stubby finger slipped beneath my chin, urging my face to his. "I promise you'll be happy. I swear."

"I am happy," I said with a grin. Caden stumbled back, catching himself on the edge of his tiny desk. "So feckin' happy."

"*You.*"

"What? No kiss to seal the deal?" I braced my hands on my hips. "And after I went through the trouble of squeezing into this gown. You wound me, captain."

"Where is she?" he snarled, searching the empty cabin as if he'd find my human hiding beneath the bed. "What have you done with Aveen?"

"My fiancée is waiting for me back at the castle." A tiny lie, but he didn't seem able to tell the difference.

His mouth gaped like the dead salmon I'd seen in the market. "She can't marry you. She's supposed to marry me. We had plans for a life together."

He could take his plans and shove them up his arse. "I may be a lot of things, but I didn't have to steal her away to make her want me." I twirled the strands of my blond wig the way some women did when they were feeling saucy. Beating this prick had me all sorts of giddy. I couldn't wait to get back to Aveen and tell her of my brilliant performance. "All I had to do was be my delightful self and she couldn't resist."

His eyes bulged. "She can't want you. You are a monster."

He was right about that. I was a monster. "And yet you thought you could come to my island and take what's mine."

"She was mine first."

"How'd that work out for you, *captain?*"

He whipped his sword free. The blade glinted in the gray light falling through the leaden windowpanes. "I will run you through."

"Go ahead." Made no difference to me. If he wanted to gut me like a fish and drop me to the bottom of the sea, I'd come back soon enough and return to Aveen. Deal done and dusted.

Uncertainty flickered across his features, followed by resolve. He returned the sword to his belt with a smirk. "Let's see how Aveen feels when you don't come back."

My heartbeat faltered.

That wasn't part of the plan. He was meant to be so incensed that I'd bested him that he threw me overboard in two halves.

"Bilson!" the captain bellowed.

The door flew open. A scrawny man in a billowy white shirt blew in, sword at the ready.

The captain's smile grew. "Bring the irons."

The man stepped out only to return a moment later wearing a pair of leather gloves and brandishing a pair of iron manacles.

He lunged, encasing my wrist in fire. A long chain stretched between me and the man called Bilson.

I may not have been able to use my magic, but I didn't need magic to destroy them both. As if he knew what I was thinking, the man holding my chain gave it a swift tug, keeping me from wrapping the iron length around the captain's throat.

When I got out of this, I would make Caden Merriweather's journey to death last an eternity. Make him wish he weren't a true immortal.

Before I could voice my threats aloud, something sharp and cold slid across my throat, and the kiss of a blade stole my final breath.

40

AVEEN

S<small>OFT FINGERS GRAZED THE BACK OF MY SHIFT.</small> E<small>VEN FROM BEHIND</small> closed eyelids, I could see sunlight brightening the bedroom. Dawn had arrived on this dark day. By some miracle, I'd managed to get some sleep, which was a blessing considering what I had to face today.

I hadn't a clue what Caden would do when he found out I had no intention of staying with him. But as long as I had Rían by my side, I would be fine. Knowing we would be doing this together made it a little easier to breathe, even though I feared for his safety. We'd spent the evening distracting each other, but this morning, there would be no time for such things.

Suddenly, the tightness that had lived in my chest since Caden had shown up in Hollowshade loosened. It felt like the times Rían had cut me free of my stay. My breaths came easier. My being felt lighter. Such a strange sensation for the heaviness of the day.

My eyes flashed open, and I stared up at the ceiling high above. When I rolled toward my prince to wake him, I found the other side of the bed empty. I'd been so exhausted from the highs and lows of yesterday that I'd fallen asleep the moment my head hit the pillow.

"Rían?"

The sheets slipped to my waist as I sat up and stretched my hands to the ceiling. My stomach let out a pitiful growl. Hopefully I had some time to eat before we left for the port. I changed quickly and evanesced down to the dining room, just to practice. This magic lark was awfully handy.

Three heads looked up from the table, not four.

Two empty place settings sat across from my sister and Ruairi.

"Where's Rían?" I dropped onto my chair and reached for the ladle in the dish of scrambled eggs.

Tadhg glanced around the table like he hadn't realized his brother's chair remained empty. "How the hell should I know?"

Keelynn sipped quietly from her cup of tea. "Was he not with you?"

I shook my head.

Across from me, Ruairi stuffed a hunk of toast into his mouth. When he caught me watching, he averted his gaze. Very suspicious.

I dumped the eggs onto my plate and jabbed the ladle toward him. "You know something."

He pointed to his closed mouth as he chewed dramatically and mumbled some incoherent response.

"Swallow it. Now. Where is he?"

The pooka winced, and I knew—I bloody well *knew*—exactly what he was about to say.

"Don't get angry," Ruairi began.

Had those words ever calmed an irate woman before? "I'm already angry. Now, tell me."

"Yer man should be back any minute."

I was sick and tired of waiting for a straight answer. I dropped the ladle and pressed my hands to my aching temples. "He went to Caden on his own, didn't he?"

Keelynn gasped and twisted to glare at her husband.

Tadhg tossed a blackberry into his mouth, not appearing the least bit concerned. "Don't look at me. I didn't know."

"We had a plan," I ground out.

"And he had a better one," Ruairi countered, going for another slice of toast.

"To go in my stead? How is that better?" And here I thought these men were better than the humans I'd known. They were all the bloody same, making decisions that affected my life without a thought to how they would make me feel. "Rían's magic doesn't work on the water. He won't be able to hold a glamour."

"I'm sure he'll be fine," Keelynn said.

On any other day, I'd have appreciated the optimism, but not today. Rían could have been locked in an iron coffin at the bottom of the ocean for all we knew. And yet here we were, sitting down for breakfast. What if we never found him? If we'd gone together *as planned*, I would've at least had an idea of where to look for his body.

Perhaps the ship hadn't left the port and there was still time to talk him out of this asinine plan. I shot to my feet and ran for the glass doors, barely remembering to throw on a glamour before emerging onto the sun-drenched patio. My boots thudded against the sandstone slabs as I ran past the entrance to the gardens toward the gates. Ruairi called my name, but I was already through the wards and evanescing to Hollowshade. Not the portal —there wasn't time for that—but to a tiny alleyway I'd once spotted when going to the market for a pint of milk.

Thanks to Rían's lessons, I ended up exactly where I wanted to go, emerging from between the buildings and darting around market-goers on my way to the grassy area overlooking the port. Small, colorful fishing boats bobbed at the docks and a handful dotted the deep blue bay. I scanned the horizon for a ship with black sails but found only dark gray clouds and dismay.

Dammit, Rían. None of us truly knew what Caden was capable of. The man was a pirate for goodness sake, and pirates were notoriously ruthless. Rían may have been a murderous prince, but he was out of his depth in the water, and with no way to safely evanesce...

Someone came to a stop next to me. I glanced over my

shoulder to find Ruairi staring out at the sea. Black and white birds swooped toward the water and back up to the low-lying gray clouds.

"He's gone," I breathed.

"Don't fret, human. He'll be back soon enough."

He couldn't possibly know that. "And when Caden finds out Rían isn't me? What then?"

"Your promise has been fulfilled. We made sure of it."

The strange sensation that woke me this morning, had that been Caden's hold on me breaking? Oh, Rían…

"You were with him, then?" I assumed.

Ruairi nodded. "So the pirate can come back all he wants, but he can't make ye go with him."

I didn't care about *me*. If I'd known what Rían was going to do, I would've kept my mouth shut yesterday and come on my own as planned. For a man who claimed to be a villain, he was certainly good at playing the hero when it was most inconvenient.

Ruairi, of all people, should've known better. He was supposed to be *my* friend, on *my* side. And here he was, making secret plans with Rían. *Traitor.* I rammed my fist into his bulky arm.

Ruairi leapt back with a curse, rubbing where I'd struck him. "Feckin' hell. What was that for?"

"Siding with Rían over me."

His eyes shuttered before he looked back toward the lapping waves, still massaging his arm. "I may not be yer soulmate, but that doesn't mean I care for ye any less."

There they were, the words he'd never spoken aloud, words I'd felt in every cheeky grin and each moment of patient silence stretching between us.

He glanced from the sea to my face and back again, his golden eyes searching, his expression unsure. When he spoke again, his voice came out gruffer, thick with all the words still left unsaid. "If I can keep ye outta harm's way, then ye'd better believe that's what I'm going to do. Having magic doesn't make ye invincible."

Since I didn't know how to deal with the first part of his statement, I focused instead on the second. I knew magic didn't make me invincible. What's more, I understood that these men had been wielding their power for centuries. I couldn't compete with them in strength or experience—I wasn't sure I'd ever be able to. "I know I'm not invincible, Ruairi." I was reminded of that fact every single day I had to hide behind a bloody glamour so that the Queen didn't find me. "But that doesn't mean you can disrespect my wishes. If the two of you thought of a better plan, the least you could have done was include me in the final decision."

His proud shoulders dropped when he nodded. "Yer right."

Someday, I hoped they realized I usually was.

Four days had come and gone, and there was still no sign of Rían. Millie minded Hagan, Ruairi had taken over Rían's trial duties, and Tadhg and Keelynn were busy meeting with Danú and relocating those who had been run out of their homes by the spreading blight.

At my wit's end, I descended the stairs into the kitchens, where Eava hummed and scrubbed a pot big enough to boil a whole pumpkin.

"Do you want any help with dinner?" I asked, desperate for something to do with my hands.

"Oh, no, child. It's nothing I can't handle." When Eava glanced over her shoulder at me, her black eyes softened, and she gave me a small, knowing smile. "But if ye'd like to peel those potatoes, I can get to work on the roast."

Working with a sharp knife would require concentration, keeping me from thinking about how angry I was at Rían. I chose anger because it was the only emotion strong enough to mask my fear.

I gripped the knife and picked up a potato to slowly work the blade around, revealing the ivory flesh beneath the reddish-brown peel.

Eava unwrapped a hunk of meat wrapped in brown paper and set it inside a deep pan. "I'm surprised yer not out in the gardens. It's a lovely day."

Every day in Tearmann was lovely. But being surrounded by life and beauty no longer brought me peace when I felt so barren inside.

Tears sprang into my eyes.

"Oh child," Eava sighed. "Let's put that knife down." She took the blade from my clenched fist and set it aside before folding me in a warm, sugary hug. "It'll be grand. Just you wait and see."

"You can't possibly know that."

"But I do. My boy's smarter than any thieving pirate out there."

Rían *was* smart—even if he had no regard for his own safety. "I just wish he would've stuck to the plan."

"Wishin' won't pay the bills. My boy's changed a great deal since he met ye, but he's still the same hero in a villain's waistcoat." She chuckled to herself and shook her head. "I knew from the moment I heard yer plan that he had no intention of letting ye set foot on that ship. He'll always protect what's his. And nothing's gonna change that."

I'd known that about him, hadn't I? Perhaps some small part of me had known that he never would've allowed Caden to take me and that's why I'd slept so well that night. With all the doom and gloom surrounding us, I knew without a shadow of a doubt that Rían wouldn't let any of it touch me. But now he wasn't here…and perhaps *that* was the real reason I felt so unsteady.

"Plans to get ye back are all well and good, but plans fail," Eava went on, going back to the counter to dice carrots. "Our Rían needed to control the situation, and that meant throwing himself in harm's way instead. Not saying it's right or fair, but that's the way he is."

Rían wouldn't have been able to predict Caden's reaction or the aftermath of the exchange. He'd been genuinely worried that I would choose to be with Caden over him.

And why wouldn't he be? I'd been holding back my heart ever since Leesha had returned. A part of me wondered if I would be enough for him. If he would regret his decision to choose me over her. I should've jumped at his proposal among the coffins and married him that very same night.

Instead, I chose to break his heart.

Something I would need to remedy when he returned.

If he returned.

No. I had to cling to hope, to tell myself and the fates that no matter what, Rían and I would find one another again.

After all, we had forever to search.

I just prayed it wouldn't take that long.

41

TADHG

Hagan snored quietly in his cot. Every so often, a sleepy smile would grace his pudgy face. The lad loved his grub—like his father. That word, *father*, still didn't sound right on my lips, but here I was, responsible for raising another person. Heaven help poor Hagan having myself and Rían as role models. Maybe Keelynn's influence would take over and he'd have a hope of growing up with some semblance of decency.

Keelynn rose from where she'd been reading on the bed and came to stand next to me. Her head fell to my shoulder as we stared down at the little boy. "He's perfect," she whispered.

"He really is."

Her fingers slipped around my arm and squeezed. "Come. Let us take a turn about the gardens while he rests."

"I'd rather not." Going out there only reminded me of my failures as the ruler of this land. Here, looking at my son, I could focus on the good. The same could not be said for outside. The blight surrounded the castle on all sides now. Even from the tallest tower, not a speck of green could be found for miles. We were running out of everything: space, food, *time*.

"Hiding away won't fix anything. Your people need to see you at least attempting to make this right."

Attempting, not actually doing anything of use. Because no one knew how to stave off the darkness. The entirety of our land would be dead by spring. We had to take action now. If only I knew what that action should be.

Rían and I had met with elders from every faction of Danú and none of their remarkably few ideas had worked. Without the Queen's help, the blight was here to stay.

I let Keelynn lace our fingers together and started for the hallway. Together, we descended the staircase and emerged into yet another glorious day. No one milled about the courtyard. No carts of fruit and veg sat parked in the gravel, waiting to be added to the dwindling stores. The castle had become silent as a graveyard with a black sea of death looming outside the warded gates.

"Oh no…" Keelynn breathed, her trembling hand lifting to her parted lips. She wasn't looking out onto the expanse of the rolling fields but at her own boots.

I glanced down, and my heart stalled.

No.

The roots of the ivy clinging to the inside of the walls had turned black, and a small stretch of ground along the stones matched the earth outside.

The blight had penetrated the wards.

My hammering heart filled the silence that had been roaring in my ears. "Shit."

I should've known we wouldn't be safe in here forever. I should've feckin' known.

And I'd been so preoccupied with Hagan and the wedding and happiness that I'd let it get this far. Cormac had been right to damn me. With the way the blight was spreading, we'd have no gardens or grass by the end of the week. If Rían were here, he and I could have shifted the castle, but he was gone, and I hadn't the foggiest idea when he'd return.

Even if I managed to shift the castle on my own, where would I put it? We'd need to drop the wards, and even if I created new ones, they wouldn't be as strong as these.

"I'm so sorry," I said, knowing the words would do nothing but fall short.

"Look at me." Keelynn used her hold on my hand to turn me toward her. "This isn't your fault," she said. "It's *hers*."

My throat started to burn, and the only thing I knew would quench the fire was drink. But since I couldn't handle my drink, I had to settle for cursing instead. This may have been the Queen's doing, but the fault remained on my shoulders. For so long, I'd been content to let Rían handle the parts of ruling this country that seemed difficult when I should've been the one taking charge. Maybe if I'd been more present over the last century, I would've seen this coming and been able to prevent it. Maybe I would've listened to him about the threat the Queen posed and done something about her before it was too late.

It may have been too late for Tearmann, but my people still needed a leader.

I flicked my wrist, and the heavy stillness of a tost descended around us. I finally let my gaze drop to my wife's, expecting to find contempt and disappointment. But all I saw in Keelynn's gorgeous gray eyes was love. And that love gave me the strength to make the only choice left to us.

"We need to leave."

A tiny wrinkle appeared between her arched brows. "Running away isn't the answer. We must find another way."

"That's just it. There *is* no other way. Even if we manage to kill the Queen, the blight will continue to consume until all of Tearmann has been swallowed. This is a battle we cannot win. I need to think of our people's wellbeing. Of my family's survival." And we could no longer survive here.

Her lips rolled together as her gaze left mine only to snag on those blackened vines. "Where will we go?"

The north of Airren was an option, but an influx of that many Danú was sure to be noticed, and taking the land by force would be in direct violation of the treaty. With all the unrest on this island, I couldn't ensure their safety.

Meaning our best bet would be to leave Airren altogether.

The neighboring island of Vellana wouldn't work—that forsaken country made Airren seem like a holiday resort for Danú. Which left the southern island of Iodale or the continent to the east.

Iodale was closer, and there were fae lands on the northern-most tip, though I had no idea if they would have room for all of us or what problems that might cause. The continent would give us more room to spread out, but the king there would likely see us as invaders instead of refugees.

"We'll go to Iodale." I would send word to the fae council there and explain the direness of our situation.

Keelynn nodded. "Iodale it is. How will we get there?"

Since we couldn't evanesce across the water, we'd have to commission ships. Our coffers were filled with gold, so payment wouldn't be a problem. I could speak to those who smuggled drink and goods and ask if they'd be willing to act as ferries. I'd need to discuss the plans with the merrow, of course, get permission to dock in the bay. And then we'd need to spread the word to our people so they would have time to gather their belongings before we left.

"What of the cattle and livestock?" Keelynn went on.

I'd forgotten about the animals. *Dammit.* And this woman thought she wouldn't be a good ruler. She'd been born for this. "We'll tell people to sell what they can to the farmers and butchers in Airren. They'll be able to use the money to buy new animals when we get settled in Iodale."

She pursed her lips, no doubt considering this from all angles. "That's a good plan."

Relief spilled through my chest, calming my thrashing heart. "You think so?"

Her hands slid up and down my arms, warming my skin with each stroke. "I do. I'm proud of you."

"Hold that thought until I save my people."

"Until *we* save your people," she countered. "You're not alone in this, Tadhg. I'll be by your side every step of the way."

Wind blasted tiny shards of ice at my cheeks beneath the hood of my cloak. Although I hated Airren year-round, I despised it even more in the winter, with its wind and rain and miserable gray skies. The only gray I cared to see lived in my wife's beautiful eyes.

Stones scraped my shoulder when I eased against the wall, peering into the twisting rain, waiting for—

A man with a bulbous waist and chicken legs waddled beneath a nearby streetlight.

Him.

Predictable as feckin' clockwork. I stepped from the alley, blocking the pub's door. The Green Serpent sign above creaked on its rusted hinges. When the man noticed me, his footsteps slowed.

"Greetings, Oran," I said with a friendly smile. "It's been a while."

The man's jowls shook when his head jerked toward me. "Yer Lordship. I…um…" He smoothed a hand over the three hairs left on his bald head as his beady eyes scanned the shadows. "I wasn't expecting to see ye here." I imagined his throat bobbed when he swallowed, but there was so much flappy skin hanging from his neck, it was hard to tell.

I pointed my thumb toward the alley at my back. "Let's go around the corner for a little chat, shall we?"

Oran's boot splashed into a slushy puddle when he took a stumbling step back. "I'm actually in a bit of a hurry—"

Brilliant. So was I. I caught his collar with stiff, frozen fingers and dragged him into the alley toward the green-door pub at the back. When I tried the door, it didn't budge.

"Ye didn't hear?" he choked.

"Didn't hear what?"

"Yer one was hanged for witchcraft a fortnight ago."

That couldn't be right. Orla and I had known one another for ages. If I'd seen her name on the list of those convicted in Airren or in Rían's ledger, I would've remembered.

How many others had been missed? Killed without witnesses. Cast into death and forgotten.

Oran took my distraction as an opportunity to wiggle free. My magic snapped out like a shadowed lasso, cinching around his protruding waist, making him look like a pig tied to a spit. He even squealed like one when he fell forward.

I shoved my own spiralling emotions aside and knelt onto the stones. Icy sludge seeped into the material at my knees. With another flick of my wrist, the man flipped over onto his back.

"Y-yer s-stronger than b-before," he stuttered.

"Best not to forget it." Now, on to business. This probably wasn't the best way to convince someone to help, but here we were. It wasn't as if I expected the man to do this out of the goodness of his heart. Hopefully his greed would win out over his hatred for me. "I'm interested in commissioning a ship," I explained, trying to keep the extent of my need from bleeding into my tone.

Oran's brows snapped together. "Fer what?"

"Moving items from Tearmann to Iodale." No sense overwhelming the poor man with unnecessary details. His tiny brain could only handle so much.

His thin lips pursed as he pretended to mull it over, even though we both knew he had little choice in the matter. "Suppose I could be persuaded. Fer the right price."

When I withdrew my magic, Oran let out a wheezing gasp and clutched his soft middle, still panned out on the disgusting ground. Feeling mildly guilty for manhandling him, I stood and offered a hand. He hesitated before accepting and nearly bowled me over with his weight as he struggled to his feet.

"I have a better idea," I said, straightening the crooked collar on his black coat. "You give me use of your ship *for free*, and I will forgive the monumental debt you owe and pay you a flat fee for any additional ship you can convince to join you in this little endeavor."

His beady eyes sparkled as he pretended to think about my proposal. "And how many ships would ye be needing?"

I bared my teeth in a vicious smile, letting him know exactly what would happen if he tried to cross me. "As many as you can get."

After visiting the lovely town of Dreadshire, I had one more stop to make, this time to the coast above Longshadow. Most humans believed the Merrow made their homes in Tearmann's seas—and a good few did. But the leaders lived in the frigid depths off Airren's northern shore.

The sky was so black, it was impossible to tell where it ended and the murky sea began but for the frothing waves splashing the tips of my boots.

If this plan had any hope of succeeding, we'd need the merrow on board.

The only problem was—

"You think I'd give you anything after what your brother did to my daughter?" the man across from me snarled.

That. That was the problem.

Manann MacLír, leader of the Merrow, was apparently not a big fan of my little brother. Not that I could blame the man considering Rían had gutted his favorite daughter like a—for lack of a better word—*fish.*

I'd forgotten how ugly the King of the Merrow really was. Pointed teeth the same shade of dried-seaweed as the slimy, damp hair sticking to his brow. The pale blue skin of a drowned corpse. Gills flapping with each labored breath. Oran may have sounded like a pig, but Manaan had the snout.

The golden crown on my head slipped when I straightened my shoulders. Keelynn had suggested I wear the thing to remind the merrow king that he might rule the seas, but I ruled these lands. "Your daughter kidnapped a woman in my brother's charge," I explained. "Her death, while regrettable, was entirely justified."

"Justified," Manann muttered with a humorless chuckle. "It's a good thing my decision to keep every single ship from reaching Tearmann is justified as well."

"What would it take to change your mind?"

He seemed to consider for a moment, his flat nostrils flaring as he glowered down at me. "Syren Isle."

What in the hell did he want with that useless rock in the North Sea? A few selkies made their homes there, but other than that, the place was uninhabitable. The merrow rarely went onto land—for good reason. I tried not to grimace at the king's knobby blue legs.

When I asked him straight out, he told me that his reasons were his own. But I couldn't just give him part of Tearmann without consulting someone first. "Choose something else."

"I don't want anything else," he rasped. "It's Syren Isle, or any ships that enter the bay and all those aboard will meet their just end on the ocean floor."

I couldn't even appeal to his compassionate side—if it existed.

He'd always been friendly with the Phantom Queen—as friendly as one could be with a murderous witch—so I couldn't tell him my plans and show all my cards at once. Looked like we'd have to evanesce to a port in Airren and leave from there.

Except Keelynn couldn't evanesce.

Back when I first bargained with the Queen to bring Keelynn into Tearmann, the witch had promised to give her safe passage to and from Tearmann exactly once. I had no doubt that if Keelynn left, she would not be allowed to return.

One problem at a time.

Manann returned to the sea, leaving me staring out at the horizon. I never thought I would miss my brother this much. "Where are you, Rían?"

Unfortunately, the sea didn't answer.

42

RÍAN

The daring captain didn't want to share a bed after all.

Which was too bad because the accommodations in the bowels of the ship were severely lacking. The iron manacle had been removed from my wrist, replaced by a cell of iron bars barely big enough for me to stretch my legs and definitely not big enough to lie down in. Not that I'd *want* to lie down in the inch or so of suspicious smelling liquid sloshing around in here. My boots were waterlogged, and the bottom of my dress was soaked. I would've shifted something else if I'd been able, but since my magic didn't work on the water, I was left in this.

The only upshot was that I still looked fabulous.

The two scrawny men standing guard against the far wall didn't seem the least bit concerned by the fact that their ship had clearly sprung a leak. Maybe they hated it here so much that they were looking forward to a watery grave. Or maybe they possessed merrow blood as well and liked the idea of always being wet.

When they noticed me staring at them from my stool, their hands dropped to the swords at their hips. Always nice to know my reputation had preceded me. At least I'd done something right in my centuries on that island.

"Any chance I could get something to drink?" I rasped,

gesturing toward the green bottles in the crates stretching along the sides of the ship.

"That's the captain's wine," the taller one said with a frown.

"And since I am your captain's most special guest, I'm sure he wouldn't mind."

Apparently, neither agreed because instead of wine, the shorter of the two poured something from a jug and held the tin cup toward me. When I stood, the ship suddenly jerked to the side, sending me careening into the bars. A terrible *hiss* erupted when my hands connected with the iron. Just what I needed. More feckin' scars.

"There's a storm," the man with the bottle said in a voice as shaky as his hand.

Feckin' brilliant. Not only was I stuck in this dank, damp, smelly cell, there was a good probability that I was going to make it even smellier by retching all over the soggy floor.

I took the drink. The man yanked his hand away, jumped back, and collided with his fellow guard.

And here I'd thought the shite Tadhg drank smelled rank. Whatever the man had poured smelled like turpentine. Ah, well. Beggars couldn't be choosers and all that nonsense. I saluted the pair with my cup. *Bottoms up.*

The first sip scorched my innards like I'd swallowed a fireball. I didn't cough or make a fool of myself by spluttering, but there wasn't a hope in hell I was going to finish that. I set the cup aside only to have it spill with another violent tilt of the ship. Not that a little extra liquid mattered when this hovel was one giant puddle.

The other guard kicked a plate toward my cell. The hunk of moldy bread rolled off and onto the wet floor. "Dinner's served, yer *highness*," he sneered.

As soon as I freed myself, I was going to shove that disgusting lump down his throat, carve his belly open, and strangle him with his own entrails.

The floor went out from under me, and I landed flat on my ass in the muck.

After every person on this ship was dead, I was going to set the feckin' thing on fire. Maybe I'd burn it first and watch them all throw themselves overboard to be eaten by sharks and merrow.

For now, though, I had to focus on not expelling the contents of my stomach. I dropped my head into my hands, wishing there were some way to stop this infernal rocking and thumping of waves against the hull. Why weren't their faces green? Did they not notice we were being thrashed about like a toy in a feckin' hurricane? "How long until we reach land?"

The man who'd given me the drink answered. "Should arrive by tomorrow morning."

His companion, with a face not even a mother could love, jabbed him in the ribs with his elbow.

"Ow! What the hell was that for?" the first muttered.

"You're not supposed to be talkin' to the prisoner."

"The man asked a question. The least I can do is answer him."

Did they have to bicker so loudly? Everything down here echoed like a feckin' cavern.

Since it usually took three days to reach Iodale, I assumed I'd been dead for two. Aveen was not going to be impressed when she learned the truth. I couldn't wait to see the rage flashing in her eyes and taste the anger on her tongue.

All of this could've been avoided if she had confided in me.

It still rankled that she hadn't said a word.

I had let her down with Leesha, sure, but hadn't I done more than enough for her to trust me before and after that little lapse? Hell, she'd told me about her problem with Robert when we barely knew each other. Why not this? Had Ruairi been right? Had part of her wanted to leave with her captain?

I swallowed the bile climbing my throat. "What happens when we arrive?" I asked the forthcoming guard.

"They'll be bringing you to His Majesty."

His Majesty? Iodale didn't have a king... "We're not going to Iodale, are we?"

"There's been a change of course, mate," the one with the face sneered. "The captain's bringing you to Vellana."

Brilliant. I had a few things to discuss with the king.

BANG.

My eyes burst open.

Captain Merriweather waited on the other side of the bars, looking as pleasant as ever with a scowl on his face and murder in his shite-brown eyes. He threw a bundle of cloth at my lap and ordered me to change.

I held up a yellowed garment that stank as if it'd already been worn by a man who'd never heard of a bath. When I pinched the material between my thumb and finger, I could hear it scrape. "Is this supposed to be a shirt? Feels like sandpaper. I have very sensitive skin, you know."

Our dear captain's smile tightened. "You won't need to worry about your skin once they peel it off your bones."

Someone was in a mood. I stood and fixed a smile on my face as I twisted to show him the back of my dress. "Care to help me with these laces? They're awfully hard to reach."

He whipped out his dagger and cut clean through the back, nicking my spine in the process.

"You cut me."

His teeth flashed. "Good."

"No one likes a sore loser, sailor."

"I haven't lost, only been delayed."

It was awfully optimistic of him to think so. As long as I lived, he wouldn't be getting within shouting distance of my soulmate ever again. I changed into the "shirt" and loose trousers. To be honest, losing my skin would've been preferable to wearing garments of such poor quality. The bastard hadn't even given me a belt. I had to use a piece of rope through the loops like a peasant in order to keep the trousers around my hips.

"Now for your jewelry." Merriweather held out a set of manacles in a gloved hand.

Wasn't that precious? He was so worried about the iron burning his skin that he covered his hands. "Pretty gloves. Do those come in men's sizes?"

His jaw flexed and pulsed. The iron burned like feckin' crazy when he tightened the manacles around my wrists, but I didn't so much as flinch. My hands would fall off before I let him see me blink.

With my non-existent power bound, he withdrew the cutlass at his hip and swung it toward the ladder at the far side of the room. "Ladies first."

I breezed past him with my head slightly bowed so I didn't end up knocking myself out on one of the worn beams. Caden prodded me with his blade, grumbling to hurry it on. I only complied with the order because I could smell fresh air. Well, not *fresh*-fresh air. Everything still reeked of fish and seaweed, but at least it didn't smell like a privy in Dreadshire.

After so long in the dark, I had to squint against the daylight. When my eyes finally adjusted to the brightness, I saw twelve broad-shouldered soldiers in red and gold livery waiting on deck beside the gangway.

The one at the front with the fancy hat and a handlebar mustache stepped forward. "Captain Caden Merriweather, you have some nerve returning to our shores after escaping the king's prison."

Oh, brilliant. Fresh air *and* a show. I folded my arms over my chest and waited for my captor to respond. For some reason, he didn't look the least bit worried.

"I trust the king received my message?" Caden asked.

The man nodded. The officer's mustache twitched as he glared down his nose at me. "Who is this?"

The fecker shoved between my shoulder blades, sending me stumbling forward. "Rían O'Clereigh."

The man's brows arched. The soldiers at his back shifted and exchanged glances. Nice to know they'd heard of me all the way on this forsaken island.

"You're certain this is him?" the officer asked in his stuffy accent.

"Would I lie to you?"

"You're a bloody pirate. You'll do anything to get what you want."

Caden looked right at me and smiled. "You're right. I will." He tugged down my shirt, exposing the scar over my chest before I could stop him.

Nodding, the soldier gestured for my chain.

Caden sneered down at the man's hand. "Before I give him over, though, I do believe you owe me a pardon."

Where'd he get off, exchanging my life for a pardon? I'd make him rue the day he ever crossed paths with me.

The soldier handed a rolled up piece of parchment to Merri-weather, and that was that. The officer became the proud new owner of my chain, and we were off, traipsing down a swaying wooden plank to a steady dock.

I would've dropped to my knees and kissed the ground if it hadn't been Vellanian soil.

The sweaty men bustling in the port paid us no attention as they loaded and unloaded vessels and peddled fish and rum. The guards walked me like a dog on a lead all the way to an arched gate before stopping next to a covered wagon with windows encased by iron bars.

The officer handed my chains to another before pulling parchment from inside his red crushed velvet coat with gold tassels. I looked fabulous in red. Maybe I'd grab one before returning to Airren. One never knew when a soldier's uniform would come in handy.

"Rían O'Clereigh," the officer said, far louder than necessary.

I may have been half deaf in one ear, but I was still standing close enough to feel the man's spittle splatter over my cheek.

"You are hereby under arrest by order of his majesty, King—"

"On what charge?"

He glowered at me before scanning the missive between his hands. "Multiple counts of premeditated murder and inciting a rebellion."

What rebellion? Where had they gotten that load of bollocks? Premeditated murder, certainly. But I refused to be held accountable for crimes I hadn't committed.

One of the soldiers stepped forward with a black sack in his hand and shoved it over my head. No matter. I didn't need to be able to see to kill them. I didn't struggle as their hands dug into my arms and they lifted me into the wagon. What was the point when they were bringing me where I needed to go, albeit in a little less luxury than I preferred?

Somehow, the hood made the scents of the port even stronger, like the vile, fish-laced air had gotten trapped inside and refused to disperse. I ended up on the floor without so much as a feckin' cushion for my arse. I may have been a prisoner, but I was also royalty. Vellanian pigs, the lot of them.

I felt every bump and knock but managed to bite back each curse.

The list of grievances I had for their king continued to mount when the hood was ripped away and I found myself at the entrance to a staircase cut into the base of a mountain. The peaks of the castle rose high above, but these stairs didn't lead upward. No, they twisted down into the bowels of the earth to what I assumed was the dungeon.

A smoky haze clung to the narrow passages. Firelight from the torches flickered off the water and mold weeping down the stone walls. Iron chains dangled from brackets at varying heights.

While I appreciated the terrorizing effect the vast array of torture devices dripping with blood would likely have had on anyone else, to me it seemed sloppy. Honestly. How hard was it to clean a scythe?

And the rust on their iron maiden screamed laziness.

The leather straps on the chairs had been chewed through—likely by the rats slinking around in the shadows. They wouldn't hold a feckin' child in place, let alone a full-grown man. If they tried to strap me down, I'd snap the straps without breaking a sweat even with my iron bracelets.

Groaning men hung in cages from the ceiling, their bare skin covered in red welts and dried blood. I would have to remember to ask who made the cages. The spikes at the bottom were a nice touch. Unfortunately, the ceilings in our dungeon weren't high enough. Maybe I could get one for the oubliette.

"I take it we're not seeing the king today," I murmured.

The soldier holding my chain laughed. "No, lad. Ye won't be seein' much of anythin' once we're through with ye."

That wasn't going to work with my schedule. Aveen would be worried sick, and I had too much shite back in Tearmann to deal with. I wasn't above cutting off my own hands to get out of these manacles, but that seemed a little unnecessary considering there were only five soldiers.

I rolled my wrist and caught the chain in my hand. With a flick and a little finesse, I had the heavy chain wrapped around the closest man's throat. He clawed and cursed, but it was hard to hear over the hissing of the metal melting my skin. I couldn't wait to get these things off.

The man's weight slumped. One down, four to go.

I stole his dagger and plunged it into the next man's gut. He fell forward, clutching his torn abdomen as he landed next to his dead comrade. The other three had the good sense to look proper worried.

I loved this part, when they realized that even shackled in iron, I was stronger than all of them combined. "I don't suppose any of you have the keys to these?" I held up my bleeding wrist, the skin beneath pink and bubbled and—was that bone? Lovely. No wonder it hurt so badly.

"I'm in a bit of a hurry, so an answer would be greatly appreciated."

One of the men stuffed his hand into his pocket, chucked a set of keys at my head, and took off running toward the stairs. The other two chased after him.

I fitted the key into the lock and turned. With a click, my hand was free. By the time I removed the second and the chain clattered to the ground, shouts echoed off the hollow walls. No sense going back into the skinny hall where I couldn't even get in a good punch. And with the heavy iron doors leading down here, evanescing wouldn't work either.

So I went to the wall of bloodied instruments and picked up the scythe. Perfect for cutting down any obstacles in one's path.

And then I sat on one of the empty racks and waited for the humans scrambling in the hallway to get themselves together.

"Ho there!" The chains on one of the cages creaked when the man within crawled toward me. "I can help ye. All ye need to do is cut me down."

I adjusted my grip on the scythe's rough handle. Hopefully I didn't end up with a splinter. "I don't need your help."

"They'll bring the whole army," he countered.

"Your point?"

"Let me down. All ye have to do is pull the lever right there. Please."

I really didn't have time for this. For all I knew, the man deserved to be swinging from that cage. "Why are you locked up?"

"I stole bread to feed my family."

Even from down here, I could taste the sweetness of his lie. "Look, if you're going to lie to me, I'll just as happily leave you there to rot."

He groaned. "Ugh. Fine. I tried to assassinate the king. Happy?"

Not quite yet. "Why did you want to assassinate the king?"

"For the bloody money. Why else?"

Principles. Vengeance. Justice. Love. There were plenty of reasons to kill someone that didn't involve monetary gain. "If I let you go, you aren't allowed to kill the king." I needed him alive to ensure he did my bidding. Otherwise, all of this would have been for naught.

The man nodded emphatically. "If ye help me get out of this place, I swear I won't kill the king."

Too bad the man was a lying bastard. I slid off the rack and started for the door, stepping over the bodies of the two guards I'd already killed.

"Where are you going? Come back! Come back!" His pitiful cries were lost to the shouts from the humans collecting in the hallway.

"If you were in my army, I'd have you killed for being so feckin' slow," I shouted. "I could've been freeing all the prisoners and training them to be brilliant warriors in the time it took you to get down here."

The closest soldier's gaze dropped to the scythe. Whispers rippled back from where he stood, shaking in his gleaming black boots.

I gestured toward his boots with the blade. "Where did you get those?"

"M-my boots?"

"No, your legs. Of course your feckin' boots." Was everyone in this country daft as doornail?

"F-from Ellison's. On m-market street."

"What's he sayin'?" someone whispered from a few steps above.

"He's askin' Mitchell about his boots."

"His boots?"

Looked like I'd be making a stop at Ellison's on my way out of Vellana City. I slammed the scythe's handle against the stones, and the sound made all the soldiers snap to attention. "I'll make you a deal, Mitchell. I'll let you put these back on me *if* you bring me to the king." I kicked the abandoned manacles toward him.

I could've murdered them all and found the king on my own, but I didn't really feel like wasting the time and magic. Plus, the king probably wouldn't be in a listening mood if I slaughtered all his guards.

"The king may kill us if we do," one from a few steps up said, his sword wavering.

"He might," I agreed with a smile. "But if you don't bring me, I will definitely kill you. So I'd say your odds are far better if you do as I ask."

After a lengthy session of whispering between Mitchell and those closest to him, one with a gray beard pushed the others aside and descended the staircase until we were eye to eye.

"I'll bring you," he said.

He probably didn't expect me to see him winking at his companion. And he definitely didn't anticipate me being able to taste his lie. With a flick of my wrist, I robbed his body of air. He clutched his throat, his eyes and the veins in his forehead bulging.

"Does anyone else care to lie to me?"

Mitchell stepped forward in his fine boots. "I'll—I'll do it. Just let Wilton go."

Finally, someone telling the truth. I retracted my magic and let the bearded man collapse onto the floor. The other soldiers knelt at his side, checking for signs of life. He wasn't dead...yet.

I swapped the scythe to my other hand and called magic to my palm, readying the bargain. "Do you swear to bring me to the king right now, with no detours?"

One of the kneeling soldiers shook his head as he stared at my outstretched hand. "Don't do it."

"What choice do I have?" Mitchell's worried gaze bounced from me to his fellow soldiers and back again. "I want your word that you won't harm the king—or anyone in his family."

I wanted to avoid a war, not start one. Not that any of these pricks had asked. "You have it."

With a nod, the man placed his hand in mine. Magic zinged between us as the bargain bound him to his word. He sucked in a harsh breath and swore.

"Right, so. Let's be off. No sense wasting daylight." I'd been away from Aveen long enough. The sooner we got this over with, the better.

43

RÍAN

THE GUARD NAMED MITCHELL WHO HAD ESCORTED ME UPSTAIRS into the main castle glanced warily down the hall. Four red-clad soldiers held spears next to what appeared to be the throne room's entrance.

A man in black robes swept out. When he saw us, he jerked back as if the stink rolling off me had offended him.

Me too, lad. Me too.

"What is the meaning of this?" he demanded of the guard.

Poor Mitchell looked ready to piss his pants. Sweat rolled down his forehead, and it wasn't nearly as warm up here as it had been down in that dungeon. "This prisoner has requested an audience with the king."

The robed man's lined lips pulled into a sneer. "Your sovereign does not meet with vile commoners who reek of feces."

I'd have loved to see how pleasant he smelled if he went through the same ordeal. "My apologies. If I'd known I was being abducted, I would've bathed and changed my shirt."

The man's nose wrinkled in disgust. Instead of lowering himself and speaking directly to a "vile commoner" like me, he turned back to the guard. "Get him out of my sight at once or you'll find yourself in the dungeon alongside him."

The guard's gaze bounced between us, looking so feckin' terrified, I almost felt sorry for him. Who did he fear more? Me or the man who looked like he'd stuffed pillows under those robes?

"I am sorry, your Lordship," Mitchell said, "but I must bring him to the king. He was quite insistent."

Looked like I was scarier. Maybe Mitchell with the nice boots would live to see tomorrow after all.

The robed buffoon nearly choked on his own tongue. Maybe that was how I'd kill him. "You dare to speak to me so disrespect-fully?" he ground out once he stopped waffling. "I should have you whipped. What is your name?"

I stepped forward, drawing the old coot's attention back to me. "Never mind his name. Why don't I tell you mine instead? Prince Rían O'Clereigh."

"Prince of what?" the man sneered. "Spoiled rags and rats?"

Basically. "Prince of Tearmann."

That got his attention. His jaw hinged like a fish gasping on shore.

"Now, if you'd be so kind as to let your king know I'm waiting, that would be brilliant. Or I could always tell him myself?" I raised a brow, knowing damn well this man wouldn't let me get within spitting distance of their precious king.

"No, no. I will give him the news." He spun on his heel, his robes fluttering behind as he sprinted as fast as his short legs would carry him back through the doors.

"Are you really a prince?" Mitchell asked under his breath, his eyes wide as saucers as he adjusted his hold on the iron chain.

"I am many things. A prince happens to be one of them."

The steady *thump thump thump* of boots echoed up the hallway. Sounded like a lot of soldiers moving quickly. Finally, someone showing me the respect I deserved. Not that I didn't appreciate the ease of being escorted by one lowly guard, but I had been a bit disappointed that my reputation hadn't earned me a whole battalion.

Soldiers flooded into the hallway, two at a time, swords drawn and eyes narrowed, their coats the color of fresh blood.

I smiled in greeting while my escort's throat bobbed. I counted twenty so far. This was far more impressive.

The closest man had a bunch of medals pinned to his coat. He tried to take the chain from my guard, but that just wouldn't do. I'd convinced Mitchell to bargain with me but doubted this one would be as easily swayed. "He stays," I insisted.

Mitchell darted a glance my way, his brows lifted.

"I am the captain here," Mr. Shiny Pins countered. "I'll be the one giving orders."

What was it about being called "captain" that automatically made a man an arrogant little prick? "I said the lad stays." He and I had a bargain to fulfil, and the last thing I wanted was these upstarts thinking they could bring be back to the dungeon without saying my piece.

The doors swung open, revealing an airy great room decorated in reds and golds. I never liked the colors much, but at least their tapestries didn't depict the Phantom Queen decapitating humans or banshees escorting souls to the Underworld.

The guards surrounded me on all sides, with Captain Shiny Pins leading us down a red stretch of carpet between courtiers in fine clothes. Say what you wanted about this shite island, but they certainly knew how to sew a frock. I saw more than a few waist-coats I'd have traded my soul for. If only I wasn't in a hurry to return to Tearmann. I could spend a great deal in the shops here.

Gold dripped everywhere, from the tops of columns to the sconces on the wall to the chandeliers and crown molding. What a joy it must be, ruling three islands from this golden castle atop a golden throne, sending minions out to do your bidding. Never having to set a foot outside. Not worrying about the land being consumed or the people destroyed.

A man sat on the throne, younger than I'd imagined. Fitter as well. For some reason, I had expected him to be round as a barrel. Speaking of rounded barrels, the flaxen-haired beauty on a smaller throne pressed a hand to her bulbous stomach. Looked like they were expecting another generation to take the island into the next century.

We stopped at the foot of the dais, and my escorts parted slightly, allowing me to step to the front of the crowd.

The king's brows slowly rose as we traded stares. "Your reputation precedes you, Prince Rían," he said after looking his fill.

"Brilliant. I hate lengthy introductions." No sense mucking about. Everyone in the room sucked in a collective gasp. "Where is King Brosnan?"

"My father passed a fortnight ago."

I bowed my head and said, "My condolences." I meant, *Good riddance.* Hopefully this new king would be more sympathetic to the Danú's plight.

"I remember Father telling me stories of meeting your brother, Prince Tadhg."

Lucky him. Unfortunately for the new king, he got to meet with me.

"You asked to see me. Why?"

"First off, I was wrongfully imprisoned in your dungeon."

His light brows arched toward the golden crown on his head. Tadhg's was bigger. "Is that so? From what I've been told, you have murdered countless Airren citizens. I don't know how you do things in Tearmann, but in Airren, murder is a capital offense."

The men and women gawking by the bay windows tittered, like speaking of death was the most delightful of subjects. Eejits. The lot of them.

"Those I've murdered were guilty of breaking Airren law. I did you a favor."

His lips turned down. "So you're claiming to be innocent?"

"Far from it." The manacles on my wrist met fresh flesh when I reached for my collar, revealing the thick scars across my throat left by my brother's blade. One for every crime I'd committed that hadn't been in the name of justice. And there had been quite a few. "But I've paid for my crimes."

The queen sucked in a breath, her pale hand lifting to her own throat.

Something flickered across the king's eyes. "If that is true, then why are you here?"

"Because Airren is in chaos and innocents are being slaughtered every day."

"You are referring to the Danú trials?"

"They aren't trials. They're executions of innocent people who have lived in peace for far longer than you've been alive. Ninety percent of the witnesses are lying through their back teeth." If not more.

The king rested his elbows against the arms of his throne and steepled his fingers in front of his pursed lips. "What would you have us do? Let every criminal go?"

Sure. Let them all go. Since *that* made sense. "Give the accused fair feckin' trials."

"How dare you speak that way to your king," Sir Robes snarled.

He did *not* want to get into this argument with me. Not today. I peeled back the curtain and let him see the monster in me, the son born of the Phantom Queen, black eyes and bloodlust. "I am a son of Tearmann. I have no king."

"And if we do not agree to your demands?" Sir Robes asked, as if he held the authority here instead of the king.

"Then I will visit every town in Airren and take the heads of each and every royalist fecker your king appoints as judge until I find one who will give us what we want."

Robes' face went red as the soldiers' coats. "Or you could tell your people to leave Airren."

Who the hell did this prick think he was? We had been there long before the humans, and we'd still be there when they were dust beneath our boots. "Would you like to lose half the physicians, apothecaries, fishermen, farmers, milliners, and seamstresses in your country? Think of all those taxes." I clicked my fingers. "Gone. Just like that. How will you gild your ceilings without their money?"

"How do you expect the trials to be fair?" the queen asked in a soft, melodic voice. She had a strange accent I wasn't familiar with. Maybe from the continent somewhere.

Something warm and fluttery that felt an awful lot like hope swelled in my chest. I knew better than to believe making such large changes would be easy. Still, at least this was a start. "Hold them in a central court one day a week. I will preside alongside one of your judges." That would give me time to deal with any other shite fate decided to throw my way.

The king gestured toward me with a bejewelled hand. "Why you?"

"Because I can smell lies."

"Poppycock," Sir Robes muttered.

I was really getting sick of his acidic asides. No one had asked for his opinion. Maybe I should. "What do you think of your king?"

The wrinkled old prune bristled. "He is my holy sovereign. I would give my life in service to the crown."

"Liar."

The vein pulsing across his forehead looked ready to explode. "I beg your pardon."

"Have you ever gone behind your king's back and done anything untoward?" I pressed.

"Never."

"Liar." Sniveling, sniffing liar. "Are you married?"

"I don't see what that has to do with—"

"Answer the question, Reuben," the king clipped.

"I am."

Poor woman. She must have been miserable with such a sweaty pig heaving atop her in bed. "Have you ever been unfaithful to your wife?"

"Absolutely not."

"Liar."

The queen stifled a tittering laugh with her pale hand. The king snorted but quickly concealed the unkingly noise behind a cough. "While I appreciate the entertainment," he said once he'd regained composure, "there is no way for me to know if you're telling the truth or if a man I've known my entire life is secretly plotting my demise."

The man in the robes dropped to his hands and knees at the foot of the throne. "Sire, I would never—"

The king held up a hand, silencing his advisor, then looked to me. "Ask me a question."

He asked for it... "How old are you?"

The heavy gold chain across his mantle glinted when he shifted on his throne. "Twenty."

"Lie."

"Very good. I am twenty-two. But that's a detail anyone would know. Ask me something else."

Let me see... "Are you glad your father is dead?"

His jaw pulsed. "He suffered in his final days. It is a blessing to no longer see him in pain."

A careful truth spoken like a true politician. I couldn't have done it better myself. "Are you happily married?"

He glanced at his wife, the barest hint of a smile gracing the corner of his mouth. "Yes. Blissfully so."

Well, weren't they feckin' adorable? Somehow I managed not to roll my eyes. Time to strike at the heart of the matter, the entire reason I'd allowed myself to be brought to this castle. "Have you ordered attacks on the Danú in Airren?"

His head whipped back to me. "Leave us." The others in the room traded startled looks. "I said leave us," he bellowed.

"Sire, you cannot be serious. This man is a beast," Sir Robes said from the ground. "He will kill you."

"I won't kill you." I jangled the chain connecting me to my dear friend Mitchell. "I already gave this lad my word, but you can have it as well." I held out my hand.

The king pushed from his throne and started down the dais

stairs, his black and white mantle dragging along behind him. I liked fashion as much as the next man but this young man wore far too many layers. Just looking at him made me sweat.

The chatter grew louder as men and women shuffled toward the entryway, casting wary glances back toward where I waited. A few of the guards left their posts to get them moving along.

"Think of your wife and unborn child. Sire, you cannot bargain with a fae."

"Enough, Reuben. The prince has given his word." The king took my hand in his. With a gentleman's agreement between us, the king dismissed the guards. The men traded worried glances before following the crowd into the hallway.

Escorted by the captain himself, Sir Robes tried once more. "Sire, please! Take away the guards and he will kill you."

"If I wanted the king dead, he'd be lying in a pool of his own blood by now."

"Says the one chained in iron, surrounded by guards," he shot back. "Even if you did manage to escape, our castle wards neutralize magic and haven't been breached in centuries."

Wards my arse. Whoever created them must've been lying about their strength. Aveen's cottage was safer than this castle.

I could've told them that straight out, but where was the fun in that?

I stuffed my hand into Mitchell's pocket and stole back the key before the poor lad knew what had happened. By the time his hand dropped to the hilt of his sword, I'd unfastened the manacle and shifted the advisor's robes right off his back, leaving him in a thin white shirt and silky breeches that left nothing to the imagination. "You were saying?"

The king nodded once more, and the doors closed with a resounding shudder. Only four of us remained—five if you counted the prince or princess inside the queen's womb.

The king's expression turned harsh, and his eyes narrowed. "What attacks do you speak of?"

I let the robes drop to the ground. "Massacres, not only of

Danú but their human mates. Businesses and houses burned."
Twenty dead in Mántan and another seventeen in Sirk.

"This is the first I am hearing of it."

Truth. *Dammit.* That made no sense. If the Vellanians weren't
killing the Danú, who was behind this? "What about your father?
Could he have ordered the attacks?"

The king's crown slipped when his head shook. "Not that I'm
aware of. He's been sick for quite some time, you see, so I've been
the one making the decisions for the past six months."

More truths and no answers. "Why has he been sending extra
troops to Airren shores over the last three years?"

"To help deal with the Danú uprising."

That was the second time someone here had mentioned a
rebellion. There *was* no Danú uprising. But if the killing didn't
stop, there sure as hell would be.

"Whoever is attacking your people wasn't sent by Vellana," he
said.

Then I had to be missing something. But what? "How do your
people know who to arrest?" Most of the Danú in Airren lived
under glamours when they could. The majority of humans
walked around blissfully unaware of exactly how many of them
lived in Airren.

"Mostly from letters with anonymous tips."

"Do you have any here at the castle?"

"I do." He hurried to the door and called for one of the
guards. A few moments later, the man returned with a stack of
letters. The king handed them to me for inspection. I didn't need
to look any further than the looped handwriting on the first page.

Dread slithered down my spine.

The Queen had written these letters.

Anger and fear were brilliant motivators. With Airren in such
a dangerous state, more people would be tempted to try and cross
the Forest. But with the land in Tearmann being swallowed by the
blight, there would be nowhere for them to go. Too many people

in too small an area was a surefire way to create dissention and more unrest.

Look at what had happened after Tadhg's wedding.

A fire was coming.

And the Phantom Queen had been the one to light the match.

44

KEELYNN

WITH THE LAST OF MY DRESSES STUFFED INTO THE TRUNK, I HAD to sit on the lid to close it. We'd be leaving so much behind, but with room on the ships so scarce, there was nothing to be done. Perhaps someday the others would return to the castle and find everything still in place. Not that I'd be here to see it. Once I left Tearmann soil, I would never again set foot in this land. The Queen would make sure of it.

Or perhaps those who were refusing to leave Tearmann would loot the entire castle and there'd be nothing left to come back to. Assuming those who remained didn't die of starvation first.

With no crops of their own, they'd be forced to venture beyond the border for sustenance. Winters in Airren were already hard on those who lived there. There wouldn't be enough for them all.

Thankfully, most of the Danú had been receptive to our plan to relocate to Iodale. Word had spread like wildfire, no doubt reaching the Queen in the Black Forest.

Let her rule this empty land.

Let her reap the darkness she'd sown in this once magical place.

Tadhg and Ruairi had been evanescing to towns across Airren, extending invitations to the Danú and their human partners there as well. Not everyone agreed to join us, but some had.

It would have to be enough.

I was about to latch the leather straps when I heard Ruairi's low voice in the hallway. "She sent another one?"

What was he doing here? Shouldn't he be packing up his house like the rest of us? I tiptoed across the bedroom to peer through a gap in the door.

Tadhg stood on the staircase, a piece of parchment clutched in his fist.

I pushed the door aside and stepped out. The two of them looked like children caught with their hands in the sugar cannister. "Who sent another what?" I asked.

Tadhg flicked his wrist, and the parchment vanished. "Nothing."

I really missed the days when he couldn't lie. "I am a Princess of Tearmann, and as such, I deserve to know what is happening in my country. What's more, I am your wife and perfectly capable of withholding all carnal pleasures until you tell me the truth."

"She sounds serious," Ruairi muttered under his breath.

"I am serious." I clicked my fingers and held out my hand.

Although he cursed, Tadhg shifted the parchment and placed it in my palm.

My stomach twisted as I read the letter twice, each ornately looped letter like a brand on my soul. "The Queen wants me in exchange for stopping the blight..."

Tadhg plucked the letter from my grasp and sent it away again. "And I have made it clear that she cannot have you."

A mortal cannot sit on Tearmann's throne...

A slap in the face to all who have lost their lives...

This wasn't just a note. It was a bloody ransom letter.

"How many of those letters have you received?"

Tadhg's jaw worked beneath his short stubble.

"Tadhg!"

"Just three."

Three demands to denounce me as Princess of Tearmann—to end our "sham of a marriage." My throat felt drier than the dead soil surrounding the castle. Soil that could once again be rich and fertile if I was willing to sacrifice the happiness I'd found and leave this place once and for all. Tadhg would keep his kingdom. Little Hagan could grow up in a safe land once more. The thought of leaving him, of not being present to witness his first words. First steps. First *anything*...

Somehow, I managed to swallow past the lump in my throat. "Shouldn't we at least consider her proposal? She's promised to stop the blight."

Tadhg's expression hardened. "I don't care."

"Well, I do." As if the people didn't already hate me enough. If news of this caveat spread, they'd despise me even more. And I couldn't even blame them. Not when I could stop this once and for all. "If I leave, she'll save your land. Your people."

My happiness in exchange for so many lives seemed a low price to pay.

Ruairi vanished, no doubt wanting to be far away from this discussion.

Tadhg's eyes shuttered, and he blew out a breath before taking my hand in his. "I don't think you understand the vows we exchanged. The only way to end our marriage is for you to..." His Adam's apple bobbed when he swallowed.

I didn't need him to finish that statement. Unlike the other times we'd married, our recent vows were for eternity. The only way to break them was for me to die. "Oh..."

His grip tightened. "Now you understand."

I didn't want to die, but what was my life compared to all the souls trying to escape this blight? "I suppose I have some thinking to do."

His fingers strangled mine. "There's nothing to think about. We're not giving in to her irrational demands."

That was all well and good for him to say, but this wasn't really his decision, was it? "If your death would save all your people, what would you do?"

His head shook. "That's different. I can come back. You can't."

"It's not all that different, Tadhg." I slipped my hand from his, my head and heart at war between the duty I had promised to this land and my love for this man with devastation painting his face. "This is not your decision to make. It's mine."

Sunlight glistened off my sister's flaxen hair as she stared out the window. "The gardens are almost gone," she murmured, no inflection in her tone.

I'd been thrown across the settee in the family room for the last hour, contemplating my choices, and yet I was no closer to making a decision. "It's not fair." That the Queen should have so much power she could damn an entire country over her own prejudices.

My sister sighed and turned away from the withered gardens beyond the windowpane. "I know."

Was there no justice in this world? Did good truly have no hope of triumphing over evil?

Was there no room for negotiation? For finding common ground? For giving people a chance to change their minds?

I'd been like the Queen once. Not as murderous, but certainly as hateful.

And it wasn't until I spent time with Tadgh that I learned better. Until I realized Padraig, a man I'd known and loved my entire life, had been one of the people I had feared all along. That I'd only feared them because that was what I'd been taught. Because of my ignorance. Because I hadn't known any better.

How could these people know better if they didn't see humans capable of doing good as well as evil? I thought of those men rotting away in the dungeon. Their hearts so full of hate that they had stormed the castle intending to do me harm. They didn't even know me. If they'd given me a chance, perhaps I would've surprised them.

Perhaps I still could.

"Do you know how to get into the dungeon?" I asked Aveen.

Her brows jumped in surprise. "Why would you want to go there?"

If I told her my plan, would she try to stop me? Better to keep it to myself for the moment. "I would like to speak with the prisoners."

Like the brilliantly supportive sister she was, Aveen asked no more questions. She simply glamoured herself before bringing me through the kitchens and out the back entrance of the castle to where the dungeon door loomed. With a flick of her wrist, the door flew aside.

What I would've given to have such power.

Down the stairs we went, firelight flickering from the torches on the wall courtesy of Aveen's magic. The foul smell of coppery blood and unwashed bodies permeated the air in the skinny hallway.

All manner of wicked looking instruments hung from hooks on the wall, their sharp blades shining. The men had been penned in like animals, five or six to a cell. I searched their haunted faces for one I recognized. Near the back of the third cell crouched the pooka who had come to the great hall that day.

"You there," I called. His golden eyes raised to mine. "What's your name?"

He blinked a couple of times before responding. "Cormac."

"I would like to speak to you in private, please."

Aveen's slender fingers gripped my elbow. "Keelynn—"

I ignored the warning in her tone. My mind was made up. "Please let him out."

"Perhaps we should get Tadhg…"

"My husband is busy."

The murmuring started, like the quiet buzzing of bees inside a hive, as everyone watched Aveen fetch a large key from behind some iron contraption. Those in the cell parted, letting Cormac to the front. The key turned in the lock, and the pooka slipped through the gap before Aveen slammed it closed once more.

I motioned for the key. Although her lips pursed with disapproval, she set it in my palm.

"I'm here, human," Cormac spat, holding his blood-and-dirt-smeared hands out at his sides. "What do ye want from me?"

"My name is Keelynn."

He lifted a shoulder. "Don't care."

He'd learn to care if he knew what was good for him. Such contempt when I held his fate in my mortal hands.

"I may be human, but you do not know me. To dismiss me because of my lineage is exactly what humans have done to your people for centuries. You have threatened me, and yet here I stand, willing to hear you out. All I ask is for the same courtesy."

"Courtesy?" he drawled, as if it were some filthy word. The rest of the men sniggered. "Your kind are a blight on this island. A curse."

My people were not—

Wait a minute.

A blight…

A *curse*…

Bloody hell.

It couldn't be that simple…could it?

All this time, we'd been searching for cures for poison when the land wasn't poisoned at all.

It was *cursed*.

If the darkness plaguing this land was a curse, there was only one way to break it.

True love's kiss.

I threw my arms around the pooka. His body went stiff as a board. "Thank you," I said, meaning every word.

When I let him go, he stood there gaping at me as I hurried to the closest cell and unlocked the door. The men inside fell silent and still as the stones around us. I unlocked the second door, and the third. Aveen asked what I was doing. Wasn't it obvious? "I'm letting these men go." No good would come from their imprisonment, and I refused to let them become martyrs because of me. That would do more harm than good. Perhaps a bit of faith in their ability to change their minds and witnessing kindness from someone they hated would be enough.

"Rían will…"

"He will get over it." And if he didn't, he could take it up with me.

"Not likely," she muttered under her breath.

The men started to gather outside the cells, filling the cramped space around us. I met Cormac's wide stare with my own. "We aren't all monsters," I told him. "I hope in time that you can see that for yourself."

With that, I whirled and caught my sister's hand, dragging her up the stairs with me. Outside, the sun shone even brighter than before, as if it, too, had hope.

"What's in your head?" Aveen asked, struggling to match my longer strides.

"Did you hear Cormac? It's not a blight, it's a curse. It's a bloody curse!" We were running scared, abandoning our country, when we should've been doing the exact opposite: showing this beautiful place that we cared. That we were willing to fight. That we loved this land and these people with our entire being. "And what's the only force strong enough to break a curse?"

Aveen's lips lifted. "True love."

"Exactly." I hauled her to where the roses had dried and withered between their thorny stems.

This land was *cursed*.

It didn't need more spells.

It needed love.

I removed my shoes and left them next to the blackened laurels. If my theory was correct, Tadgh's ring on my finger would repel the curse. I'd have nothing to fear. I stepped onto the burnt, barren ground.

"Keelynn! You can't—"

"I'll be fine." The curse writhed beneath my feet, searching for a way through the magical barrier created by Tadhg's mother's ring. One it would never find. Aveen remained on the patch of gravel, her gaze fixed on my toes peeking from beneath my skirt.

I knelt right there on the ground and buried my hands in the onyx dust. "I love this land," I said to the cursed earth, the sky and the blazing sun high above. "This is my kingdom. My home." From the rolling hills to the cliffs defying the sea and everything in between. I loved it all.

Aveen sank down next to me, spreading her fingers over the dying grass. "I love it too."

The prisoners I'd freed lingered at the gates, looking on with wary expressions. I could practically feel their doubt and confusion like a weight upon my shoulders.

Tears stung the backs of my eyes as I leaned forward to whisper words of love for this land of magic and mythical monsters, its leader, my beloved coachman Padraig, and every single Danú who had been wrongfully persecuted. For my friend Ruairi. For Millie and Nettie May. For Eava and Oscar.

Aveen's murmurs lifted into the rancid air.

I screwed my eyes shut and reached deep down within myself, past the fear and the mistakes I'd made, pouring the love from my heart into my fingertips.

I may have been human, but I had more love in my being than the wretched witch who'd sent this blight. I'd been the one strong enough to break the Gancanagh's curse. Me, no one else.

Love was its own brand of magic. Overcoming impossible odds. Bringing hope to the hopeless.

The Queen had sown seeds of despair and hatred, intolerance and fear.

From my weak human heart, I would give this place all my hope and love, to restore peace and prosperity.

It wasn't until my lashes fluttered open that I realized I was crying. I looked over my shoulder to where Aveen knelt, her hands and arms radiating like the sun. My hands may not have glowed but the stretch of green beneath me was proof enough that what we were doing was working.

Tadhg ran out the castle door, his face a mask of confusion as he took in the prisoners who remained. I expected him to shout or go after them, but when he saw me, he ran to where I knelt instead. My husband fell down beside me, his eyes the color of glittering emeralds. Pure magic.

"Tell me what to do," he pleaded.

"Love the land...and let it know."

With a brusque nod, he splayed his hands in the grass and closed his eyes. Ruairi dropped beside him, followed by Eava and Oscar. The rest of the prisoners fell to their knees as well.

I watched in awe as the dead blades grew fat and green. Beyond the warded gates, a phantom breeze shuddered the tufts. Like catching a bucket of paint and throwing it across a canvas, green shot from where they knelt into the fields beyond. Within the walls, the ivy climbing the gray stone slowly regained its color. In the garden, withered flowers burst to life as if kissed by eternal spring.

I pushed to my feet and ran for the gates. Color stretched as far as the eye could see. I brought my hands to my trembling lips. Joyful tears streamed down my cheeks.

Tadhg collected me in a soul-mending embrace, wrapping me in the scent of sweet almonds and freshly cut grass. "Have I told you how feckin' brilliant you are?" he murmured against my temple.

I laughed into his soft shirt.

He eased back and tilted my chin up with the tip of his finger. "Although I believe we will need to have a chat about you releasing our prisoners." Sure enough, all the prisoners had gone. When Tadgh's smiling lips claimed mine, everything else fell away.

"Do ye mind?" Ruairi grumbled from the garden entrance.

When I opened my eyes once more, I found Aveen beaming beside the pooka.

Eava hobbled next to her. When she saw the green hills, she threw up her hands with a shrill *whoop*.

"Looks like we won't be needin' those ships," Ruairi said with a smile.

The Danú may not have to leave Tearmann, but where did that leave those living in Airren with their humans? Tadhg's brow knitted as he seemed to consider the same question.

"What if we brought everyone here?" I asked. At least the ones who wanted to get away.

His emerald eyes met mine, and his lips tilted into the most beautiful smile. "Looks like I need to set another meeting with the merrow."

He kissed me once more before dragging Ruairi to check how far the magic had spread. Eava went inside to bake a cake worthy of such a joyous occasion. Knowing her, we'd be eating cake for weeks.

I offered to help, but when I turned for the castle, Aveen remained where she stood, staring out at the hills.

I slid a hand across the small of her back and pulled her into me. "He'll be back soon."

Her head fell to my shoulder, and she sighed. "I hope you're right."

45

AVEEN

I'D NEVER BEEN AS PROUD OF MY SISTER AS I WAS WHEN SHE SAVED Tearmann. Three days had passed, and all the scouts had reported that the blight remained contained by the Black River bordering the Queen's Forest. The curse had been well and truly broken. Tearmann had been saved from a grave threat.

And yet I couldn't find it in my heart to celebrate with the rest of my friends and family.

I stabbed the slice of cake on my plate with my fork. Who knew it was possible to be sick of eating chocolate? Three days of cake and music and dancing and singing and rejoicing, and yet it felt as if the curse had burrowed into my very soul. Had they forgotten that one of us was still missing?

I felt Rían's absence with every breath. Searched for him in every room I entered, scanned the horizon from the cliffs for signs of a ship. So many sleepless nights spent tossing and turning and wishing, all for naught.

I set my fork aside, unable to stomach another bite, and reached for my wine glass instead.

"I like what you've done with the lawns," a deep voice drawled from the open doors leading to the patio.

My head snapped up, and as if I'd conjured him myself, my

prince stood beside the open glass doors, his boots gleaming and smile as wicked as ever. I launched from my chair, knocking it clean over in my haste to get to him. I ran, and so did he. We met beneath the flickering chandelier. I threw my arms around my love, breathing in the spicy cinnamon clinging to his starched collar, desperate to feel his heart beat against mine.

"Tell me this is real. That you've returned to me."

"This is real," he whispered against my temple before dipping his head and laying claim to my mouth. The soft pressure of his lips grew firmer, more insistent. I found his tongue with mine, relearning this dance we knew so well. His hands slipped from the small of my back to my backside, gripping and lifting and fitting my legs around his hips to show me *exactly* how much he'd missed me. And bloody hell was it a lot.

I clung to him, losing my hands in his thick hair and soul-stealing kiss until Tadhg's voice cut through the lust-filled haze. "Do you mind doing that elsewhere? Some of us are trying to enjoy our cake."

Chocolate be damned. This man would be my dessert.

"Hush," Keelynn hissed, followed by a loud *smack*. "Leave them be. We can eat our dessert in the kitchens."

Chairs scraped and footsteps retreated, but neither of us paid them any mind. A moment later, the door slammed, and we were alone.

"I've missed you so much," I murmured against Rían's mouth, loath to draw away long enough to get the words out.

His grip on my backside tightened as he moved me up and down his solid length. "I missed you more."

My hand slid into his breeches at the same time my back slammed against the wall. Rían ground himself into me, nudging my thighs apart with his. He thrust up into my grasp, rocking his hips and bunching my skirts, finding my center with his fingers.

Our panting breaths filled the still night air.

"I have thought about being inside you every single day I was gone," he murmured against the swell of my breast before pulling down the front of my dress and teasing the rigid peaks with his teeth.

I tightened my grip on his manhood, stroking hard and fast. "What are you waiting for?"

With a curse, he set me back on my feet long enough to yank his breeches down to his knees and draw my knickers to the side.

He teased the head of his thick erection against my folds. "Always so ready for me. So feckin' wet."

"Yes." All for him, always and forever.

With a thrust of his hips, he stole my breath. Such fullness. Such delicious pressure. Such a tremendous ache deep in my core.

Our hips aligned, hitting deep, striking the most beautiful chord over and over again, dragging moans and whimpers from my throat.

Beds were overrated.

Give me a sturdy wall any day.

His head dipped, his tone back to teasing once more. "I should get abducted more often."

I caught him by the jaw, dragging his mouth to mine. "If you ever pull something like that again, I'll kill you myself."

"Yes," he growled, taking my bottom lip between his teeth. "I love it when you're murderous."

His thumb worked quick circles above where we joined. Desire blazed through my veins, my magic swelling like a living, breathing entity all its own.

Incorrigible, that's what he was. And I loved him all the more for it. I splayed my hands against his dark shirt, the scar left by his mother thick beneath my palm. His heart thumped hard and fast, galloping alongside mine as we raced toward the edge of this cliff.

"I'm so close." To falling. To flying.

His hips rocked harder, and those skillful fingers knew exactly what I needed to get me there.

Rían growled my name, his body convulsing into mine, filling me with warmth and pleasure and happiness. He rested his forehead on the cool stones and panted into my neck as we both came down from the high.

My lips grazed his chest. His collarbone. His neck.

That was strange.

I drew back to study the scars stretching across the tanned skin of his throat. I could've sworn they hadn't reached all the way around. The lust-filled fog crowding my mind dissipated. He had a new scar. The revelation shouldn't have surprised me. He had defied a pirate, after all. Caden may have shown me mercy, but the same courtesy would not have been extended to Rían.

My prince tugged up his breeches but didn't bother with his belt.

I traced my fingertip along the silver flesh. "He hurt you…"

Snorting, Rían fixed my skirts back in place. "Please. It's hardly a scratch."

The "scratch" was as thick as my little finger and reached from one ear to the other like a sick silver smile. The thought of Caden taking a blade to my beloved's throat… "I'm going to kill him." If ever our paths were to cross again, he would rue the day we met.

Rían's forehead rolled against mine, his light laugh fanning across my cheeks. "You know what that does to me. Looking to go another round, murderous Aveen?"

He could tease me all he wanted; I wasn't jesting.

Rían's arms snaked around my back, holding me to him. I wasn't sure how long we clung to each other, filling our lungs with every breath. My mind drifted to the last time we stood like this, when Rían had offered his roundabout proposal of marriage.

I'd never felt the need to be attached to another, especially to a man who would expect me to be placid and silent, a "proper" lady. My prince had never been that man. He liked when I snapped. Reveled in my bite. The fury that lived within me turned him on. He may have requested I glamour myself to keep me safe from the Queen's wrath, but not once had he asked me to change who I was deep down.

And wasn't that the kind of partner we all should strive to find? One who loved you for you, weeds and all. Why had I been so afraid to tie myself to this man? Our marriage didn't have to resemble my parents' or any of the unions back in Airren. It could be whatever we wanted it to be.

It really was so simple.

I pressed a final kiss to his heart before stepping back and taking his hands in mine. His cerulean eyes sparkled with more love than I ever thought I'd find. My throat thickened with tears, but I swallowed them away. Now wasn't the time for tears, not even happy ones. I'd wasted far too many while he was gone. "Before you left, you asked me a question."

Rían's smile faltered with his heavy sigh. "You were right to turn me down. Why would you want to marry a man who doesn't respect your wishes?"

Oh, we would be discussing that at length. But not right now. "I really shouldn't," I said. "But I do all the same."

His dark brows came together. "Aveen—"

I lifted my hand to cover his beautiful mouth. His swollen lips curved beneath the press of my palm. "Allow me to get this out. Please." When he nodded, I let my hand fall. "Growing up, living with my father, marriage was always this looming threat, a reminder of a woman's purpose and her place in this world: beneath a man. I never wanted any part of it. But you're not some stuffy old lord trying to use me as a brood mare or for my father's estate. You're a man I've chosen for myself and will continue to choose for the rest of eternity. And seeing as I'm the one doing the choosing, *I* have a question to ask *you*." I let go of the hand I was still holding and dropped to one knee. Despite the layers of my skirts and shift, the stones still felt hard beneath me. "Rían Joseph O'Clereigh. Will you do me the tremendous honor of becoming my husband?"

His lips lifted, revealing the deep dimples in his cheeks that I loved so much. "Aveen Cora Bannon, I thought you'd never ask."

RÍAN

Moonlight seeped through the open window, gilding my fiancée's sleeping form. As tired as I was after journeying across the sea—on the King's personal ship, might I add—there wasn't time for sleep. I didn't bother tiptoeing across the room or easing onto the mattress. No, I stomped right over and plopped down next to Aveen. Not that it mattered since my human slept like the dead. And for good reason. I'd thoroughly worn her out after her proposal and again after gorging ourselves on Eava's cake.

I drew the coverlet down, revealing the soft skin of her shoulder, and gave her a shake. "Wake up. Hurry!"

Aveen shot upright, her hair a mess of tangled gold where it fell over her bare chest. "What is it?" she rasped in a voice thick with sleep, peering into the darkness. "What's wrong?"

For once I could say, hand on heart, that nothing was wrong. "Your sister needs you downstairs."

She scrubbed a hand down her face, blinking at me as if I'd spoken ancient fae. Her gaze swung to the window and back. "What time is it?"

"Four o'clock."

With a groan, she flopped back onto the bed and covered her face with her hands.

That wouldn't do at all. We had important business to attend to. I poked her hip. "Get up."

She caught the corner of the quilt and threw it over herself.

If she wanted to do this the hard way, I was more than happy to oblige. I got up and went to the end of the bed to tug up the coverlet and tickle her feet.

"No. Go away." She kicked like a feckin' mule and screeched like a banshee. "Stop!"

"Not until you get up." I caught her ankles with magic so she didn't accidentally catch me in the bollocks and tickled harder.

The curses she came up with were particularly creative. So feisty, this human of mine. And so very different from the woman I'd met back in Graystones.

She pushed upright, her icy eyes blazing with the magic coursing through her veins. The flush of her cheeks highlighted the freckles across the bridge of her nose. "I hate you," she snarled.

A lie as sweet as honeysuckle candy. "No, you don't." Since she was reluctantly sitting, I let her feet go. "Here. Put this on." I shifted the blue silk robe I'd purchased on the day I left Vellana. One couldn't travel all that way only to return empty-handed. I'd bought myself boots as well as a handful of dresses for Aveen too fine to pass up.

Still cursing, she stuffed her arms into the sleeves and cinched the tie around her waist. "I hate my sister too."

"Brilliant. So do I." The comment earned me a swift kick to the shin.

Before she could disappear into the hallway, I called her back. "Aveen?" She glowered at me from over her silk-clad shoulder. "No glamour tonight."

Her eyes widened. With a bob of her head, she slipped out the door.

I evanesced out to the gardens, where my brother waited, a smile pinned to his lips. Normally, I'd want to break his teeth, but seeing as this was a special day, I smiled back.

"You have everything you need, correct?"

Tadhg nodded and patted the breast pocket on his paisley printed waistcoat—courtesy of my closet, of course. He may no longer have been cursed, but his sense of style remained as tragic as ever, and I couldn't allow him to bring down the tone of this glorious night.

Aveen and Keelynn stepped into the garden. Aveen's bare feet peeked from beneath the hem of her silk robe. Her eyes widened as she took in the gobs of fuchsia surrounding us, spilling from pots, threaded through the arbor, reminiscent of our first night together in the townhouse in Graystones.

"What in heaven's name…?" Aveen's eyes flew to mine.

Keelynn handed her a bouquet of fuchsia tied with a blue ribbon, and Eava settled a crown of white flowers over my soulmate's golden curls. And here I'd thought she couldn't get more beautiful. Looked like I was wrong. No music lifted into the night, no crowd stood or cheered as Eava took Aveen's arm and led her down the aisle.

My heart sang louder than any melody. My soul erupted with each forward step.

And when my soulmate took my hand, my black heart wept with joy.

"I didn't mean for you to marry me tonight," Aveen said under her breath.

"Now you can't change your mind," I whispered back with a wink, only half kidding.

The crescent moon glimmered in her mischievous eyes. "I can always kill you."

"Not after these vows." Neither death nor any power on this earth would be able to separate us from one another. We would be forever bound, her light and my darkness, no longer two souls but one.

Aveen's lips curved into the most stunning smile.

I withdrew my dagger, and she turned over her palm without a word of prompting, letting me drag the blade along the length of her left hand. Deep red welled from the wound, leaking down the creases in her palm. I cut myself and pressed my palm to hers. The heat of our mingling magic felt like grabbing a hot coal. She sucked in a breath but didn't pull away.

When Tadhg pulled out a twisted ball of ribbons from his pocket, I could've strangled him with them. I'd given them to him separately for this very reason. It took him and Keelynn an entire minute to untangle them from one another. Eventually, they did, and he offered a sheepish smile before wrapping our joined hands.

Technically, the handfasting wasn't necessary, but I didn't want there to be any question that the two of us were wed.

My throat thickened as I stared down at my new bride. "My light, my love, my world, I have been intrigued by you, hated by you, and saved by you. To be loved by you is my greatest joy. To spend eternity at your side is my greatest honor. I stand before you of my own free will and offer you my hand and my heart from this day until my last. For you, I forsake all others. To you, my soul is forever bound."

Silver tears glistened on Aveen's impossibly long lashes and yet her words never faltered. "My wicked, devious prince. I have hated you and loved you in the same breath. If I'm your light, then you are my dark shadow, always by my side. I stand before you of my own free will and offer you my hand and my heart from this day until my last. For you, I forsake all others. To you, my soul is forever bound."

I needed no throne, no kingdom, no castle, no crown so long as this woman remained by my side.

When our lips finally met and magic marked our ring fingers with a thin black band, I finally found my missing piece.

46

AVEEN

I was married.

To a *prince*.

Bloody hell.

Who would've thought when I first stumbled upon Rían in that shed back in Graystones, one day I would be his wife? Certainly not me.

I traced the magical tattoo encircling my finger. Solid, black, and infinite, like my love for my new husband.

No fanfare followed the ceremony, only a handful of hugs and well-wishes and a plate of cherry tarts on a tray beside Rían's bed. How he'd pulled this off in such a short amount of time I would never know. Another plan perfectly executed.

Rían reached into the drawer of the bedside table and tossed something toward me. A glinting gold band hit my knee. The sapphire on top looked familiar. "Is this the ring you gave me when we were pretending to be engaged?"

His lips twitched with the barest hint of a smile. "Maybe."

"I appreciate you tossing it at me as if it means nothing," I teased, slipping the cold band over my finger, concealing the tattoo.

"I might point out that you're the one who proposed to me, so really, you should be the one giving me a ring."

"Oh, please. We both know this marriage is a sham. I only proposed to you because I've always secretly wanted to be a princess."

A startled laugh burst from his chest.

Warmth spilled through my own. I was so happy, I could've spontaneously combusted.

His dark brows arched, and dimples appeared with his crooked smile. "Is that so? You're only interested in me for a crown? My cock has nothing to do with it."

"That's right."

His bare chest expanded with his deep inhale. "Mmmm. You tell the sweetest lies."

I collected my second tart and took a bite to hide my grin. My eyes sank closed as pure bliss swirled on my tongue. When they opened again, I found my husband smiling around a bite of his own tart.

A husband.

I'd never wanted one of those, and yet here I lounged, perfectly content.

When I took a second bite, my finger poked through the buttery crust to the warm gooey center, spilling crumbs over the sheets. "There's only one thing I don't like about these tarts."

Rían's chin jerked back. "Blasphemy."

"What happened to hearing all the evidence before making a ruling?"

He gestured toward me with his tart. "Fair point. You may proceed."

"Tarts, while delicious, are quite messy."

He rolled his eyes. "That's because you eat like a heathen."

I'd give him a bloody heathen. I swiped my finger across the top of my tart and smeared sticky red goo over his smirking lips. His mouth popped open, and a sound of utter disgust tore from his throat.

"I'm so sorry, *your highness*. Let me get that for you." I eased forward and traced his lips with my tongue, licking the filling right off.

Something warm landed on my neck. When I glanced down, I saw a dollop of filling sticking to my collarbone.

Rían grinned back at me. "Whoops."

"You'd better clean that off." Otherwise, he'd be wearing a new tart hat.

His head dipped, and his tongue swiped across my skin. He didn't stop there, continuing down to the swell of my breast.

"I don't think there are any cherries down there," I breathed.

He glanced up at me, his pupils wide and dark. "Best to be sure, just in case."

He did have a point.

Rían tugged the lapel of my silk robe aside and clicked his tongue. "As I feared. Crumbs everywhere."

What was he on about? "I don't see any—"

His teeth scraped my pebbled nipple.

When I fell onto the mattress, Rían fell with me, still devouring my breast.

"Still hungry?" I dipped my finger into the tart and painted a sticky line from my ribs to my hips.

"Ravenous."

"Oh…ravenous Rían." Definitely a new favorite.

My husband didn't miss a beat, cleaning every last drop with his mouth. And when he finished, he plucked a plump cherry off the tray and placed it right atop my center. When his soft lips connected with my overheated skin, my eyes rolled back in my head.

"Delicious," he murmured, hooking his arms beneath my thighs and pulling me closer to his hungry mouth. My knees spread wider, making room for his toned shoulders. His tongue swirled slowly, as if savoring, finding and flicking against my most sensitive spot. How did he always know exactly how to touch me?

My lashes fluttered open so I could watch this wicked prince work me into a ball of tension and desire until my stomach began to quiver. "Rían…"

His finger slipped inside me, stroking in and curling time with his tongue, making room for a second. The more he teased, the closer I drew to the edge of that coveted precipice. Only tonight, I didn't want to fall alone.

"I need you inside me."

"Ah-ah. You said you only wanted me for a crown."

Really? He wanted to tease me *now*? That wicked, beautiful tongue…"Your cock is…adequate."

He tsked and curled his fingers once more before sucking hard at that bundle of nerves. My spine came clear off the bed. "I mean it's glorious! I love everything about it, and if you don't put it inside me this instant, I shall expire."

His chuckle vibrated against my swollen flesh. "We can't have that, now, can we?" He let go enough to sit back on his heels and free his thick length from his breeches. I stroked him from base to tip, urging him toward where I needed him most.

Instead of giving in, he caught my waist and flipped me onto my stomach. "Get on your knees."

The command in his tone had me doing exactly that. Anchoring his hands on my hips, he nudged my entrance, the soft hairs on his legs tickling the backs of my thighs. He eased inside slowly, drawing out the torture. My body barely had time to adjust to the beautiful invasion when he pulled out, only to push back inside even deeper.

How could I have been with this man so many times and have everything still feel so new?

When we found our pleasure together, our broken threads didn't unravel; they knotted tight, binding as one for the rest of our days. Before we fell asleep in each other's arms, I dragged a limp hand down Rían's spine, utterly at peace, and whispered, "I may have been wrong about the merits of a messy tart."

The curse may have been gone, but our problems continued to mount. Rían and I had slept away most of the day, and when we forced ourselves out of bed, reality struck like a ton of bricks. More fires had been set, this time in Niloc, killing three Danú and their human partners. We had to act, to save those we could from their dismal fate in Airren.

"The plan hasn't changed," Keelynn explained over dinner beneath a soundproof tost. Despite our quiet conversation, Hagan snoozed away in her arms, the picture of contentment. "We've already commissioned ships that will be sailing to ports in Airren," she went on. "Instead of having Danú evanesce from Tearmann to the docks, we'll have the humans who wish to come to Tearmann board and ferry them to the bay."

Another brilliant plan born of my sister's brilliant mind. She really had stepped seamlessly into the role of princess.

"And when the Queen finds out?" I asked.

"We'll disperse them before that witch can do anything about it," she responded with a hopeful smile.

Tadhg picked at the few remaining carrots on his plate. "Our people are stubborn. I can't see a whole pile of them wanting to make the move."

At least they'd have the option.

Rían's fingers drummed against the table. "Before we can move anyone, we need to deal with the merrow."

Tadhg nodded. "I've spoken to Manann once, and he refused to let our people board here in the bay. I highly doubt he'll be welcoming to humans."

"I could always speak to him," Rían offered.

Tadhg's brows climbed his forehead. "If he turned me down, do you really think he'll say yes to you?"

"I can be very persuasive. Just ask her." Rían shot a knowing glance my way and winked. My face felt as if I were holding a flame to my cheeks.

"I'm not sure your new wife will appreciate your usual negotiating tactics," Tadhg said with a half-laugh.

Hagan twitched at the sound. All of us held our breath, waiting to see if he would stir.

It took a moment for me to catch his meaning. When Rían and I had first met in that shed, he'd been supposed to meet with Lady Eithne instead. From what he told me, the two of them had been intimate together multiple times simply so that he could glean information about her husband's affairs.

Surely he didn't think he could employ the same methods with the merrow now that we were wed. "As said wife, I can agree that I would not." I thought of Muireann, the merrow who used to reside in the castle fountain. Slimy siren. I wouldn't trust any of those fish near my husband.

Rían laced our hands together and brought my knuckles to his lips. "You're the only woman for me, jealous Aveen."

And he'd better not forget it. "So how do we convince them to cooperate?" I asked.

Rían eased back in his chair. "I suppose we figure out what the merrow want and give it to them."

Silence filled the dining room. I didn't know much about the merrow other than that they were vicious and lived in the sea. What could we possibly have that they would desire enough to convince them to open the waters?

Tadhg dragged a hand down his face. "They want Syren Isle."

Rían's brow furrowed. "Why?"

"Your guess is as good as mine."

"What's Syren Isle?" Keelynn asked.

Tadhg shifted on his seat like he couldn't get comfortable. "A tiny rock in the northern sea."

"Have you been there?" she pressed, toying with a lock of Hagan's hair.

Both princes shook their heads. The mystery compounded.

Keelynn glanced between them, her lips pursing. "Should you go before you agree to give them an entire island?"

"Probably. But there really isn't time. The ships will be arriving at port in two days." Tadhg narrowed his eyes at Rían.

"Don't look at me. I'm not setting foot on another ship for as long as I live."

Thank heavens for that. We'd narrowly avoided disaster the first time. No need to court fate again so soon.

"Do we do this?" Tadhg asked. "Do we give them the island, sight unseen?"

Rían shrugged. "Why not? It's not as if I plan on taking my wife there for our honeymoon."

Tiny butterflies took flight in my stomach. "Are we going on a honeymoon?"

He gave my fingers a squeeze. "Once everything settles here, I'll bring you anywhere you wish to go."

"And if it requires traveling by sea?" I teased.

Rían grimaced and I laughed.

Tadhg sat forward and splayed his hands on the table, his expression grim. "So we're agreed. If the merrow want Syren Isle in exchange for safe passage, it's theirs."

We traded glances before nodding.

I crossed my fingers and sent up a silent prayer that this would work.

It had to.

47

TADHG

WAVES KISSED MY BOOTS WHERE I WAITED ON THE SHORE, watching the setting sun paint the bay orange as the last of the humans disembarked from the final ship. Negotiations with the merrow had been blessedly swift. Once I offered the craggy island in the northern sea, Manann had nearly snapped off my hand to take the bargain, making me wonder if I'd given away something I really shouldn't have.

Despite the magic binding the merrow king to his promise, part of me still worried the other merrow would attack the ships. All of us had waited on the clifftop with bated breath while the ships landed, but not one shimmering tail had appeared.

Ferrying the humans from ship to shore had taken all day, but now that it was through, I felt proud of what we'd accomplished in such little time.

With the lateness of the hour, they'd have to spend the night in the field near the castle, beneath a cloaking ward Rían and I had created. Tomorrow morning, we'd begin rehoming them across Tearmann.

Finding enough canvas tents had been no mean feat, but my amazing wife had managed to do just that. Between Airren and

Tearmann, I'd say there wasn't a tent left unused. Ruairi had been up at the crack of dawn getting posts staked and canvas stretched. At sunrise, Rían and I would begin the painstaking process of shifting cottages from Airren to set up villages across Tearmann for everyone who had made the move.

A pooka lifted a little black-haired boy clutching a stuffed bear into his arms and evanesced, reappearing a split second later at the top of the cliffs.

The steep paths up the cliffside were too treacherous for anyone without a death wish. Thankfully, the Danú had met their humans on the shore. Those with enough power evanesced straight to the top, while Rían and I helped those without.

Oran waddled over, his boots sinking deep in the wet sand. "That's the last of them Yer Lordship," he wheezed, as if he'd run a mile instead of walking a couple hundred feet.

I shifted the coins owed and handed the purses to the smuggler. "It's been a pleasure doing business with you, Oran." For the first time in our acquaintance, I meant it.

His shifty little eyes glinted with greed as he opened the first purse for a quick glance at the gold inside. Enough for a king's ransom. "The pleasure is all mine," he muttered, closing the purses once more. Once they were safely stuffed into the bag across his sagging chest, he looked up expectantly. "And the debt I owe ye?"

"Forgiven as promised." Hopefully, this would be the last time I ever dealt with the pig.

He made it to the tiny boat that had brought the last passengers to shore, and the two lads who'd come with him rowed back to the ship bobbing in deeper water.

Today, Tearmann gained one hundred and seven more residents. There were still far too many who'd chosen to remain in Airren, but with the negotiating Rían had done with the Vellanian King, I felt confident their lives would improve with the much-needed change in Airren's judicial system.

Trials were to be held on the first of every month in Swiftfell, a central location that would be convenient for everyone. The accusations might not stop, but at least the convictions would be impartial.

I'd never been very good at this ruling lark, but I would get better.

I didn't want Hagan to be ashamed of being my son. I wanted him to be proud.

And I couldn't have asked for a better start.

On my way back to the castle, I stopped briefly at the camp. What looked like an empty field one moment transformed into a bustling hub as soon as I crossed beneath the wards. Thanks to the magic keeping our climate mild, those staying within shouldn't have been too uncomfortable while we built or shifted places for all of them to live. Two families had already taken up residence in Anwen's vacant home.

People nodded as I passed, all seeming content with the current arrangement as they built fires for cooking the rations Aveen and Eava had organized. Children darted beneath tent flaps and leapt over the ropes tied to the stakes in the ground.

I found Ruairi at the center of it all, kneeling next to a stack of wool blankets donated by a few of the Danú who had come by the castle to show their support for this endeavor. Not that there had been many, but with the curse broken, my people seemed in more generous spirits.

I came to a stop next to my friend. "All going well?"

"As well as can be expected," he replied, standing up and dusting the grass and dirt from his breeches. "Folks seem optimistic."

"For once."

He chuckled. "For once."

Between a gap in the tents, I could make out the start of the trees leading to the Black Forest. The Queen hadn't sent any letters since the last one, and I still wasn't sure letting the dissenters go had been the correct course of action, but there was nothing to be done about that now. "We have to get them all moved by tomorrow night."

"I know. Rían's already found homes for twenty. Another thirty or so only have small cottages back in Airren that shouldn't take too much to shift."

"That's feckin' brilliant." We'd already decided to spread out the cottages across our land. Having them all in one place would make them too easy a target. Still, I believed that my people would be more welcoming of the newcomers than those in Airren had been to us. Hopefully, my faith in them wasn't misplaced.

Ruairi nodded his agreement.

I scanned the sea of faces busying themselves around the camp, some I recognized, most I didn't. The one I was searching for was nowhere to be found. "Have you seen my wife?"

"Last I heard, she was taking the little lad back to the castle for a nap."

Two young women in brown muslin dresses strolled up to Ruairi, their cheeks painted pink with a blush as they exchanged excited glances. "Excuse me?" the one with dark brown hair said. "Is this where we come for rations?"

Ruairi didn't seem to notice the way their gazes raked over him like he was a thick slice of blackberry cobbler. "Afraid I've only blankets here. The rations are down that way." He gestured between the tents.

"There are an awful lot of people," the other woman remarked after a quick glance in the direction indicated. "Would you be so kind as to show us where to go?"

I bit back my smile and left him to it.

After what felt like the longest day of my life, I finally made it to my bedroom only to find my wife stepping out of the tub. Talk about brilliant timing. Water cascaded from her dark curtain of hair to her round backside. She must've heard me in the doorway, because she turned to throw a knowing smile over her shoulder and asked me to retrieve the towel from beside the fire.

I'd never moved as fast, grabbing the length of linen and bringing it over to the porcelain tub. When she went to reach for it, I eased her hand back to her side. "Allow me."

Her smile grew as she took my proffered hand and stepped out of the tub. I ran the linen over her shoulders and arms, down her back to the swell of her hips. Gooseflesh prickled her skin as I moved to dry her chest, taking extra care to catch every single drop from her perky breasts.

"I think you've got it all," she giggled.

"No. I missed a spot. Look right there."

"Where?"

I bent to capture her nipple with my tongue. Her hands made their way into my hair, holding me as I teased her until we were both out of breath. When I eased back, her dusky nipple glistened. "See? All wet." I grazed the soft linen across the very tip. "I'm only being thorough. Is there anywhere else that may be wet and need some attention?"

Her gray eyes darkened as she sank onto the side of the tub and spread her creamy white thighs.

The towel fell next to my boots, and I braced one hand on the edge of the tub. Water droplets from the damp waves clinging to her shoulders dripped onto my knuckles. I dragged my free hand from her knee to her silken center. "As I suspected," I whispered, dipping a finger inside her heat. "You're soaked."

Keelynn's head fell back with her sensual moan.

My cock strained against my breeches as I added a second finger. "What's it to be, wife? Shall I finish drying you off…or give you a reason to take another bath?"

Her legs spread wider, urging me to kiss the inside of her knee.

Her inner thigh. I guessed that meant she'd chosen the second option. She whimpered when I replaced my fingers with my tongue, working her into a frenzy until she tugged at my hair and demanded we move to the bed. I scooped her up and carried her over. Her body slipped down mine when I set her back on her feet. She clawed at the buttons on my waistcoat, unfastening them while my hips ground into hers, my cock desperate for any friction it could find.

I adjusted myself, not quite ready to give in. "Get on the bed."

Keelynn went to lie on the pillows, her hand trailing down her flat stomach, past the black scar left from Fiadh's attack.

"Sit up. Wouldn't want to get the pillows all wet." The mattress dipped when I climbed in next to her. "Good, woman. Now lift up and hold on to the headboard."

"Why? What are you—"

I laid down and slipped my head between her thighs. She stared down at me, her lips parting with surprise. My hands cradled her hips, urging her to lower herself right where I wanted her. With a tilt of my chin, my mouth met her glistening core once more. Her moan was absolutely feral as she started to rock against my face. What a way to end a glorious day.

It wasn't long before she came apart for me, trembling and pulsing against my tongue.

"That was…" She shoved her damp waves back from her flushed face. "God, Tadhg…"

"It's prince, actually."

With a burst of laughter, she let go and climbed down my body to cup my aching length inside my breeches. "What's that?" she gasped.

My hips lifted. "You're about to find out."

She shook her head. That was when I noticed she was no longer looking at me but toward the window. Reluctantly, I sat up and peered outside. "I don't see anything—"

The words died on my lips.

A plume of black smoke lifted in the darkened sky. She rolled off me, and I shot to my feet. In the distance, orange light flickered beyond the wards. It looked like it was coming from the camp. Which didn't make any sense because the camp should've been hidden. If I didn't know better, I'd say it looked like—

"Something's on fire!" Keelynn shoved my shoulder. "Do something! Hurry!"

"Rían!" I shed my waistcoat and sprinted into the hallway.

My brother appeared at my side, not a hair out of place and his eyes gone black. "I saw."

Aveen hurried down the stairs behind us, pulling the tie on her robe tighter. Rían and I ran into the courtyard and through the wards, catching each other's hands and evanescing to the camp where angry flames licked the starlit sky.

The wards hadn't just been broken; they'd been obliterated.

Screams of terror ripped through the air as humans darted around like headless chickens.

We needed buckets for water—and a lot of them. I was about to shift the ones from our stables when a figure cloaked in black streaked between tents, a torch clenched in his fist.

"Get him!" I bellowed.

Rían took off after the man, but by the time he caught up, the bastard had already tilted the writhing flame toward the nearest canvas wall. The material burst into flames.

Rían caught the bastard's hood and yanked. The man stumbled back and tried to replace the hood, but it was too late. I'd already seen his face. The black pits of his eyes stared back, chilling in their vacancy.

More figures in black cloaks appeared down the line, setting canvas after canvas alight.

I had to stop them but couldn't get my feckin' boots to budge. Why had I thought smuggling people across the border would be safer than leaving them in Airren?

Every death tonight was on my head.

Ruairi skidded to a halt at my side, a short sword in each

hand. Rían appeared next to him, a dagger in his fist. His black gaze swung toward me. "Same as before?" he shouted.

These villains didn't deserve a trial. They deserved death.

Icy darkness leaked into my veins as I focused my rage on those black cloaks and shifted a sword of my own. "No. Tonight, there is no mercy."

48

RÍAN

I EVANESCED BEHIND A SHORT MAN WEARING THE SAME DAMN black cloak as the rest of the bastards attacking the humans and dragged my dagger across his throat. He went down hard. When I glanced down at my weapon, no blood coated the blade...just like when I'd killed the men who'd set fire to The Arches. I went to kick the dead man lying on the ground when his hand shot out, catching my ankle and clawing at me like a feral animal.

I shifted a sword and relieved him of his head.

Only then did he finally fall still.

There wasn't time to stop and think. I ran to the next man and cut him down in a similar fashion. His body and head thumped to the ground, one after another. Behind me, a woman shrieked. I whirled around to find her bashing a villain's skull with a broom handle. The handle snapped, but the man continued coming for her...until she impaled him in the eye with the broken hunk of wood, and he collapsed onto the grass.

With burning eyes, I scoured the mayhem for another culprit, but there seemed to be no more.

If these were same monsters from The Arches, whoever had sent them would surely steal away their bodies like the ones in

Gaul. I needed to ensure we had some evidence to study after this disaster was over.

So that was what I did.

To my right, a man in a singed tunic darted inside a flaming tent. He returned a moment later through the rolling black smoke carrying a small, limp body. I ran to him, my own thunderous heartbeat flooding my ears.

"Are there more inside?" I bellowed over the cracking inferno.

His blown-out eyes met mine as he settled the little girl onto the grass far from the flames. "My son."

I handed him my sword in case any more attackers appeared and headed into the blaze. Heat engulfed me, doing its best to melt my skin clean off. Thick black smoke clung to the air, making it impossible to see. I made the mistake of inhaling too deeply and choked on the acrid air. "Hello?"

The toe of my boot collided with something solid. When I knelt, I found a small body curled beneath a wool blanket. I scooped the child into my arms, turning his head toward my shirt to keep the smoke from his face. Before I could evanesce, a tremendous boom rang through the air. One of the beams holding the canvas roof in place collapsed in a ball of flames. I barely made it out before it landed on top of me.

Outside, the screams had turned to soft sobs and quiet wails, punctuated by the fires still raging. I laid the boy on the grass next to the little girl. His father dropped to his side. "Dalis?" No response left the boy's small lips. The man smoothed his hand across the boy's blackened forehead. "No…No, please…"

I called magic to my palm and pressed it to the lad's chest, but when the magic refused to leave me, I knew. I hadn't been quick enough to save the little boy.

"I'm so sorry." Such inadequate words to offer a man who'd lost his son. My nephew slept soundly in the safety of the castle, while this boy would sleep no more.

Tears tracked down the man's ruddy cheeks. "He was a good lad. Such a good lad…"

I stood, having nothing left in me to comfort the grieving man.

The tents and everything in them had been lost. Countless bodies remained twisted in the grass, blackened and burned. Innocent victims caught in this war that none of us had wanted. Humans with no hope of winning in this game of immortals.

Bringing them here had been a mistake. Leaving them with only wards for protection, even temporarily, had been foolish. If I'd been here while the plans were being made, maybe I could've put a stop to it. I should've spoken up when Tadhg had told me. Instead, we'd gathered all of them in one place, ripe for the picking. And our enemies had taken every advantage. The smoke would clear, daylight would come, but the terror from this night would never fade.

Ruairi appeared at my side, sweat dripping down his forehead, his damp shirt clinging to his muscular frame. "Did yours bleed?"

"Not one."

Tadhg made his way through the devastation, the shadows on his face having nothing to do with the lateness of the hour. The survivors began to gather where we met. Men with slumped shoulders, women with tear-streaked faces, and children clutching their skirts.

Ruairi drew his forearm across his brow. "What now?" he asked Tadhg.

"We can't leave them here," I said to my brother.

Tadhg heaved a weary sigh. "Bring them into the castle."

Ruairi's eyes expanded. "All of them?"

With a flick of Tadhg's wrist, the sounds around us faded to nothing. "Until we come up with a better solution, we have no other choice. I brought these people from their homes in Airren, promised them a fresh start and safety, and they haven't even gotten through one feckin' night." He blew out a frustrated breath. "The ones who don't fit can camp in the courtyard behind the wards."

"We cannot continue to keep them in one place. They're too clear a target for the Queen." We may not have known for certain my mother had been the one to send these *things*, but I didn't know anyone else in Tearmann with this sort of power.

"We don't have a choice tonight. Gather what you can salvage." With another wrist flick, the tost evaporated, and the stench of death and smoke flooded around us anew. I stood by while Tadhg announced to those gathered that they would be moving to the castle.

"We've been told the wards won't let us through," a woman near the front said, her voice devoid of emotion as she rocked back and forth, clutching a tiny bundle in her too-thin arms.

Having all these unknown people near Aveen left my insides in knots, but since it couldn't be helped, I promised to open the wards. I shifted a cart from the stables, and Ruairi traded forms, shapeshifting into a horse to pull the cart laden with crying babies, screaming toddlers, and terrified young ones. Their mothers followed closely behind, their eyes as dead as those bodies left in the field.

Tomorrow, we'd return to bury the dead. Tonight, we needed to think of the living.

As those remaining shuffled toward the castle in the distance, Tadhg turned to me. "Did any of yours bleed?" he whispered under his breath.

I shook my head. We both looked down at one of the bodies lying on the ground near us. Humans and Danú both bled. Meaning these things weren't either. "What are they?"

Tadhg squatted next to the cloaked form. "There's only one way to find out." Before he could throw back the hood, the body vanished, just like at the fire in Gaul. "You've got to be feckin' kidding me." He shot to his feet and dashed his fingers through his matted brown hair. "Not again."

My poor brother. Always two steps behind.

He glanced up at me, his brow furrowing. "Why aren't you cursing as well?"

"Because unlike you, I plan ahead."

"What does that mean?"

"It means we're taking a trip to the dungeons."

A ghost of a smile found its way to his lips. "You saved a body, didn't you?"

"I saved a body."

Hours passed before we had time to head to the dungeons where I'd shifted one of the attackers' bodies. By the time we returned to the castle, Keelynn and Aveen were already in the courtyard assigning rooms for families with the smallest children and sorting a midnight meal with Eava. The humans would be eating break-fast in two shifts, with the women and children first and the men to follow afterward.

Tadhg had moved Hagan into his room, and Aveen had given up her space for four children left orphaned by the night. Eava and Keelynn were with them now, while Aveen accompanied Tadhg and me to the dungeons.

Whimpers and broken sobs echoed off the damp stone walls. I didn't bother glancing toward the cells farther down the hallway, where only two of my captives remained chained to the wall. I still had yet to discuss my displeasure with the dear princess over releasing prisoners.

"Do I want to know what's going on down there?" Tadhg murmured with a tilt of his head toward the noises.

"Probably not." Whatever he saw would likely turn his stom-ach, and with food in short supply, he shouldn't be wasting it by vomiting all over the floor.

Luckily, I'd shifted the attacker's body into the cell closest to the door, so we didn't need to pass any other guests.

Aveen peered into the gloom. "Who else is down here?"

Only two bastards I'd caught trying to break through the castle wards intending to assassinate our dearest Princess Keelynn.

"You promised if I let you accompany us, that you wouldn't ask questions," I reminded her, withdrawing a key from my pocket and unlocking the door. I stepped inside and knelt beside the body chained in iron. Time to find out once and for all what sort of monster hid beneath these hoods. I gripped the rough wool and tugged.

Long, strawberry-blond hair spilled out.

The attacker didn't look like a monster at all, but a young woman with freckles sprinkling the bridge of her nose, set in a face I knew.

Aveen gasped. "She looks human."

Shit. Shit. Shit.

"She is. This is Leesha's sister."

"Feckin' hell," Tadhg whispered, squatting down next to me. "I thought you killed Leesha's sister."

"I did. Two hundred years ago." And then the Queen had cut out her heart. I'd assumed that meant her body would rot into worm food. Instead, she looked like she hadn't aged a day. *Just like Leesha.*

I nudged Tadhg's shoulder. "Check her chest." We needed to see the scar to be sure, but I wouldn't be undressing any women, dead or alive, except my wife.

He shoved me back. "You check her chest."

"You two are such children," Aveen muttered, dropping beside me to unfasten the silver clasp at Gilly's neck. The black cloak fell away, revealing black leather armor I was all too familiar with.

Tadhg must've recognized it as well. "She's one of the Queen's guards."

I couldn't even bring myself to nod. I'd already suspected the Queen, but to have such evidence in our possession meant there was no doubt.

Aveen slipped free the straps holding the armor across the dead woman's torso, revealing a black shirt beneath, unstained by blood or grime. A silver scar adorned her throat, and sure enough, a second scar marked her left breast.

A human without a heart.

Meaning the Queen had been able to control her the same

way she used to be able to control me. And she'd used that power to force this woman to attack her fellow humans. But while the Queen had had my heart, I'd been able to bleed, so maybe the spell she used to reanimate the humans and keep them from rotting was different.

"That's what she's been doing with all those hearts," Aveen whispered, her face paling in the dim light. Her gaze snagged with mine, full of the same icy dread coursing through my veins.

"The Queen must've killed hundreds, if not thousands of humans through the years," Tadhg remarked. "Surely she hasn't kept them all."

"Oh, but she has," I said, my throat as tight as a fist. "And we know where they are." The creepy hall of caged hearts where mine had been locked away.

Tadhg nudged Gilly's shoulder with a fingertip.

Aveen stood slowly and pressed a hand to her stomach. "What would happen if we returned their hearts?"

Good question. "The Queen would no longer be able to control them, and they'd go about living their boring lives, I imagine."

That was what had happened with Leesha, wasn't it? She woke up not knowing any difference, believing no time had passed, when in reality, she'd been gone for centuries. I'd always known the Queen was powerful, but this…this was unheard of.

Aveen smiled, such hope in her soft blue eyes. "We can save them."

Forever the optimist. Leave it to my wife to think about rehabilitating those who'd wrought such devastation. "Not while the Queen lives," I countered. "Even if we managed to enter the Forest without her finding out, she's strengthened her wards, and there's no way through without the Queen's blood."

After all that had happened, there was only one choice left for us to make.

A weary breath blew through Tadhg's lips as he stood and said, "Then we find a way to kill the Queen."

49

KEELYNN

WITH THE FAMILY ROOM BEING USED TO HOUSE HUMAN REFUGEES, the five of us had retreated to Rían's room, where he'd shifted the sofa and chairs from downstairs. A fire crackled in the hearth, but I barely felt its heat.

I was too bloody disheartened. Too bloody useless. Yes, I'd helped serve breakfast and lunch and organized enough bedding for those who still had no homes, but that wasn't enough. Every single person I cared about was preparing to risk life and limb, and I was sitting here like a plod, twiddling my thumbs. There had to be *something* I could do to help them in their endeavors to take down the Phantom Queen.

Tadhg slumped in his wingback, the picture of defeat as he massaged his temples. No matter what any of us said, he continued to blame himself for what had happened last night. He glanced over at Rían where he leaned against the mantle, staring into the flickering orange flames. "You still have the dagger, don't you?"

"No, I lost it. What do you think? Eejit," Rían muttered.

Aveen sighed from beside me on the settee. "Let's save the fighting for the Queen, shall we?"

Rían rolled his eyes, and Tadhg harrumphed. Ruairi sipped

his whiskey from the other chair, his booted foot thrown over his knee. While the princes spent the day shifting cottages, Ruairi had spent the day digging graves.

I tapped my nail against my glass of water, wishing it were wine instead. If ever there was a time for wine, it was tonight. "Who's going to stab her?"

The men exchanged looks. "We'll have to find someone without immortal blood," Tadhg said eventually.

My heartrate kicked up a notch. "You know, *I* don't have immortal blood."

Tadhg's head swung toward the settee, his face pale and eyes bulging. "In what world do you think I'll let you near the battlefield?"

"In what world do you think you can stop me?" This was my home—he'd crowned me a princess of Tearmann—it was my right to defend this place however I could. If that meant stabbing another witch, then so be it.

Aveen patted my knee. "While I support your right to choose, the Queen would kill you before you got close."

Rían straightened and tilted his glass toward his wife. "You're not going near the Queen either."

Aveen's eyes narrowed into slits. "Excuse me?"

I leaned back against the cushion, flashing my sister a victorious smile. How quickly she'd forgotten how it felt to have someone else make her decisions.

"I am a true immortal," Aveen insisted. "She cannot kill me."

"And I don't give a shite," Rían said over the rim of his glass.

"You and I will discuss this in private." Aveen's mouth flattened when she turned back to me. "Keelynn, you're too fragile—"

"I'm not fragile. Yes, I can die. But so can he." I gestured toward Ruairi. "And I don't hear anyone telling *him* to stay out of the fight."

Tadhg shook his head with a groan. "You do realize you're

comparing yourself to a pooka who has lived and fought for centuries, right?"

Insignificant details. "The curse will kill any immortal who kills another immortal using that weapon. So, in this at least, I am the strongest one of us all."

Rían tapped his lips as he stared at me. "She's has a point, you know."

Tadgh shoved himself upright and leveled his brother with a murderous glare. "You can feck right off with that shite. She's not going near the Queen with that cursed dagger."

"It's not your choice. It's mine." And if this was the only way to keep my family and our people safe, I would do it.

Blackness bled into Tadgh's green eyes. He could throw a strop all he wanted, but on this I refused to sway. I fixed him with my most bored expression. Apparently, the two of us were due a private discussion as well.

My husband had the good sense to look away first. "How do we even know the legends are true? That one of us will die if we use the dagger on another immortal? Do we know of anyone who has tried?"

The men exchanged glances and shrugs.

"How are we supposed to know?" Aveen asked. "It's not like there's a safe way to test it out."

Rían's eyes seemed to ignite, and he vanished without a word.

Aveen launched to her feet, her head whipping this way and that, searching the bedroom. "Where the hell did he go?" She balled up her fist and punched Tadgh in the arm. "Get off your backside and find him before he does something reckless."

My poor husband cursed as he massaged his bicep. "Feckin' hell, Aveen. Stop worrying. He'll be fine."

Rían reappeared a moment later and tossed something at the coffee table. The long object landed with a loud *thud*, rattling the empty bottles and glasses. Good god, was that an *arm*?

"What did I tell you about bringing severed limbs into the castle?" Tadgh muttered, not the least bit fazed by the fact that there was a bloodied arm lying across the remaining tea cakes. And not just any arm. One covered in dark hair, with blackened fingers and blackened veins leading to where the elbow would be if it were…attached.

Bile scorched the back of my throat. I'd seen blood and gore before, but there was something particularly gruesome about watching blood drip into white icing like strawberry sauce. None of the men batted an eye, like this was just another Tuesday in Tearmann.

"It'll kill us," Rían said mildly, sinking onto the arm of Tadhg's chair and lifting his wine glass, leaving bloodied smudges against the stem.

"Whose arm is that?" Aveen hissed.

That was a question I never thought I'd hear coming from my sister's mouth.

Rían took a slow sip before smirking over the rim of his glass. "One of the prisoners from downstairs."

Aveen's lips pursed. "Is he dead?"

Rían's teeth gleamed when he grinned. "He is quite dead."

No one in his right mind would've used that dagger to kill someone else if he knew the consequences. "How did you convince him to use the dagger?"

Rían's head tilted toward me, a maniacal gleam in his too-blue eyes. "I told him that if he stabbed his cell mate, I'd let him go free. He did, and now they're both out of my hair."

My stomach churned. Terrible, but effective. Those should have been Rían's middle names.

Rían leaned forward, resting his elbows on his knees. "So, that brings us back to the question: How do we kill the Queen when none of us can use the dagger? We have no army and cannot hope to win against a legion of shadow guards. And you know I want the Queen dead more than anyone in this world, but she cannot be killed unless we use that dagger. So unless you're willing to let Keelynn wield it—"

I opened my mouth to volunteer once more, but Tadhg got there first.

"Keelynn isn't getting near the Queen," he said.

I rammed the toe of my boot into his shin. The irritating man didn't even budge. When I went to kick him a second time, he caught my ankle and lifted my foot onto his knee.

"What about paying someone?" Tadhg suggested.

Ruairi rubbed his hand along his bearded chin. "That seems a mite deceitful, doesn't it?"

At least there was one moral man in the lot.

"Too bad ye killed yer last prisoners," Ruairi added.

Never mind. None of these men had a drop of morality between them.

"Too bad someone let the others go." Rían gave me a pointed look.

Brilliant. Now I was the bad guy for doing what was right. Honestly, I couldn't win.

My brother-in-law swirled what remained in his glass before finishing the deep red liquid in one final gulp. "I think we can all agree that anyone we could convince to do this will end up running scared in the other direction."

Aveen's palm slapped against her thigh. "I've got it! What if we cut out someone's heart?"

Slowly, I turned to my sister. Had she just said she wanted to cut out someone's heart? *Bloody hell.* What had happened to the person who used to spend countless hours tending flowers in the garden? When had she gone from pulling weeds to carving out organs?

Our father would be so disappointed if he knew how our lives had ended up.

"Hear me out," Aveen went on, setting her own glass next to the bloody arm. "If we take someone's heart, we can control that person the way the Queen controls her guards, correct?" Her questioning gaze flicked between Tadhg and Rían. "Do you know the spell she uses to remove a heart or just the one to restore it?"

Rían's eyes darkened as he stared down at the goblet in his hand, as if the empty glass held all the answers. Why was he hesitating? Hadn't he just professed to wanting the Queen dead more than anyone? After a few more beats of silence, he let out a heavy sigh. "I know the spell."

Tadhg eased back against his chair, a pensive expression on his handsome face as he looked up at his brother. "It's settled, then. All we have to do is decide whose heart to take." He rolled his glass of water between his hands, his brow furrowing. "I really wish Robert were alive."

Rían sighed wistfully. "Yes. This would've been the perfect task for dear Robert."

I raised my hand once more. "I'll do it." Tadhg could glower all he wanted. This was an excellent idea. "If I don't have a heart, I can't die, right?" Unless someone took my head.

Tadhg squeezed my foot still resting on his knee. "I love you, Keelynn. But I really wish you'd get it through your beautiful skull that you are *not* getting involved. No one is taking your heart. You aren't stabbing the Queen. The only reason you're in this room is because I cannot bear to be apart from you. But if you don't stop volunteering to be a martyr, I will lock you in our room."

"I bet Ned has someone we could use," Rían offered.

"Who is Ned?" I asked.

"The Dullahan," the others said in unison, as if discussing some mundane topic instead of a murderous fae who stole the wickedest souls for the underworld.

"The headless monster is *real?*" What was I saying? I was married to the bloody Gancanagh. Why should this be such a stretch to believe?

Aveen's lips rolled together as she shared a knowing look with Rían. "He is."

The hairs on the back of my neck lifted. Hold on one bloody minute. "How do you know?"

"Rían had to save me from being his next meal when he came to kill Eithne."

"*That's* who killed Eithne? Good heavens, Aveen. Why didn't you tell me?"

Aveen winced. "It wasn't relevant at the time."

"You and I are going to speak after this, and you are going to tell me everything I don't already know."

A smirking Rían wiggled his brows. "*Everything?*"

"Minus the bedroom talk." I did not want to hear about their romps. Just the thought of his hands on my sister turned my insides. I preferred to imagine them in separate beds, thank you very much.

"Are you sure?" Rían drawled, no doubt determined to get a rise out of me. "Maybe Tadhg could learn a thing or two."

Tadgh's lips curled into a knowing smile, the same one I first saw back in that pub in Dreadshire, wicked and full of sinful promises. "If anyone needs to learn a thing or two, it's you."

With a loud groan, Ruairi dropped his head into his hands. "I'm sure ye are both magnificent lovers in yer own rights. Now quit yer bickering and let's finish hashing out a plan so I can get some sleep."

Poor Ruairi was the real victim here, being stuck hanging around with two newly wed couples. After all this was over, Aveen and I would have to find him a love of his own.

"Why don't I just do it?" Ruairi said suddenly.

I didn't want Ruairi to put himself in danger just like I didn't want the rest of my family to risk their lives. Except maybe Rían. But if he were gone, Aveen would be sad, so I supposed I'd have to deal with him. I hated that this situation had come down to who would risk his or her life to save the others. Not for the first time, I cursed the Phantom Queen. Silently, of course.

Aveen gasped. "You can't do that."

Rían's lips flattened as he glanced between the pooka and Aveen.

The way Ruairi's eyes softened when he looked at my sister made my chest ache. His feelings for her were so bloody obvious. If only the two of them had been fated to be soulmates instead.

"I don't think we should force someone against his will," Ruairi said. "Besides, what have I to lose? I am on my own, no family, no wife, no offspring. The three of ye would be the only ones to miss me if I were to fall." He gestured toward Aveen, Tadhg, and me. "Take my heart to keep me from dying and we'll be on our way."

Tadhg and Aveen started speaking at once, but then Rían's authoritative tone cut across them all. "He's right. The Queen won't suspect it."

Aveen whipped toward her husband, her brow furrowed with concern. "How do we know it's safe?"

Rían looked Ruairi dead in the eye and said, "There's only one way to find out."

50

RÍAN

OUR PLAN WASN'T GOING TO WORK.

Not that I spoke those damning words aloud—it would kill the morale. And that thought wasn't only borne of my own innate pessimism but from facts. The Queen had survived for millennia and thwarted countless attempts on her life. What made us think we could defeat her with a plan more full of holes than a feckin' sieve?

Yet here I stood with sweaty palms, ready to rip the heart from Ruairi's chest. I wouldn't say I respected the pooka for putting himself on the line like this, but it did make me hate him a little less.

Aveen patted the mattress. "You should probably get on the bed."

"I thought ye'd never ask," Ruairi said with a wink before dropping onto my bed and stretching out on *my* feckin' pillow. Had I said I hated him less? I meant more.

At least he hadn't put his filthy head on my wife's pillow. Then I'd have to burn it, and pillows were few and far between with all the humans skulking around.

Aveen's laugh didn't sound forced. She didn't honestly find this dog funny, did she?

Suddenly, the thought of her being here for this made my throat tight. I'd only ever returned my own heart and had never taken one. What if something went wrong and I accidentally killed Ruairi? The thought of what I was about to do filled my chest with dread. No one should have this sort of control over another person. No one.

I pressed a hand to the small of Aveen's back. "Maybe you should leave for this next part."

She shook her head and sank onto the bed by Ruairi's boots. "I'm staying."

Fine. "Shirt off, dog." The sooner we got this over with, the better.

Ruairi's grin widened as he unbuttoned his shirt. I glanced over at Aveen to see if she was impressed, but her expression gave nothing away. Probably because there was nothing to be impressed about. Sure, he was larger than me in the chest, and his stomach looked like a feckin' washboard, but he was also a mutt, so—

The pooka folded his hands behind his head, his smile widening. "Enjoying the view, Little Rían?"

"Actually, I'm deciding what I'm going to make you do first: shave off all your hair or punch yourself in the bollocks."

Ruairi's laughter boomed, but I could've sworn he winced when I stepped toward him. Was all of this for show? False bravado to conceal his nervousness? He must have been shaking in his shite boots, putting his life in my hands.

I closed my eyes and began the Queen's spell for removing hearts. My hand heated until it glowed bright red. When I pressed my finger to Ruairi's chest, he let out a low curse.

"That really feckin' hurts."

"Good."

Aveen poked my side. "Be nice."

That was me being nice. He wasn't dead, was he? Not yet, anyway. Once I flayed his skin and called forth his heart, *then* he'd be dead. Thanks to the reanimation spell rife with dark magic, he would still be able to walk and talk and wear those terrible grins, but he would technically be dead and therefore unable to die if he found himself, let's say, stabbed in the gut.

Sweat beaded on his brow, and the smile slipped from his face when I called to his heart. His body grew still and eyes dulled.

Aveen stood, her hip pressed against me when she stepped closer. "Is everything all right?"

How was I supposed to know? I'd never feckin' done this before.

I squeezed my eyes tighter and forced myself to concentrate. I spoke the words once more and felt something heavy in my palm. Warm wetness leaked down my wrist. The coppery tang of blood left my tongue tingling. When I opened my eyes, the pooka's still-beating heart waited in my hand.

So far, so good. We just had to keep it somewhere safe and under my control so no one used him against us—especially seeing as he'd be the one carrying the only weapon in this world capable of killing us all.

I shifted the box Eava had spelled to keep anything it held within safe and tucked the heart inside.

"Where will you put it?" Aveen asked.

I summoned a tost to keep out any prying ears and told her exactly where I planned on hiding the pooka's heart. The exact same place I'd left the dagger. If anything happened to me, someone else would need to know how to bring Ruairi back to himself. As much as I despised the bastard, he didn't deserve to be controlled the way I had.

Aveen's hand fell to Ruairi's boot as she stared at his body. "What now?"

Good question. I'd never hung around the Queen's victims long enough to see what happened after she'd stolen their hearts. "Now, we wake him up." I sounded far more certain than I felt. I disbanded the tost and used magic to close the wound, leaving a nasty new scar on Ruairi's chest.

Aveen's golden curls spilled over her shoulders when she leaned closer to his face. "Should he be waking up yet?"

Maybe? Maybe not? When the Queen had stolen mine, I'd been unconscious, so I couldn't speak to how long it would take Ruairi to come back to himself.

She gave my arm a shake. "Rían?"

"I don't know."

Her nails bit into my bicep. "What do you mean you don't know? You just ripped out his bloody heart and you don't know how long he'll be dead?"

My stomach twisted even as I lifted my shoulders in a shrug. "I stab hearts, I don't steal them. This was my first time using the Queen's spell."

Her hand flew to her throat, her face paling. "What if you did it wrong?"

I'd gone over the feckin' spell at least twenty times. "I didn't do it wrong."

"Then why isn't he waking up?" Her voice rose with panic.

"Because it takes a little time."

"It does?"

"Probably." What if I *had* done something wrong? What if I'd actually killed him?

She dragged her hands through her curls, then started gesturing wildly toward the dog. "Put it back. Hurry. Before it's too late."

"Stop panicking. He'll be fine." Hopefully.

"This is all my fault. Why did I suggest taking someone's heart?"

Ruairi sucked in a breath, and relief spilled through my chest, loosening my lungs.

Aveen gasped and reached for the dog's hand. "Ruairi?"

His eyes opened, no longer a golden hue but black as pitch. The fang-toothed grin was the same, though. "Did ye miss me, human?"

I stuffed my hands into my pockets so neither of them could see how they trembled. "I told you he'd be fine."

Aveen ignored me completely. "How are you feeling?"

He was awake and talking. What more did she need to know?

Ruairi stared down at their joined hands with his lips pressed together. "I feel...empty."

Ah, yes. The emptiness. Sometimes—especially at times like this—I missed the peaceful side of that hollow feeling.

After a beat, he withdrew his hand from hers, sat up, and swung his legs off the edge of the bed. Pink stained Aveen's cheeks as she watched Ruairi stand and start buttoning his shirt without so much as a second glance in her direction.

She eased to her feet and swiped her hands down her skirts. "Right. Well..." She cleared her throat. "I suppose that is a good thing. Wouldn't want you scared when you face the Queen."

Ruairi snorted but didn't comment.

"I suppose...I should...um...go down and see if Keelynn needs any help serving lunch." Her skirts swished and swayed as she hurried toward the door.

The thought of her being upset left my own heart breaking. I might not approve of their closeness, but I couldn't bear to see her distraught. I evanesced into the hallway, catching Aveen before she reached the stairs. "Don't worry. The moment we return his heart, he'll be back to his normal, irritating self."

Her lips rolled together, and although she looked away, I saw the tears clinging to her lashes. "Do you promise?"

I collected her in a hug, squeezing her tight. "I swear."

The castle's crowded courtyard reminded me of a cattle mart. The men who'd been standing guard outside the gates had come inside to join their wives and children hiding behind the wards. Together, Tadhg and I had shifted thirteen cottages. Nothing to be sniffed at, but it wasn't enough. Every night these humans stayed together was another night their lives were at risk.

I would've evanesced straight to my room, but I'd already expended too much magic. My arms were heavier than lead, and my legs felt as if they could give out at any moment. Keeping my head down, I squeezed between men and women who smelled of sweat and smoke.

My boot barely met the first step leading up to the castle when someone called my name.

I twisted to find the man whose son I hadn't been able to save pushing his way through a group of nattering women. Memories of what it had felt like to hold that small, lifeless body would haunt me for the rest of my days.

"I was wondering if I might speak with ye for a moment," he said when he got closer.

After what had happened, the least I could do was hear him out. Schooling my features into stone, I gave him a brusque nod.

"I've been talking with a few of the other men here, and we were wondering if we might be of any help if ye decide to go against the Queen." Five other men sidled up next to him, all of them with the same haunted look in their darkening eyes.

I gestured for them to follow me into the foyer. Once the final man came through the door I summoned a tost. "What makes you think we're going after the Queen?" I asked. No one but the five of us knew the plan to draw the Queen from her castle. Tadhg and I would use our magic to hold her in place while Ruairi stabbed her. We would likely have to contend with her shadow guards before we got to that point, but I wasn't exactly sure how these men thought they could help.

The man I'd failed answered. "My wife said those were the Queen's guards who set the fire that stole our little lad."

So someone else had recognized the cloaked attackers. Hopefully none of them decided to do something stupid and go after the Queen themselves. At least these men had come to me first.

"No offense, but humans against an army of shadow guards are as good as a spoon in a sword fight."

"I have military training," said a man with his arms wrapped in white bandages.

"As do I," said another with more wrinkles than a dried grape. And was that a wooden leg?

A couple of humans, Tadhg, me, and a heartless pooka. May as well commission a tapestry commemorating our victory straight away.

The door swung open, and Oscar stumbled through the gap. His mouth moved like he was speaking, but with the tost, I couldn't hear a word of what he said. I withdrew my magic, dissolving the barrier. "What is it, Oscar?"

He waved a hairy hand toward the open door. "Yer needed in the courtyard."

Not another feckin' emergency. All I wanted was my wife and my pillow, in that order. The joys of being a prince in a time of turmoil. I followed him outside to where the crowd of humans had parted on either side of the gravel path. Beyond, I could see a horde of Danú waiting at the gates.

Tadhg appeared behind me. "What do they want?"

"Let's find out." Maybe we'd get to kill them and I could drain their magic to refill my empty well.

Our boots crunched the gravel as we stalked toward the gates. There had to be at least a hundred people. Pooka and witches. Grogochs and leprechauns. Abcans and clurichauns.

"We heard what the Queen did to the humans," said the grogoch at the front. Hold on. Was he one of the bastards from the mob the night of the wedding?

"And how Princess Keelynn broke the curse," another chimed in.

"We are willing to fight."

"Feckin' hell..." Tadhg murmured.

Our plan might work out after all.

51

TADHG

A FINAL HEADCOUNT PRODUCED ONE HUNDRED AND ELEVEN MEN and twenty-eight women willing to fight for our cause, the majority of them Danú. Even though the likelihood of surprising the Queen with our small force was slim, we chose not to train in the fields or courtyard. We'd broken our volunteers into groups of thirty to meet in the great hall at various times throughout the day.

"These people are pathetic," Rían muttered. "The one over there brought an actual pitchfork. Not saying you can't kill someone with a pitchfork, but it's hardly ideal."

Sure enough, Milton Brandford had a pitchfork with rusted tines clutched in his fist.

Unfortunately, these people were all we had. "We'll do our best." And pray it would be enough. We had plenty of weapons in the armory. Now to teach our "army" how to use them.

Rían's narrowing gaze sent those at the front back a step. If they couldn't face him, how did they hope to fight against the Queen?

"Most of them are grogochs," he said. "What are they going to do? Weed the enemy to death?"

"All they have to do is hold off the guards long enough for you and me to end her. They're little more than a distraction." And a lot like moving targets.

Guilt sat heavy in my gut. Many of these men and women wouldn't survive this fight. But if they remained here, they were as good as dead anyway.

With a groan, Rían stomped forward to where Ruairi stood with his arms outstretched so Rían could show our audience how to strike. "Shadow guards are mindless minions, controlled by one witch," he said, pacing at the front of the ranks. "They have one mission and one mission only: to destroy. They feel no pain. They show no mercy. Don't bother begging for your life; they will not spare it."

So much for boosting morale. Those whose faces I could see were visibly paler than they had been a few moments ago. Telling them the truth of what they were about to face was important. I only wished it wasn't so dire.

"Your job is to draw them away from the Queen by any means necessary," he announced.

A grogoch near the back raised a trembling hand. "If they never stop, then how do we defeat them?"

Rían came to a halt in front of Ruairi. "Excellent question, Mortimer. You cannot kill a shadow guard by stabbing them in the heart because they don't have one. There's no sense trying to disembowel them, they'll continue striking." Rían spun around and pressed the tip of his blade to Ruairi's gullet. I still hadn't gotten used to the blackness in my mate's eyes. "The only way to keep them from attacking is to impale their brains or decapitate them."

Murmurs lifted into the air as those gathered exchanged confused glances.

"Decapitate, sire?" someone at the back asked.

Rían dropped his dagger and loosed a resigned sigh. "You know, lop off their heads. Make them this much shorter." He held his hands apart at approximately the size of a human head.

A woman's voice lifted from behind the dais. "But if you can find a way to stop them without cutting off their heads, that would be far better."

My stomach tightened. Keelynn sauntered in from the door behind the dais, her eyes narrowed on my darling brother. What was she doing here? She was supposed to be helping Eava in the kitchens.

I jogged down to meet her, lightly gripping her arm and steering her back into the dark room. "My love—"

"You told Aveen we were going to try and save the guards. You promised."

"And once the Queen is dead, we will. But until her hold on them is severed, we cannot restore their hearts." And even then, we'd need her blood to access the wards and ensure each individual heart had been returned to its rightful owner. The amount of magic we'd need to expend was astronomical. I wasn't even sure it was possible.

At this stage, there was only one thing I knew for certain. "You haven't seen these guards fight. They're vicious, merciless creatures." I gestured back toward the room, the clashing of swords ringing through the air. "We are already asking so much of those who've volunteered to help us. They must be able to defend themselves."

"I know...I just..." A sigh. "Those guards are human, like me. I cannot help but feel so sorry for what she's taken from them."

I slid my hands up and down her arms, stealing some of her warmth. "I may not be human, but I feel the very same. We will save as many as we can, I swear." Even if it took a decade, we would find a way.

Back in the great hall, the volunteers had split into pairs to practice wielding their weapons. The longer I watched, the more disheartened I became. *It's only the first day. It'll get better.*

A shattering crash echoed to my left, where one of the men

had put his sword straight through the feckin' window. If this was the quality of the next group too, were in right trouble.

I shifted the glittering shards to the bin, but the panel would need to be replaced by someone who knew what he was doing.

Ruairi demonstrated how to properly swing a short sword to the women. All of them looked appreciative for the tutorial— although I had a feeling they appreciated the instructor more.

Where had Rían gone? He wasn't in here, that was for sure. Because if he had been, he'd be cursing up a storm and calling everyone pathetic.

I found him a few moments later in the hallway, with a young man backed into the corner next to the staircase.

"How old are you?" my brother snarled.

Was he trying to make the poor man piss himself? The lad looked whiter than a feckin' sheet.

"N-nineteen," the boy replied.

"No, you're not."

"Fine. I'm eighteen."

Rían's scowl morphed into a sneer. "I can smell lies."

The boy's shoulders wilted. "I'm only f-fifteen," he finally confessed, his gaze dropping to his crusty boots.

The lad was tall for a fifteen-year-old. So tall, I would've believed him when he claimed to be nineteen. "Where are your parents?" I asked, crossing to the staircase. I couldn't imagine his mother and father approving of him wanting to join the battle.

The boys eyes widened when they found me. "N-never knew my Da, b-but the Queen killed my mam in the fires. I-if it's all the same to ye, I'd like to help."

With no one to look after this boy, the responsibility fell on our shoulders. Losing an able-bodied fighter wasn't ideal, but I wouldn't have this boy's death on my head the way his mother's was. "You will stay with the other children."

His chin jerked up, and he shoved his sleeve to reveal toned arms almost as big as my brother's. "But I'm strong, my prince. I can fight."

"Just because you can fight doesn't mean you should," Rían said, leaving me in a state of utter shock. Who knew he could speak to another person besides Aveen without his tone oozing contempt?

"With all the able-bodied men and women out on that field, there will be a whole heap of little ones vulnerable if we cannot hold the line," Rían went on. With a flick of his wrist, a short sword appeared in his hand. The young lad's eyes widened when Rían held it out to him, but before he could take it, Rían said, "I want you to promise me that you will use it to protect the children. And I want your word that you will not leave this castle unless given permission by an adult."

"Ye have it, sire."

The sword was so heavy, the lad had to hold the hilt with two hands. The awed look he gave my brother before practically skipping out the door left me chuckling.

Rían whirled, pinning me with a glower. "What?"

"Oh, nothing." I smirked—I couldn't help it. Each day, joy seemed a little harder to find, so I had to grasp it when I could.

"I want to gouge out your eyes right now," Rían muttered, stomping back into the great room.

The sentiment only made my smile widen.

As predicted, my brother cursed and grumbled for the entire hour. We'd decided to keep the training sessions short. No sense exhausting everyone on day one. Besides, they would need to build up their stamina before we fought the Queen. However, since time wasn't on our side, we had given ourselves three weeks to prepare for our final battle.

I wiped the sweat from my brow, my own arms stiff as stone as I shifted my sword back to the armory beneath the castle. It had been a long time since I'd trained like that. My muscles could do with a long soak.

I clapped one of the grogochs on the shoulder, his shirt wringing wet beneath my palm. "Well done, everyone. We'll reconvene at the same time tomorrow. Take your weapons and send in the next group. Lunch will be provided at the rear of the castle."

The volunteers shuffled past on heavy limbs, sweat beading their brows and staining their clothes. Time to do it all over again. But first...

I shifted a plate of biscuits Eava had left on the counter just for us. Rían and Ruairi grabbed for them like they hadn't eaten in days. I only allowed it because I was feeling magnanimous today. These two men had been at my side for the entirety of my rule, through thick and thin, helping me get by on the hard days and taking over completely when I couldn't handle life. The least they deserved was a biscuit.

"That was awful," Rían murmured around his bite, dusting crumbs from his shirt.

The biscuit crunched loudly when Ruairi bit into it. "The next group has to be better."

One could only hope.

A loud bang echoed from the hallway. Oscar skidded into the room, his face as red as his scraggly beard. "Prince Tadhg! Prince Rían!"

"What now?" Rían groaned.

Oscar's next words sent ice through my blood. "It's the Queen. She's here."

52

KEELYNN

WE'RE NOT READY.

That was all I could think as I stared through the gates to where the Queen waited on the hill, flanked by shadow guards and Danú. The plan had been to bring the war to her. We'd wanted to separate those who could fight from those who couldn't. To put up a line of defense around the castle.

Instead, all that stood between us and the Phantom Queen were ancient stone walls that could easily crumble and wards that wouldn't keep her out. It wasn't a matter of if she would breach our defenses but when. Those of us hiding here wouldn't stand a chance.

Ruairi filed in next to me, the fresh scar across his chest hidden beneath his white shirt. Since Rían had taken his heart, the pooka had been quieter than usual, more pensive. Then again, we all had, so perhaps it was the heaviness of what we were about to face and not his missing heart at all.

"Feckin' hell," Ruairi whispered. "How are there so many?"

I was thinking the same thing. Hundreds of guards fanned out behind the Queen, an impressive show of force against any army, let alone one made up of untrained men using borrowed weapons, only a quarter of whom had actual fighting experience.

And next to the Queen stood the pooka I'd freed, along with others I recognized from that day in the dungeon.

My throat constricted.

After all she'd done, how could they choose her side in this fight? The guards had no choice, but those men did. And they'd chosen hate.

Tadhg adjusted his grip on his sword, his jaw flexing beneath the layer of dark stubble. "We knew the odds wouldn't be in our favor."

Not in our favor? It was almost as if the curse had returned, turning the earth black. Only these weren't blades of grass. These were shadow guards, the Queen's countless victims forced to serve in her army against their will.

These odds were impossible. *Doomed.* That's what we were.

Rían's hand flexed on the hilt of his gleaming sword. "She won't be able to control them all individually, that would drain too much magic. They should attack and move as one."

Should? They were basing their whole battle strategy off of *should?*

We'd had no time to prepare. At least twenty of the people who had agreed to fight with us had gone home for lunch.

We'd planned to send the children away. To let Eava and Millie take Hagan to Eava's home near the coast. But with the Queen blocking the only exit, Tearmann's heir was as trapped as the rest of us.

"Remember to aim for the head," Rían added.

Tadhg nodded.

Had I really given out over wanting to save the guards? This was a mistake. We shouldn't be here. When I'd stabbed Fiadh, it had been—not a fair fight, but at least the odds hadn't been *this* bad.

Tadhg took my fingers in his and raised my knuckles to his soft lips. "I love you, Keelynn."

I held tighter, loath to let him go. "Don't say it like that. This isn't goodbye forever. Tonight, we'll be gorging on cake, celebrating our victory."

His answering smile didn't quite reach his dull eyes.

My sister's glamour never faltered as she stared through the wards to where the Queen waited. "That vile witch needs to die," she said under her breath.

The Queen's voice rang with authority, echoing across the glen. "For centuries, I have protected you, and this is how you repay me?" She held something aloft. The head of a man with black eyes and long, lanky hair the color of seaweed. Pointed teeth protruded from his gaping mouth, twisted in an eternal scream.

"Is that the merrow king?" Ruairí asked under his breath.

Tadhg and Rían both nodded.

Blackness spread from beneath the Queen's feathered skirts, slowly devouring the earth, her curse now truly returning with a vengeance to reclaim our land.

The people at our back shifted on their feet, their nervousness matching my own.

The head dropped to the ground and rolled down the hill, disappearing between the guards. "You're lucky I am in a more forgiving mood this afternoon," she said.

Rían snorted. "I can taste her lies from here."

"Because you have yet to betray me, I will give you one chance to lay down your weapons and abandon this foolish pursuit. The humans you're harboring have entered Tearmann without my permission. The law says their lives are forfeit. If you choose to raise a hand against me, this battle will be your last."

Although the men and women who had joined us seemed to shrink back, not one person left.

We had one thing the Queen's army of shadow guards didn't: hearts. And one man battling for the people and land he loved was worth a hundred heartless minions.

"Grant all humans safe passage across the Forest, and we will let you leave this field alive," Tadhg shouted back.

The Queen's answering smile sent chills down my spine. "After the humans have slaughtered your people for centuries, you want me to allow more murderers into your midst?"

Tadhg never faltered, his words and tone resolute. "The humans aren't the problem. You are. You've been giving names to the officials; you've been orchestrating the massacres in Airren."

The men next to the Queen traded looks, and the crowd behind us let out a collective gasp.

The Queen's smile faltered, but only for a moment. "On this day, you will draw your final breath, Tadhg Alexander O'Clereigh. And when you do, I want you to remember: You brought this upon yourself." With a flick of her wrist, the first wave of guards raised their weapons in unison and charged.

Tadhg twisted toward Aveen, his emerald eyes searching. "You're with Keelynn. If at any point she's in danger, take her away."

He pressed a quick kiss to my lips, crossed the wards, and vanished. With my heart in my throat, I scoured the field, searching for my love. Tadhg reappeared in the center of the horde, swinging his sword and cutting down anyone who came close.

Rían winked at Aveen and crossed the wards as well.

My sister grabbed my hand, squeezing tight.

Rían appeared to Tadhg's right, stabbing and slicing, cleaving heads from bodies. The rest of the Danú leapt into action with a piercing battle cry, sprinting through the wards and evanescing closer, weapons swinging at the charging guards and the few who'd chosen the Queen's side. The humans followed after them, running on mortal legs toward a fight we had no hope of winning.

Ruairi left without a word, his broad shoulders easy to spot among the mele as he rushed in, sword swinging.

Bodies fell to the ground, most of them belonging to the guards. Rían had been right. They fought, but not well, swinging haphazardly, while even the smallest of the Danú darted this way and that, evanescing behind and beside to cut them down.

Three guards rushed Rían all at once, surrounding him. Aveen sucked in a breath, her hand flying to her chest. Rían spun, taking them all out in one fell swoop.

"I should be down there too," she murmured.

"To do what? Distract him?" As much as I hated being behind these wards with the other women and children, Tadhg had been right to leave us behind. Watching them fight, I knew I wouldn't have a hope of taking even one guard, let alone fighting multiple at once.

More guards fell. None turned away. With the Queen controlling them like puppets, they couldn't have even if they'd wanted to. Our side fought with such ferocity, and if they continued, perhaps we would leave this field victorious after all.

Then Aveen gasped. I checked Tadhg and Rían, but the brothers seemed well able for the guards. But when my gaze flew to Ruairi, my stomach bottomed out. Four guards swarmed over him, and he went down hard and did not rise again.

My heartbeat thundered in my ears. He may not be able to die, but if he didn't make it to the Queen, he couldn't stab her with that dagger. She could leave to build an army stronger than this one, slaughter more humans for their hearts, convince more Danú to fight on her side. If we had any hope at all of winning, it had to be today.

The guards who'd attacked Ruairi moved forward. His body remained on the ground.

I turned to my sister, her grim expression matching my own. "We need to get the dagger," I whispered.

Although her lips pressed flat, she nodded. "If you stay close, I might be able to create a ward around us both. But I won't be able to hold it and my glamour at the same time."

If she dropped her glamour, the Queen would know she lived. I hated putting her at risk, but with all the Danú out fighting, I couldn't see a way around it.

Tadhg and Rían had almost reached the Queen. Once they broke through whatever protective barrier she likely had around herself, there would only be a short window where she'd be powerless enough for us to kill her.

"Are you sure you can evanesce with me in tow?" I asked. She'd barely mastered evanescing on her own.

She glanced back at the field. "I can at least get us close."

Close would have to do.

I held out my hand, and Aveen laced our fingers together. "I can't lose you," she said, her gaze piercing mine.

"You won't. I can do this. I know I can." I hadn't been put on this island to become some rich lord's wife, pandering to his every whim. I'd been born to be a Princess of Tearmann, and I would save these people and this land from the Phantom Queen once and for all.

I'd killed Fiadh, hadn't I? This witch would be no different.

The wards tickled my face when my sister and I stepped through together. A soft breeze cooled the sweat collecting on my neck. I closed my eyes, and the world fell out from beneath my feet. My stomach dropped, and when my boots connected with solid earth once more, the shrill sounds of clashing metal and scent of coppery blood consumed my senses.

Ruairi's body lay between two guards, face-down in the grass. My limbs locked in place as I took in the devastation around us. Bodies coated the hillside, Danú, humans, and guards, all still in eternal sleep.

Aveen knelt beside Ruairi and retrieved the dagger from his belt. The emerald glowed as she stood, tears streaming down her cheeks when she handed it to me.

My fingers wrapped around the cold hilt before I concealed the dagger inside my skirts. It would do no good to have the Queen discover that I possessed the only weapon capable of destroying her.

Aveen wrapped me in a fierce hug. "I love you."

"Love you too."

Twenty or so guards remained standing; our men had surrounded the hill on which the Queen stood, her face a mask of fury as her hands spun in the air, words in a language I didn't know pouring from her lips in a low hum.

Aveen gripped my hand once more, and we were off, falling through darkness, landing on a spot behind the Queen. "Glamour yourself," I ordered. "Quickly! Before she sees you."

With a nod, Aveen's face became that of our cousin's. Only her clear blue eyes remained the same.

By some miracle, Tadhg and Rían had reached the Queen. Rían threw out a glowing hand. The Queen's arms snapped to her sides. She squirmed and cursed, bound by Rían's magic.

"You weak, pathetic fool," she spat at her son, the blackened veins in her arms swelling as she strained against the invisible bonds. "Your magic cannot hold me forever."

Rían's lips curved into a malevolent smile as he tapped his dagger against his thigh. "It doesn't need to hold you forever. Just long enough."

"You think I'm afraid of your blade?" she hissed at Tadhg where he extended his sword. She writhed and tugged, but to no avail. "I am the Phantom Queen. A true immortal. You cannot *kill* me."

"I'm not going to kill you," Tadhg said with a smirk before his gaze shifted to where I stood. When our eyes locked, the color drained from his cheeks.

The Queen's piercing onyx eyes landed on me, flickering with confusion. And when I withdrew the dagger, I saw fear there.

With a deep inhale, I closed the distance between us and plunged the cursed dagger between her ribs. She let out a screeching wail, an unearthly sound that sent us all back a step as she collapsed to her knees. I stumbled away from her, and the dagger slipped from my grasp and tumbled into the grass. Tadhg caught me in his warm embrace. The smell of blood overwhelmed the scent of candied almonds still clinging to his shirt.

We'd done it. We'd won.

Tears flooded my eyes until suddenly, Tadhg was ripped away. Something tight gripped my throat, crushing my windpipe. I scraped at whatever it was, but the thing only tightened. Blackened shadows clawed at the edge of my vision. Tadhg's face swam in and out of focus.

That's when I saw them.

There had to be... *oh god*... there had to be *thousands*.

Shadow guards surrounded us on all sides of the hill. We were trapped.

The Queen laughed.

How could she laugh? She was dead.

Tadhg raced toward where I struggled, arms stretched toward me, but he was too slow. A gut-wrenching wail tore from his throat.

I heard a sharp snap. Felt a flicker of pain in my neck.

And everything faded to black.

53

TADHG

I lunged for Keelynn, catching her body before she hit the ground. "No, no, no, no, no." Her head twisted at the wrong angle. Her gray eyes refused to focus on my face or the sky or anything else around us.

She couldn't be dead. She couldn't.

And yet here she was, lying in my arms. Not cursed. Not dying. *Dead*. Lifeless. No more.

The Queen had killed my wife.

My world had been stolen along with the breath from my lungs and the next beat of my heart and every beat thereafter. I remained frozen, unable to think or feel or understand the mayhem and carnage surrounding me.

I'd known falling in love with a fragile human would only lead to heartache, but not once did I consider her death would arrive so soon. We should've had seventy—hell, maybe even eighty years together. Instead, I was kneeling in mud with my love's broken body draped across me like a shroud.

The Queen's cackling dredged the darkness in me to the forefront. And then she evanesced, breaking through the magical bonds Rían had weaved as if they were mere threads, appearing on the next hill over. More guards swarmed from the forest's edge. Hundreds…maybe even thousands.

Tears streamed down my cheeks as I clung to the most precious thing in the world, praying death came quickly and never let me go.

Rían grasped me by the shoulders, gripping hard enough to leave bruises. "Look at me. Dammit, Tadhg, I said look at me!" I raised my eyes to his, peering through my tears to find Rían's blood-splattered face. "You cannot fall apart on me now."

How could he possibly expect me to keep myself together when my heart had been shattered? "She's gone," I choked. "She's gone."

"I know. I know she is. But we can get her back if we kill the Queen."

Kill the Queen and use her immortal life force to resurrect my love. Keelynn would return as a true immortal. She'd be mine, not just for a lifetime but for forever.

"She must be wearing some sort of protection spell," he went on, his words coming in a rush. He peered over my head to where the Queen commanded her army. "If we can get her isolated once more, you can hold her steady while I undo whatever spell she has in place. Then we'll get one of the humans to stab her. But, Tadhg, I cannot defeat her on my own. We must do this together."

"Together," I repeated dumbly, his words only half penetrating my grief-stricken mind.

He nodded. "Together."

What other choice did we have? It was either do this here and now or accept defeat and live an eternity without the woman I loved.

I shifted Keelynn's body to the castle for safekeeping and took my brother's hand. Stumbling to my feet, I glowered across the blood-drenched fields toward the witch who had started this fight, vowing to put an end to her reign once and for all.

Darkness that I'd worked so hard to keep at bay soared through my veins. I lifted my sword and sent fire coursing through hilt until the blade glowed like it had come straight from the blacksmith's forge. My arms screamed as I hefted its weight and cut through the closest guard, cleaving him in two.

A man appeared in front of me, not in the black uniform of a guard but in blood-drenched chainmail. The pooka who'd come for Keelynn the night of our wedding faced me, fighting not for us but against us. When he saw me, he lifted his sword as if aiming for my heart.

The rage vibrating in my voice was only a fraction of the seething anger boiling in my blood. "You were shown mercy, and *this* is how you thank me? By siding with the witch who tried to destroy our land—our people? My wife let you out of that dungeon, and yet you fight for *her*?" I swung my sword toward the distant hill.

The pooka's nostrils flared, the brightness of my blade reflected in his golden eyes. "I never should've been imprisoned in the first place," he shot back, both hands clasping the hilt as he stalked toward me.

I bared my teeth and let my shadows free. They shot out like phantom arms, wrapping around the pooka's legs before he could evanesce. "You're right. I should've killed you the moment you threatened my wife."

The only sound he made was the quiet thump of his head hitting the ground.

I stepped over his headless body and cut through the next guard in line. Four more came for me, and I sent enough magic into the earth to break through the crust and swallow them whole.

No one would stand in my way.

I was darkness, and I would destroy the Queen for what she had stolen from me.

I would stop at nothing to bring Keelynn back.

54

AVEEN

ALL THE AIR HAD BEEN SUCKED OUT OF THE WORLD, AND I WAS drowning. Tears clogged my throat, blurring the body-strewn field. Tadhg sobbed while he held my sister's lifeless body in his arms. I tore my gaze away from them, refusing to acknowledge what I'd witnessed.

This wasn't happening.

Something glinted on the trampled ground. The dagger. With numbness seeping into my soul, I bent to retrieve the cursed weapon. Black blood painted the blade.

Keelynn had stabbed the witch; I'd been close enough to see the dagger sink between the witch's ribs. So why was the Queen still living while Keelynn—

I screwed my eyes shut, pushing the visions of the Queen snapping my sister's neck from my mind. Silence settled over me, dulling the sounds of war and loss.

This was all some terrible nightmare.

I would wake any moment, warm and safe in Rían's arms. I would find Keelynn curled up in the family room with a book. She'd smile at me, and we'd make plans to stroll through the gardens.

Hands clamped onto my shoulders. "Give me the dagger."
Rían.

My eyes met a sea of black, no sign of blue or gold in my husband's stare.

His hands cupped my face gently. His thumbs stroked my wet cheeks. "The dagger, Aveen. Give it to me."

If I gave him the dagger, he would use it to kill the Queen and lose his life as well. I couldn't let him do that. "No."

"You beautiful, stubborn woman. Can't you see? If we don't kill her today, all our lives are over."

I knew he spoke the truth, but that didn't change the facts. "We have to find another way. The dagger doesn't work."

His brows snapped together as his eyes fell to the dagger still clutched in my fist.

The only weapon capable of killing a true immortal had proven useless against the Queen. "What are we going to do?"

He stumbled back, his hands raking through his hair, leaving the mahogany strands standing on end. "Shit."

"How will we win?" I choked.

Wide black eyes locked with mine. "We can't." With a flick of his wrist, the clash of swords and shrill screams erupted around us. "You need to leave."

I couldn't leave him all alone. I refused to go on without him. "No. If I am to die, I will do so by your side."

Guards swarmed us from all sides. Rían cursed again, his gaze darting toward the approaching attackers. With a final curse, he shifted a sword and cut off the head of the closest guard. Another two came at my back. I raised the only weapon I had. The guard's sword swung so swiftly, his blade blurred. I braced for a strike that never came. The weapon hit a ward I hadn't created.

The guard must've realized he couldn't breach the protective shell and set his sights on Rían instead.

A scream tore from my throat. My love whirled in time to cleave the guard's head from his body.

Every single drop of magic Rían sent my way made him that

bit weaker. When he made his final stand against the Queen, he would need every advantage.

Think, Aveen.

Our forces were overwhelmed, no hope of winning as long as those bloody guards kept coming. We may not be able to stop the Queen, but we could cut off her forces. The Queen couldn't control them if she no longer held their hearts.

Suddenly, I knew what I had to do.

A pile of bodies stretched from where my husband stood only a few feet away, wiping sweat from his brow.

"Rían?"

He turned to face me, the darkness in his eyes stark against his pale face.

"I love you."

His brows came together; tears swelled in his endless eyes. "And I love you."

I took a few steps toward him, until my boots met the leg of a lifeless guard. "You must conserve your magic. Remove the ward."

He shook his head. "I'm sorry, but I need to keep you safe."

"I'll leave."

He evanesced to my side, and his hand slipped to the nape of my neck. "Do you swear?"

"I swear. This isn't goodbye," I vowed, my voice catching. "I will see you again."

More guards ran toward us, quickly closing in.

His forehead fell against mine. "You will," he whispered.

I didn't need to taste lies to know he didn't believe a word of that promise.

Before I could talk myself out of this, I evanesced—not back to the safety of the castle, but to the home of terror itself—the Black Forest. Only in my panic, I must've done something wrong, because I didn't land next to the gates as planned but in the Forest itself. *Dammit.* I turned in a circle, searching the sky beyond the twisted trees. The Queen's onyx tower peeked through barren branches.

I took off in a sprint, the cursed earth writhing beneath my boots, clawing at my ankles. My pounding footsteps matched my thundering heart. My harsh breaths screamed in the utter silence.

Until my feet began to sink, as if swallowed by quicksand. I tried to evanesce, but whatever spell held me would not let go. I pitched forward, my knees crashing onto the vile earth. My grip on the dagger slipped, and the blade skidded past the decaying bodies of rodents, landing next to the roots of a twisted black tree, too far out of reach. Holding my breath against the stench of rot and death, I flattened my body over the ground and stretched as far as I could. Slicing pain screamed through my arms. Sharp shards of white bone protruded from the earth, leaving tiny wounds oozing along the exposed skin.

The spell tightened around my calves. My knees. My thighs. Until I could no longer move.

I'd failed.

This was where I died, swallowed by cursed earth.

Cursed earth...

As dark and terrifying as this curse may have been, it was still only a curse. And all curses could be broken with true love.

The Queen knew nothing of love. That even on the blackest of days, if you had love, you felt like you'd won. Look at her life, having lived for centuries in this Forest, despised and feared by humans, revered yet feared by the Danú.

What a lonely life she would've led, out here all on her own, only her heartless minions for company. A woman who'd witnessed her sister brutally murdered by humans, beings without power. Who had presumably held some affection for Rían's father only to have him wed someone else.

At the end of the day, if Rían succeeded in ending her life, would anyone miss her? She'd be spoken of in whispers, but those whispers would soon fade.

To die and have the world rejoice. How devastating.

The Black Forest didn't just keep out humans. It kept out everyone.

Had this place always been so terrifying, or had it once been full of beautiful trees and luscious grass? Squirrels with twitching tails and birdsong drifting from a thick, green canopy?

I stopped trying to reach for the dagger and spread my fingers through the barren soil instead. Like that day at the castle when my sister had saved the rest of this country, I closed my eyes and focused, not on the fear of impending death but on the love that lived in my heart.

In my short time alive, I'd found more love than the Queen had in her eternity. I loved an old coachman who'd been hiding behind a glamour. I loved an old witch who made the best cherry tarts. I loved a faithful pooka with a heart of gold. I loved a cursed fae prince who had suffered years of abuse. I loved my sister so much that I had been willing to give up my life for her.

And I loved a man who'd lived for centuries without a heart. A man who had sacrificed himself for me again and again.

I loved them all.

And I loved this land. The wild abandon in the constant breeze. The reckless cliffs jutting from the turbulent sea. The sunshine, the flowers, the butterflies and blades of grass.

This land gave life to everyone in it, a place for castles and cottages to rest. Food for our tables.

I even loved this Forest, that it had kept the Danú safe for so many years.

But there was no longer a need for this barrier between our worlds.

I turned my head, not to the sky but to the ground.

"Thank you for giving me a home," I whispered. "For all you've done to sustain my family. I love you." I called on my magic, the seeds of power, willing them to take root not in me but in this soil. I thought of every good thing that had happened in my life, letting the happiness in my heart pump through my veins and spread to my fingertips.

I gave and gave, cracking myself open, letting love and joy and peace and passion spill into this place of death and destruction.

I could've sworn I smelled grass but didn't dare check until I could give no more. When my lashes finally fluttered open, they met soft green blades. A grassy green carpet stretched from where I lay all the way to the castle gates. It would take more than the love of one person to heal this place, but at least it was a start.

My legs wobbled when I stood upright. I collected the dagger from the ground and started down the path toward the castle of death.

The last time I'd stood at these gates, Rían had used his own blood to enter. I may not have had Rían's blood now...but I had something better.

The Queen's blackened blood still coating the blade.

If only I knew some sort of spell to turn it back into a liquid.

Instead, I spat on the end and rubbed my thumb across the dried black blood. Sending up a quick prayer, I smeared the mixture across the lock. A clicking noise pierced the silence, and the gate opened.

About bloody time something went right today. With hope burning anew, I crossed beneath the gates and returned to the Queen's bedchamber where I'd found Rían's heart. Through the hallway filled with unused children's toys to the secret door. I didn't know if it was my own heart pounding in my ears or the hearts on the other side of the wall, but the air seemed to hum with life. I found the protruding stone, but when I tried to press it, my hand met resistance.

The Queen had been tricked once. I was a fool for thinking she wouldn't have taken precautions against the same thing happening a second time.

Still, I hadn't come this far to fail.

If she'd warded the door, perhaps her blood would unlock this one as well. Couldn't hurt to try.

I swiped my thumb over the damp blade and then painted the stones. This time, when I pressed the lever, the wall shifted aside.

Hearts locked in cages stretched as far as the eye could see. The dagger's cold hilt bit into my palm as I tightened my grip. I didn't want to kill these people, I wanted to save them. That had been our plan. Kill the Queen and save the humans.

Except this would turn the tide in a war we never wanted.

They're already gone.

You're not killing them. You're setting them free.

There was no time to hesitate. It may already be too late.

I adjusted my grip on the hilt and plunged the blade between the cage's bars and into the closest heart. Blood sprayed across my hands and arms. The organ gave one final thump before falling still.

Each heart that ceased to beat stole a piece of my soul. *For my sister.* A sob escaped. For Keelynn, I would kill them all. To give the man she loved and the man I loved a chance.

To save them, I would destroy myself.

I stabbed and stabbed until so much blood painted my hands that the dagger slipped from my fingers. The emerald winked out, tumbling into darkness until it came to rest next to two empty cages at the very rear.

One that used to hold Rían's heart, and the other, marked with the same date, that must have belonged to Leesha.

Only one heart remained.

When I picked up the dagger, the emerald ignited, glowing brighter than ever before. In the blinding green light, I could find no date adorning the simple black cage. I slipped the dagger through the bars. Blackness stained the thick arteries and veins surrounding the organ.

Bloody hell...

I knew why we hadn't been able to kill the Phantom Queen.

55

RÍAN

Tadhg and I fought back-to-back, throwing power toward the guards. They kept swarming like ants, overwhelming in a black flood. There was no escaping this hilltop. The Danú and humans who had fought with us had either fallen or fled. And I couldn't even blame them. They'd known as well as I that this was a fight we couldn't win.

The Queen watched from a distant hill, an iridescent ward shimmering around her.

She wouldn't make the same mistake again by letting us get too close.

The moment we died, the Queen would take our hearts.

She would win.

This was the end.

Death spread from beneath her feathered skirts and spells flew from her lips as she lifted her hands, directing more of her army toward us. The muscles in my arms screamed each time I lifted my blade to swipe across another throat.

There were too many. They were too fast. I was too feckin' tired.

My hand started to cramp, and my dagger slipped from my

grasp, the blade piercing the ground by my boots. I needed to pick it up. I needed to shift another. I needed to do *something*.

Instead, I did nothing.

Hands closed around my arms. A pair of guards dragged me toward the Queen's hill, and I didn't have the energy to fend them off. Tadhg's vicious curse pierced the air. Two guards had him as well, his boots leaving streaks in the cursed ground as they hauled him behind me.

This was it.

At least Aveen had had the good sense to leave. I only hoped she'd made it wherever she was going. That she'd find sanctuary and, eventually, happiness. Eternity was a long time to live without joy.

Blackness swam at the edge of my vision. I blinked slowly. By the time my lids lifted, the Queen appeared a few feet away, peering down at us with a sneer twisting her lips.

Without warning, the guard gripping my right arm stilled, but the one holding my left continued, stretching me like I was on a feckin' rack.

Then the man's grip loosened, and he fell straight back, landing with a loud thud.

What the hell?

I pressed my heels into the ground. The guard who still held me pulled harder. I balled my hand into a fist and somehow managed to send my weary arm flying, slamming my fist into the bastard's face.

He let go, and I went down like a sack of stones, my chin cracking off the feckin' ground.

The guard's body went stiff as a board, and he fell onto his back as well.

Tadhg crawled over to me, his eye black and bruised. "What's happening?" he rasped, spitting blood onto the grass.

Good feckin' question.

One by one, the guards surrounding us fell. Bodies as far as the eye could see, blending in with the blackened grass.

Tadhg glanced at me, the green in his eyes dull as his life flickered. "Kill me."

Not this again. "Now isn't the time for your suicidal tendencies."

"Use my life force, you eejit," he hissed, pressing his own blade into my palm. "You're the only chance we have."

That was...actually a pretty good plan. I cut his throat and inhaled his magic before his head hit the ground. More power than I'd ever felt before flooded my depleted stores. It felt like someone had lit my innards on fire. Feckin' hell. I felt...invincible.

But would it be enough?

I shifted Tadhg's body to the castle so that at least one of us would awaken after this day.

The Queen's wide, black eyes met mine, and she smiled. "The kingdom is ours, my son." She stretched her blackened fingers toward me. "Take my hand."

Ours? She couldn't be serious.

She clicked her fingers. "Take it!"

I slid my hand into hers...and pulled. She fell forward, landing on her knees next to me. With a surge of magic, I kept her from evanescing, holding her unholy power beneath mine. The muscles in my arms quivered; sweat and blood dripped down my brow.

She cursed and writhed in a pathetic attempt to get away.

The tide in this war had finally turned. This ended now.

For every single human who had died trying to reach our land. For those forced into servitude against their will. For Leesha and her sister.

For Keelynn.

For Aveen.

I plunged Tadhg's dagger into the Queen's chest.

This blade wouldn't kill her forever, but she'd be dead long enough. All I had to do was shift her body to the dungeon in the Black Castle and chain her in iron. As powerful as she was, no one could escape those dungeons.

Her nostrils flared and eyes bulged as she tugged and tugged to no avail. "You foolish boy! I wanted to give you everything. Everything! And you fought me every step of the way."

With her free hand, she caught the neck of her gown and tugged it aside, revealing the edge of a thick silver scar across her upper chest. A scar that could only mean one thing.

The Queen had no heart.

"You cannot kill that which is already dead," she cooed.

Her glowing hand slammed against my chest, throwing me to the ground. Her hot breath flamed over my cheek as she leaned forward, the first words of her favorite spell falling from her bloodred lips.

"Let him go!"

The Queen's head snapped up, and her eyes narrowed at something behind me.

"*You*," my mother snarled, the veins beneath her skin pulsing with black.

"I said, let go of my husband."

I could've sworn I heard Aveen. But she wasn't here anymore. She was gone. She was safe.

From the corner of my eye, something shifted. I peered through my swollen eye, seeing an angel, her blue skirts drenched in blood.

The Queen twisted my collar, forcing me to my knees and taking my jaw, angling my head toward the woman I loved. "Look where your cursed love has gotten you now," she spat. "My worthless son will never again see the light of day. Never again know a moment without pain." She jerked my head until I stared at her. "Your eternity is mine."

Aveen's laughter chimed like a bell. "Your reign of terror is over," she said. My sweet, beautiful viper. Always so feckin' optimistic.

That's when I saw the dagger with a glowing emerald in her hand.

"No," I rasped, choking on my own blood dripping down the

back of my throat. She couldn't stab the Queen because the Queen couldn't die.

The Queen's cackle sent chills racing down my spine. She stood slowly, my dagger still protruding from her chest. "You wish to kill me, girl? You wish to slay the Phantom Queen?"

A hint of a smile played on the corners of my wife's lips. Instead of lunging for the Queen as I'd expected, she held something aloft. I blinked past my pain, desperate to know what rested in her palm.

A heart.

The Queen let me go and lunged for my wife.

My body hit the ground with a sickening crunch.

A blood-curdling scream echoed through the sky as Aveen pierced the heart with the cursed blade.

The ground beneath me trembled. Thunder boomed. A black mist twisted from the Queen's body as she fell to her knees, her arms outstretched toward my wife, her once youthful face wrinkled and contorted in fury. The shadows collided with the emerald.

The Queen fell down beside me, her eyes finding mine. "I win," she whispered as her body melted into the blackened earth beneath her.

Arrogant fool. How could she win when she was no more?

My wife flicked her wrist, and Keelynn's body appeared at her feet. Blood-drenched skirts billowed when she knelt next to her sister and cut Keelynn's pale hand with that cursed dagger.

The gray sheen over Keelynn's skin vanished, and she sucked in a ragged breath.

A cry broke from Aveen's throat and she hugged her sister close.

My human had done it. She had saved us all.

If only I could move my legs to carry me over to where she knelt. If only I could lift my arms to hug her close. Soon enough. For now, I'd settle for the smile lifting my lips...

Tears streamed down Aveen's cheeks as she embraced her

sister. Then I saw the blackness spreading from beneath her short nails to her knuckles, over the backs of her hands, twisting through her veins.

No.

I win...

No.

Aveen had killed the Queen with the cursed dagger.

NO!

Aveen was a true immortal.

A growl wrenched from my chest. "No!" I couldn't lose her. I refused to.

Aveen's eyes locked with mine; tears streaked down her blood-splattered cheeks. "I'm sorry."

She'd wasted the Queen's life force on her feckin' sister when she should've saved it so I could bring her back. And now...

Now she would die.

Aveen swayed. I crawled toward her, stones scraping my knees, ripping my breeches. I caught my wife, easing her onto the ground. "I love you, Rían," she murmured. "More than life itself."

"Don't say that," I managed through my own tears. "This isn't goodbye."

Blackness had reached her upper arms. It was only a matter of time before the curse reached her heart.

Her heart.

If she didn't have one, the curse wouldn't be able to take her from me.

My tongue seemed to swell as I tried to speak the words of my mother's spell. My hand began to glow, but I didn't have enough magic. My final stand against the Queen had depleted my stores. I'd let myself grow so weak that I couldn't even save the only person in this cursed world worth saving.

A hand landed on my shoulder. Keelynn's. A rush of magic filled my empty well from the Queen's life force thrumming through her veins.

Another hand pressed against my back. Tadhg's.

Magic swelled. I whispered the words as quickly as I could, watching in horror as Aveen's eyes drifted shut and praying to anyone who would listen, begging them to save my soulmate.

56

Pity the girl from Graystones
Who loved a heartless prince.
For the only way to save him
Was at her own expense.

57

AVEEN

I KNEW WHERE I WAS WITHOUT HAVING TO OPEN MY EYES. RÍAN'S cinnamon magic danced in the air, filling my lungs from my first unsteady breath. The soft silk of his sheets enveloped me in a delicate caress. My head no longer rested on unforgiving ground but a downy-soft pillow.

He'd brought me to his bed. In his room. In the castle.

Memories from the battle with the Queen came in flickers, candles on a moonless, windy night.

"She's waking," a familiar voice whispered.

My sister was alive. I should have felt happy. I should have felt joyful. Instead, I felt numb. As if I could see all those emotions fluttering inside a box made entirely of glass with no way to break inside.

"Don't crowd her. Give her space." *Rían.* I'd saved him from the Queen. The Queen was dead. Destroyed. Defeated. Neither relief nor elation followed the revelation. Two more emotions to fill that glass box.

When I opened my eyes and saw Ruairi grinning down at me from behind Tadhg, I should've been relieved that they'd been able to revive him after his fall on the battlefield.

So many warm feelings should have been coursing through my veins, but instead, I felt nothing at all.

The mattress dipped when Rían sank down next to me. He braced a hand behind my back, helping me sit upright and propping pillows against the headboard. So careful and attentive. So devilishly handsome.

And yet when his warm lips grazed my temple, my heart did not skip a beat.

It wasn't until he laced our fingers together that I saw the blackness. The veins in my hands looked as if they'd been filled with ink. The markings stretched all the way to my elbows, like gloves made of black spiderwebs.

I'd killed the Queen with the cursed blade, and yet I was not dead.

I was not dead, and yet I did not feel alive.

"What am I?" I whispered, my scratchy voice harsh against the silken silence.

Rían's brow furrowed. "What do you mean? You're you."

I pulled myself from his grip, turning my hands over and back again, but the color did not fade. "But I don't feel like me."

Tadhg's hand slipped around the small of Keelynn's back, and he drew her close. Red splotches covered her pale face, as if she'd been crying. The longer I stared, the more I noticed the toll this battle had taken on them all. Darkness ringed their eyes. Tension bracketed their smiling mouths and lined their worried eyes. Their happiness wasn't *real*. This was all for show.

If I didn't know any better, I would have said they looked scared.

Scared of what, though?

Rían's eyes shuttered. "How do you feel?"

My father used to own an antique vase from a famous glass blower on the continent. I could never remember the artist's name, but the way the oranges and yellows mixed and swirled was like looking at poetry. The fluted top had always reminded me of daffodils, the first flowers marking the end of a long Airren winter.

They used to be my favorite, once upon a time. I couldn't remember how old I was—seven, eight maybe—but I'd picked a whole handful of those bright, cheerful flowers the day they bloomed and carried them in my chubby fist all the way to the parlor where that vase sat on a shelf all on its own.

That had never made sense to me. Something so beautiful sitting up there, empty and collecting dust. That hadn't been why the artist had created the vase. That hadn't been its purpose. So I'd climbed on a footstool to take it down, fill it with water, and stuff those green stems into the top. I knew nothing of arrangement but did my best, spreading the trumpets so you could see them from every angle. And then I had placed that vase proudly on the center of the coffee table for all to see.

What'd my father do when he found it?

He'd snapped at me for touching something so valuable, carried it right out onto the patio, and dumped it out. Back on the shelf it went, empty and devoid of life, and to this day, that was where it remained.

That was how I felt. Like that beautiful, empty vase.

"I feel hollow."

Keelynn sucked in a breath. Tadhg and Ruairi no longer smiled false smiles but wore matching frowns.

Rían gathered my hair from my face, tucking the curls behind my ears. "Do you remember what happened?"

Did I remember? How could I forget? "I killed the Queen."

His beautiful mouth hitched at the side. Those dimples winked. "Yes, murderous Aveen. You did."

More pieces locked into place, but not the one I felt missing deep inside of me. "I used the dagger. I shouldn't be here."

"The curse was ravaging your body, but I figured out a way to stop it."

On any other day, I would've been afraid to ask. But not today. Today, I didn't feel afraid of anything. "How did you stop the curse?"

Clear cerulean eyes tangled with mine. "I took your heart."

Slowly, my gaze fell to the front of my shift. My hand did not tremble as I drew down the lace at my throat. More poisoned veins surrounded a fresh scar across my breast.

I had no heart.

The same darkness that had lived inside the Phantom Queen now lived within me.

Was I destined to become a monster like the Queen? Were my friends and family scared of *me*?

Rían leaned over to collect a golden box from the bedside table and place it in my lap. There was no need to open it when I could hear the steady thump of what was kept inside.

"This belongs to you," he said.

"And so does this, my Queen." Tadhg held something between his hands. The Phantom Queen's onyx crown.

"I don't want that." Turned out I *could* feel something: contempt. The thought of putting something on my head that had belonged to that wretched witch made me want to kill her all over again.

Rían's soft chuckle fanned against my cheek. "You slayed the Phantom Queen. Her throne and her crown are yours, whether you want them or not."

"But that thing is hideous."

"Then we shall find you one that suits," he promised.

Her throne and her crown are yours...

"Are we certain it's a good idea for another heartless murderer to take the throne?" I asked. "Wouldn't someone like Keelynn be better suited?" At least she had her heart. And as far as hearts went, hers was one of the best.

Tadhg set the crown on the bed beside my heart. "First, it's the law. Second, the fact that you are concerned with your own suitability despite being a 'heartless murderer' makes me confident that you'll be just fine."

Perhaps he had a point. The guilt over killing all those people no longer weighed me down. I'd done what was necessary to save my family and the Danú. If I had a chance to do it all over again, I wouldn't change a thing.

Was this to be my fate for the rest of eternity? This emptiness? Was I to never know the joy of finally defeating the Queen? Of finally being free to live and love the man sitting next to me?

I reached for Rían's fingers. "Is this how you felt without your heart?" I asked him. "Hollow. Empty. Devoid of life."

His eyes softened as he took my hand once more. "For a long time, yes. But only because it was easier. The Queen stole a piece of me, but it was my choice to let darkness take root. Until you came into my life with your tiny shovel and weeded that shite right out."

"So there's hope that I will learn to love once more?"

His forehead dropped to mine. "My Queen, if there's one thing you have taught me, it's that there is always hope."

EPILOGUE

TADHG

I'D ALWAYS BEEN TAUGHT THAT TRUE HAPPINESS WAS A FANTASY. Considering I myself was a creature of legend, I'd hoped the authority on life was wrong. Nine months after defeating the Phantom Queen, I could say with my entire being that happiness *was* attainable…if you were patient. For a man who'd spent most of his life cursed, that lesson had been hard earned. But as I sat at this table, I could think of nothing else in this world that I needed. Hell, that I wanted.

Mitchell Geara, the newly appointed Vellanian Ambassador, chuckled at something Ruairi said. As far as Vellanians went, he wasn't the worst. And the fact that my brother approved of his appointment was a miracle in and of itself. Then again, they both owned the same pair of fancy boots, so perhaps Rían hadn't been completely impartial.

"Are you pleased with the trials, sire?" Mitchell asked.

Although the number of trials had gone down considerably, there were still far too many in my opinion. At least with my brother serving as a judge, we knew those convicted were actually guilty. "There seem to be no problems as of yet. If that changes, I'm sure Rían will let you know."

That earned another chuckle. "I am certain he will."

"What about your king? Is he happy?"

"The king is pleased as long as his citizens are safe."

Such a diplomatic answer.

"Have you spoken to the merrow?" he went on.

Ah, the merrow. After their king had been slain by the Phantom Queen, the sea-dwelling folk were more open to negotiations with my brother and me. One of the king's daughters took his place, ready to usher in a new era of peace and prosperity. While they still patrolled Tearmann's waters, they allowed ships to bring their cargo and even tourists to our bay—for a price, of course.

"They'll charge a toll, but they'll let your ships pass safely through."

He nodded. "And the Queen?"

"She is pleased to welcome those without ill intent to our shores."

The door burst open, and Hagan came tearing in like a banshee, a very pregnant Keelynn waddling after him. She caught him by the dirt-smeared collar and offered an apologetic laugh. "Pardon the interruption. This little devil gets faster by the day."

I thought it best not to mention that she was slower as well. I couldn't tear my eyes from her form. Even splotchy-faced and winded, she was still the most stunning woman I'd ever seen. The spark of magic in her eyes only made her more so. Hagan let out a loud howl and ducked out of his stepmother's grasp, taking off for the gardens.

Groaning, Keelynn pressed both her hands to her lower back but did not give chase. Her feet must've been aching something fierce. Last night I'd forced her to soak in the tub for an hour to get the swelling down.

I stood from my chair and gave Ruairi and Mitchell an apologetic smile. "Excuse me for a moment."

I found my son in his usual hiding spot, in the middle of the garden maze, trying to climb into the fountain. Wouldn't be long before he succeeded. I'd have to ward the thing the same way I had the well and the tower windows.

He squealed when I caught him beneath the arms and heaved his writhing body atop my shoulders. Keelynn appeared next to me, still a little unsteady on her feet when she evanesced.

She gave Hagan a mock frown. "You're a little heathen. Just like your father." He did one of those deep-belly laughs I lived for when she started tickling his toes.

I leaned in close and nipped her ear. "I'll show you a heathen."

Laughing, Keelynn leaned in closer, her head falling to my chest and her swollen belly nudging mine. My family, whole, healthy, and happy. And soon we'd have another little terror running around the place, filling these castle walls with more laughter.

If anyone would've told me a few years ago that I'd be standing here, free of curses, with only hope and love in my heart, I would've called them a liar.

But now I knew the truth. Happiness would find you...if you were willing to fight for it.

EPILOGUE

RÍAN

THE DOWNSIDE OF LIVING IN A FOREST TEAMING WITH LIFE WAS that you had to keep an eye out for random piles of rabbit and deer shite. At least it was an improvement on bones and dead bodies.

Birds and butterflies danced between leaves of green and stretches of wildflowers more colorful than the brightest rainbow. Faeries had claimed more than a few of the larger trees as their own—with the Queen's enthusiastic permission, of course.

The black gates had been torn down, replaced with laurel hedges that grew like wildfire in the fertile soil. Climbing ivy slowly claimed the Black Tower, replacing the darkness with life. Flowers burst from window boxes all the way to the very top window.

Except for all the leaves and bits of grass constantly being dragged into the foyer, I liked what Aveen had done with the place.

An indignant yelp echoed from the parlor. "Da! *Da!* Joshua's pullin' my hair again!"

I stepped over the mound of shoes that must have been spelled, because every time I shifted the things into the closet, they magically reappeared right in front of the damn door.

Joshua sat on his hands, eyes lifted to the ceiling. If the dictionary had had an illustration of guilt, it would have been of this little boy's face.

Mae fumed in the corner, her face red as her frock and eyes murderous as she clutched the left side of her head, the end of a pigtail peeking through her chubby fingers.

Nine children had been left orphaned by the final battle with the Phantom Queen. And since the tower happened to be left vacant after the battle, my wife had convinced me that we should bring them to live with us.

I squatted next to the settee and looked into the little boy's bright blue eyes. "I'll give you one chance to tell me the truth. Did you pull your sister's hair?"

His lower lip wobbled as those eyes filled with tears. "She said my ears were big!"

"They *are* big," Mae muttered.

"That's enough. Both of you are on dish duty tonight. And if I hear any more arguing, you'll be up at dawn to help Eava with breakfast."

They traded glares and grumbles but knew better than to protest once I'd passed judgement. Bernie and Tarren screeched as they flew down the banister, landing on a pile of cushions at the bottom.

Heaven only knew where the others had run off to. I only hoped they didn't bring home any more stray animals. The children I could tolerate. The mangey dogs and cats I could do without.

I crossed the loud hallway into the Queen's sun-drenched throne room.

My wife smiled from her throne, where two humans fawned over her stunning golden crown, created to resemble a bunch of roses—a gift from the Vellanian queen. Aveen wore her black veins with pride, and the smile on her face, though weary, was as genuine as the love in my heart.

The humans thanked Aveen, bowed, and gave me a wide

berth before going on their merry way.

"Is that the last of them?" she breathed.

"It appears so."

More visitors would arrive to the Border Forest tomorrow morning, keen on paying the entry tax that went to the safety and care of the Danú both in Tearmann and Airren. My mother's curse still remained along the outer edge between our countries, mostly to deter large movement of people all at once—like an army. Not that we were anticipating an attack. Better safe than sorry though.

I had yet to hear of Aveen denying a request. Families who had never met their half-human relatives had been united. Trade between approved vendors had soared. Towns were growing in our small section of land, complete with inns and new pubs for tourists. There had never been as many opportunities for the Danú to earn fair wages.

I braced my hands on the arms of her throne and leaned in for a soft, sweet kiss.

"How were the trials?" Aveen asked when I drew back, sliding her stained hands up and down my arms.

"Some human prig tried to blame a witch for his disastrous love life. He was laughed out of the courtroom."

Her soft chuckle puffed against my cheek.

We could talk about trials later. First... I nuzzled into her throat, breathing in the rose oil on her skin. "How are you feeling?"

Her head tipped back, a smile playing on her lips. "Tired. Happy."

Truth never tasted as sweet. "You still love me, even without this?" I pressed a hand to her still chest.

"It's impossible not to."

My mother's words drifted on a warm breeze.

"Look where your cursed love got you."

Look indeed. A loving wife, a job I finally enjoyed, a family I was proud to call my own.

448

Love, even one as cursed as ours, was always worth the risk.

AFTERWORD

Long live the princes from Tearmann,
the princess and the heartless Queen,
for they brought peace to all the land
the likes of which had never been seen.

ACKNOWLEDGMENTS

Well? Did I do it? Did I break your heart?

But then I put it back together again…right?

Let's face it, these characters all needed some more growth and character development and what better way for that to happen than to torture them?

Rest assured, dear readers, Tadhg, Keelynn, Rían, and Aveen have found their happily-ever-afters.

Ruairi, however… I think he deserves one too.

Until then, let me thank all of you who've taken a chance on this series and fallen in love with Airren and these flawed characters as much as I have.

I think we can all agree that the covers for these books are what drew you in—and we have Fran (@coverdungeonrabbit) to thank for her brilliant talent. Without her designs, I'm not sure we would have found each other.

And Meg, my spectacular editor who helped me polish this mayhem into a coherent book: Thank you for all you do, you wonderful comma goblin.

Lastly, to my street team: I couldn't have done this without you. Thank you for hyping my writing and this series when I was in a slump and for braving this finale before everyone else.

NO ROBERTS ALLOWED!

ABOUT THE AUTHOR

Jenny has been a lover of love stories ever since she picked up her first romance novel one summer vacation with the family. She enjoys breaking reader hearts and sewing them up by "the end". See that smile on her face? She's secretly plotting her next heartbreaking fantasy romance.

ALSO BY JENNY

THE MYTHS OF AIRREN

(Adult Fantasy Romance)

A Cursed Kiss

A Cursed Heart

A Cursed Love

Prince of Seduction

Prince of Deception

THE PAN TRILOGY

(YA Sci-Fi Romance with a Peter Pan Twist)

The PAN

The HOOK

The CROC

CONTEMPORARY ROMANCE

(Co-written with Natalie Murray)

Hating the Best Man

Loving the Worst Man

MORE BOOKS YOU'LL LOVE

If you enjoyed this story, please consider leaving a review.
Then check out more books from Midnight Tide Publishing.

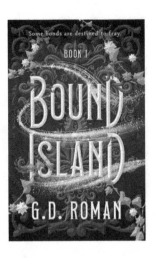

Some bonds are destined to fray.

BOOK 1

BOUND ISLAND

G.D. ROMAN

Until the Knots of Avalon break.

Brye, Lenna, and Tara have lived their entire lives on an island surrounded by mists and protected by magical bonds. Nothing could be more perfect. Until one night, when magic begins to fray at the seams, and their lives change forever.

The Healer–Brye's healing abilities are her pride, making her the best match of the season. If only someone were interesting enough for her. Until she catches the eye of Prince Gareth, the least interesting one of all.

The Mist Maiden–Lenna has lived her life in the shadow of her sisters. Until Beltane, when her magic explodes. Now, she has been chosen to be a Mist Maiden, protector of Avalon. A role she was never destined to play.

The Warrior–Tara knows that she is meant to be more than being someone's mate. A warrior through and through, Tara strives for the extraordinary. No matter the cost. Even if that means she might have to sacrifice her growing feelings for Aiden.

As Avalon slowly becomes an island lost in the mists, will the sisters strengthen their bonds and save their home, or will they break apart forever?

Life for Eden is simple—until she's given to the nightmare king.

Wishing for more adventure in her life, and hoping to escape from under her overprotective mother's thumb even for just a night, Eden accepts an invitation to a ball in another king's court. Despite her mother's ire, it all seems worth it as their travels take Eden away from home for the first time and into the middle realm.

Draven, known as the king of nightmares and ruler of the dark realm, Andhera, desires only to remain in his kingdom and maintain control and order over the ravenous creatures that lurk in the shadows. However, he finds himself drawn away by the mysterious summons of his brother, who appears to need his aid desperately.

In one evening, thrust unwittingly together, Lady Eden and King Draven find themselves beguiled, betrayed, and betrothed. Neither is prepared for what it means for them, or for the immortal realms.

As politics and death intermingle, can two entirely different fae learn to rely on one another? Or will the dark realm destroy all that is held most innocent and precious within the realms, and Eden herself?